MW00617890

THE FOX HOLLOW ENCOUNTERS

A Historical Fiction Novel

Nilish Gupte

E.T. Pug Publishing

Copyright © 2023 Nilish Gupte

All rights reserved

No part of this book may be reproduced, or stored in a retrieval system, or transmitted in any form or by any means, electronic, mechanical, photocopying, recording, or otherwise, without express written permission of the publisher.

ISBN-13: 978-1-961363-01-4

Cover design by: Nilish Gupte
Printed in the United States of America

First Edition 2023

AUTHORS NOTE

This book is a work of fiction. All incidents, dialogues, and characters, except for some well-known historical figures, are products of the author's imagination and are not to be construed as real. Where and when real-life historical persons appear, the situations, incidents, places and dialogues concerning those persons are entirely fictional and are not intended to depict actual events or to change the entirely fictional nature of the work. In all other respects, any resemblance to persons living or dead is coincidental.

Dedicated to my Grandfather D. B. Karnik,
Journalist and Freedom Fighter.

Where the mind is without fear and the head is held high.....

Into that heaven of freedom, my Father, let my country awake.

RABINDRANATH TAGORE

CONTENTS

CAST OF CHARACTERS

India

Jeev Sen - Freedom Fighter

Amee - Plantation Worker

Arti - Amee's Sister

Ramu (Bhalu) - Freedom Fighter; Jeev's Friend

Swamy - Indian Leader

Agni - Amee's Friend

Maryland

Emily Calvert - Daughter of McBride

Benjamin Calvert - Maryland Farmer

McBride Calvert - Benjamin's Son / Farmer

Emma Calvert - Benjamin's Wife

Chogan - Algonquin Warrior

Segenam - Algonquin Warrior

Chief Eluwilussit - Algonquin Chief

Louis - Cowhand

Chet - Cowhand

Elizabeth & Lionel Burke - Parents of Sean Burke

Claire Calvert - McBride's wife

Craig Baker - US Intelligence

Germany

General Mueller - German General

Commander Koenig - German U-boat Captain

Franz Von Oppenheim- German Diplomat

England

Sean Burke - Captain British Army

Mr. Sarkar - British Merchant
James Mason - Friend of the Viceroy

Guyana
Odeyman Brown - Scarface, Plantation Manager
Amir & Meera Chaudhary - Guyanese farmers

Virgin Islands
Jimmy Riley - Plantation Owner
Captain Riley -Jimmy's Father
Freja and Mo - Managers of the Riley Plantation

New York
Stan and Norman - Editors of the Workingman

Rangoon
Saharilal and Shawarilal - Merchants
Kyi Kyi - Burmese girl

Mexico
Juan Carlos - Publisher of Voz De La Gente
Mariana Alvarez - Mexican Fighter
Felix Diaz - Mexican Military Officer
Jacinto Kan - Mayan Guide
Xochitl - Jacinto's Wife
Logan - Crew member on Cargo Ship

HISTORICAL FIGURES

Lord Curzon	Viceroy of India
Abraham Lincoln	President of United States
Thomas Hunter	College President
Baroness Mary Curzon	Wife of the Viceroy
Jawaharlal Nehru	First Prime Minister of India
David Jackson	Labor Leader, Virgin Islands
Frida Kahlo	Mexican Painter
Guillermo Kahlo	Frida's Father
Alvarez Obregon	General/President of Mexico
Venustiano Carranza	President of Mexico
Winston Churchill	First Lord of the Admirality

MAP OF BRITISH INDIA

CHINA

AFGHANISTAN

NEPAL

DELHI

GANGES

BRITISH INDIA

CALCUTTA

MANDALAY

IRAWADDY

BOMBAY

ARABIAN SEA

BAY OF BENGAL

RANGOON

PORTUGUESE
GOA

ANDAMAN
NICOBAR
ISLANDS

CEYLON

PROLOGUE

The most dangerous question a person can ask is Who am I? It scathes the soul, questions every decision, tears at the fabric of relationships, and lays life bare in its naked truth. It was the question Jeev asked himself as he sat on a rocky ledge overlooking the clear blue-green sea. The waves below crashed in rhythmic succession, as they had for millennia, the froth splashing over, smoothening the rocks, only to start again. An angler's boat, tied to a dock by a single rope, danced in the waters. The waves tugged at the boat to set it adrift and drag it into the ocean; the rope stretched to its limit, held on. Without the rope, the boat would sail into the ocean, following the winds and the currents, until its eventual destined demise in a tropical storm. Yet the rope, holding back the call of the ocean, had in mind a different destiny, one of a peaceful existence. Peaceful, however, could not coexist with purposeful.

Jeev walked away from the cliff towards the road. To his left, the dirt road snaked upwards, curving its way into the plantation above. An idyllic farmhouse looked over the ocean. Coconut and banana leaves danced in the wind, a white hammock swung in the distance, and a woman sat in a chair on the porch playing with a puppy. To the right, the road led down to the town and the docks. Rows of houses and a couple of church steeples formed the perimeter of the city. A cobblestone path led to the Misty Tavern, where a German officer was waiting for him.

The Misty Tavern, at one time, was a favorite haunt of pirates. It started out as a shack on the beach facing the ocean. Every night a fight, a stabbing or worse, was common. The place reeked of cheap liquor; the floors were wet and muddy, and the food stale. Yet after being on the ocean for months, this was the place everyone longed to visit. Over the years, a sturdy timber structure replaced the shack. There were proper floors, and customers upgraded from pirates to officers and plantation owners. They had to be well off to afford the smooth whiskies and marbled steaks. Plush velvet upholstery, chandeliers and fine China had replaced the broken chairs, melted candles and wooden mugs. Commander Koenig sat at a corner table, nursing a glass of rum. His vantage point let him see who entered the tavern. To his right, a window with wrought iron bars overlooked the waves breaking over jagged rocks. Frustrated with his contact's tardiness, he impatiently tapped at the wooden table, making a spoon jump in the air.

Jeev stopped at the crossroad. In front of him was a collapsed tree, its branches lying across a hollow in the ground, with blooming pink bougainvillea shrubs covering the trunk. A small, silver-gray fox stood by the tree, its bushy tail resting on the fallen leaves. It stared at Jeev, and Jeev stood still, staring back into the blue infinity of the fox's eyes.

Mesmerized, Jeev saw himself diving into a gentle ocean. As the water covered his body, there was a sea of humanity before him—men, women, children, all struggling to breathe, their hands stretched upward towards the waters' surface with their legs tied down by ropes to rocks on the seabed. Observing him enter the waves, they turned to look at him with desperation. Further down on the seabed, thousands lay lifeless. He grabbed a knife that appeared before him and slashed the binding ropes. One by one, the people floated up to the surface to breathe again. Jeev became desperate. There were multitudes of people to save, and he too was running out of air. As suddenly as it had started, Jeev catapulted back onto land, his lungs burning. He crumpled to the ground with exhaustion. The apparition was over. As his vision ended, he broke the fox's stare. He again glanced back at the boat; the rope had gripped it to the dock. Suddenly, Jeev knew what he had to do. He turned his back to the plantation and purposefully strode down towards the town.

CHAPTER 1: JUNIOR YEARS (1899)

T he boy, Jeev, stared out towards the streets of Calcutta. It was a typical afternoon. The sun beat down on the metropolis. No rain had fallen in the last two years, and no one could understand why the normal monsoon season had changed to a new weather pattern. Dust hung in the air like a dry blanket, seeped through clothes, and attached itself to every inch of uncovered skin, creating an almost unbearable itchiness, which Jeev resisted as scratching only made the irritation worse.

He watched as crowds, gathering in large numbers, headed towards the Government House, which was the Viceroy's Palace. Mostly bare footed, the people trudged forward, kicking pockets of dust into the air which hung suspended by invisible strings. They were coming to see the new ruler with a mixture of curiosity, fear, and a desire to be associated with royalty, if merely from a great distance. They would then go back to their villages and tell tales of seeing the white man who was now their supreme commander. He was the new Viceroy of India, Lord Curzon, the First Marquess Curzon of Kedleston. He was the chief executive, who governed the country in the name of the English throne. Being the Viceroy was like being the king of India, except that he had to answer to an even higher power, the monarchy of Great Britain.

In the 1890s, a terrible famine raged throughout the country. Rampant malnutrition existed even during good times, but now entire villages were dying from starvation, and an untold number of farm animals had perished. Luckily, Jeev could feed himself, but he could not fully understand why the British would not help. For the Crown, India was merely a source of iron, diamonds, and other mineral wealth and the Indian people were homeless in their own birthplace.

Finally, Jeev sprinted forward and melded into the crowd. He zigzagged with his tall, lanky frame and oversized arms and legs, through the throngs of mostly men wearing white or off-white kurtas and a splattering of a few women in colorful sarees. He was intent on finding a good place to view the ceremonies.

When he reached the Viceroy's Palace, he saw red coated British soldiers standing at attention their rifles ready to fire. Jeev knew they would never let him in, but he also knew of a large banyan tree around the corner whose branches overlooked the compound. The multiple roots provided an easy wall to traverse the palace wall. He ran around the corner and climbed up the tree. The next step, though, was dangerous. Jeev looked around to make sure no one was watching, then leaped from the branch onto the wall and slid down to the ground. He made his way towards the front of the mansion, mingling with the sizeable crowd that was already inside the palace grounds.

The crowd was divided into three parts. The first, a small gathering of governmental elites of the government and the Viceroy's entourage, were in the immediate vicinity of the palace grounds. The second crowd, consisting of hundreds of civil servants, stood within the palace compound, and the third and largest, a vast crowd of thousands of Indian natives, congregated outside the gates. A string of armed Sepoys and chain-link fences separated the elites from the commoners.

Jeev looked up and gazed in awe at the neoclassical magnificence of the palace, which was built about a hundred years ago by the East India Company. Numerous columns in the middle of the building supported a Roman Dome, and two massive wings protruding outwards, also with columns and passageways.

He found a spot with an unobstructed view of the podium. The main door to the palace had large stairs leading to the palace grounds, with a lush green lawn covering most of the area. Jeev wondered how the British could water the lawn, when outside the palace, people were dying from thirst. A red carpet led up to the ornate stage. On either side of the carpet were soldiers in their finest red and white military uniforms. Drummers, bagpipers, and flutists were playing songs that were foreign to the listening public. Then, cannons fired from the back of the palace, announcing the Viceroy's entrance.

Jeev observed a man, in a flowing cloak with a plethora of medals adorning his chest, coming up to the podium, followed by a thin woman in a long blue dress and an entourage of officers. *This must be Lord Curzon!* He did not have a hat on, so Jeev could view his balding head and sharp facial features. His wife, Baroness Curzon, was just behind the new viceroy. She was as tall as her husband. Her pale white skin was yet untouched by the strong Indian sun. A lady-in-waiting trailed behind, furiously fanning the Baroness to keep her cool.

The gathering inside the fences politely clapped as the Viceroy entered and waved a white gloved hand towards them. The crowd outside the barrier was raucous, and thunderous protests were hurled at the new viceroy.

Jeev, moving closer to the chain-link fence, wondered, *if he had a gun, would be able to shoot the Viceroy?* His eyes studied the pattern of the guards. *It would be impossible,* he reasoned; *the security is too tight; they would not let me get close enough. There will be other opportunities.*

Unknown to him, however, Jeev was being watched. On the second floor of the palace, Captain Sean Burke took out a small telescope and stretched it out, surveying the crowd, observing his troops stationed at strategic points. He had accompanied Lord Curzon on his expeditions around the world, from Russia to the Middle East, from Korea to Indochina and through the Himalayas to Mongolia. Lord Curzon trusted him and promoted him through the ranks. Now Sean was Head Captain and personally responsible for guarding the Viceroy in British India. As he gazed over the sea of people, he saw a young man weaving his way through the crowd, moving closer to the Viceroy. Sean tensed slightly and trained the telescope on him, seeing his movements. Once he stopped moving, Sean turned away and checked other areas.

Curzon spoke to the crowds gathered in front of him. "India is the crown Jewel of the British Empire. Without India, England cannot retain its superiority in the World. All of you who have gathered here are an essential part of maintaining England's greatness. Baroness Curzon and I are honored to be here in Calcutta. I have grand plans for this land, for its military, and for the part it will play in the glory of Britain." His voice, although booming, was dim beyond a few hundred feet. Then again, the message was only for his select group of people.

Having satisfied his ceremonial duties, Lord Curzon then stepped into the shade of a large white tent just outside the palace. Servants had laid out long snow-white clothed tables bursting with roast venison, lamb, oysters, fish, colorful vegetables, and fruits. To drink there was hot punch, tea, coffee, wine, and liquors. All this was for the invited guests, the princes, princesses, British officers, their families, and the wealthy merchants of Calcutta to guzzle. Rows of fences and chains cordoned the feast off from the public. Even from a distance, Jeev could see the heaving plates, and full bottles. Soldiers shouted and moved forward with menace pushing the commoners away from the banquet and out of the palace compound.

Lord Curzon glanced at the overfilled tables and gluttonous crowd. He was not interested in eating in the stifling heat, so he hurried back inside the palace. He smiled to himself as he entered the building, which the British government designed to look like his own Kedleston Hall back in England.

Before heading to his office, Lord Curzon knocked on his wife's door. Her lady in waiting, a small, sallow woman with a warm smile, answered the door. "Good day, Lord Curzon. Lady Curzon is laying down. She is quite overcome by the heat."

"George? Is that you, George?" Lady Curzon's American accented voice was weak, yet distinct.

"Yes, it's me, Mary," Curzon replied. The lady in waiting stood back, allowing Curzon to enter the room and approach his wife's oversized four poster bed which was surrounded by mosquito nets. Lady Curzon lay on the bed, uncovered, while two maids with large fans twirled them around her to keep her cool.

"Why, oh why did I have to come to this godforsaken country?" It's simply too hot to move, eat, or even breathe!" Lady Curzon wailed, hot tears running down her cheeks.

Lord Curzon reached through the mosquito netting and took her hand. He did not say anything, but his presence calmed Mary, who soon fell asleep. He then slowly released her hand and tread softly out of the room. Curzon had a critical issue bothering him, which he wanted to discuss with his generals. He thus quickened his pace and headed to his office.

After Curzon arrived at his office, a small group of British personnel, including Captain Burke and James Mason, his chum from Eton, entered. They all sat down at a broad mahogany table on which was spread a large map.

"Here is a problem," said Curzon, pointing his fingers at a section of the map. "We have to govern almost eighty million people in this province of Bengal. This is too big a region; we need to split it up."

"How do you plan to split this region?" inquired Captain Burke.

There was silence for a moment, then James Mason spoke up. "Do it along religious lines, with the Muslims in one, the Hindus in another. Keep them divided and fighting. Fewer troubles for us," he said with a smirk. Curzon smiled without letting the others know of his approval. Divide and conquer had worked for the British in their colonial conquests, whether it was the East India company or the Monarchy itself. By separating the population along religious lines, they could suppress the growing nationalist movement, as well as breaking down the region into units that were easier to administer. It changed the focus of the region from being anti-British to pro-Muslim or pro-Hindu, depending on the religion. This would lead to religious violence, as each group tried to benefit from being the majority while oppressing the minorities. *Trust Mason to always come up with a solution*, thought the Viceroy. They discussed the details for a while longer, but the decision was already made.

The Viceroy dictated an announcement that was scribed by his secretary, who then read the proclamation aloud to the group. Curzon nodded his approval, took out a large seal from his desk, and affixed it to the scroll. The deed being finished, the group walked down the hall to enjoy their afternoon tea and get ready for a game of polo.

Outside the palace, Jeev mingled with the retreating crowd and made his way back to Swamy's house. This was his safe place. He glanced down the street to verify no one was looking, and then quickly jumped over a low fence. It was one of many two-story houses in the lane. The facade was gray and weather-beaten from years of monsoon rains. An open sewer, its stench stifling in the tropical sun, ran in front of the houses.

As was the custom, he removed his chappal sandals before entering. The front door opened to a rickety, carved staircase with a banister well-worn from years of greasy hands. Jeev bounded up the staircase to the top landing. There, the house expanded into a rectangular courtyard, the size of which could not be seen by someone looking from the outside. There were rooms on both the first and second floor overlooking the courtyard. At least fifty young men lived in the house. They came mostly from torn-apart families and were united in their quest to rid the country of the British rule.

On one side of the courtyard, a group of teenage boys sat cross-legged around a heavy-set man with long hair, piercing eyes and three horizontal lines of ash painted across his forehead. Affectionately called 'Swamy', very few knew his actual name. They were listening intently to his speech. "The famine that we are facing today, *they* caused it, the British and the East India Company. It has nothing to do with the rains. The Gods have delayed the rains many times before in the past. We did not have these famines till the British took over."

The boys nodded in silence, happy to be fed here at Swamy's house. The villages they had escaped from were hellscapes. Cows and buffaloes were reduced to bones and ribs. Human corpses littered street corners. Many of the men moved to other areas of the country to find work. The farms lay burned in the sun. The children and women were forced to fend for themselves. It was common to be hungry for days. They had seen entire families wiped out by the famine. The youngest children, the frailest, would die first. Many died from infections caught due to their weaknesses. The death toll in the region rose every day. Relatives dumped bodies into the river. There was no firewood for the pyres.

When Jeev entered the room, Swamy called him over. "Did you go to the Viceroy's palace?" he asked.

"Yes," nodded Jeev. "I got close enough to smell the food. *How* can they indulge when our people are dying of starvation?"

Swamy closed his eyes. When he opened them, they were dark with anger. "It is up to us to put an end to their rule," he thundered. "You must get angry, all of you." He pointed his finger at all the boys in the room. "You are part of the future that will rise and drive the English from our shores." He then handed Jeev a stack of letters. "Deliver this to the usual warehouse near the docks." Jeev had delivered items to the warehouse many times before, so he placed them in a small bag, tucked the bag inside his shirt, and made his way to the docks.

The road to the docks ran parallel to the Hooghly River. An offspring of the Goddess Ganges, the Hooghly River flows down through Bengal past Calcutta into the Bay of Bengal and then the Indian Ocean, carrying the holy water all along its length. As Jeev approached the bank, he saw corpses scattered along the riverbed, some humans, some animals, as the putrid, muddy waters made their way towards the Bay of Bengal. He turned his face away from the river to avoid the gruesome sights of the bodies drifting downstream. A long dusty road stretched out into the distance. The sun rose high in the cloudless sky, uninterrupted by clouds. All the trees in the area had been cut down, the leaves used for fodder and the wood for pyres. On his right, along the wall, was the compound for the army barracks. Further down the road was the harbor where there were the 'godowns' or storage facilities for the ship's cargo. He headed to the harbor to deliver letters for the Swamy.

Jeev grew more alert and tread lightly as he approached an area with guards who would search and beat up anyone they thought might steal from their warehouses. A boy of Jeev's age would arouse suspicion and be labelled a perpetual criminal. There was no concept of innocent until proven guilty. His kind were thought to be guilty all the time.

If the soldiers found the letters on him, unimaginable torture would follow, and his body would be dumped into the river. Jeev imagined seeing himself floating by as a bloated corpse, with a bloodied, unrecognizable head, and mangled limbs. He shook his head in disbelief as he tried to get those ugly thoughts out of his head, as a pungent stench from the river permeated all who passed by.

Up ahead, as the army compound ended, he saw the godowns beginning. He knocked on a door. A large woman wearing a bright blue and gold saree, her mouth red from chewing betel leaves, opened the door. Jeev saw that everything about her appeared swollen, including her large, fat hands. Her head merged into her shoulders with no visible neck, her broad shoulders and the rest of her body stretched out into the fabric of her outfit. Scared by the image and his hands shaking, he handed her the letters. "This is… from…er… Swamy," he said hesitatingly.

She looked up and down the street to see if anyone had seen her and snatched the packet. "Get out, you rascal," she hissed under her breath, "if anyone sees you, we are both dead. Get lost!" Spitting the red betel liquid from the corner of her mouth, it splattered on the side wall, as a fresh coat of gooey liquid, and she slammed the door shut.

CHAPTER 2: THE DOPPELGANGERS (1845)

The fox was curled up under the fallen tree, its eyes shut, with his bushy tail wrapped all the way down his front legs, chin resting on tail, and ears swooping downwards. A dirt road snaked down a small hill from where he lay. Beech, oak, and sweet bay magnolia trees surrounded the road. There was a puddle where the runoff from the last few storms had washed parts of the road away. Attached to a rotting tree stump was a crude hand carved sign. Someone had used a sharp blade to slice the words 'Fox Hollow' with the straight lines in each word cutting upward, resembling the edge of a knife.

Uphill from Fox Hollow, Benjamin Calvert, sat on a bale of hay, feet dangling, chewing tobacco in a staccato rhythm. At twenty-five, he was already balding. His deep brown hair was slicked back revealing a giant forehead. Shirtless, his well-toned body glistened in the sun as sweat dripped down his face. He spit the tobacco on the ground and then glanced at the farmhouse to his right. It was a log cabin with a tall stone chimney towering over the house. Two steps led up to an open porch held up by four uneven logs. A single door opened into a two-room interior, consisting of a bedroom for him and his wife, Emma, and a sitting area and kitchen. From the back door, a path led to an outhouse a few feet away. A horse impatiently shook its head, wanting to be released from the midwife's carriage.

The midwife was inside the room aiding Emma who was screaming in pain, "Dear God! Someone do something. Help me with this baby. The pain! I can't take it anymore!"

A neighboring woman peered into the bedroom, wringing her hands in helplessness. "What can I do to help you?"

The midwife shook her head at the bystander and whispered, "Shhhh, Emma, a few more pushes and your baby will be out. Come on, Emma, there you go, breathe, and push hard. One more time." The next shriek from the bedroom shook Calvert to the bone, and then he heard wailing. *The baby is born!*

He jumped off the hay and ran into the house, stumbling over the front steps. Inside the bedroom, the midwife was wiping down a bawling baby. "How is she?" Benjamin demanded. "Did she make it? How 'bout the baby?" He looked over at Emma lying on the bed, covered in bloody bedsheets, eyes closed, and breathing softly.

He glanced again at the midwife, who nodded, "Emma and your son are fine." She placed the baby boy in Emma's arms.

"Let us name him McBride, after my grandfather," declared Emma weakly. Benjamin Calvert certainly had no objections. He would be the first child born with the Calvert name in the family.

Benjamin's eyes welled with tears. His memories of his own parents were dim shadows, as they both died of an incurable, wasting sickness in 1828 when he was three years old. His parents' home, and Benjamin himself, passed to the care of an uncle. Benjamin faintly remembered the man's aggravation with his mere presence. As Benjamin grew older, however, the boy developed a cunning mind and a talent for acting. His uncle found these helpful in his robbery, forgery, and gambling schemes. He taught Benjamin all that he knew. The boy soon became adept at stealing cattle, cheating at cards, and especially forging documents and seals. Benjamin's life thus settled into a steady routine of more complicated schemes.

This came to a sudden end one evening when Benjamin was about fourteen. Benjamin was standing in the hallway outside the drawing room door, peering in watching his uncle and companions playing cards. Even though he watched from a distance, his hearing was sharp, and he knew how his uncle was cheating. Suddenly, one of the players, a dark headed man with a long beard, slammed his hand of cards on the oaken table.

"Dammit, Smith! You're a cheating bastard!" The other men leaned back in their seats, not moving even an eyelash.

"What did you say, Sharpe?" Benjamin's uncle rose slowly, reaching into his waistband. Before Benjamin, or his uncle, knew it, Sharpe pulled a handgun from his pocket, and shot Benjamin's uncle straight in the heart, killing him instantly. His body fell to the floor knocking over his chair as he went down. Benjamin was too startled to scream. He ran outside, behind the outhouse and threw up until there was nothing left except dry air.

From then on, Benjamin stayed in his birth home which was on the outskirts of unclaimed land. With all the confidence, wariness, and skills of a street-smart kid, he followed in his uncle's perilous footsteps and lived a mundane life except for his uncontrollable anger, which often landed him in trouble.

Through skillful forgery, he changed his name to Benjamin Calvert, which gave him high status and recognition in Maryland, where the Calvert family had settled in the early 1600s, and later became governors of Maryland. The Calverts established goodwill with Maryland citizens at the turn of the 18th century by giving land to homesteaders.

Those days, however, had long passed. Agriculture was booming as farmers found new ways to make the land more productive. So, seeing a lucrative opportunity, Benjamin created documents to claim an undeveloped tract of land north of the Potomac River. With the help of a few strategic bribes, the governor's office in Baltimore authenticated the documents, deeds, and seals he had carefully drawn.

Benjamin then got to work clearing the land for cattle and horses, which he stole from farms in neighboring Virginia and brought to his farm by boat. His stock multiplied, and Benjamin began selling some of them to merchants and farmers in Baltimore. He would often make cattle runs to farms in Baltimore to deliver the animals. On one such run, he walked into the farmhouse to let the owner know his cattle had been delivered. As the farmer accepted the papers, his daughter walked into the room and smiled at Benjamin. He felt as if he had been hit by lightning. Emma was wearing a light summer dress that twirled around her legs as she moved. An intoxicating sweet perfume that he could not identify floated past him. "This is Emma, my oldest daughter" said the farmer introducing them. Benjamin hastily removed his hat and managed to blurt out a "Hello." The farmer continued "My bad leg is acting up today. Emma will go with you to inspect the cattle." As Benjamin and Emma rode to the corral, his eyes were on Emma. When Emma pointed out the number was one less than he had counted, he readily agreed with her. "Could I call on you this Friday?" asked Benjamin. "I have choir practice and I sing at the Basilica of the Assumption on Saturday and Sunday" replied Emma. "Yes, I know that Church, maybe I will see you there," said Benjamin. "Are you Catholic too?" Emma asked. Benjamin who did not know his religious background nor had he any interest in the Church readily replied, "Yes born, baptized and raised Catholic."

Benjamin became regular at the downtown Baltimore Church. Emma and Benjamin would frequently talk after the service. They took long walks together along the seashore. On one such walk he asked her to marry him. Emma was not surprised, as she had been expecting Benjamin to propose. She had, however, visited his farm and was appalled by the small cabin he lived in. "Yes" she said, "under one condition, you build me a new home for us to live." Benjamin was thrilled "I promise my dear to build a mansion worthy of your stature."

A few weeks before the planned wedding, Benjamin called on Emma's father to finalize the plans. As he was coming up the house front steps a Black servant, descending the steps carrying a large pot of water, bumped into him, and they both tumbled down the stairs, the pot splashing water all over Benjamin. Furious, a dripping wet Benjamin shouted, "Damn you fool, look where you are going." The servant stayed down on the ground, held up his hands in apology "Sir I am very sorry, very sorry." Benjamins' eyes started to twitch in anger, he lashed out with his foot, hitting the man on his face. Blood spurted out from his mouth as Benjamin repeatedly kicked him in the stomach. Emma's father ran out and pushed Benjamin aside "Stop this" he shouted as he called on one of his farm hands to take care of the man on the ground. Emma saw the whole scene play out from her window. Benjamin now ashamed of his behavior and not knowing how to explain this to Emma, turned around and walked out of the farm.

He showed up unannounced the next day as Emma and her father sat on the porch. Getting down on his knees he said "I hope you will forgive me Emma. I can assure this will never happen again." Emma's father looked at her "This is your call, Emma. I will support your decision." Benjamin unrolled a parchment paper with drawings on it and pointed at them "This is the house I want to build for you. Where we will raise our children and build a grand future." Emma knew she had invested many months in her relationship with Benjamin.

This was the only bad incident. Her Church had taught her she must forgive those who trespass against her. She would use her faith to guide Benjamin to be a God-fearing man. She nodded her head "Yes." The two were married later that summer in a small but beautiful ceremony at her church in downtown Baltimore.

The south side of Calvert's farm had a thick forest leading down to the river. The small cabin that Benjamin and Emma initially lived in on the edge of the forest remained in disrepair as Benjamin started but never finished his construction projects. They cleared the north side for rearing cattle. There was a Patawomeck tribal village nestled nearby on the cliff side, overlooking the Potomac River, Despite the great river being named for this tiny settlement, most of the city people did not know of its existence and the few that knew did not care about the inhabitants of the village as long as the natives kept their distance.

After Benjamin got title to the land, he hired people to lay markers and signposts showing the boundary. It was too big to fence in. The natives, oblivious to the fact that their land was no longer theirs, continued to hunt the local deer and fish in the Potomac. Being the only occupants of the land, Calvert and his family left the natives alone but not for long.

CHAPTER 3: PATAWOMECK VILLAGE (1859)

O ne day a couple of braves on horseback ventured too close to the Calvert homestead while chasing a deer. The deer cleared the forest and bounded into the open meadow, then ran up a slope, and looked behind as the two hunters continued their chase. One hunter fired his arrow, which flew over the deer's head. As they followed the deer uphill, they pulled back their horses and came to a halt. Up ahead was the Calvert Cabin. Outside, a white woman was hanging clothes to dry while a young boy played with a dog. The dog saw the hunters and started growling.

Emma looked up, and fear spread across her face. Standing downhill from her were two men from the Patawomeck tribe, with bows drawn and arrows nocked, riding astride unsaddled horses, wearing only loincloths around their waists. Their bare chests were painted white and red, with their long black hair tied back in ponytails. The deer had long since disappeared, so Emma could not tell they were hunting. They too were startled to see the woman and boy. Normally they did not come this far to hunt, avoiding Calvert's land near the house.

The dog barked viciously and rushed towards the hunters. Emma ran to her son, "Come on, McBride, run! Run to the house NOW." She grabbed him by the arm and sprinted towards the cabin. *On the shelf next to the front door is a rifle.*

I need to get to it, Emma thought. Emma was close enough now to get through the front door, pushed her son inside, and bolted the door. "Now you stay inside, you hear me?" she whispered. "These are dangerous people." The hunters, out of curiosity, drifted towards the house.

Benjamin and the cowhands rounding up cattle were not too far away from the house. *If I am lucky,* Emma thought, *they will hear shots from the rifle.* Out of breath, she leaned against the closed door to recover from the run. Still breathing hard, she lifted the rifle from the shelf. It was a new gun; the wood smelt fresh, and the stock, barrel and trigger were a shiny silver. She grabbed a handful of cartridges from a wooden box and slid them into the breech. Unlike older rifles that needed to be loaded from the muzzle, this one had a special tube under the barrel to load multiple bullets. Satisfied that the gun was loaded properly, she peered out of the side of a window. The two hunters were still there surveying the property.

Slowly she opened a window and slid the gun out, resting the barrel on the windowsill and the stock on her shoulder. She had hoped the riders would go away, but they inched closer to the house. She pulled the lever to load a fresh cartridge into the chamber barrel and pulled the trigger. Not being an excellent marksman, the bullet strayed wide. The horses reared instinctively at the gunfire. One hunter raised his bow as if to shoot in the window's direction. Emma loaded a new bullet and fired. Again, she missed by a large margin. The other hunter shouted a command, and they both prodded their horses and galloped away. Left behind on the side of the house was an embedded arrow, the one that had missed the deer. The sharp stone arrowhead with black feathers had penetrated a log, the feathers now gently swayed in the wind.

Chogan, whose name meant blackbird, was the brave riding the white horse. He decorated and balanced his arrows with black feathers. When he killed, everyone knew whose arrow had struck the prey. The son of the village chief, Chogan was brash, brave, and fearless. He knew he would someday be the chief, so everything he did was with the intent of proving himself. He went overboard and pushed the limits of what he should do. The chief had assigned Segenam, whose name meant lazy, to be Chogan's partner on expeditions. Segenam, however, was far from lazy. Slow and thorough, he thought before he spoke or acted, considering the options and the situation, which the tribe interpreted as lethargy. The chief knew that Segenam's personality balanced to his impetuous son, hoping this would prevent Chogan from harming himself or others. The two, growing up together, formed a close friendship. Chogan knew he could always count on Segenam.

Segenam was riding a grey mare when they were chasing the deer. Once he saw they had inadvertently stumbled upon the Calvert home, which the chief had told them to avoid, he realized they had strayed far from their normal hunting route.

"Chogan, we are not allowed here. The Chief has already told us. What are you doing? We need to leave!" Segenam shouted.

"No," Chogan argued, "Let's get closer. I want to see the white man's house."

Segenam tried to hold him back. "No. You know the rules. You cannot break them. Your father has commanded us. Leave now!" When he saw the woman shooting from the house repeatedly and now Chogan ready to release his arrow, Segenam decided they had gone far enough. He rode up to Chogan and looked him straight in the eye. "We are leaving now!" Chogan reluctantly lowered his arrow, and they both galloped into the woods.

They rode back to the village in silence, each thinking about the day's events. There were about fifty people, men, women, and children, living in the village. The huts had their sides and tops stitched together with branches and shrubs, were built in the form of an inverted 'U' with a large firepit in the center space. On the periphery, tall trees provided a natural boundary. Beyond the trees, a steep cliff overlooked the Potomac River. The village was hidden from anyone fishing or traveling down the river. As they rode towards the clearing, Chogan beseeched, "What happened today stays between us. Please, let us tell no one."

Segenam, retorted, "Listen, I am going to tell the chief about today with or without you. It will not look good for you if you don't come with me."

Chogan did not have a choice and reluctantly followed Segenam to Chief Eluwilussit's hut. The elderly and well-respected chief, whose name meant 'the holy one,' had protected his clan for over fifty years.

The braves alighted from their horses and bent down at the low entrance to the chief's hut. Inside it was dark and smokey. A few rolls of bedding, a small fire in the corner for warmth and cooking, and headgear made from turkey feathers, seashells, and deer antlers hanging from bark covered branches made up the wall. The chief listened while Segenam narrated the day's events. He focused on the arrow that Chogan had shot. "The arrow missed the deer and hit the house?" the chief inquired.

Chogan responded, "We don't know for sure where the arrow hit."

Segenam interjected, "I am sure I saw it embedded in the house's wall."

The chief narrowed his eyes and stroked his chin. Then he waved his hand towards the door. "Go now. Leave me alone. I need to think."

Dismissed, Segenam and Chogan got up and slowly walked backwards to the door, staring at the chief. Lost in thought, Chief Eluwilussit took a deep breath and sighed. He had seen the white man come for many years. As the chieftain of the tiny village, he always wondered when the two cultures would clash. Hidden away in the cliffs and behind thick trees, no one had bothered them so far. He knew their bows and arrows were no match for the guns the white men carried. Hiding amongst the leaves, he had watched the forest being cleared for pastures and farmland as the newcomers moved closer and closer to the Patawomeck habitats. Up in the shallow hills of the forest surrounding the river, he saw them place cruel metal traps that snared rabbits, foxes, and bears by mutilating their legs. He had seen the white man shoot deer for no reason and leave the carcass in the fields. Over the years, news that other villages of his tribe further north that had been annihilated made him shiver. There were stories of chiefs who had tried to make peace with the white man, to live together, but it never ended well for them. The greed of the white man always superseded his best intentions. The white man broke the agreements based on trust. These foreigners were stealing Patawomeck land. When the Indians fought back, it ended in their own slaughter.

The chief picked up a basket containing a handful of brightly polished stones, shook the basket, and then turned it upside down, sending the stones spinning on to the floor like dice. He carefully studied the pattern stones made across the floor. He shook his head in disdain. *The stones foretell a time of great upheaval for the tribe. I pray the great Spirits will guide me to make the right decision.* Not happy with what he saw, he picked up his bow and arrow and strode out into the now darkening forest.

A fox scampered towards the river. As he approached the Patawomeck village, he paused. There was someone up ahead staring at the moon. It was Chief Eluwilussit standing on a cliff overlooking the Potomac River. The fox darted towards the man.

The river, forced into a narrow gorge, turned the slow-moving water into a torrential waterfall. The water gurgled and screamed as it tore through the rocks, making its way down the ravine. It fashioned a deep chasm between the rocks, creating a natural boundary for the village and protecting it from one side. The water appeared a dark blue in the moonlight, with specks of white foam where it crashed against the rocks. The fox came closer to the man standing over the waterfall. Sensing something nearby, the chief turned to see the fox. The fox stared directly into the eyes of the chief. The chief shuddered at the sight reflected in the fox's eyes. He saw a campfire with villagers gathered around the fire, talking, laughing, and sharing food. Suddenly, the gunshots from outside the circle shattered the peaceful evening. One man clutched his chest and fell over. A further volley of gunfire came from the surrounding forest. It was a bloodbath, men, women, and children gunned down without mercy. and then their huts were set on fire. The remaining stunned warriors responded bravely with bows and arrows, but they were no match for the blazing rifles. The chief abruptly broke contact with the fox's eyes as he could not watch the massacre anymore. He bowed slightly to the fox in gratitude. The fox slinked back into the brush.

The chief walked back to the village. In the middle of the hamlet, most of the inhabitants had gathered around the fire, with the men sitting in the center discussing hunting and farming matters, the women at the periphery cooking food, and the children frolicking here and there between the elders. The chief strode to his traditional seating place and raised his hand, stopping all conversation. A few stragglers, seeing the Chief, ran to sit around the fire. He scanned the crowd sitting in front of him, satisfied that all who needed to be present were there. He spoke. "Do you know why we have a body?" Some shook their heads. Others responded, "So we can sense what is happening. We can see, we can smell, we can taste, and we can hear." Pointing to his skin, eyes, nose, and ears as he spoke. "Yes, there is all that, but there is more to what we can sense. We who have lived off the land and acknowledge what our mother land gives to us — that noble spirit that flows in our river, which speaks to us when we need help, when we need guidance." He placed his hand on his heart and continued, "There comes a time when we must listen to the noble spirit. I was in the forest today and the noble spirit spoke to me." The crowd looked at him expectantly. His eyes glowed as the flames silhouetted them. He stood up and held his pole, chiseled with carvings of various faces, some scarier than the others. The colorful feathers at the end of his pole fluttered in the wind. Holding it high over his head, he shouted, "The time has come! The white man has been moving closer and closer to us. Our way of life is being threatened. We must act because the greed of the white man knows no boundaries and his cruelty knows no limits. We know what needs to be done." He discussed his plan with the group and then dismissed them to do their jobs. They swiftly moved to their huts to prepare, gather their bows and arrows, corral their animals, and protect the women and children.

CHAPTER 4: A TENSE SITUATION

That same morning, Benjamin Calvert and his workers were rounding up cattle. The morning was sunny but not too warm yet. Benjamin glanced at one worker, Chet, who was riding on the far edge of the field, herding the cattle to the center. Chet was tall, pale, and thin as a stick with unruly, dirty blonde hair. He wore a wide-brimmed hat and chaps over his trousers. Notorious all over the county for being quick on the draw, he had come back east after a failed gold venture out in California. Benjamin gave him a job as a cowhand so he could repay his debts.

Further into the field, another cowhand, Louis, steered the cattle through the open gate into the next, greener field. He was the opposite of Chet, black-skinned and muscular with broad shoulders, he considered himself a 'free' slave. His family had worked for Benjamin's uncle's ever since he could remember. When the uncle died, Louis came to work for Benjamin, who paid him, provided him a roof over his head, and permitted him to carry a rifle, making Louis the freest he had ever been.

The hectic pace of the morning was shattered when Benjamin thought he heard gunfire. Unsure of his hearing, he stopped and raised his right arm, signaling his workers to pause and listen. A couple of minutes later, he heard another shot. This time, he was sure it was a gunshot from the direction of his house. His adrenaline rushing, Benjamin shouted, "Louis! Chet! The cabin! I heard shots!" The three men leaned forward on their horses, braced their knees, and galloped at high speed toward the Calvert home. As they rode up the hill, the men saw clothes scattered all over the backyard. Benjamin's heart skipped a beat, and his hands grew cold, as he feared the worst.

Inside the house, Emma heard the riders coming up the hill. Thinking the natives had come back, she grabbed the rifle, and debated what she should do. Soon, however, she saw Benjamin, and ran to open the door. "I am so glad to see you!" she cried out, swinging her arms.

Benjamin dismounted, and Emma hugged him close enough to smell the sweat caked into his flannel shirt.

"Emma, what happened? Where's McBride?" Benjamin's eyes scanned the yard, looking for his son.

Emma turned towards the door. McBride stood at the entrance, and seeing his father, ran out to greet him. Benjamin smiled and scooped him up in a big hug. He then put the boy down, and Chet and Louis walked over and joined him. "Now, Emma, tell me what happened? Did you fire the rifle? Benjamin's voice was gentle, as he looked his wife straight in the eye.

Emma swallowed. "Yes. Two Indians came in the yard on horseback. They didn't get into the house, but I wasn't going to let them." Emma pulled her son close under her arm.

Benjamin took hold of Emma's hands in a soft yet firm grip. "Listen to me, Emma. Nothing bad is going to happen to you or McBride. I won't let it.". He nodded to Chet and Louis who went to survey around the house.

The pair returned shortly. "We saw two tracks heading up to the house and then back into the forest," reported Chet. "Also, come out front. I want to show you something."

Emma, Benjamin, and young McBride followed them to the front of the house, where Chet pointed to an arrow embedded in the wood. Benjamin grabbed the arrow with his gloved hand and pulled it out, his face turning violet red. McBride noticed arteries twitching violently in his dad's temple, his mouth clamped with the lower lip turned over his upper lip and a foreboding look. It was a grimace that McBride would never forget. "Those damn Injuns have gone too far," Benjamin yelled to Chet. "Go get the others from the cattle roundup. We are forming a posse. I will teach them a lesson." Chet nodded. He had learned a thing or two about tracking and forming gangs to hunt down outlaws and Apache when he was out west. With this knowledge, he felt superior to the easterners and their so-called ability as fighters or even hunters.

"Look Ben," Chet drawled, glancing at Emma for her approval. The words came out soft and calm. "Let Louis go back to the others and finish his job for the day. I will scout around and track where the Indians' trail leads. I assure you we will find them. Let's talk tonight after I gather some information. "

Emma placed her hand on Benjamin's shoulder and nodded. "I agree with Chet," she said. She knew her hot-headed husband would fly into the face of danger without thinking of the consequences. She, on the other hand, dreaded fighting of any sort, especially a bloodbath between the cowhands and Indians. "Ben, there's no need to act before you know what's really happening. Let Chet do what he does best. You'll know what you need to do then."

Benjamin looked at his wife. "I guess you're right, Emma, but if anything happens to you or McBride..."

"With Chet's help, it won't," Emma reassured him. Benjamin took her hand without saying a word, and she pulled her husband and son back into the house before Benjamin could change his mind. Meanwhile, Louis headed out to the fields. Chet led his horse by the reins and walked down the slope, following the horse trail left by the two hunters.

That night there were two campfires, one at the Patawomeck village and another at the Calvert homestead, both burning brightly and briskly. Benjamin, Louis, and five other cowhands sat around the Calvert bonfire. Benjamin had sent notes to neighboring farmers to help form a raiding party. Soon, Bruce and James, two nearby tobacco farmers, joined them.

Benjamin chewed angrily on a piece of straw. "You know, we have been too good to these redskins. It's time to act. What do they mean by coming to my property? They could have killed my wife and son. What if they had kidnapped and enslaved them? I have heard stories of them scalping our people for no reason."

Bruce answered, "Now come on, Ben. You don't mean that. They ain't done nothing to us all these years. They don't mean no harm. You are jumping to conclusions. You don't know why they came on your land; maybe they were chasing an animal."

"Hell, yes, I do," retorted Benjamin. He stood up. "They were trying to scare us. Well, I will show them."

James jumped in. "I agree. This is an all-out war. One day it's Ben's property, and if we do nothin', next thing you know it will be mine and then yours, Bruce. Come on, man. You gotta nip this in the bud." Tempers rose as opinions were argued.

Just then, Emma came out of the house with a large pot of pea soup with ham and chunks of bread. "Dinner is ready, boys." One by one, she ladled the soup into tin cups and passed them around. The warm soup felt good to the group on the chilly autumn night. A bit later, she served a supper of hot, steaming corn bread and juicy, tender steaks. The men, somewhat satiated, settled into peaceful conversation about the day's events, the earlier heated exchange temporarily forgotten. As Emma gathered up the empty plates, there was a rustling noise downhill from the house. The men got up and moved their eyes away from the fire to adjust to the darkness. Some of them pointed their weapons in the direction of the noise. "Who goes there?" roared Benjamin.

"It's me, Chet!" boomed a voice from the darkness. The men lowered their weapons as Chet rode into the light and alighted from his horse. Louis grabbed the reins and led the horse away. Emma brought him a cup of warm soup and filled the dinner plate with food, which he graciously accepted. As Chet wolfed down the food, he explained, "I followed the tracks all the way to the river. Those two Indians came from the village by the forest there. I did not get too close or else they would catch me. There are around ten or fifteen huts and about fifty people, including men, women, and children, living there. They have a herd of about twenty horses and some goats. I can lead you to the village; it's just a few miles from here."

Bruce spoke first. "Not now. It is not the time. Let's ride to the village tomorrow and speak with the Chief there. We need to come up with some understanding of why this happened and how close to our houses and farms they can come. I can bring ten men with me for protection."

James chimed in, "I agree. I can bring another five-armed men, between mine and Benjamin's men. We will have over twenty able-bodied fellows. We can handle anything that those Indians might try to do. Let us ride to the village tomorrow and threaten the chief."

Benjamin had other thoughts. "That village is on my property. I had an arrow stuck in my house. It could have been me, my son, or my wife. They started the fight. Now I will finish it. They must suffer the consequences. We will ride as a posse tomorrow night. Chet can guide us there. We will launch a surprise attack on them. They will not know what hit them."

As the men argued about what to do next, a moon rose over the forest. Night creatures stirred in the woods. A silver fox crept out of its den and went down a hollow among the trees. From the distance, he could see the men gathered around the fire. A tantalizing smell of cooked meat rose from the fire. The fox moved closer to the flames, waiting on the periphery of the woods, surveying the area for food he could steal or kill.

Benjamin got up and peered into the dark forest. "It's decided! We attack tomorrow night." The others nodded in acceptance. He noticed the fox staring at him in the distance. He lifted his rifle, looked through the sighting, loaded the cartridge and fired. The shot startled the men. The bullets kicked up a cloud of dirt between the feet of the fox. It jumped up in the air, turned around airborne, and scuttled into the bushes.

"You know, the natives here consider those foxes sacred," warned Chet. "I would not play games like this if I were you."

"Too bad I missed," challenged Benjamin, "but trust me, tomorrow night I will be luckier.". Emma walked up to the group with two large apple pies. The men dug into the dessert, agreeing to meet later the next day, all other matters forgotten for the time.

CHAPTER 5: THE AMBUSH

The next evening, Benjamin Calvert and his crew gathered in front of the farmhouse. Heavily armed with two rifles and a six-shooter each, the mob was ready to attack. As the sun set, Bruce and James rode up the hill with their groups. Emma and a petrified McBride stood on the porch watching the crowd. Benjamin called McBride over and ordered, "You, son! Get on your horse. You are coming with us."

Horrified, Emma objected, "No! He is still a child. Ben, I beg you. Please let him stay home."

"He is old enough and needs to learn." Benjamin gave her a stern look and nodded to Louis, who saddled a horse for McBride and held the reins as McBride mounted the horse. "Louis will be by his side throughout, so don't worry," reassured Benjamin as Chet led the men into the forest.

They rode slowly and silently in a single file as they passed the place, they called the fox hollow. Camouflaged under the fallen leaves, the fox watched as the lengthy line of men made their way towards the river.

About half a mile away from the village, Chet gestured that they dismount and tie their horses to the trees. One of Benjamin's men stayed behind with the horses as the rest of the group silently walked towards the village. It was dark but the full moon allowed them to see clearly. Chet signaled to stop. He slowly moved ahead and then returned a few minutes later.

"The village is very close now. We will stop at the ridge ahead. I see a few people in the center sitting around a fire," he whispered. The men, crawling on all fours, gathered and looked down at the village. There was not much movement. They saw a few men sitting and staring into a central fire encircled by reed and bark huts; *the others may be in the huts*, thought Benjamin. They were within shooting range of the village. Louis brought McBride to his side so he could see what was happening.

Before anyone was prepared for the next step, Benjamin impulsively yelled, "Fire!" and started shooting at the natives around the fire. Astonishingly, they all toppled over easily. In the confusion, the rest of the men started shooting. They targeted the huts too and for a few minutes the shots from the rifles, the ricocheting of the bullets, and the smoke from burning wood and reeds filled the air.

As the men reloaded their guns, Chet commanded, "Everybody, stop!" The main fire now seemed minor compared to the larger blazes of several huts. A few Indians lay lifeless in the middle of the settlement. Yet something was wrong. It was eerily quiet. Even the foxes and owls were silent. The villagers did not return the gunfire. The expected shower of arrows did not happen. *What happened?* Chet thought. He took his rifle, stepped over the clifftop, and walked down to the village.

I swear to God that man has lost his mind! Benjamin reasoned as he saw Chet trudge straight into the carnage.

Chet pushed over the dead bodies of the people in the village. "Holy cow, these are all effigies. The people are gone. Nobody is here!" he shouted to the onlookers.

The rest of the men now bolted down to the village. In the middle, by the fire pit, clothes and hats stuffed with straw lay dispersed on the ground. The huts, a few on fire and others with immeasurable holes from the bullets, stood empty. Chet squatted over some tracks near the cliff side of the village. As

Benjamin and the others approached him, he pointed at the prints and explained, "They must have left over a day ago. Horses, goats, people, all of them escaped. They have gone too far ahead. There is no point following them. Once they wade through the river, we will lose their tracks. We should head back home."

As the group walked back to the horses, they stumbled on the man assigned to guard them. He lay unconscious on the forest floor. Around him, the slashed horse saddles were scattered on the ground. The group dejectedly began the long walk home. Benjamin was furious. *They had been made fools! The horses were gone. Outwitted!*

In the underbrush, the fox lay on the ground with his face nestled between his feet watching the men trudge back to the farmhouse, his mouth turned up at the corners into a smirk.

CHAPTER 6: FRIENDS FOREVER (1900)

The hot Calcutta sun glared down without mercy as Amee and her sister Arti stared at a straight-backed woman with thick black hair piled in an elaborate top knot woman talking to their father. She wore a jade silk sari embroidered with gold thread that sparkled in the bright sun, a strange sight. Rich people did not visit impoverished huts, nor did they talk to the destitute villagers. Their mother, head and face covered with the tail of her faded blue cotton sari, huddled in the distance, seeing the interaction between her husband and the stranger. Just one of her deep brown eyes was visible. Like deep abysses, they showed a story of submission and surrender. Times had been hard, their crops had been destroyed, and as their money ran out, they had sold all their animals. Mother had resorted to cooking any plants or leaves she could scavenge. It was a tough time now. The visitor got up to take her leave, bowing slightly and folding her hands in a namaste. As she passed the two sisters, she smiled at them.

Amee felt shivers going up and down her spine. *Something did not seem right. This woman seemed evil. Why do I feel this way?* She cautiously approached her father. "Baba, what did that woman want?"

Her father answered softly, "That woman had a message from your aunt. You both will go to stay with her until things get better here."

"*Aunt?* What aunt? We have never met her. Why? Where does she live? And for how long? " Probed Amee.

"Don't ask questions," snapped Baba.

"I don't want to go. I'm staying here," muttered Amee. Baba got up, grabbed the front of her shirt and slapped her hard on the cheek. The force of the slap sent her sprawling to the ground. Shocked, she held her palm to her ear to subdue the ringing in the ears. Her head hurt. Horrified, Arti and her mother ran to help Amee as blood trickled from her ears.

"You will do as I tell you. Don't argue with me. It's done," roared Baba and walked away.

A few days later, as Amee was walking by a field, she saw Jeev, who sprinted up to meet her. They ran on an embankment parallel to the dry sugarcane field. It had a crudely carved irrigation canal which led water from the river into the fields. From time to time, they jumped into the canal. There was no water now, but it was a game they had always played. When there had been water in the canal, they had splashed each other as they hopped from the ridge. Today there was no water to ease the heat, so they pretended to spray water thriving in the momentary bliss of freedom.

Jeev had grown up with Amee, who lived a few doors down from his family home. The families were good friends, and Amee was often over at his house with her mother. Their childhood friendship continued, with Jeev now a tall, awkward boy, and Amee a blossoming young woman.

They stopped at the edge of the farm, and both sat down cross-legged. As far as they could see, the ground was dry and cracked from the heat, with the plants burnt to a crisp golden color. For two years, the rain gods had forgotten about them. All agriculture relied on the monsoons. No rain meant no food and no drinking water. Their favorite tree, a giant oak, was now a pile of firewood. Somebody had chopped it down after it died. They reminisced about the rope swing they had made on one of its branches and how they would swing higher and higher until euphoric and then splash down into the canal.

Amee absentmindedly stared off into the distance. Jeev looked at her and realized something was wrong. She turned to face him, and he saw a large bruise across her ear. He inquisitively pointed at it.

She just shook her head and replied, "I bumped into something while I was cleaning the cowshed."

Jeev doubted it. *It was something to do with her father.* Amee's father was a farmer, prone to heavy bouts of drinking, and was always borrowing money. He never understood the concept of interest, nor could he read the documents he was asked to place his thumb print on, so the money lenders charged him exorbitant amounts. *What if her father had lost his land? They would take land as collateral. Amee and her family would be homeless.* Jeev trembled, and then spoke "What happened, Amee? What really happened? I know you, and you don't do dumb things!"

Amee lowered her eyes so that Jeev couldn't see her tears. "We have to give up our land, maybe even the house, to pay back the loans. Also, the crops have died in the heat, so we have nothing anyway. I don't know what is going to happen."

"You can always come live with us. Please! I am sure my family will be thrilled," entreated Jeev.

Amee gave a halfhearted smile and looked at Jeev with a faraway glazed look, her eyes red. Jeev had a gnawing in the pit of his stomach, a premonition of unfortunate events to come. He put his hand around her, and she rested her head on his shoulder. They watched the sun set in the distance as darkness enveloped the riverbed.

He never felt closer to Amee than he felt that night. The stars were brighter than usual on this moonless night. Despite the tranquil beauty, there was a sadness in Amee that Jeev could not lessen. He knew it was getting late. Dejectedly, he stood up to go back home and helped her up. She held on to his hand and then pressed against his body in a hug. The aroma of coconut oil from her hair filled the air and he could feel her breasts as she held him even tighter. He nestled his nose into fragrant black hair. Just as suddenly, she let go and started running home. He chased after her until she turned into her house. *Why did she leave so abruptly? How bad is this? I must find out!*

The next day, Jeev made his usual trek to Swamy's house. There was another delivery for the harbor area. He placed the package in his bag, swung the bag around his back and started walking towards the harbor. It was about an hour away and he wanted to get there before the noon sun made it unbearable.

"Saheb, Saheb!" Suddenly, Jeev was surrounded by a group of naked, dusty children with swollen bellies, coming out of a ramshackle colony of huts made from dry coconut leaves. "Do you have any food?", asked a small boy with big black eyes. He looked down at his clean white shirt and brown trousers. Compared to these kids, he was well to do.

"Yes," Jeev replied, reaching into his bag, he found his lunch He reached into his bag and found his rations of molasses cake, raw green peas, and cucumber. The children snatched the food eagerly and wolfed it down before anyone or anything else could grab it.

Jeev walked on. Warehouses surrounded the harbor. They originally belonged to the East India Company. Over time, rich Indian merchants bought many of the warehouses and the British government grabbed the rest. The area was bustling with laborers carrying sacks of goods on their backs, transferring them from the ships or taking them to storage areas. Spices were loaded on to one ship while workers offloaded another ship's sacks filled with English made clothing. Looking up, he saw a large warehouse with a big red sign above the front doors saying New World Trading in English. He nodded at the turbaned guards standing at the entrance, who knowing him, returned his nod and let him pass. Jeev strode through a large, grey, open area which was dim except for a few rays of sunlight streaming through small, barred windows. Grains of dust and fibers danced in the sunbeams, and gave the building a stale, musty odor. He reached the middle of the warehouse, where a man dressed in a white kurta and pajamas sat on a desk piled with papers.

Sitting next to him was a large woman wearing a peacock blue sari with speckled stones that glittered like diamonds. Her blouse was a dark blood red that contrasted sharply with a gaudy gold necklace with a malachite pendant around her neck. She looked up from the paper she was reading, and her eyes met Jeeves' and scanned the length of his body, evaluating the boy's worth. Satisfied with what she saw, she went back to reading her paper.

Jeev was quite perturbed. He straightened his back and walked up to the man at the desk. "Here you are, Sir", he said as he removed the package from his bag and handed it over.

The man took the package, staring at him through glasses perched precariously on his nose, and handed Jeev a note. "Make sure you give this note to Swamy," he instructed. He waved Jeev away.

On the other side of the warehouse Jeev saw an earthen pot likely filled with cool water. The heat and dust had made his mouth and throat dry. "Could I get some water from there?" asked Jeev, pointing to the container.

The man looked annoyed. "Yes, yes, go ahead" he waved with his hand. Jeev walked across the room. The pot was indeed full and refreshingly cool to the touch. He took a steel cup, dipped it in the pot and holding the cup a few inches from his mouth, poured the chilly water down his parched throat. As he finished, he noticed someone was looking at him.

"Jeev," he heard his name being whispered. Amee was peering at him through a window behind iron bars.

Astonished, he ran over to her and asked, "*What* are you doing here?"

She placed her finger on her lips. "We are leaving soon. My father has sent my sister and me to live with my aunt. She will take care of us," she whispered.

"What aunt? When and where are you going?" he asked, horrified by the situation.

"I don't know the name of the town, but we have to go by boat. It will take many days to get there. You don't know my aunt, but she is well off and will provide for us until things are better for my father and then we will come back."

"What aunt?" persisted Jeev. "You don't even have an aunt! And you are leaving without saying 'goodbye'?"

"What can we do? It is not my choice! They brought us here last night. Baba said the ship was leaving today. I had no time. I am so glad I got to see you," blurted Amee.

On tiptoes, Jeev peered into the room Amee was in. It was dark, with two small cots. He could see a tiny figure huddling in the corner, sobbing silently. *Oh my god, that's little Aarti! He reached his hands through the bars to touch Amee.*

As he did this, he heard a whoosh, followed by a sharp pain in his leg. Swinging around, he saw the man from the desk standing next to him with a huge stick. "Get out of here!" He yelled as he lifted the stick to strike Jeev again. Jeev's leg stung and throbbed, but he did not take time to check his wounds. The large woman followed behind glaring at Jeev in a heinous manner. Holding on to the rough, dirty wall while dragging his bad leg, Jeev limped out of the warehouse. As he passed the entrance, he looked back. Amee was no longer at the window.

Horrified, he staggered back to Swamy's house. The Swamy was seated with two other men in the courtyard. Swamy's eyes briefly widened when Jeev entered the courtyard, panting, and he raised his right hand and beckoned him. Jeev approached the Swamy, stepping gingerly with his sore leg, careful not to show any sign of pain. He reached into his bag, pulled out the note and presented it to the Swamy. The Swamy read the note and the corners of his mouth turned up in a slight smile. "I have another task for you tomorrow," he said. "Something very worthwhile for our cause."

Jeev nodded. Worriedly, he stammered, "Swamy, I have a question. I saw my friend Amee in a room at the warehouse where I delivered the package, and she told me she is leaving on a ship today. Do you know anything about this? Where is this ship going?"

The two men next to the Swamy suddenly stiffened and looked anxious. Swamy hesitated, sighed, and then said, "The ship is going to Guyana in South America, and the people who are on that ship will work on the farms there." Jeev racked his brains to see if he could visualize on the map where Guyana was but could only picture South America.

"But Amee told me she was going to stay with her rich aunt, who will take care of her. This is just for a while, right, while her father returns the money. I don't think she is working on a farm!" The two men now turned their heads away from Jeev and stared out of the window.

Again, the Swamy said, "Yes, yes, she will be in excellent hands. May God protect her."

CHAPTER 7: TO AN UNKNOWN LAND

Amee and her sister walked a dusty path from the warehouse to the harbor. The sun was so bright that it was hard to see, and the heat was stifling as rows of warehouses blocked the sea breeze. The woman in the fine-looking saree led them. "Everyone, stay in your lines," she commanded loudly. Amee and Aarti were a line of about seventy-five women, mostly teenage girls, and some in their early twenties. Her sister was one of the youngest. There was another, about three times longer line of men, mostly teenagers or young males, led by the man from the warehouse. Two men carrying sticks watched the line and whacked anyone who lagged or stepped out of line. Most of the men and women carried knapsacks slung over their shoulders, a few carried old, worn suitcases. As they approached the docks, Amee and many others caught their breath when they saw a giant ship with three towering masts, two smokestacks, a freshly painted white hull and cherry red keel. Amee had to stretch her neck all the way back to see the top of the mast. Cannons protruded from both sides of the ship. The name of the ship, Indus Princess, was painted on the side of the ship in brilliant blue.

The area around the Indus Princess bustled with activity. Workers were loading cargo onto the ship using heavy ropes and pulleys. There were two gangplanks attached to the ship. On one, a group of elegantly dressed English men in crisp, tailored suits and jackets strolled onto the ship, along with women in long gowns, most carrying parasols to protect their fair skin from the sun. The dock was packed with trunks and suitcases, waiting to be loaded. Amee noticed an English woman leading two fluffy white dogs, followed by a short man with glasses. Both dressed in bright white clothes. They looked at the line of ragged men and women waiting to board the ship. Amee felt the woman's gaze bore straight through her. She could not tell if it was a look of pity or disgust.

The woman with the expensive saree beckoned to the girls "Follow me" as she walked towards the gangplank away from the English people. As they boarded, she led them across the deck to a doorway and then down a steep set of stairs into a chasm of darkness. Gingerly, they stepped down the stairs, precariously clutching their belongings as their eyes slowly adjusted to the low light. Amee wanted nothing more than to look around, but there was no room to move, and she could not see anything except what was directly in front of her. The women were guided to the left of the stairs into a large room with gray walls. A few small portholes cast just enough light to see. There were plank wood bunk beds lining the sides of the room. In one corner, there were heaps of thin mattresses.

"Each one of you grab a mattress and place it on a bed. This will be your place for the duration of the trip. Keep your luggage close to you," yelled the woman in the expensive saree. Amee grabbed two mattresses and ran as fast as she could to a bunk bed on one side of the room. Quickly, she eyed what she thought would be a safe place for her and her sister and slapped the two mattresses on adjoining bunks amid a mad rush as the bunk beds filled up. The remaining women had to place their mattresses on the floor.

Peering out from her bunk bed, she noticed the men were now descending the steps and being led to the other side of the room. On one side of her bed was a porthole. She and her sister peered out of the round window, watching people embarking, and cargo being loaded. Other women also crowded around the small number of portholes in the room, looking out. The woman in the expensive saree had disappeared. A few hours later, the loaded ship was ready to embark. Amee was startled by large bells ringing from the ship and the dock. With a loud groan, the ship moved forward, spewing dark black smoke into the air, some of which found its way into the room sending many into a coughing frenzy. Amee placed her long dupatta over her nose to filter the smoke and smell penetrating the room. As the boat sailed out of the harbor, she stretched out on her thin mattress and settled in for the journey. A straight-backed sailor in bright white pants and shirt with blue neckerchief and white cap came down the stairs, surveyed the men's room, and closed the door. He then did the same for the women's room. One girl walked up to the door and pushed on the handle. It did not budge. They were trapped inside.

The first few days of the journey were uneventful. A strict schedule was followed. A sailor came in the morning to open the door, and the women could go to the deck for about an hour. For Amee, it was a relief to breathe the fresh, salty sea air and see the wide, blue ocean. The expanse of water fascinated her as it stretched infinitely onto the horizon. They ate on deck, usually white rice gruel with flat wheat bread. Amee hid whatever she or her sister did not eat, so they could eat later in the hold. When the bell sounded, the women had to go back. They would get another chance to go on deck later in the evening, again eating a rice broth meal. The men went on deck at separate times from the women.

While on the deck, Amee noticed there were cabins above their floor and some large rooms towards the aft of the ship. A large rope cordoned these areas off. She wondered if these areas beyond the thick ropes housed the people with the lavish clothes. Amee had sneaked a copy of a 'book' of about twenty-five pages stitched together using a jute rope that Jeev had given her as a birthday gift a year ago. It was a book of poems that Jeev found in the Swamy's house, where it had sat, unread, on a bookshelf for many years. The printed title on the cover was 'Poems of William Wordsworth'. Curious, Jeev had torn pages from the book of poems that had titles that caught his eye. He then took a blank sheet of paper and hand wrote the table of contents. He sketched the front cover using a lead pencil and charcoal. On the front cover was an illustration of a girl sitting on a hill surrounded by flowers which had long stems coming out of the ground with a star-shaped outer petal and a bulb like inner petals. Jeev had told her these were 'daffodils' and if he had some colors, he would have painted them a bright yellow. The girl on the hill looked suspiciously like a silhouette of Amee.

The porthole provided her with light to read the book. She read slowly, trying to understand the meaning of each word. It offered her an escape from the monotony of the voyage. By the time the voyage was over, she had read the book more than a hundred times and etched Wordsworth's poetry into her mind. One poem in the book was about a cloud that chanced upon a field of daffodils. She wondered what it would be like to dance amongst the daffodils.

CHAPTER 8: RAMU - BHALU

Jeev walked out of the house, still confused. What was going on? He blundered down the street, not paying attention.

"Hey! Where do you think you're going?" Jeev almost collided with his friend, Ramu, a large boy, with thick, black hair down running down his cheeks, hence the nickname, Bhalu, or Bear. Ramu's eyes widened with concern.

"Sorry, Bhalu." Jeev grabbed Ramu's large hand, dragging the taller, older boy into a side street. Jeev's heart pounded and his lips were dry as he backed up to a stone wall far from the main street. "Ramu, you introduced me to the Swamy, and you know everything about everyone…"

Ramu's eyes narrowed. "I don't know about that…"

Jeev spoke quickly before he could lose his courage. "How long will it take to go to Guyana by ship? What do you know about Guyana?" he asked breathlessly.

Ramu said, "Slow down, my friend, why are you asking these questions?"

Jeev told him what had transpired. Ramu's eyes narrowed further, and he placed his hand on this friend's shoulder. "There is something you should know. They send the people to Guyana as servants. Hardly anyone comes back. They work there on the farms, usually sugar cane, but also doing whatever their master wants them to do. Amee's father sold her and her sister. There is no aunt, who is just a fairy tale.

He needed the money to pay his debts. I know there are many men, women and children who are being taken on that ship today. I should not tell you this, but the fate that awaits Amee will not be good. She can never repay the money that was given to her father. She will be indebted to her new master for all her life."

"I have to warn her and stop her from going," said Jeev, as he turned around and ran towards the harbor.

Ramu yelled after him, "Stop, it's too late", to no avail. Jeev was sprinting away from him. Breathlessly approaching the guard at the warehouse, he asked, "Where are the girls?". The guard, knowing exactly what Jeev was asking, pointed to a ship that was streaming out of the harbor. Jeev ran towards the edge of the docks. Suddenly, he felt nauseous and drowsy. The earth started spinning. Jeev sank to his knees and watched the ship glide out to the open sea.

Ramu, who had gone after him, finally caught up with Jeev and sat down next to him. They both sat silently by the bay, watching the ship until it disappeared onto the horizon. "There are things beyond our control," he prophesied. "The universe wrote her destiny even before she was born, just as your and my destiny have already been written. What will happen to all of us is predetermined. Nothing you can do or not do will change what was meant to be." Despite being just a few years older, Ramu spoke as someone more mature than belied by his youthful appearance.

"So, do we then do nothing?" sobbed Jeev, wiping away his tears. "We leave everything to a predetermined fate. We just go about our lives like a ship lost in a storm. Like the villagers we pass every day, who wake up in the morning and repeat the same ritual day in and day out. They work tirelessly in the fields, they eat the same food every day, they meet the same people, the same landlords take advantage of them. When the rain does not come, they starve. They sell their daughters to the highest bidder. Then they go back to the same daily ritual. They go to the temple and pray to the idols. The priests tell them they should accept their destiny. Tell me, should I accept my destiny." He looked up at the sky and complained "God, why did you bring me this misfortune?"

Ramu smiled. His round face mocking Jeev, through eyes that expressed sainthood at first sight and then a glint of evil as Jeev stared longer "I believe our destiny differs from that of the farmers. That we met, that we see things differently, is destiny telling us we need to search for our purpose. Your destiny does not lie here on the banks of the river. You were not born to waste your life in a small village cutting sugar cane for the rest of your life. Your destiny is something big and relevant. Search for that destiny. It will not just come to you. Expand your wings and fly, my friend."

Jeev looked out onto the far horizon, then back at his friend. There was something special about Ramu. He had a body that was strong from years of arduous work. He carried himself with the confidence of a maharaja. Ramu pulled off his shirt, getting ready to plunge into the harbor and get a respite from the heat, revealing the black shaggy hair that covered his front and back. There were two thoughts about why people called him Bhalu, the first because he was a large boy with thick black hair that covered his body, the other was a story about Ramu killing a bear single-handedly. Jeev wondered if the story was true.

Jeev's mind wandered to remembering Swamy telling the boys the legend of Ramu. "Did Ramu really kill a bear?" One boy asked Swamy during a lecture.

"Yes, that is correct, boys," said Swamy. "Ramu fought and killed a bear. When he was visiting his village, he and some other villagers were hunting for a bear that was terrorizing the village. The bear had already killed quite a few chickens and some goats as well. The villagers were afraid children might be next. He went out with a group of people in the night looking for the animal in an area where the bear had struck a few nights before. He became separated from the group, yet the word fear had no meaning in Ramu's vocabulary. As he walked around the farmland, looking for footprints, he realized there was a rustling noise nearby. He froze, as the only weapon he had was a Gurkha knife. His sight settled on a patch of sugar cane where a pair of eyes were looking straight at him. It was a brown bear; its hair had camouflaged the beast perfectly amongst the sugarcane plants. In the night's stillness, he realized it was just him and the bear. The enormous animal was on the hunt that night, and Ramu was its next target. With a roar, the bear sprinted out of the field and lunged at Ramu. As the bear leaped on him, he placed both his hands on the bear's throat to keep the bear's teeth away from him. The bear's nails penetrated his skin on his shoulders and legs as he fell to the floor. He knew he had little time, as the bear was going to overwhelm him. Keeping one hand on the bear's throat, pushing the bear's head away from him, he reached for his Gurkha knife and plunged it into the animal's neck. The sharp knife sliced into the bear's neck. The bear let go of Ramu and tried to get away but collapsed after a few feet. It was a fatal cut. The bear's claws had cut deep gashes into Ramu's hands, shoulders, and legs. He was losing blood fast and needed help. Some members of the group had heard the Bear's roars and headed in his direction. They found Ramu, bleeding and unconscious. Wrapping his wounds with pieces of cloth to stop the bleeding, they carried him to the local doctor. The wounds became infected, and he had lost a lot of blood. While the doctors were treating him, the news of his bravery spread. It took several weeks for Ramu to recover from his wounds. Soon they were 'whispering his name as 'Bhalu Ramu'. Political leaders and local dignitaries came to visit him in the hospital." After hearing the story from Swamy, the boys looked up at Ramu with eyes of reverence.

Jeev met Ramu when he was living in the house with Swamy. By then, the legend of Ramu and the bear had become common street lore. When Ramu walked into the room, they regarded him with awe and trepidation. He took a liking to Jeev right from the start. There was a chemistry between them to an outsider, to Jeev one of student-teacher, and to Ramu one of confidant and colleague. Ramu recognized in Jeev an intelligence and drive not present in the other boys living in the house. Jeev looked at life differently than others. He had an altruistic vision that longed to make an impact beyond the daily rigor of domestic life that permeated his surroundings. Ramu knew he needed to guide that internal force in the right direction.

"Look across the Ocean, tell me what you see?" he said, sweeping his hands across the horizon.

"I see water as far as the eye can see," replied Jeev.
"The vast expanse of the World is waiting to be discovered. You see ideas that no one has thought about waiting to be written, you see philosophies waiting to be told, you see systems you can use to better the life of your country's people. You see freedom," exulted Ramu. "That's the most important thing we need right now. Freedom from the colonist powers, freedom from oppression, freedom for our faith, freedom for our people and freedom for our ideas. There are things we need to do to get freedom. Some you will like, others you will not. Yet they are necessary. I am saying the means justify the end. I say that from my heart. You could not help Amee because you did not have the means and the freedom to help her. How does that make you feel? And what are you going to do about it? How many more Amees will need to be sold as servants to horrible masters? What about the farmers who will lose their lands because the rain does not come? How many more people will die of starvation because the English do not see them as people? They see them as cheap and disposable labor. Become awake, open your eyes, your destiny is calling you." Ramu took

a flying leap and jumped into the sea.

As Jeev watched Ramu swim, the ship was a barely visible speck in the ocean. The cold tears of grief that were solidifying on his face, turned into embers of anger. An anger that would last many years, driving a quest for freedom. In some ways, his anger was not unlike that of the earth, cool on the surface with a molten core beneath that spluttered and rumbled.

CHAPTER 9: BROTHERS AT WAR (1862)

Hearing the rumble of hoofbeats, McBride Calvert mounted his horse and rode out into the field. The sun was bright, so he used his hand to shade his eyes, and relaxed when he saw a line of blue uniformed Union soldiers' approach on horseback. The country was at war, and in Western Maryland, both sides came and went across his farm as many battles were fought close by. He rode up further and reigned in his horse and the soldiers did the same. "Welcome," he said to the dark headed captain who sat straight-backed at the front of the line. "Please come to the farm for some supper and rest".

The captain smiled, his blue eyes crinkling. "That would be most agreeable, sir." McBride led them to the farmhouse where the soldiers dismounted and strode into a large, weathered barn. The fragrance of beef stew, cornbread, and hot coffee wafted out from the building, enticing the men to move quickly. The Captain and McBride rode towards the cabin, where Benjamin sat hunchbacked in his rocking chair, crutches at his side, watching the soldiers from the cabin porch. His expression was solemn, but his grey eyes were intense.

"Who is that?" asked the captain, pointing towards Benjamin.

"My father," replied McBride. "He suffered a horse-riding accident while hunting. He was chasing a fox near the hollow. A fallen tree loomed ahead. The fox scooted under the tree. In pursuit, my father did not hesitate and lurched his horse forward, racing towards the tree. At the last moment, the horse came to a full stop as it decided the tree was too tall to jump over. The momentum carried him forward, and he landed with his legs crashing into the tree trunk, shattering bones in both legs. He lay on the forest floor for several hours before my mother, Emma, sent the cowhands to look for him. They found him lying under the tree, unconscious. Unfortunately, his legs did not heal properly. He can never ride again. He is confined to shuffling between his bed, the outhouse, and his rocking chair on the porch."

The captain looked at Benjamin and tipped his hat in his direction. Benjamin replied with a defiant shake of his fist. "Ignore him," said McBride. "He has not been the same since his fall. He sits on the verandah with his rifle or shotgun and takes pot shots at squirrels, rabbits and especially the fox that he had taken an extreme dislike to. Not being able to move much, he spends his days brooding about life." McBride did not tell the captain that Benjamin, being a slave owner, hated Lincoln and that he secretly provided the Confederate troops with ammunition and cattle as they moved northwards.

As Benjamin drowned in his own misery and could no longer physically or financially take care of the farm, McBride took on his father's responsibilities. The day-to-day affairs fell on the young man's shoulders, and he had a natural acumen for management. He did not like being a slave owner and treated all his workers, regardless of color, extremely well, providing them with good accommodations, food, and listened to their concerns about working conditions. They repaid him with high productivity and ideas on how to improve the farm. His workers thus happily stayed on as tenants and laborers after slavery was emancipated in

Maryland. McBride expanded his numbers of livestock and started growing tobacco which he alternated with wheat. He also built new barns for dairy cattle and opened a blacksmith's shop. He had one of the best run farms in the region. With his revenue and wealth rising, his reputation and prestige in the state increased.

Benjamin did not take part much in running the farm, yet he did sometimes give orders that McBride was told about but did not override. McBride did not question Benjamin's distribution of cattle and supplies to the Confederate troops.

As the war progressed, McBride worried about the farm. One morning, a few visitors came to see Benjamin. McBride peered out of his bedroom window as he saw four horses ride up. They dismounted and huddled around Benjamin on the porch. He saw his mother walk up with cups of coffee. "Emma, please close the door behind you. I have to talk to these gentlemen." Emma quickly left the room. Benjamin addressed one man, a well-groomed, dark, good-looking man and said, "So John, how is the acting career going?"

"Well, I have been travelling all over the country with my theatrical troupe. We have performed in New York, Albany, Chicago, Cleveland, New Orleans, and Atlanta. We have been getting excellent reviews wherever we go."

Benjamin wrinkled his brow in disgust. "I think you should go back to your farm and build it up. Help the Confederate troops. This is no time for traipsing around in fancy clothes."

John's lower lip trembled with anger. "You know I care about this country as much as you do. You don't think I am not appalled by the politics of Seward and Lincoln! They are destroying us."

All four men stared out at the distant fox hollow, lost in their thoughts as they sipped their coffee. Then John spoke up. "You know Lincoln comes to stay at the Old Soldier's House often. When he goes from there to the White House, he has a troop of soldiers protecting him. However, at night here are only a few guards on the grounds."

"What are you saying?" asked Benjamin, scooting forward in his seat, "You are going to assassinate him?"

"No kidnap him. Bring him across the river and then hide him on your farm. Force him to stop the war. The North will surrender to the South. The Alliance will be restored," said John.

One man turned to Benjamin and said, "I know you are helping the Confederate forces. You can have them sneak into the farm and guard Lincoln."

Benjamin was excited to be part of the conspiracy. It gave meaning to his pitiful existence of sitting on the porch, cursing at his misfortune. "I will do whatever it takes to make this happen", he said cackling with anticipation.

McBride, curious about the conversation, opened the front door and walked out onto the porch. The conversation at once died, and Benjamin looked at him, annoyed. "Talking to some of my friends," ignoring McBride's look for introductions, "Anything you need?" McBride shook his head and walked out towards the barn. He could feel holes being drilled in the back of his head.

A light rain fell as McBride headed back to his home. The guests had left. He now decided to build another house for himself. He did not think he could live with his father any longer. He gazed at the flat meadow overlooking the fox hollow, the perfect spot to build his new abode. He often rode his horse there and would sit amongst the tall grass, looking over at the clump of trees surrounding the hollow. Somehow, the peacefulness of the location always cleared his mind and helped him resolve whatever was troubling him.

The next day, he walked over to his father and sat in the

chair next to him on the porch. "So, who were those people who came to see you yesterday?"

"Just some friends who were passing by. No one you would know." Benjamin stared straight ahead, not looking at his son.

"I know of your sympathies towards the Confederates. You should be careful. We could be in a lot of trouble with the Union if they found out about your helping the enemy troops. I have worked really, really hard to build this place into what it is today."

Benjamin's eyes narrowed as he wondered how much his son knew, and anger burned within him as he blurted out, "I built this place. Just so you understand," his voice increased in volume. "*I* built this place, all of this is *my* doing, you were just lucky to have this handed to you, and by the way, this is still *my* place, I will run it *my* way even if I have to run it to the ground." Emma, hearing raised voices, stopped her cooking and walked up to the front door, wiping her hands on a towel, listening to the father-son argument.

"Those damn Yankees have gone too far. They have no right to tell the other states what to do. They have no right to tell my state what to do. I bought the slaves, and they will remain mine. You watch, there is a storm brewing. The right people are getting involved. Lincoln and his bunch will never know what hit him. I know that General Lee's army will soon be here," Benjamin chuckled, "And when they are here, I will help them with whatever they need."

McBride silently lowered his head and cupped his face. How could his father support the slave holding Confederacy when the Union were fighting for the freedom of all men? Emma stood on the doorstep, fighting back tears, torn between her husband and her son. All she wanted was for them to live in peace as a family.

Peace did not last long. As General Lee's army moved

up towards Northern Virginia, Union scouts came by the farm, looking at the terrain and seeing what resources were available. McBride welcomed the troops and did what he could to help them. He sold the Union army grain, cattle, and tools. He became friendly with the local quartermaster, and because of his value in supplying the army, they did not draft him. Meanwhile, his father, sat on the porch and pouted and yelled obscenities at the Union soldiers when they passed through the farm.

In September of that year, there was a huge battle, a few miles away at Antietam. Emma huddled in the corner of her kitchen as they heard cannon blasts in the distance, fervently praying the battle would not come to their house. Benjamin stayed on the porch all day and night, watching the fires and smoke in the distance. Periodically he shouted at the exploding cannons, "Die you bastards, die!". That night the western sky was ablaze with red and orange fire and the air was heavy with smoke. Union troops commandeered McBride's barns for a makeshift hospital. Dozens of injured soldiers, some on stretchers, others carried by their fellowmen and still others limping, trudged into the barn seeking medical attention. Emma brought boiled water by the buckets to the barn. She bundled up all her linens and gave them to the doctors to use as bandages. From time-to-time ear piercing screams emanated from the barn as they performed amputations on someone's leg or arm. McBride and his workers gathered all the straw they could and made improvised beds for the injured. For three days and nights, the battle raged. The kitchen staff worked day and night to cook food for the soldiers.

On the fourth day, Benjamin sat on the porch as the first light of dawn broke through the trees, three soldiers, carrying rifles and bayonets, passed by the house. They did not wear the familiar blue uniform. Rather, they were shabbily dressed, much of their clothing torn. One had blood dripping from his shoulder, another's face was caked with grime and blood and the third limped on a poorly bandaged leg. Startled, Benjamin blinked, and he recognized them as Confederate soldiers. they must have become lost as chaos descended on the battlefield.

As Benjamin peered through the dim light, he softly called out to them, "Hey you, come here". The soldiers scared and confused, pivoted to see a man with a shotgun sitting on the porch calling them out.

"Men, this is Union land. We haven't come this far to be captured or killed," whispered the grimy faced man. His stomach hurt from lack of food, and his skin was burnt from the raging heat of battle fires. He lifted his rifle and fired at Benjamin. The bullet hit the old man in the chest, and he toppled forward in his chair, his weak legs unable to hold him up, his arms clutched across his chest. "Run!" the grimy faced soldier shouted, and all three men, including the one with the injured leg, sprinted towards the woods.

McBride and Emma heard the shot and rushed out to the porch, just as the Union soldiers came running from the barn. They all saw Benjamin on the floor of the porch lying in a pool of blood, his eyes open as if in surprise. Several of the guards who had come out fired at the escaping soldiers. None of the Confederate soldiers made it to the wood line. Emma cried, cradling Benjamin's head in her lap. It was too late. The soldiers carried him inside the house and laid him on his bed. Emma sat next to the body on the bed and continued to sob, tears running down her face and wetting her bodice. McBride stood next to her; stone faced. He felt nothing, but he laid his hand gently on his mother's shoulder to comfort her. She, however, was oblivious of his presence. He then walked out of the room, softly closing the door. He strangely felt no sorrow.

CHAPTER 10:
THE MAN WITH
THE TALL HAT

A few days later, as Emma and McBride sat on the porch next to Benjamin's empty chair, they heard hoofbeats coming from the north. Both straightened up, and McBride put his hand on his rifle, which he kept next to his rocker. They then saw a convoy of mounted troops come to the farmhouse and felt relieved when they saw the blue uniforms. The captain, riding at front, dismounted and approached McBride. "We are bringing in more soldiers," he explained. "We have orders to secure this area."

McBride nodded to the captain and quickly took Emma inside and said, "There may be another battle coming. Stay inside and go hide in the cellar if you hear any gunshots." He then went out to warn his workers about the possibility of an imminent battle.

That evening, another large contingent of Union calvary and a horse carriage pulled up to the barn housing the wounded troops. Out stepped a tall man with sideburns and a beard. He wore a white shirt, black bowtie, a long black coat, and his signature tall hat. Towering over everyone else, Lincoln stepped into the barn to greet the wounded. He walked around the barn, speaking to the wounded and shook their hands. In one corner of the barn, a group of wounded Confederate soldiers were being treated. Lincoln walked over, spoke to them and shook their hands. Emma and McBride stood politely on the cabin porch, watching the scene unfold through the open barn doors. As he left the barn, moving to see the wounded closer to the battlefield, Lincoln raised his hat towards Emma and McBride with a gesture of thanks. His assistant whispered to him, "They are the owners of the farm."

He nodded, strode towards the porch and up the small flight of steps. He shook Emma's hand and then McBride's, "Sorry for your loss. And thank you for your support."

As he spoke, McBride looked into his grey eyes, behind which lay a grey mist. They seemed to perceive everything. McBride also sensed a great burden, stretched from the president's wrinkled eyebrows down to his shoulders. Despite this, his outward body language was one of defiance and confidence. His handshake was warm and firm. Conveying the confidence of a man who knew his destination. He then boarded his horse carriage and proceeded further into the battlefield.

As Lincoln and the soldier rode away, McBride took his mother's hand and held it in silence. Both he and Emma were dumbstruck. In the eyes of the Union soldiers, Benjamin was a hero, a victim of senseless violence by the Confederates. They, as his surviving family, had received condolences from the leader of the country.

The battles moved further south as the Civil War continued. However, with a steady stream of wounded soldiers coming back from the war front, McBride's barns continued to be used as makeshift hospitals. Eventually, however, as with all wars, this war too ended.

CHAPTER 11:
EMILY (1887)

McBride wiped the sweat off his brow and took a deep breath and gathered his horse, Prince's, reigns in his hands. Saddled astride Prince's muscular back, he gazed at the ripening wheat in his field, which was turning from green to gold underneath the clear blue sky. Not far from the field, there were several barns, pigpens, a mill, and a blacksmith shop. He remembered when it all was bare land. First, he dreamed, then he then plowed, sawed, and hammered his dreams into reality, increasing the yield, and quality and variety of his crops and livestock and even making tools to sell. The local quartermaster provided him with steady orders for supplies to the Army, which despite the newly established peace, still had an immense appetite for supplies. For McBride, this meant more money for more improvements. With his father gone, McBride could work on his plans free from interference.

Even McBride's best laid plans, however, could not meet the Army's great demands. McBride pulled the reigns and leaned his body slightly forward, and Prince began to trot. After a steady twenty-minute ride, McBride saw his neighbor's farm in the distance. As he approached the farmhouse, McBride saw a heavyset man sitting in a straight back chair on the front porch. The man stood up as McBride approached, and then came down the steps. His shoulders were stooped, and he moved slowly, but his eyes were clear, revealing a sharp mind behind them.

McBride stopped his horse and dismounted. "Hello, Evans. I could use some help. Do you have any hogs ready for butchering? The soldiers are hungry, and I don't have any pigs or cattle to spare."

The corners of Evans' mouth turned up in a wry smile. "You're in luck. Calvert, I've got a couple of fat swine that are ready for slaughter."

McBride tied Prince to the front porch railing. "Good! How much do you want for them?"

"How about $40?"

"That's good. I'll bring you the money when I collect them." Unlike his father, McBride did not have a cold enough heart to barter for a better price. John Evans was too good a man to cheat.

Evans nodded, sealing the agreement. "Do you want to come in? Claire has dinner about ready."

The scent of pork chops in gravy, green beans, and fried potatoes wafted through the open windows, making McBride's stomach grumble. "Thank you. I'd like that." McBride replied.

"I'll let her know." Evans walked into the house, and McBride took a seat on the porch. He looked out at the Evans farm. Unlike his own, it was weedy and dusty, with a single weathered barn with a sloppily patched roof.

As McBride mused, he heard the footsteps behind him, and Evans spoke. "I know my place isn't as pretty as yours, but it's enough to do me in. I'm welcome to any offers I can get for crops and livestock." The older man set down, staring straight ahead, not looking at McBride. "Sallie's passing right after Joe was born hit me hard. Then he was killed at Antietam."

McBride shuddered, remembering the smoke that had covered the farm for days while that battle raged nearby.

"And then Robert died when those damn Rebels sank

his ship off the coast of South Carolina. Only Claire remains." Evans spoke in a clear, distinct monotone, giving no hint of the emotion underneath his words.

"Father, McBride, dinner's ready." McBride turned to see a slim, fair-haired young woman with deep blue eyes wiping her hands on a white apron. She smiled and blushed when she saw McBride and quickly lowered her eyes.

McBride's heart melted, and his tongue felt thick. "It smells delicious, Claire. You're a good cook." Evans glanced at his daughter, with a tinge of hope mixed with sadness.

After dinner, Claire walked out on the porch with McBride. She smiled when she saw Prince, went down the steps, and rubbed his glossy brown neck. "What a handsome horse! He rides well, doesn't he?"

McBride chuckled. "He does indeed! Would you like to try?"

Claire sighed. "If only I could. I've got dishes to wash and barn chores to do."

Suddenly, McBride was inspired. He knew what he had to do. "Claire, how would you like to have Prince for your very own?"

Claire gasped. "No! I couldn't! That's far too generous!"

"I don't know about that. You'll have to take me as well." McBride spoke so rapidly that the words almost tripped over each other.

Claire's eyes grew misty, as she looked McBride straight in the eye. "Yes, I'll have you and the horse too."

McBride, ecstatic, embraced Claire, wetting the shoulder of her gingham dress with happy tears. They were soon married at the All-Saints Church in Frederick, Maryland in the presence of friends and family, including Claire's overjoyed father.

After the wedding, John Evans was eager to turn over the day-of-day operations of his farm to his son-in-law. McBride extended his management style to the Evans' farm, combining it with his own. He streamlined the crops, the cattle and pig barns, the grain mills, and the iron works factory, organized all the workers into a hierarchical organization reporting to him at the apex and promoted trusted staff such as Chet and Louis to supervise specific areas. By paying higher wages than the neighboring farms, he ensured the loyalty of his workforce and never had trouble finding good new workers as needed. This held true even after the Emancipation Proclamation and the eventual Thirteenth Amendment abolished slavery. McBride never accepted that fact that one human could own another as property. He treated all his workers with equal respect. For him, skills, work ethics and character were important, not skin color.

One day, after working on his extended farm, McBride walked up to the meadow overlooking Fox Hollow. He sussed the lay of the land. It was firm and level with a spectacular view of the surrounding landscape. It was the perfect place to build a home for him and Claire. The next day, McBride and his wife rode up to the meadow. He pointed out the surrounding landmarks, including Fox Hollow.

"It's beautiful!" exclaimed Claire, squeezing McBride's big, rough hand with her small, delicate one.

"I'm glad you like it. I'm going to build our home here."

"McBride! Really? This is… simply perfect!"

McBride smiled. "I think so too. In fact, I've always thought so. You don't mind not having a porch, do you?"

Shocked, Claire said, "I've never thought about not having a porch, or really thought about wanting one either. I'll be happy either way."

"Well, I don't want one." McBride shuddered as he remembered his father sitting on the cabin porch day in and day out, taking potshots at the wildlife that passed by.

Having received Claire's approval, McBride built a stone and brick mansion above Fox Hollow. Soon after construction started, Claire found out she was pregnant. Riding and walking quickly tired her, and she could not return to the meadow. McBride and Claire's daughter, Emily, was born about a year after the wedding. Claire was then consumed by the responsibilities of new motherhood. McBride was sympathetic, doing what he could to make sure that Claire got what rest and care she could manage.

One day, he said, "Claire, you haven't ridden in a long time. It's a fine spring day. My mother would love to take care of Emily for a couple of hours or so. So why don't we ride up to Fox Hollow?"

Claire's tired eyes sparkled. "Oh, that would be lovely!"

So, they left Emily with her grandmother, and rode up to the meadow. The sun was warm and bright with fluffy clouds dotting the pale blue sky. Both McBride and Claire felt free. Finally, they reached the meadow, and Claire's eyes widened in amazement.

"Oh, McBride! It's... it's... magnificent!" She stared at a massive stone and brick mansion. They rode up to the front, got off their horses, and walked around. Claire stared there was a large circular pond at the front with a stone carving of a horse and fox walking together in the center of the water. She circled around the pond on a driveway paved with bricks. She and McBride then mounted brick steps which led up to a large wooden door inlaid with carvings.

Claire brushed her fingers over the carvings. "What are these? They're lovely, but so unusual."

McBride looked pleased. "They're carvings of totem poles, feathers, animals, and birds. I hired Indian carvers. I wanted it to be New World American, not that Old World

European drivel everybody else has." McBride then took out a key and unlocked the front door. He then swooped Claire up in his arms and carried her over the threshold. When he put her down, Claire was silent with awe.

Inside was a magnificent room with marble fireplaces at both ends. A huge dining room, kitchen, office, and ballroom made up the bottom floor. The upstairs had seven bedrooms, bathrooms, and the third floor had servant's quarters and storage areas.

When McBride and Claire returned from their ride, Claire ran to her mother-in-law. "Emma, you won't believe what McBride's done for us! It's a mansion and it's gorgeous!"

Emma cried, a clapped her hands together. "Finally! Good for you, son!"

McBride hugged his mother. "Mother, you're moving in with us, if you want."

Emma gazed into his eyes. "Yes, I want to. You can raze that old cabin to the ground if you like." McBride did, and the old cabin was flattened.

As the years passed, the Calvert fortune, the mansion, and Emily grew. One evening, McBride leaned back in his favorite chair with a brandy as Claire sipped tea and worked on her embroidery. A large fire crackled in the fireplace. Emily was at the other end of the room, reading a book, oblivious to her parents' watchful eyes. The girl grew up on the farm, home schooled by tutors who were brought in from nearby schools.

"McBride, what are we going to do with Emily?" Claire sighed.

McBride looked puzzled. "What do you mean? She's a quick learner. She's too smart for the local schoolmasters, so I've hired college professors. We have the money, and lots of people here and in Washington who want to do us favors, so why are you concerned?"

"It's not that she's bright." Claire whispered, so that Emily's sharp ears would not pick up the conversation. "I'm concerned about her comportment, as a lady."

"She is a tomboy, I must admit, but she's healthy and strong. She'll calm down as she gets older."

I hope so, for her sake. In the meantime, I'm keeping a close eye on her, and having the maids to help."

At the other end of the room, Emily could hear her parents' fervent whispers. Silently, she crept close enough to catch what they were saying and crouched in a dark spot behind a chair. They were so involved in their conversation that they did not notice she had moved. Emily spent most of her time sequestered in the house, which now had many extensions added to it, a garage to house the motor wagons, another wing that served as offices for McBride and his expanding businesses and the attic converted to a mini museum to showcase art, hunting trophies and gifts from his wealthy acquaintances. McBride also added a new wing for the servants' quarters. Although the house and estate were vast, Emily yearned to know what was outside the gates. She resented her parents' protectiveness and her wealthy isolation. Emily's ears burned as she listened to her parents talk. How dare they say she was unladylike! She was never alone, always under the vigilant eye of her mother or a maid. She watched a steady stream of politicians; Army officers, and local farmers visit her father's office. She would often station herself in the room above her father's office, pretending to study, but instead listening to their conversations, which she understood all too clearly.

CHAPTER 12: AMEE'S VOYAGE (1901)

Several days after leaving Calcutta, the ship stopped. Sunlight poured through the open porthole, which was the only source of fresh air for Amee and her roommates. They had rounded the Indian cape and were now on the other side of the country, in Bombay. She heard the bustle of voices and rattle of luggage and cargo being loaded. Curious, she squeezed close enough to the front to peer out of the porthole. The bright sunlight hurt her eyes, making it hard to see more than dark shadows on a bright background, but she made out the straight-backed figures of elite passengers, moving in a smooth, elegant line. The men wore hats, and the women carried parasols to protect themselves from the harsh sun. This same sun poured into Amee's quarters creating stifling heat that prickled her skin and made it hard to breathe.

Amee rubbed her stinging eyes, turned her head stared at the locked doors to the communal cabin. She and her shipmates could not leave their quarters while docked in Bombay harbor. The only break in the monotony was when two sailors brought them salted meat, flatbread, and water. Sleep came fitfully and uncovered, as the heat made even the thinnest sheets unbearable. Before the break of dawn, just as Amee was drifting off to sleep, the bellow of the ship's engines awakened her and the other women, as the ship lurched forward, heading out towards the coast of Africa and their lives, for the present, went back to the former routine.

The ship lurched and rolled as Amee looked out over the

railing at the choppy waves. A strong breeze whipped up, ruffling her long hair in tendrils around her face. She was nonchalant. Squalls and storms were now normal, and Amee had learned to hold her footing by shifting her weight.

Growing tired of watching the waves chop, she glanced over at the cabins beyond the thick, red ropes and saw a black suited butler hold a pair of heavy teak doors wide open. A slim blonde woman in a green dress with yellow flowers came out with two small, white, curly haired dogs on leashes. She looked straight ahead, not even exchanging the briefest of glances with the butler. Her luxuriant hair was piled high on her head which was topped by a green hat with white and yellow flowers. Looking through the doors, Amee saw a teak lined room with white covered tables and red velvet seated chairs. The tables had silver teapots, cups, and saucers. An immense variety of food in shapes and colors she had never seen or imagined was displayed on round china platters that were three feet tall. Soft, melodious music was playing in the room, and the aroma of freshly baked goods swept across the deck, making Amee's stomach rumble. A few minutes later, the butler closed the doors, and the woman walked her dogs along the top deck towards the back of the ship, barely glancing at Amee and the scores of bedraggled women lined on the side of the ship.

Amee turned her eyes out to sea again. In the distance, the horizon was gloomy and menacing. She shivered at the thought of what the darkness might hold. What unknown creatures lived there? Amee suddenly felt small and insignificant. The waves were getting bigger, and their crests were now frothy white. She had to hold on tightly as the ship shuddered and bounced upwards. Then a wave hit the ship, spraying Amee and everyone near the side of the ship with cold salt water. Amee shivered, as her eyes blurred and stung, and her mouth tasted of salt. A sailor called out, "Get down back to your rooms everyone" waving his hands to herd the women below decks. Amee stumbled, following the crowd more by sound and touch than sight, and made it back to the cramped, communal quarters.

Over the next few hours, the high winds developed into a full-blown storm. The waves crashed above the porthole, as the ship heaved from side to side. Amee kept her eyes tightly shut and muttered prayers to Durga for protection. She was now too scared to look out, as water made its way across the floor, soaking the beds and belongings of those sleeping there. Pandemonium ensued as there was a mad dash to salvage precious and needed possessions, and many women doubled up in the bunk beds. Unfortunately, there was not enough space for all, and several women huddled in the corners, curling into tight balls as water splashed around them. Amee shook with cold as the temperature dropped. She grabbed a green sari from her bag and handed it to her sister, Arti, who stared at her with wide eyes, wondering what to do.

"Put this on. It'll keep you warm". Amee spoke rapidly and efficiently. Her sister put on the sari. Both girls then ransacked their bags for more clothing.

"My head is cold!" Arti cried. By now, only the thinnest and dullest clothes were left. Amee had a flash of inspiration.

"Try this." She said, taking an old blue cotton shawl and wrapping it around her head. Her sister grabbed a faded gray one and did the same. They then cuddled close together as the ship tossed and turned in the stormy seas. The air smelled acrid as many of the women became sick, turning the floor into a putrid mess.

The storm lasted for two days during which there was no food or fresh water. Amee had dozed off, her head resting on the porthole, her sister lying next to her, and two other women unsteadily balanced on the bunk bed. Suddenly, she noticed the ship was no longer tossing. In fact, it was quite calm. Amee gazed out the still wet porthole. In the distance, the sun was rising, drenching the clouds with gold, orange and red, melded into a hazy, dreamlike seascape. It was as if the Sun God, the wind God, and the sea God had finally made peace and let the travelers through. Amee heard the doors open and turned over on her other side, to see who entered. She saw two sailors pick up two lifeless bodies. One woman had a bloody mass where her forehead had bashed into the side of the ship. The other was unnaturally thin and had likely perished from an unknown disease.

"Three men died next door." She heard a woman in the bunk behind her whisper to her bunkmate, who began softly sobbing. Amee heard faint splashes as the bodies were unceremoniously tossed out to sea. Amee swallowed hard as she contemplated how these lives had ended so suddenly and their common grave was the cold, dark ocean.

Amee's thoughts soon lifted, as she poured cold, fresh water harvested from the storm, over her sweat drenched body. She then washed her and her sister's clothes. After completing these chores, Amee curled up in her bunk and went back to her reading. Today she read and re-read the "Solitary Reaper". Jeev had crossed out William Wordsworth and added himself as the author. She whispered to herself, "Behold her, single in the field, Yon solitary Highland Lass" then paused as she pictured a young girl working in the sugarcane fields of Bengal, then continued to the end of the poem, still whispering to herself "The music in my heart I bore, long after it was here no more." Amee closed her eyes and imagined the story of the poem as a young girl working alone in the fields, singing a sad song, pondering if she was the only one singing the melancholy tune, about leaving her homeland, her family, and her friendship with Jeev.

The ship continued its journey through the Arabian Sea, towards the coast of Africa. They passed several idyllic looking islands with white beaches and coconut trees. *If only they would stop here so I could taste the sweet coconut water*, Amee wondered as she looked at her meager portion of stew, which had only two chunks of tough, gray meat. There had been three chunks of meat yesterday, and her bowl had been two-thirds full. Today it was only half full. Amee glanced at Arti's bowl. She had only one chunk of meat. Amee heard her sister's stomach rumble. Using her fingers, she picked up the largest meat chunk in her bowl and tossed it in Arti's.

Arti looked up and turned the corners of her mouth in a smile. "Thank you," she said, as she started chewing the gristly lump. Amee reached over at patted her back. Amee then spooned a piece of overcooked carrot and thin broth into her mouth, and as she swallowed the tasteless fodder, she mused on the declining portions of food and water, which were less and less each day.

"Amee, I'm still hungry," Arti's black eyes were filled with tears as she looked into her empty bowl. "I can smell food. Why can't the rich people share just a little bit with us?" She spoke loud enough for the girls around them to look at her with pity.

Amee's stomach rumbled. She could smell roast beef, lamb, vegetables, and sweety, yeasty bread. "I don't know, Arti. I wish..." Amee sighed. Something had to be done, but all she could do was pray.

Later, in the middle of the night, Amee woke to soft giggles and hushing sounds. The door was open, and four sailors were in the room, several women climbed out of their bunks or rose up off the floor and left with them. Amee turned over and went back to sleep.

About an hour later, Amee was jostled awake. "Amee, Amee! It's me, Agni. I've got something for you and Arti." Amee opened her eyes. Agni was holding a large burlap bag. Curious, Amee sat up and rubbed her eyes. Agni reached into the bag and pulled out two large hunks of buttered bread and cheddar cheese.

Amee gasped, reached over and shook Arti awake. "Arti!

Food!" she whispered eagerly, as she grabbed the bread and cheese, giving the biggest one to her little sister. Both Amee and Arti wolfed down the soft, crusty, buttered bread and tender cheese barely pausing for breath. Agni watched them and smiled.

After finishing, Amee said, "Thank you, Agni! I don't know how you got this, but I'm grateful. What can I do to repay you?"

"Well... Agni hesitated. "The floor is awfully cold and wet. Would you share your bunk with me?"

Amee scooted over. "Come here. You're welcome to stay with us."

Agni grinned sheepishly. "Thank you!" She tucked herself in. Her body was warm and soft.

"So, how did you get the food?" Amee asked.

"By being friends with a sailor." Agni replied. "Everyone needs a friend."

Amee started to ask another question. Before she could speak, Agni continued. "Do you know where we're going?" Amee shook her head. "The ship is passing islands off the coast of Africa. There's lots of pirates in these waters, so the crew must be incredibly careful."

"What would happen if the pirates caught the ship and us?" asked Arti.

Agni shivered. "They would kill all the men and sell us women to brothels in Zanzibar."

Arti giggled and Amee joined in. Agni looked stunned.

"Zanzibar! What kind of name is that?" Arti's body rolled with laughter. Agni caught the joke, grinned, and started chuckling in concert with the sisters.

The ship made a stop in Zanzibar to pick up supplies and passengers. Amee gazed out the porthole at the white buildings that lined the port. Agni scooted up beside her and peered over her shoulder.

"This must be Zanzibar. The sailors are going to be having some good times…" Agni whispered, her voice trailing off softly at the end.

Amee's back straightened with a sharp shock. She looked around the room for Arti and called her over. The young girl climbed up on the bunk, her eyes wide.

Amee placed her hands gently on Arti's shoulders and looked her straight in the eye. "Agni, you and I are going to stay down here while the ship is docked. No going up on the deck. Do you understand?"

Arti swallowed and nodded. "I understand".

She peered through the porthole at the white buildings that lined the port. Many of the people walking the street by the harbor were of a dark skin and crinkly hair that she had never seen before. They had features vastly different from the villagers back in Bengal. The men wore a tall squarish hat and long white robes. There were several women also in a multicolored robe like garments, carrying baskets of bananas on their heads. A few British soldiers walked by carrying guns, smartly dressed in their black shoes, white pants, red jackets, and tall military caps.

Amee moved her hand under the thin wool blanket and reached inside her bag. Tucked among her clothes was a waterproof oil cloth that her mother had painstakingly made for her by soaking a heavy canvas sheet in oil and drying it in the scorching sun. She gingerly untied the strings wrapped around the bag and unrolled the canvas. Inside were two gold earrings. The jewelry her mother had handed to her as a future wedding gift or as currency she could use in her unknown land. The other was a sealed envelope that had two letters. They addressed it to 'Sir Isaac Thompson, City Hall, Georgetown' and inside were two letters, one signed by her father, and another signed by the lady with the expensive saree. They contained an introduction to an important man in City Hall who would take them to her aunt's farm where the two of them would live and continue their schooling. Her father had told her that her aunt had been advised of their arrival and was anxiously awaiting the ship. She carefully wrapped up the letters and earrings, retied the package and hid it under her clothes in the bag.

After a couple of days, the ship sailed back out to sea and trips to the deck resumed. Amee spent most of her time on the deck, breathing in the fresh sea air and basked in awe of the immensity of the ocean. Her stomach rumbled. Although rations had increased, most of them were rice and bread, with truly little meat or dal. Amee gave most of what little chicken or mutton she had to Arti, so hunger was constant. Agni's late-night rendezvous with the sailors supplied additional food from time to time. She was also able to get them an extra blanket which helped on the cold damp nights. Her conversations with the sailors were also the source of pertinent information.

"In a few days, we'll be going around the Cape of Good Hope." Agni's voice startled Amee out of her reverie.

"What is that?" she asked.

"I think it's at the bottom of Africa. The seas there are always stormy, so you and Arti should be ready for the boat rocking immensely."

Looking out at the placid, blue sea, with the sun creating sparkles on the crests of the gently rolling waves, Amee found this difficult to believe, but she knew it was best to be prepared.

Sure enough, in a few days, the skies darkened. They saw bolts of lightning on the horizon; the sea churned, and the ship headed directly into the ominous clouds on the horizon. They had been out at sea for a month now since leaving Calcutta and were getting used to the tossing and turning. Rarely did anyone become seasick.

Outside, the waves grew larger. Amee, her sister, and Agni clutched each other to prevent them from being thrown off the bed. The ship rocked from side to side, the wooden beams groaning in protest. The hands of the ocean seemed to grab the boat and pull it into the dark depths. An equally unseen powerful force dragged the boat upwards. The water lashed from different directions to the passengers as they were being thrashed around right, left, up, down, all at the same time. The spray permeated into all levels of the ship. Not a single dry person or floor. The weary sailors tugged and pulled at the sails, endeavoring to keep the boat upright. An enormous wave crashed on the deck, washing a sailor overboard and rocking the boat so violently that it sent the passengers sprawling across the room. Cuts, bruises, and concussions abounded among all. She could not tell how long the storm lasted. Most had willed their fate to providence. At the deepest, darkest moments when all hope is lost, humanity usually finds religion. As the sea violently lurched them around, a feverish grasp of prayers extended out to whatever super spirit that rules the world, to beseech it for salvation. Like all storms, this one, too, ended. As the sun's rays peaked through the clouds, they felt relieved. One sailor unlocked the door to their room so they could go up to the deck. The air on the deck was chilly, refreshing, and uplifting as most felt their prayers were answered and their lives spared. They looked back at the path travelled and saw in the distance the dark clouds through which they had passed. Flashes of lightning strobed through the dark veils of the distant storm.

CHAPTER 13:
GOLD COAST

"The ship has rounded the tip of Africa and is heading North," Agni informed Amee. "My sailor friend had also told me they would make a stop in a few days to repair and resupply the ship. There had been some damage, however, they could not stop until they reached a friendly port. Unfriendly nations govern the nearby ports, such as the French, the Portuguese, and the Dutch. The captain and his elite passengers did not trust these ports would welcome a British ship."

The damaged ship hobbled on for almost two weeks, fortunate in not encountering another devastating storm, and reached the Colony of Gold Coast in West Africa. They headed to a harbor in the town of Port Coast. The British regiment that ruled the city from the Cape Coast castle and fort would provide them shelter while they performed repairs. They dropped anchor in the deep waters near the fort. Amee watched through the porthole as several small boats came out to meet the ship. She saw men in suits and women with parasols and hats move toward the boats. The men took long strides, while the ladies' steps were shorter, as their long skirts did not allow for free movement. All these elite passengers were first placed in the boats, along with their luggage. It took most of the day for them to be transported to the port.

The next day, the captain came down to the belly of the ship. "Everyone, gather your things and come to the deck. You will be placed in boats and taken across to the port."

They waited on the deck as the small boats ferried them to the port. Amee, her sister, and Agni boarded one of the small boats, along with about ten other people. Two men, again quite dark-skinned as Amee had seen in Zanzibar, rowed the boat to the shore. One man yelled out, "Form a single line" and led them up a rocky road towards the fort. There were soldiers on guard at every corner. The fort walls were tall and painted white. As they walked through the fort entrance, they noticed cannons on either side of the gates. Glancing up and around, they saw there were also cannons protruding from openings in the walls. The women trudged into this foreboding place, in single file, carrying their worldly belongings on their shoulders. Soldiers led them into a courtyard, then through another gate and down a flight of stone stairs. They entered a cave-like area that was damp and dark. A musty smell saturated the air. Before them was a long corridor with prison cells on both sides. They steered the women into the cells, about ten to fifteen per cell. Inside, black and grey rock covered the walls and floors. Pierced into the walls were hooks, with chains hanging from them. In some places, water trickled down from the ceiling. Each cell had a small window with an iron grate overlooking the beach below. Amee, Agni, and Arti were pushed into one cell, along with several other women. The soldier shut the doors of the cells with a loud clang.

Terrified, Amee and Agni moved towards the back of the room, near the small window, and sat on the floor, their backs against the wall. The wall was damp and cold; the stone floor was hard and uneven. Tired from the journey, Amee placed her bag near her for support and dozed off. When she woke up, it was dark, with faint moonlight coming from the window. Most of the women were asleep, though they stirred constantly, unable to find a comfortable position. The pale light cast shadows on the wall, making its aberrations look like monsters, ready to attack and eat the cell occupants. She glanced over at her sister asleep on the floor next to her. On the wall behind Agni appeared a grotesque figure with a long thin face, covered by a hood, large beady eyes, and a large, slender hand with tapering fingers and long fingernails. Amee shuddered and rubbed her eyes in disbelief. Haltingly, she stretched her hand out towards the wall to protect her sister. Her head touched the cold damp wall; the realization sunk in that her mind was playing tricks on her. She scanned the room. There were many anomalies on the wall. Sometimes they appeared as monsters, and at other times as the god figures on her mother's shelf in the kitchen back home. She concentrated on the figure behind her sister, mentally banishing the beast from the wall and transforming it into Durga the Goddess, a beautiful, powerful woman with many hands, some carrying weapons. The Goddess was astride a lion. She continued to look at the wall and the figure of the Goddess remained. With the same concentration, she then distorted the other beasts in the room until they no longer resembled evil beings, but rather harmless figures like rabbits, elephants, tables, chairs, or kites. Smug with her powers, a slight smile on her face, she dozed off again.

The sun's rays cast a bright light into the cell, waking up the women. They took turns looking out of the window. Before them was a white sand beach filled with black skinned fishermen and fishing boats. Blinding sunlight flickered on the blue waves, a gentle, steady breeze swayed the palm trees, and sounds of singing, shouting, and talking in strange tongues came through the iron bars that made the window. Some fishermen were heading out to sea. Other fishermen stayed ashore to fix their nets, and those who had just returned were unloading their catches into baskets. A rough road lined with fisherwomen in bright robes and headscarves selling fish, crabs, and shrimp in wicker baskets ran parallel to the beach. A steady stream of shoppers strolled from one fisherwoman to the other, reviewing the catches and bargaining for the goods. Further up the road, there were tables where more women were selling fruits and vegetables.

"Amee, my stomach hurts," Arti whined, looking at Amee, her wide eyes shining unshed tears of frustration.

"Mine too," Amee replied. "We'll have food soon, I'm sure." She stroked Arti's hair and tried to smile but could only manage the briefest flicker. It had been three days since they had been fed, and all the women were feeling weak and irritable. If only they could go outside and barter for some vegetables and fish! Amee sighed and waited.

Later that day, as the sun was lowering in the sky, two uniformed men unlocked the cell. "Form a queue and get out," one of the men barked and turned his back while his partner watched the women line up. Both men then led the women out to a courtyard. Amee's spirits picked up when she smelled fish and vegetables, food at last! She saw a large metal bucket full of hot fish stew concoction and a basket filled with round white balls made from boiled plantains. Bowls and spoons were eagerly grabbed and passed around and then filled with the spicy fish stew and starchy sweet plantain balls. The women furiously devoured the food. Amee had never tasted anything so delicious.

Out of the corner of her eye, Amee saw Agni stroll over to some sailors standing at the edge of the courtyard. She spoke to them, smiling at first but then growing somber. A few minutes later, she came up to Amee. Her expression was serious.

"What's the matter, Agni?" Amee said with concern.

Agni took a deep breath. "The *Indus Princess*'s repairs are going to take much longer than expected. We're being transferred to another ship that will be here in a few days."

Amee glanced back at the cramped cell. "We'll just have to make the best of it, I guess."

Over the next few days, conditions in the cell were indeed

hard, however, food was delicious and plentiful, and the women had freedom to walk about the courtyard for extended periods.

The new routine was broken a few days later, when a crisply uniformed sailor arrived at the holding cell. "Pack up your belongings. It is time to board."

The women complied. As they continued in a line to the harbor, they noticed there were two ships docked. Both were much smaller than the Indus Princess. As they came near the ship, they saw a group of soldiers directing them, men, and women on to which ship to board. Amee clenched her sister's hand, determined that they stay on the same ship. Agni was right behind and placed a hand on Amee's shoulder. Their anxiety rose as they moved closer to the group of soldiers. One soldier pointed at Arti and commanded her to join the other line.

Amee screamed, "No, she stays with me," and dragged her sister back in her direction.

A soldier stepped up, lifted his gun, and slammed the rifle butt into Amee's head. It caught her between her ear and the back of her skull, momentarily stunning her. The soldier grabbed Arti by the hand and pulled her into the other ship. Agni held Amee up to prevent her from falling and helped the semi-conscious girl on to the boat. Blood poured from her ear and the back of her head swelled up. She did not fully regain her senses until the boat was well out to sea. As she slowly opened her eyes, she felt a splitting headache. Her first question was, "Where is my sister?"

Agni, who had stayed by her side, shook her head. "They divided us up between two boats." "The two boats are going to the same place, right? Inquired Amee, we can meet up at the next stop."

Again, Agni sadly shook her head. "That boat is heading to an island. I don't know the name. We are traveling to

Georgetown in Guyana."

Amee felt a pain in the pit of her stomach as tears rolled down her eyes. "I have failed her. She was my responsibility. She will not survive without me looking after her." The spasm of sobs continued well into the night.

The ship 'Carib Dream' differed from the 'Indus Princess'. It had two large sails and a smaller one up front. There were no smokestacks or elite cabins above deck. Some parts of the ship carried bags of cargo. The other parts of the ship were for the men and women on their long, ongoing trip from India. Once again, the men and women were separated, their living quarters much smaller, and there appeared to be chains everywhere.

One sailor told them with a cruel smile, "In the old days, they would chain slaves on the boat for the duration of the trip. These days, the crew is much nicer to all of you."

Amee did not get the reference to the word slaves but kept quiet. She did not want to get into trouble with the crew, needed to stay strong for her sister and knew somehow, somewhere, the two of them would be together again.

The voyage lasted for almost two months. Winds often blew the ship off course. The passengers, all occupying a small, confined space, formed many friendships. Someone would later recount these bonds as 'Jahazi' or fellow boat travelers. Agni knew most of the women in confinement. They came mostly from the Indian territory of Bengal or its surrounding areas.

There was Sura, who was travelling with her mother. Their two brothers were with the men on the other side. Their father had died by suicide after the crops had failed, as he could no longer pay back the loans he had taken from the landlords. There were the sisters, Amba and Ambu, both lucky to not have been separated, thought Amee. They were in their late teens, around the same age as Amee. Their parents had been killed in a clash with British soldiers, and after staying with relatives for a year, they were being sent to live with another relative in a faraway land. There was Baruni, a single woman close to thirty years of age. Never married, her life in her small village was turning perilous as a much older unmarried woman. Shunned by the women her age who were all married, devoid of marriage proposals, pursued by nefarious men, she tried her luck elsewhere and volunteered for this journey. Jabli was distraught over the entire journey. She was travelling with her husband, who was now on the other boat. They were victims of the famine, their livestock wiped out by lack of food and water. This journey was their hope to start a new life, yet without her husband, she did not know how she would cope. Vaagdevi belonged to the lowest caste in India, the Dalits. Her family cleaned the village streets. When people saw her walking, they crossed over to the other side of the street. Classified as an untouchable, she soon realized her life would start and end in the same way. There was no hope, so she ran away to the big city of Calcutta. Befriended by a lady in an expensive sari, she was told of a promising voyage that would give her a better life. All the stories were like Amee's, being sold by the family, running away from danger, devastated by the famine. When the streams of hope ran dry, they chose to face the unknown.

Trapped in a confined cabin, lurching on the turbulent waves of the Atlantic Ocean, hidden feelings bubbled to the surface as strangers confided in strangers. Tales of emotions and hidden sentiments, suspicions, and treacheries, despair, and dreams created a chain of intimacy and binding bonds. Agni, using her skills of persuasion and seduction, befriended sailors, who provided Amee with information on what was happening as well as better rations from time to time. She desperately wanted to find out where her sister was being transported. She pressed Agni to talk to her sailor friends.

One evening, Agni snuggled up to Amee with a big smile.

"I found out about your sister. The boat is going to an Island called Tortola."

Amee's brow wrinkled in puzzlement. "What does that mean? Where is this place?" She stared blankly at the wall for a few minutes, then continued, "How will I get to this island? I wonder every day about Arti's condition. Hoping she is not sick. I tremble at the thought of sailors taking advantage of her. What will become of her after they reach the island?"

Agni placed her hand on Amee's hand and gripped it tightly. "We should reach Georgetown in a few days. You said there are relatives of yours there with whom you will stay. They could help you find her. At least now you know where she is." That became Amee's hope. *My aunt in Guyana will help.*

"What about you Agni? Do you know where your relatives are?" Amee realized she had never asked Agni where she was headed.

"I don't have relatives like you do. My father and mother told me I would be living with a nice family there. But I know that they just do not want to have the burden of a girl living with them. They sold me when I was younger to an Anglo-Indian family in Calcutta. I worked there as a servant, cleaning the house, washing clothes, whatever they wanted me to do. It was a long day's work, and I often got blamed if something was wrong. Sometimes their children would break things and blame it on me. They would hit me with a stick, even though I did nothing. When I told them the children broke it, they would hit me even harder. "You are lying," they said. Then one day when I was about sixteen years old, they caught me holding the hands of a boy who was a servant in the neighbor's house. I think the stick that they were beating with me broke, and that was the only reason they stopped. They forced me to go back home. My family obviously did not want me, so a year later, they sold me to the people on the ship. I could have run away, but I went. I will have a better life, far away from home. I will work again as a servant somewhere." Agni paused, swallowed hard, and wiped the tears from her eyes. "You know what, I am going to make a better life for myself. I don't know how, but I will. You watch, I will have my home, my farm with goats, cows, dogs, and vegetables. Even a horse. And any girl who has been sent away by their parents to work as a servant can run away and come and live on the farm, in peace. A place where all can be safe. With plenty of food." They continued their chatter far into the night, building the utopian farm as a shelter for runaway girls.

CHAPTER 14: LABORERS

The ship approached the port of Georgetown at night and anchored offshore until daylight, when the docking would be safer. The next day, shortly after sunrise, the boat sailed into the harbor and the crew threw ropes on to the dock to tie it in place. Amee and the rest of the passengers descended the narrow gangplank, squinting from the already bright sun. They were herded into a large open area where they were told to wait. Amee stared up at the vast, blue sky, where a few puffy clouds floated.

Her focus was broken as she saw a brown-skinned man with center-parted slicked back black hair climb onto a rock overlooking the crowd. Although he looked Indian, he wore a suit and tie and carried a sheet of paper in his right hand. A group of well-dressed white men and women stood to the side of the rock. The men wore suits and hats. The women wore high necked dresses with long sleeves. The men carried umbrellas and the women parasols to shield their pale skin from the harsh tropical sun.

The man on the rock looked down at his sheet of paper then shouted "Mr. Daniel!" One of the standing white men raised his hand and kept it raised. The man on the rock then called out the names of several of the Indian men and women who had disembarked from the boat. "You will all go with Mr. Daniel. First, he will take you to the immigration house, there" he pointed towards a low structure with several desks on the porch. "Your arrival will be recorded there. Now, follow

Mr. Daniel." Agni's name was among the group. She quietly squeezed Amee's hand, then walked away. Mr. Daniel led the group to the house to be registered.

The man on the rock then called out, "Mr. Oliver." A stout man, with his gut poking out of his white jacket and beige pants tucked into his big black shoes, moved towards the rock. His head was mostly bald. Long sideburns and a thick mustache covered his pudgy white face. Sweat rolled down his neck and settled in large puddles on the front of his white shirt. The man on the rock rattled off another set of names, including Amee's. He then pointed towards Mr. Oliver. "Follow him!"

Amee moved with the others who were called and stood by Mr. Oliver, confused and scared by what was happening. She wanted to go to the City Hall so that they could notify her relative as per the letter, instead; she was told to follow a strange man. Gathering up her strength, she reached into her bag and produced the letter. She walked up to Mr. Oliver and thrust the letter towards him. "I am supposed to meet someone in City Hall."

He looked at her with a glint of humor and some disgust. "Let me see that," he said, grabbing her letter. Amee's heartbeat quickened and her breath became shallow as her senses heightened. She did not want that important document snatched away from her. Mr. Oliver glanced at the letter, then looked at Amee. To her horror, he then tore open the envelope. Inside were two papers. He looked them over twice before flinging the envelope and the papers at Amee. "This is rubbish," he exclaimed, and beckoned the group to follow him.

Amee, crying, bent down on her knees and gathered the papers from the floor. The papers were blank. Not a single word on them. She double checked the papers, aimlessly placing the envelope and papers back in her satchel. She followed Mr. Oliver and the group, numb with shock as anxiety and fear replaced hope. The group walked towards the immigration house. Groups of passengers from the ship were huddled around makeshift tables made from wooden barrels and flat pieces of wood. Men sat behind each of these desks asking questions and writing into a large notebook. Amee scanned the passengers, looking for Agni, but she was not there. The man leading Amee's group introduced himself to them. "You can call me Mr. Oliver or Sir". Then he paused. Any kind of physical activity, even long sentences, seemed to tire him, as he often stopped to catch his breath. He led them to one table, then said, "Give the man your name and date of birth." Several of the passengers looked confused, as they did not understand the instructions.

"Let me help," volunteered Amee. "I can speak, read, and write English. Also, I speak both Hindi and Bengali" Amee's words spilled out quickly, her eagerness to help alleviating her anxiety about her new life. No one else spoke up.

Mr. Oliver looked at Amee and nodded. "Good. Help, then."

Amee took a deep breath and started interpreting. When someone could not remember their birth date, she made it up. Before she knew it, registration was complete. Mr. Oliver then led the group to a pair of black carriages, harnessed to sleek, brown horses with short legs. Amee and the others boarded the carriages which then lurched forward down a muddy road. They travelled through dense, green jungle for a few days, sleeping out in the open along the way. Amee lost track of time and dozed off in a stupor, looking up from time to time. Hope, the panacea that had kept her strong, was rapidly fading, draining her resolve.

Amee woke with a start when the coach suddenly stopped moving. Bleary-eyed, Amee gazed out at the landscape. The sun had set, and shadows were encroaching on an open clearing filled with sugar cane. On one side of the field was a group of huts that formed a semi-circle around a large tree. Near the base of the tree, a roaring fire was burning in a square shaped pit, topped by a sizeable metal pot sitting on a pile of logs. A heavy-set woman was stirring the pot in slow, rhythmic motion. Looking ahead, she saw the dirt road continuing past the open land into the distant jungle. Just beyond the cane field, a large house was visible, however, none of the group had any strength left to take in their new surroundings. They were exhausted after the long and arduous journey, first on the ships and then the carriage. They had left their homeland with hope and anticipation of a better life. Those hopes were being slowly cut down, like sugar cane, one by one.

"Attention!", yelled a booming voice in a thick accent that Amee and the others could barely understand but was imposing enough for the group to go quiet. A tall thin man with ebony skin, oversized lips, and a scar that ran from the bottom of his left cheek to part of his lip over his nose and ended at his right eye appeared in front of them. He was dressed in loose-fitting white clothes with a blue cloth wrapped around his head. "Get out of the carriage now!", he commanded. Amee and the other passengers scrambled to gather their meager belongings and stumbled out onto the edge of the field. The ebony man called out to Mr. Oliver, "Sir, should I take the new workers to their quarters?" Mr. Oliver nodded in acquiescence and headed out down the road towards the house in the distance.

The man then turned to face the newly arrivals. " My name is Odeyman Brown. You can call me Master Brown. I am the overseer of this plantation. Sir tells me what to do and I will tell you what to do. When I say something, you will listen to me. Or else..." He reached and picked up a whip lying at the base of a tree. Then, with a flourish of his arms, cracked the whip around the tree. The firecracker-like sound startled them all as they watched pieces of bark flying to the ground. "That would have been your back," his eyes sparking with malice. "Follow me. I will show you where you will live." He led them to a large, empty hut and told the men they would sleep there. He then led the women to another hut. "You all can sleep here until you get married, then you can join your husbands" and laughed at his own joke.

Still chuckling, he grabbed Amee by the shoulder and led her to a room on the far side of the hut. He shoved her inside. "This will be your room for now. I have my eyes on you. Sir owes me a wife. If you are good, you can become mine. I will take care of you. " In the darkness, the scar shone red, and his eyes turned a deep shade of black. Amee slid to the back of the room, cowering in the corner, unsure of what would happen next.

A woman's voice called out, "Master Brown, the food is ready."

The man hesitated and then walked out of the room. "Come out to get your food" he yelled at no one in particular.

The group streamed out and formed a line by the heavy-set woman standing next to the large pot, which emanated a sour, musty odor tinged with cinnamon and old mutton. She now had a ladle that she dipped in the pot and filled the bowls of the people as they came up to her. A small nervous boy stood next to her and handed a piece of bread to each of the workers. When Amee stepped up to the woman, she looked her in the eye. "Ok, you are new. Here is a bowl. You lose it or break it. There will be no food." With that, she handed her a tin bowl. Amee held it up, and she served a ladle full of watery stew. The little boy handed her a piece of hard, stale bread. She walked over to the group of women who had come journeyed with her, sat on the ground, and took a sip of the brew. She saw beans, chili peppers, cassava chunks, and a few tiny bits of gray meat in a thin, peppery sauce. Regardless of the quality of the food, it felt good. The solid food chunks and the warmth of the broth brought some of her strength back. No one spoke as they ravenously ate their allotted share. She wiped down the bowl with the bread and finally looked up. Some people had gathered around the fire to keep warm, others were heading back to their huts, bowl in hand. Amee got up and started walking back to her hut.

As she passed the heavy-set woman, the woman whispered to her, "come here and help me with the pot." The woman held one side of the handle of the pot and told Amee to hold the other side. They carried the now empty pot back to the kitchen building. As they placed the pot on the floor, the woman spoke in a hushed tone, "Now you be careful dear, scar face has his eyes on you. I see everything that goes on here. Do not want to scare you, but the last girl he kept in that room turned up dead just a few weeks after coming here. You need to be strong and think about how you can get out of here." She handed her another piece of hard bread, patted her on the shoulder and, with a sigh, led her out.

Amee hid the bread in the folds of her skirt as she headed back to her room. There was a thin mattress on the floor. She lay down thinking about the words of the heavy-set woman. Outside, a full moon rose over the sugarcane field. Exhausted from the day's events, she fell into a deep slumber.

CHAPTER 15:
BENGAL (1903)

Swamy sat in his seat, a large armchair covered by a white bed sheet, surrounded by his henchmen in chairs behind him. The boys sat on the floor; legs crossed. All of them wore white shirts and khaki-colored shorts. Ramu took his place near the Swamy's feet, while Jeev lingered towards the back of the hall. The boys sat in silence while the older men up front talked amongst themselves in hushed tones. Jeev heard the back door open. Two men and a woman in a jade silk sari embroidered with gold thread entered. Jeev at once recognized the two men. They were with the Swamy when he had asked about the ship that Amee was aboard. Seeing the woman, however sent a chill through his body. It was the same large woman who was at the warehouse where he last saw Amee. Ramu shot Jeev a warning glance - please do nothing stupid. Jeev nodded his head and sat down in the back of the room, hidden from the front by a pillar. He clenched his fists tightly in his lap and gritted his teeth hard enough to keep the anger welling up inside from spilling out. The Swamy did not acknowledge the visitors, who stood at the back of the room. He led the group through their regular morning prayers, followed by a reading from the Vedas.

Swamy then addressed the gathering, "Today there will be a demonstration at Dalhousie square to protest the government's response to ongoing famine and farmers' appalling conditions. All the boys will attend the demonstration. This is to be a peaceful march. The police will allow the protest for an hour, then they will break it up by attacking with their long sticks. At that point, no one is to fight back. You will all return peacefully to the house." As the group broke up and left the house, Ramu grabbed Jeev and pulled him towards the Swamy. "Stay. He wants to speak to us."

The Swamy was speaking to the large lady in the jade silk sari and the two men he had seen earlier. They handed the Swamy a package. He opened it, and Jeev glimpsed a thick wad of rupee notes. Swamy hurriedly tucked the notes back in the package, noticing that the boys were still present. He thanked the large woman and her two companions. Then, with a sigh, he turned to the boys, "We have some important work for the two of you. Jeev, I want you to know that you are one of our new junior leaders. Under Ramu you will accomplish great deeds for us and for your destiny." Placing his hand on Jeev's head, he recited a mantra to the Goddess Durga, then said, "I know you have a lot of questions; I will answer them in due time. For now, trust in me and our cause. There is a fire burning inside you. Use it against those who seek to destroy our way of life. Those who mock our culture, take away our land, rob our country and oppress our people." There was confusion in Jeev's head, between believing the words of Swamy to a desire to choke the daylights out of the large woman, to trying to understand the connections between the people standing in front of him. He opened his mouth to speak, but the words would not come out.

Ramu came to his rescue and interjected, "Swamy, I will explain all to Jeev." They both touched the feet of Swamy and meekly left the room.

Outside on the street, they walked to a tea shop and sat down. The man behind the counter stirred a pot of meat and vegetables in a metal pot precariously perched on two burning logs. The smell of ginger, turmeric, cinnamon, and onion made Jeev's stomach rumble. Ramu raised two fingers at the man showing an order for two cups of tea. He also pointed to a plate of fish and rice. "We will have two plates of that." The tea arrived promptly, served in an earthen pot. It was mixed with cardamom, ginger, milk, and plenty of sugar. The warm and spicy mixture felt soothing and invigorating at the same time. As the warmth flowed down Jeev's throat, he felt a calming sensation across his chest. He felt reconnected with the world. They sat in silence sipping their tea, glancing out at the bustling street of tram cars, horse carts, cows, chickens, dogs, bicycles, and people, all sharing a thin narrow street. There were open drains on either side of the street, and a cloud of dust hovered over the street like a permanent blanket. It was a wonder that no one bumped into each other, fell in the drains, or was attacked by one of the animals. It was a mysterious rendition of a series of near misses; a clockwork of chaos that challenged the traditional sense of precision and organization yet worked with an efficiency that defied logic. Their reverie was pleasantly broken when the counter man served plates of spicy fried fish, along with a heaping of white rice and mango pickle. Jeev dove into the food, expertly removing the flesh from the fish bones and making round balls of fish and rice with a smidgen of pickle and then popping the balls into his mouth. They devoured the food, relishing every bite, a luxury few could afford. As they wiped their plates clean, the server once again arrived with two bowls of a steaming sweet milk and vermicelli dish. The dessert was a welcome change to the palate. At last, stomachs full, they pushed back their chairs, satisfied with their gastronomical undertaking. Ramu ordered two sweet paans, a betel leaf twisted around a sweet and savory filling and gave the cook money to settle the bill. Their mouths red from the paan, they walked away from the tea shop.

Ramu placed his hand around Jeev's shoulder. "There is an important job for us. I know I can trust you and you are capable. I want to know if you want to do this. Do you want to continue the fight, or do you want to lie down and give up?"

Jeev stopped walking, brushed Ramu's arm away and indignantly yelled, "I am not someone who gives up. Count me in."

Ramu smiled, "Meet me at the house tomorrow night," smacked him on the back and wove goodbye.

CHAPTER 16:
VICEROY TRAIN

J eev walked back home, shoulders hunched, focusing hard to keep tears from flooding his dry eyes. Dejection at Amee's new life, confusion about Swamy's intentions, and questions about the reason for his own existence had him trapped in a dizzying, never-ending loop. He realized there was no way out but to fight. With this thought, he lifted his head and straightened his shoulders. His purpose was clear.

The next night at the house. Ramu led Jeev into a room where four other men and Swamy were sitting. They closed the door and then Swamy spoke. "We know that Lord Curzon will take the Viceroy Train from Calcutta to Delhi. We do not know the exact date or time, but our sources tell us it will be in a few days. Soldiers will guard the train from inside and on the train stations. However, there is an isolated area where we plan to attack the train. You will all leave right away so we can get to the spot and be prepared. Ramu will be your leader for this assignment. Any questions?" Jeev had plenty, but he kept his mouth shut. Swamy continued, "I don't have to tell you the dangers of this assignment. Just a few of you will be up against hundreds of soldiers. Move fast and be brave. If you are successful, you will spark a fuse of a revolution in the country that the English cannot control. Now go pray to the Goddess Durga for her blessings." Swamy approached them and placed a white mark on their foreheads. They touched his feet, and filled with anticipation and trepidation, they walked out and went to the train station.

"The station of Durgapur is about a hundred miles away. We will get there by this evening" said Ramu. "I will explain what we have to do once we get to the forest near Durgapur." On reaching the station, they walked towards the outskirts of the town. On the way, they passed a temple dedicated to the Goddess Durga. It was a small temple carved into a rock, where worshippers left fresh flowers and fruit as an offering to the deity. Removing their shoes, they stepped inside. It was dark and cold, a ray of light shone through a window-like opening in the rock facade. The light shone on a carving of the goddess Durga at the end of the temple. She had four hands, one carrying a sword, another a shield, another a three-pointed spear and in the fourth hand was a weapon made of tiger claws, which glared at them. They sprinkled the deity with red powder. She seemed to look straight at Jeev, her stone carved eyes asking him if he was up to this task. Not just the task at hand, but life itself. He knelt in front of the goddess and closed his eyes. A fox appeared in his mind. *Listen to the fox, follow the fox*, a voice told him. He opened his eyes and thought he saw the statue smile.

The group then left the temple and walked to a small village on the outskirts of the town. As they approached the settlement, a tall, thin man in a brown kurta came out to meet them and took them to his house. Inside the house were five large canvas bags and two wooden crates. "Pick up this luggage, we are heading out to the forest" he said. The young men placed the canvas bags on their backs. The wooden boxes had handles on each end, which required two men to carry them. Hauling the luggage, they trudged out, following the tall thin man. They walked for several miles, eventually coming to a train track in an isolated area. Wiping sweat from his eyes, Jeev looked back. There was no sign of the villages and farms. A dense jungle stood on one side of the tracks. On the other side was the Damodar River. The tracks ran parallel to the river before crossing a bridge further upstream. The young men walked into the woods where they deposited the bags and crates, deep enough not to be seen, yet close enough that they could run to the railway tracks in a few minutes.

"I will set up a tent on the hill in the distance" said the man guiding them, pointing to a small hill overlooking the river and the tracks. "When I see the Viceroy's train coming, I will raise a white flag. If it is dark, I will light a torch. You will have about fifteen minutes once I give the signal before the train reaches you. The rest is up to all of you." They opened the wooden boxes. Inside were sticks of dynamite. They set up a crude shelter with branches, leaves and canvas bags, lit a small fire to stay warm and waited for sundown.

After nightfall, they headed to the train tracks. The steel rails glistened in the darkness; heavy wooden planks kept the tracks parallel to each other. The space in between the tracks was filled with gravel. They dug up the gravel in spots and placed the sticks of dynamite, then covered them with waterproof cloths and placed the gravel back over the dynamite. Attaching wires to each of the dynamite sticks, they ran a final long wire to a spot behind a tall tree. The end of the wire fed into an igniter. Pressing down on the igniter would set off the dynamite. The other wooden boxes held rifles and bullet belts with thirty bullets apiece. Each of the men picked up a rifle and strapped a belt over their shoulders. Jeev felt powerful holding a rifle. He stood straight-backed and alert with purpose and importance. He was now a soldier, fighting for freedom. He peered across the barrel at an imaginary viceroy looking out of the window of his train and pulled the trigger. The rifle boomed, and the bullet splintered the branches of a nearby tree.

Ramu rushed up to him and grabbed the rifle out of his hands. "No more antics. You will give our position away," he admonished.

Jeev mumbled, "I did not know the rifle was loaded, " and sheepishly walked away.

Lord George Nathaniel Curzon was not in a cheerful mood. He had received a letter from the Prince of Wales, George Albert asking him to go to Delhi as part of a high-ranking mission to scope the area for the future capital of British India. He had already indicated to the prince that he would send a high-level delegation to perform the survey, but the prince strongly insisted that having the Viceroy visit Delhi would increase the stature of the town, sending a message to the people of India and the commonwealth of the importance of the city. Curzon was well established in Calcutta with his palace, having all the comforts of England, and even more than the King. Servants and officials cocooned him to cater to his every need. The viceroy wrinkled his nose and grimaced when he thought of being out in the dusty country with all the brown people. The intolerable heat, dirt and smells of spices, unwashed clothes and the bodies that wore them were not pleasant. Governing from the cool and clean comforts of his palace and gardens suited him fine. This trip would also interfere with the hunting season. He hoped to nab a few tigers as trophies he could take back to England.

He crumpled the letter and threw it across the room. He then rang the bell, and his secretary entered. "You called Sir?" said the secretary.

Curzon pointed to the paper on the floor "Bring me that letter." The secretary smoothened the paper before handing it to the Viceroy. "Call an immediate meeting of my council staff. I will meet them in my office." Soon they marched in, Sir Timothy Bedford, his private secretary, Captain Sean Burke, of the Viceroy's private guard, Lieutenant Colonel M.S. Steward, the Military Secretary to the Viceroy and Sir William McNulty, the Local Affairs Secretary. As they assembled at the long table, the Viceroy stayed standing at the head of the table. "I have received a letter from the Prince of Wales to make an official trip Delhi so that we may lay the foundation for making it the capital of India. As much as I dislike this letter, we must make the trip to Delhi. I cannot disobey the man who will become the King of Britain. Get the train ready."

Captain Burke spoke up, "Sir, with all due respect to the prince, the situation in Bengal is unstable. The talk of the partition of the state and the ongoing famine has stirred up resentment in the community. We have information that several militants are active in the area. I am concerned about your safety."

The Viceroy held up a hand. "Make the arrangements, get extra soldiers. Seal the stations along the way. Do whatever you must, my mind is made up and Lady Curzon will also travel with us. You are all dismissed." The four men nodded, unable to override their superior.

As they left the room and were out of earshot of the Viceroy, Sir William said, "The news of his travel will be hard to keep secret. There are hundreds of people involved in getting the train ready. The news that the Viceroy is leaving on a trip will spread like wildfire."

"Understood," agreed Lieutenant Colonel Steward. "I will double the number of guards and have more troops positioned along the way. Sean, you will be on the train in charge of security. I will stay in Calcutta and coordinate the troops from here."

The Viceroy's order to get the train ready was passed down to his subordinates. A swarm of workers descended on the train, cleaning every inch. Even the wheels were polished. One worker wrote a note and handed it to a young boy, "Give this to Swamy, quickly." The note said 'Viceroy train going to Delhi soon' an alert to Swamy that the Viceroy was leaving. The train was a large steam locomotive, painted black, with the bumper and wheels painted a bright red with a large light on the nose of the engine. A car full of coal was attached to the engine to ensure enough fuel for the entire journey. Behind the coal car were five carriages. Two carriages for the viceroy and his special guests, one carriage for the troops, one for the servants and cooks, and the last carriage for supplies and the kitchen. At the back of the train was a second large steam engine, which could supply extra power on inclines as well as serving as a backup in the unlikely event the front engine had problems. All the carriages were painted bright red. The viceroy's carriage had large, gilded emblems and intricate designs in gold paint. Captain Burke would have preferred all the carriages to look the same, so it would not be obvious which carriage the viceroy was travelling in. He sent troops to all the stations along the way. This train would not stop at any station until it reached New Delhi. He also ordered the station platforms to be cleared when the train approached so that there were no security threats. Bags, food, and supplies were loaded onto carriages and hauled to the independent railway station built exclusively for the viceroy's train. Lord and Lady Curzon made the trip in their delicately adorned carriage, with a hundred soldiers marching by their side. The viceroy's railway carriage had two bedrooms, one for him, another for his lady. Each bedroom had its own bathroom and a sitting room. There was both a private and public office. The second viceroy carriage had a dining room and chambers for his council. Captain Burke and Sir Timothy Bedford had their cabins there. The troops piled into the soldiers' carriage, and the servants loaded the supplies. A marching band played outside on the platform, bidding the travelers farewell. With a loud whistle, the train moved forward as an enormous cloud of thick black smoke bellowed out, swallowing the spectators near the engine, and steam screeched out of the pistons, moving the wheels.

That afternoon, troops entered the station of Durgapur and cleared everyone out of the station. The man who was keeping watch, notified of the troop movement, ran up the hill and raised a red flag. Ramu always had someone keeping a lookout for the signal. As soon as they saw the flag go up, the young men sprang into action. Ramu positioned himself by the detonator. He would press it as soon as the viceroy's carriage passed over the dynamite sticks. The rest of the team armed themselves with rifles and loaded the ammunition. They added extra bullets to the belts strapped to their shoulders and crept close to the train tracks while staying hidden in the bushes.

Captain Burke was at the back of the train checking on the troops when the train passed Durgapur Station. He leaned out of the side door, returning the salute of the soldiers on the platform. Some soldiers tried to get a glimpse of the viceroy, but the curtains were drawn shut. He stayed by the door, watching the scenery as the Damodar River flowed on one side and a thick jungle began on the other side. To get a better view, he climbed to the top of the train and sat down to enjoy the ride. The breeze on top of the train was a welcome change from the heat in the troop carriage. He took out his telescope and surveyed the area ahead. As he focused in on the jungle, he noticed a glint, as if the sun were reflecting off a metallic object. One man in Ramu's group had not properly hidden his rifle. Sean then moved his telescope to the railroad tracks and saw the wires leading from the tracks into the jungle. "Stop the train! " He yelled at the soldiers standing by the door below him. Scrambling from his post, one soldier ran to the end of the carriage and pulled a chain, activating the emergency brake. Wheels scraped against the rails; sparks flew as metal rubbed against metal. The train slowed, finally coming to a halt a few feet from the dynamite sticks.

Sean and a few soldiers leaped from the train and ran to the front. "Reverse the engines! Go back to the train station!" He commanded the driver as he ran past the engine.

Ramu watched the train slow down and stop just before it reached the dynamite. He saw the troops rushing out and taking positions around the train. He pressed the detonator, but nothing happened. Repeatedly pressing the detonator did not light the dynamite. Frustrated, he grabbed his rifle and started shooting in the train's direction. Jeev and the others followed Ramu's lead and joined in the attack. The British soldiers dropped to their knees and returned fire. Jeev saw two of his fellow rebels instantly fall to the ground. He rushed over the railway tracks to the other side. There a shallow ravine provided him with cover from the bullets. He ran in the train's direction. The engine had started to push the train backwards, but it would take time for the train to gain momentum. He was in line with the engine when he saw Captain Burke fire in his direction. The shot missed, and Jeev got a foothold on the step of the first carriage. Captain Burke, right behind him, ran up the steps and grabbed Jeev by the back of his neck. They both briefly struggled before another soldier came up and hit Jeev on the head with the butt of his rifle. In that instant, Sean, who never forgot faces, recognized Jeev as the boy in the crowd. The recognition was fleeting as Ramu had now caught up with them and he fired at the soldier, hitting him in the stomach. Sean turned around and fired at Ramu, who stumbled out of the train grasping at his leg. Jeev, shaken by the hit, staggered forward and grabbed the soldier's rifle lying on the floor. He ran into the carriage, looking for the viceroy. There were two soldiers in front of him. He fired two shots, both hitting the same soldier. Lifting his bayonet, he stabbed the second solder and rushed to the back of the carriage. He needed to get to the Viceroy's carriage. Passing through the back door, he slammed it shut behind him and opened the door to the next carriage. Staring ahead, he saw several soldiers with their rifles drawn coming towards him. Behind the solders, stood a pale, wide-eyed viceroy. There was no way to get past the soldiers in front of him. The train had picked up speed. He rushed back to the exit door, bullets flying towards him, and leaped off the train, rolling down a steep slope. As he looked up, he saw the train speeding away.

Sean stayed on the train to ensure the viceroy was safe. A group of soldiers stayed continued searching for the militants. Ramu, injured and bleeding, crawled into the bushes near the tracks. Jeev rolled down the steep slope until he reached the banks of the river, relieved that he had not been shot. He saw soldiers patrolling the tracks. There was no sign of his militant companions. He heard intermittent gunfire. He wanted to find the others, so he walked parallel to the tracks. In the distance, he saw the soldiers removing the unexploded dynamite. Had they been given faulty or fake dynamite? Jeev could only guess. He wondered what had happened to Ramu and the others. He had seen at least two of them die in the first shootout. Ramu and the others may have hidden in the forest. His next step was to find Ramu and the remaining men. He traversed the tracks where they curved around the hillside. Hidden from the soldiers he scoured for his co-conspirators in the underbrush. He heard a rustling sound in the bushes and saw a silhouette of a small animal scraping through the fallen leaves. Peering closely into the vegetation, he saw a protruding leg. It was Ramu, lying unconscious on the ground. He knelt beside him and lifted his head. Blood poured from his friend's leg. Jeev removed his shirt and used it to make a tourniquet around the wound. Then he placed Ramu's hand over his right shoulder, using his back to carry most of Ramu's weight, and moved away from the soldiers. In the distance, he heard another train approaching. Through the bushes, he saw it was filled with soldiers. Jeev knew they would comb the forest, looking for them. He dragged the lifeless Ramu through the forest in search of a hiding place. Out of the corner of his eye, he saw a fox looking at him. The fox then ran down a slope to the left of them. 'Follow the fox', the saying echoed in his mind. He moved down the slope. The fox ducked under a fallen tree and disappeared. Jeev dragged Ramu under the tree, where there was a depression on the ground. He gently placed Ramu in the dip and then hurriedly twisted some branches around both him and Ramu. Camouflaged, he waited for the soldiers and held his breath as soon as he heard their loud steps marching through the jungle searching for them. The troops walked right past his hiding place.

CHAPTER 17: MISSION TO NOWHERE

It was quiet in the forest, except for the leaves rustling in the wind and small animals scurrying. Several hours had passed since the solders had been in their vicinity. As the sun slipped over the horizon and darkness crawled over the hillside, Ramu regained consciousness. He glanced at his leg and grimaced, then raised his head and looked around. "Where are we?" he muttered in a weak but firm voice.

Jeev placed his fingers to his mouth, signaling Ramu to stay quiet. Jeev then crawled out to survey the area. All his senses were alert, and his muscles were ready to spring in case of threat. When he realized that it was all clear, he helped Ramu out. He broke a branch to make a cane for Ramu to lean on.

Ramu grasped it and said, "Thanks, I know someone who can help, let's go this way." He pointed towards a small hill. They climbed up the hill, dense forest surrounding them. Soon, they came to a small derelict cabin. "This used to be a hunting cabin used by a prince decades ago, now long abandoned. Very few know of its existence," explained Ramu.

Jeev approached the weathered wooden door which looked firmly shut. He turned the rusty handle, and it easily opened. Inside was a single room, with dust particles dancing in the sunlight that filtered through the two windows at the front of the building. Cobwebs were everywhere, and tiny insects crawled around, annoyed at the disturbance. Jeev spied a small, dirty cot in the corner of the room, and helped Ramu walk to it.

Ramu smiled. "Wait till later when the villagers will be sleeping. I will tell you how to find the man who helped us in the village. He will get us medicine and food," said Ramu, as he relaxed and fell asleep.

After nightfall, with the directions given to him by Ramu, Jeev set off towards the village. The moon was low on the horizon. Stars twinkled in the clear cool night. He put his hands in his pockets to warm them. Soon he saw a small path in the woods and followed it downhill towards the village. He was looking for a blue house on the outskirts of the village, but in the darkness, it was hard to make out the house colors. There were a few people sitting around a fire in the distance. He stayed at the edge of the forest, moving stealthily in a long path around them. As a stranger in this hamlet, he would be obvious. Finally, he saw a house that looked blue. He crept close to the wall and blinked his eyes to make sure his vision was clear. It was indeed blue. He knocked softly on the door. The door opened.

"Come in. You are expected." Before Jeev could reply, he was pulled inside. Jeev stared, recognizing his host as the man who had signaled them with the flag earlier. "My name is Arjun," he said as he bustled about brewing a hot cup of tea for Jeev.

Jeev sat down on a floor mat, his back against the wall. He took a deep breath and spoke. "Ramu was shot in the leg. He's still alive, but we need a doctor to look at him and we need a place to hide." Jeev swallowed and lowered his head. His message was delivered. There was nothing more he could do.

Arjun offered him the tea in a white mug. "Yes, I will get a doctor and some food. You stay here and drink this, I will be back."

Arjun left. Jeev stayed in the house, savoring the warm cup of tea, at the same time wondering if this was a trap. Before he could decide whether to flee or not, however, Arjun returned with the doctor, a short, bald man carrying a small black bag. Arjun then packed up some naan, dried fish, and mangos in a canvas bag, tossed two blankets and pillows for Jeev to hold, and then the three of them set out towards the hunting cabin.

When they reached the cabin, Jeev opened the door, calling out "Ramu, I'm back. Arjun and the doctor are with me."

Ramu grunted in response. Arjun lit a candle, and the three men walked to the dirty cot. The doctor examined Ramu's wound, cleaned the wound, treated it with medicinal herbs and bandaged it with cotton and a fresh cloth. After he finished, he said, "The bullet went right through the leg; it will take some time to heal. Don't put weight on your leg for a few days."

As they were leaving, Arjun said "I will be back in a day with more food and will find out what the latest news is on the railway incident."

The next afternoon, Arjun returned with food and updated them on the latest news. "The Viceroy has safely reached Delhi. His train had stayed at Durgapur until an added regiment of troops had arrived. They also had a second train that travelled in front of the Viceroys train, all the way to Delhi, carrying a full regiment of almost a thousand soldiers. There was no mention of the attack in any of the newspapers, for reasons I think only the Viceroy knows. They have kept the news of the attack quiet. They did not want to encourage other militant groups to carry out copycat strikes."

Stranded in the cabin until Ramu's leg healed, Jeev and Ramu spent their time having long philosophical questions about life and its purpose. "Here's the problem..." Ramu would begin. Jeev knew this was the start of a long monologue that he should pay attention to and raise the pro or con arguments once the lecture was over. "Colonization is based on simple economics. The English, French, Portuguese, Spanish conquests are all based on the simple fact of obtaining cheap labor and physical resources. Let us say they could grow rice in England, and it takes a hundred hours of labor to grow a bag of rice. In England, they may pay the laborer hundred times more than they pay the laborer in India. So, by growing rice in India, and selling it in England, they are making a hundred times the profit. And it all comes down to the exploitation of the laborer. In Africa they took it to an even bigger extent where slaves were captured and sold all over North and South America. That's even true of the people from our area who have been sent to the Caribbean Islands as labor, they are just like slaves." He paused mid-sentence. This was not a topic he wanted to get into with Jeev, on account of what had happened to Amee. Instead, he continued, "Profit is the goal of colonialism, to make the elite of England rich. They even grow the cotton in India, take it to England to make clothes and then sell it back to Indians at exorbitant prices. Again, profit. I am not saying profit is necessarily bad. I am saying the system of colonialization that exploits other countries, does nothing for the betterment of the colonies and exists only to enrich the conqueror is morally wrong. So, it justifies us in our use of violence to fight. We have a moral right to fight."

"Do we have a moral right to take someone's life?" asked Jeev, wondering about the two British soldiers he had shot earlier. He did not want to talk about Amee.

"Yes!" emphasized Ramu. "When they take lives of our countrymen, we are justified in taking their lives. In fact, it is our duty. In the epic Mahabharata, when Lord Arjuna was hesitant to take up arms against his own family, Lord Krishna told him it was his duty to fight. So, it is our duty to fight too. Jeev, I am counting on you to take this fight to the next level. We can no longer rely on old dynamite sticks and shoddy weaponry. We need to fight them on our terms as a well-equipped military. We are losing this battle."

Jeev shrugged his shoulders in defeat "What can I do? I am just a poor boy from Calcutta."

"Something I have been planning for a while. We have people in England, America and Germany who are ready to help. We have sent them messages. What we need is someone from here to go there, meet with them and organize the details. You are the perfect candidate."

"Why me?" Jeev was unsure of where this conversation was going.

"You are young and can bear the rigors of travel and are still an unknown face. If I were to go, someone would recognize me at once and jail me or worse. Also, you can get along with people and talk with people. You have grit and don't give up or get scared easily."

Jeev smiled. It meant a lot to him, getting this praise from someone he looked up to and admired immensely. "I am ready to go."

Ramu placed his hand on Jeev's shoulder. "I know you are ready for this."

A few weeks later Arjun arrived with fresh food. He was startled to see Ramu answering the door, leaning on his stick cane, grinning. "Hello old friend. I still can't dance, but I'm getting used to walking again."

Arjun looked at Ramu with skepticism. "But aren't you in pain?"

"A bit, but not enough to mind it. We're ready to leave this place and stay with you."

"Come on, then. We can start with some tea and go from

there."

Ramu and Jeev walked back with Arjuna to the blue house in the village. The men were quiet on the journey, each lost in his own thoughts. Ramu was slow, but Jeev and Arjuna walked closely with him being careful to not let him get far behind.

A week later, Jeev and Ramu were sitting on the floor drinking tea. Arjun said "It is not safe for you both to go back to Calcutta. There are posters with your name on it accusing you both of killing English soldiers. I have your travel papers for you and a guide will take you to the mountains where you can hide until it is safe to return."

Ramu turned to Arjun "I will go with your guide to the Himalayas. Jeev will be going to Bombay to start on a new quest." Arjun nodded, knowing he should not ask any more questions.

"I'm going to miss you, Ramu," said Jeev. "Are you sure you can get around the Himalayas with your bad leg?"

Ramu smiled. "No problem, friend. I'm still alive, for which I'm grateful. Once things calm down in Calcutta, I'll go back home."

Jeev stared down at the new travel papers Ramu's contacts had brought him. "I don't know when I'll get back, or if I'll get back..."

Ramu chuckled. "Bombay isn't that far. Once you get there, you get on a ship for England, and then Germany, where you'll meet with our allies there. Then you'll plead our cause to the German Army for arms and ammunition. Just tell them the truth. Indian people are living in misery, overworked, overcharged and overly poor. By the time you've finished that, the British will have forgotten their dead soldiers, and you should be able to return home."

Jeev listened to Ramu and reasoned; *the case was that the*

rival of my enemy is my friend. It was in Germany's interest for the English rule in India to be unstable. With the proper mobilization and armaments, the militant forces could wage battle against the British and drive them out of the Indian sub-continent.

CHAPTER 18: GATEWAY TO INDIA (1907)

J eev pored over his travel papers, scrutinizing every detail of his new identity, Stephen Pereira. His mind went back to the conversation with the man who had given the papers to him, a gruff, balding man who communicated only the essentials, which did not include his name.

He handed Jeev a brown paper package containing the documents and said, "You are a teacher travelling to take a job at the Jesuit St. Mary's school in Bombay. Stephen Pereira had just finished his studies at St. Xavier college, a Jesuit educational institution. Since you, as Stephen, were born in Goa, your papers are stamped with the seal of Portuguese Authorities." The man stared at Jeev's clean-shaven face. "Of course, you will have to grow a mustache and short beard if you expect to pass as Pereira."

Jeev nodded. He knew that Goa was a Portuguese colony and the British and Portuguese had a mutually beneficial alliance, so Great Britain recognized the validity of Portuguese travel papers.

Six weeks later, with his new mustache and goatee, Jeev arrived at Asansol Railway Station, which was only four stops from Durgapur, the site of the shooting incident. He walked up to the railway counter and bought his train tickets to Bombay. Jeev found a seat and glanced around the small station. The only waiting passengers were a few women in dull cotton saris and a scattering of bored men who gazed at the tracks while smoking pipes. There were even fewer guards. His train arrived. Jeev boarded. He walked down one of the carriages and found a seat for the fifteen-hour journey to Allahabad, where he would have to change to a different train.

The train journey was without incident, and he spent his time memorizing the details of his new identity. Preoccupied, he did not notice a thin young man wearing a blue suit sit down next to him. "Hello, I'm Benoy Banerjee". He smiled and placed his bag under his seat.

Although startled, Jeev quickly realized this was an excellent opportunity to practice his new identity. He replied, "Hello, I'm Stephen Pereira. Nice to meet you."

"Have you travelled to Allahabad before" inquired Benoy. "No, this is my first time" replied Jeev.

"Did you know Allahabad is one of the oldest and holiest cities in India. It is the intersection of three rivers, the Ganges, Yamuna and Saraswathi. We can see the joining of the first two. They say the third is to be found underground. A city that has seen monarchies and civilizations thousands of years old. One of the Mogul rulers, Akbar, gave the name of Allahabad in the 1500s."

The two men kept the conversation light, not discussing politics or personal matters, until Benoy asked Jeev, "Do you go to church every Sunday?"

Jeev almost replied that he was Hindu, but checked himself, mumbling "Yes, yes as much as I can." Then he feigned weariness and pretended to go to sleep, reminding himself to buy a Bible when he reached Bombay.

The Allahabad station had a substantial number of troops. As he walked over to the platform to wait for his train, two soldiers stopped him and asked, "Where are you going?" Jeev dressed in white shirt and brown belted trousers, a rumpled grey jacket and black leather shoes, hesitated, in his mind, though, he was still the ragged kid running through the farmland, swimming in the river, and associating with militants. Sweat trickling down his cheek, he answered "Bombay, I have my travel papers" and reached inside his jacket for his travel papers. "No need for papers, Sir," replied one soldier. "The train should be here shortly, you are in the right place," and with that they walked away. He resolved to be more confident in his approach from now on. The old Jeev would have to be left behind in Calcutta. Stephen was educated, successful, and confident.

He walked past the stationmaster's office and peered inside. On the wall were posters of wanted militants. As he studied the posters, he saw to his horror a likeness of his face with the words underneath: Wanted for Murder. A similar poster had the likeness of Ramu. He quickly bolted out to the platform and sighed deeply with relief when the Imperial Mail train grandly chugged into the station.

While the train was carrying mail, its name was a misnomer. It was mostly an opulent passenger train. The steam engine was painted black and bright green. Six carriage cars made of teak wood were behind the engine, followed by two luggage and mail cars. Inside the teak cars were sleeper beds, complete with sheets and blankets. The first four cars were set aside for Europeans, while the last two were for rich Indians, as most Indians could not afford this means of travel.

A conductor greeted Jeev as he entered the carriage, and a coolie picked up his suitcase and guided him to his berth. Jeev's eyes widened slightly at the opulence of the train. It was hard for him not to stare at the teak paneled walls and brass handled doors. His footsteps fell silently on the green and black patterned carpet. The coolie stopped, grabbed a brass handle, and slid open the door to Jeev's compartment. There were three other men already sitting in the cabin. His seat was by the damask draped window. The drapes were pulled back so that passengers could enjoy the view. As he sat down, a server arrived pushing a wood and metal cart piled high with hot beverages and small food dishes. The man smiled. "Would you like some tea, coffee, or snacks?"

Unused to being waited on, Jeev hesitated. "Uhm... I'd like some tea, and do you have any hot potato pancakes?" He could smell the spicy-sweet scent of garam masala and savory potatoes emanating from the cart. His stomach rumbled in response.

"Yes sir, we do."

"Then I'll have some then", Jeev replied, with a nervous smile. The server poured him a steaming cup of orange pekoe tea and handed him a small plate of warm potato pancakes flecked with green onion. The server then left gliding out as he pushed his cart without spilling a drop or crumb.

Jeev exchanged pleasantries with the three strangers and then stared out of the window admiring the passing scenery. One man had his head buried in a book. The other two passengers were engaged in a conversation about the Indian National Congress in hushed whispers. Jeev closed his eyes and feigned asleep. The first man, who was wearing glasses, leaned forward, and said "I don't agree with the congress pledging cooperation with the British. They are just dangling the carrot of freedom in front of us, we will never have an agreement for a free India."

The other man replied "We must work with the system, avoid the deaths of countless of our countrymen. Active non-violent resistance will work in the long term." The man with the glasses raised his voice "I can only accept self-rule of Indians by Indians. The American Revolution, the French Revolution, were all carried out by force." He looked tentatively at Jeev, then lowered his voice "The only way we can drive the English out of the country is through an armed intervention."

The men then changed the subject and Jeev nodded off to sleep.

He was awakened by the attendant bringing in trays of food for dinner. After dinner, the attendant came back to make the beds for the passengers. Jeev laid down on the fluffy mattress with clean, white sheets, and pulled a soft cotton blanket over him, while the gentle swaying of the train rocked him into a deep sleep. He was grateful for the luxuries, as he had previously travelled by train on a hard wooden bench, squeezed between so many passengers that he could barely move his hands or feet. The unbearable heat of the train caused the stench of sweat and body odors to permeate the carriage. On this train, in stark contrast, an attendant periodically sprinkled jasmine scented liquid on the floor and doors, making the train carriage smell like a fragrant garden. Food and beverages were constantly being served, and a fresh breeze blew in from the window. The journey took over a day and a half. Jeev enjoyed every minute.

Finally, the train arrived at Victoria Terminus. Jeev glanced around but detected little security presence. He stepped out of the building and admired its immensity. Designed in a gothic style with Moghul influenced arches, its standout feature was an enormous clock in the center tower with a marble statue of Queen Victoria underneath. There were towers on each side of the main tower. Outside the terminus was a line of carriages for hire. Jeev climbed into one of them and asked, "Take me to the Mahalaxmi Temple".

The carriage driver nodded his head and urged the horse forward. He had in his pocket an address on Warden Road near the temple. He recalled the man in Durgapur telling him "Do not go directly to this address. Get down at the Temple and then walk." Jeev saw the sights of the bustling city until the carriage stopped in front of the temple, which was housed in a rocky outcropping overlooking the Arabian Sea. The waves lashed the rocks at the base of the structure with substantial force, spraying fine droplets of salt water on the devotees gathered within. He stood watching the waves crashing on the rocks, wondering if the rough seas were a precursor to what was to come next for him.

He then looked at the address on the paper, *1210 Warden Road*, and walked down the street studying the house numbers. Soon he was standing by a three-story house facing the sea, with two guards standing in front of an iron gate surrounded by a tall brick wall. Jeev straightened his shoulders, lifted his head, and approached the guards telling them, "I am here to meet with Mr. Jagdish Chandra."

The guards looked at Jeev suspiciously. "Wait here", barked the guard nearest Jeev. He marched into the house while the other guard stared at Jeev with steely resolve. Jeev remained calm and did not move.

A few minutes later, the first guard returned and summoned him into the house. "You can wait here" said the guard, pointing to a plush, red leather sofa. Jeev sat down and made himself comfortable. He glanced around the room and knew this was a rich person's house. The room was decorated with fresh flowers, large mirrors on the walls and intricate carpets on the floor. Shining crystal chandeliers hung from the ceiling. Jeev did not have long to admire the décor, as a short, pudgy man wearing a white topi, white shirt, and a dhoti soon strolled into the room.

Jeev started to stand up, but the short man, sat down on the sofa and said, "Mr. Pereira, thank you for coming. I trust you had a comfortable journey."

"Yes, thank you, Mr. Chandra" said Jeev wondering if this man had paid for his trip. Another man then entered the room wearing a dark blue suit.

Mr. Chandra pointed at the man, saying, "This is my assistant, Mr. Sanjay. He will help you with the rest of your arrangements. I want you to know that what you are doing for our nation is extremely important. I wish you the best for your journey." And with that, he got up, folded his hands to his chest in a namaste and left.

"Here are a few things for your journey" said Mr. Sanjay handing Jeev a small leather bag." Inside you will find English Pounds and an address in London. "Also" handing him a paper packet, "this is your ticket for the ship to England and the address of a hotel in Bombay where you will stay until your ship departs. His gaze then grew stern, "Most importantly, forget you were ever here. The guards will not let you in again. You met no one while you were here." Then he smiled and said, "We wish you a pleasant journey" and escorted Jeev out of the mansion.

Jeev stayed at a small inn near the Bombay Harbor while he waited for his ship. He found a dilapidated store that sold used books, mostly left behind by English, returning back home, who left them with their servants or tried to sell them. The bookstore owner let servants know he would pay for books by the pound. This arrangement benefited everyone. The bookstore customers got treasures of knowledge and inspiration, while the bookstore owner got a wonderful source of income. Many rich Indians who were fluent in English would frequent the bookstore, as well as college students looking for bargains. Jeev picked up a few books, some about ships, some about European and American History, and others by well-known authors such as Marx, Shakespeare, and Dickens. He read voraciously as he waited for the ship. He then packed more books with him to take on the voyage.

CHAPTER 19:
PASSAGE TO THE
EMPIRE (1908)

Jeev sweated as he stood in line waiting to embark on the England-bound ship. His gray suit jacket made his back and shoulders hotter and restricted his movement. He looked around at his fellow Indians, mostly dressed in loose cotton clothing, which allowed the air to flow through and cool their bodies. If only he didn't have to disguise himself.

Suddenly, Jeev saw something that made him forget his hot back. It was a British army officer embarking into the first-class section. He looked vaguely familiar. Jeev's senses shifted into high alert. Squinting his eyes to see the man better, he recognized him as the officer on the Viceroy train. Jeev reached into his jacket pocket and pulled out a pair of eyeglasses. Along with the facial hair, they would make him look more like Stephen Pereira. His confidence in his new identity was increasing, and he felt less anxious about being recognized. Regardless, he resolved to avoid the English officer during the voyage that was to last a month, weather permitting.

Several minutes later, after embarking, Jeev glanced around his private, second-class cabin. *Wonderfully comfortable* he thought. He stood in the middle of the room and stretched his arms out on both sides. His fingers did not touch the wall, but there was not much space to spare. Jeev smiled, thinking, *the cabin might be small, but it's all mine. For once, I don't have to share with anyone.* Jeev stepped over to the small porthole, through which the sun came through, lighting and warming the room. He gazed out at the clear, light blue sky, the bustling harbor, and beyond that, the endless horizon of deeper blue waves with sparkling crests. He sat down at the small wooden desk and pulled out pen and paper from his bag to start working on his proposal to the Germans to buy arms to use against the British. This would be a good voyage, if Jeev kept to himself, and away from Captain Burke, which should not be difficult as the upper-class cabins on the top floor of the ship were reserved solely for Europeans. No Indians were allowed there.

Meanwhile, Captain Burke sat in his first-class cabin, with a large glass window overlooking the Arabian Sea, writing out a proposal on the organization of his Southeast Asian espionage department. After a while, the words in his head started muddling together. Sean rubbed his sore eyes, turned his chair around, and like Jeev, contemplated the busy port and the serenity of the blue vista beyond it. He thought of his recent conversation with an old friend who was now a high-ranking officer in the Directorate of Military Intelligence. They were in a bar snug in the officers' club drinking gin and lime.

"Burke, you do know that a man of your skills is wasted in this god-forsaken outpost, don't you?" His friend took a healthy sip of his drink and carefully placed it on a round wooden coaster on the mahogany table.

The corners of Captain Burke's mouth turned up slightly, as he examined the contents of his glass. He took a small sip of gin and replied. "Weston, you know that Curzon isn't just my liege lord. He's, my friend."

Weston leaned slightly forward. His expression was now serious. "If Lord Curzon is your friend, he'll understand that you're wasting your time as his bodyguard. You've got *skills*. You can work with both people and information better than anybody I know."

Weston's words hit Burke hard. He set down his drink and took a deep breath. "I know what I can do, but I want to do something *meaningful*, not sit at a desk writing papers."

Weston smiled. "Do you really think that His Majesty's government would want you serving as a minion? You've traveled the world, and you know India as well as you do England. Also, you can speak and read German..."

Burke's curiosity rose. "What does my speaking and reading German have to do with India?"

"The Directorate of Military Intelligence needs a man... rather needs *you* to investigate activities of the German government. We've had reports that Indian militants are looking to buy arms to use against our soldiers here on the sub-continent. We need you to identify and eradicate German influence and espionage activities in South-East Asia."

Burke was excited but retained his composure. "What's my first assignment?"

Weston smiled without showing his teeth. "Good to have you with us, Burke! His Majesty will reward you well for your service." He stretched out his hand, which Burke shook with calm firmness. "First, you will return to London and establish an office to detect and track Indian and German mercenary activities."

Burke blinked his eyes and returned to the present. There was a lot to do before the ship reached London, so he turned his chair back to the desk and went back to work.

Two weeks later, Jeev walked out onto the deck. Bombay was far behind, and the ship had passed through the Gulf of Aden, into the Suez Canal. Jeev gazed out at the golden desert sands that flanked both sides of the canal's blue water. The sky was a paler blue and cloudless.

Lost in thought, Jeev didn't notice a man siding up to

him on his left.

"Amazing sight, isn't it?" Jeev turned around to see Captain Sean Burke standing next to him. A cold sweat passed through his body, as the man held out his hand and introduced himself "Sean Burke",

"Stephen Pereira" Jeev replied, accepting the handshake.

They both marveled at the massive size of the canal and the engineering prowess that had designed and built it.

"The journey from Bombay to London is now five thousand miles shorter, as ships no longer had to travel around the Cape of Good Hope at the tip of Africa, which is notorious for stormy weather, high winds, and massive waves. Instead, we get to enjoy scenic views from the slow-moving ship," said Sean.

Jeev gazed out at the desert, where a caravan of camels was slowly walking, loads of wares strapped to their back, the handlers nudging them across the sea of sand and a bright sun gently sinking into the horizon highlighting a small pyramid surrounded by date palm trees.

"So, what brings you on this journey? " Inquired Sean. Jeev felt the pressure lessening in his chest. The officer had not recognized him with his newly pressed clothes, glasses, and facial hair. "I am going to England to pursue higher studies," answered Jeev.

"Oh, that's a noteworthy endeavor," remarked Sean. "Where specifically?"

While Jeev was prepared for this questioning, he did not want to supply too much information to a military man, but he did not have a choice. "Cambridge University, Trinity College" responded Jeev.

He saw Sean's eyebrows rise slightly. "Well, a mighty fine institution. What will you do after you finish?"

"I hope to come back and teach in Bombay," stated Jeev.

Then wanting to end the conversation, "Excuse me, I have something I need to attend to". With that, he took his leave. He could feel Sean's eyes following him all the way back to the stairwell leading to the lower deck.

The ship soon left the Suez Canal, entered the Mediterranean Sea, and picked up speed. Sean tapped his pen on his blotter paper as he thought about his plans for the new South-East Asian office he was setting up. He lowered his head and sighed. Why had he accepted this job? He was a high adrenaline warrior, not a paper pusher. Then he realized, *I can define my own position, so why not leave room for direct participation in espionage and tracking missions?* His energy increased, he sat up straight and began writing furiously. Not only did he set up exciting opportunities for himself, but he also created foot on the ground positions to support his activities to be staffed by current and former Army and Navy officers with combat experience, especially those who had rotated in and out of Asia. He then created a cadre of administrative positions for research and analysis to be given to recent graduates in mathematics, chemistry, and justice. He also made plans to set up a group of informants on the sub-continent, as well as in mainland Europe, to feed his office with information. After completing his plans, and letting the ink dry, he placed them under lock and key in his desk.

On reaching London, Sean was to meet with Prince Louis of Battenberg, now in charge of the Naval Intelligence Department. The prince intended to reorganize the British intelligence services, but many naval officers were skeptical of his intentions, as he was a prince, not a career naval officer, and because he had been raised in Austria, Italy and Germany. England was his adopted home. Sean, however, was thrilled to meet him. With his background, Battenberg would have unique insight into the workings and operations of Imperial Germany, knowledge which could be invaluable to the success of the new South-East Asian office.

Meanwhile, Jeev sat at his tiny desk, writing his plans on a back of a postcard sized paper. He wrote in the smallest handwriting possible, the effort making his neck and shoulders ache and his fingers cramp. Being caught with such treasonous material would get him killed, so he then committed his plans to memory and tore the paper into tiny segments and tossed them overboard. Upon landing in London, he was to contact sympathizers of the Free India movement, many of whom lived near Trinity College. From there, he was to use their help and their contacts to travel to Berlin, where he was to present his plans to the Berlin-India Committee, a group of Indian freedom fighters and members of the Imperial German military establishment, who were ready to help destabilize South-East Asia. He still needed to work out the details of the plan in terms of what arms were necessary, where they would be delivered, the troops who would fight, and an entire strategy around the battle plan.

The ship sailed through the Mediterranean and rounded the straits of Gibraltar. Once out in the open North Atlantic Ocean, the weather turned. There were frequent squalls as they rode up the coast of Portugal. Touching his Portuguese travel papers, Jeev wondered what the reaction would be if he jumped ship, were to swim to Portugal, and stay there indefinitely. The waters in the Bay of Biscay, bordered by Spain and France, tossed the ship around like a rag doll. Most of the passengers became seasick. Sean Burke stood on the deck, taking the sea swells in stride, impervious to the danger of being washed overboard. He enjoyed the thrill and the danger of the situation. He had a bring it on attitude, his angular face teasing the sea. 'Is that all you got?' Jeev watched Sean from a window, his dark raincoat starkly contrasted with the white foaming sea. Little did he know that this man would be his nemesis.

Eventually, the journey ended. They disembarked at the London East India Imports port. Jeev, as Stephen Pereira, did not have any problems with the port authorities and set foot in London, where he shivered in the cold, damp weather. Leaving the docks, he walked for a while, enjoying the sights of a new city, which were mostly rows of dark brick houses with lace curtains and small shops in between. In the distance, he saw the Tower of London and London Bridge. Passing the Leadenhall market, he smelled something familiar, something Indian. Excited, he broke into a brisk walk, and saw an Indian restaurant. When he opened the door, he was greeted by the familiar fragrance of blended spices, ghee and roasting meat. The dining room walls were papered in dark red scrolled with a gold paisley pattern. He took a seat at a small table near a large window with pulled back maroon curtains. He looked out at the street, where a light rain was starting.

As Jeev was musing, a slim young woman with long braided black hair wearing a dark red sari approached him. "Excuse me sir, would you like to order?"

Jeev glanced at the menu. "I'll have the chana masala, naan and Darjeeling tea".

The young woman smiled, revealing small, perfect white teeth. "Fine, sir. I'll bring them to you."

A few minutes later, the girl returned, with a small pot of steaming tea, teacup, a small pitcher of milk and bowl of sugar. Jeev helped himself to the tea without milk or sugar. It was bracing. Jeev felt the warmth go to from his chest to his toes. A few minutes later, the woman brought a plate of chana masala with two pieces of naan bread. Jeev took a bite. The chickpea curry was not as spicy as he would have liked, but the bread was the right balance of chewy and soft. Most of all, it was nourishing and familiar, and Jeev was grateful.

After leaving the restaurant, Jeev hailed a carriage to take him to an address on Cromwell Street in North London. He alighted and stared up at the front of a dilapidated three-story brick building known as the India house.

CHAPTER 20: SCAR FACE (1901)

T he sound of Scar Face cracking his whip on a wooden pole startled Amee awake. "Time to get to work, everyone up," he bellowed.

She went outside and washed her face and hands with chilly water from a common pot all the women shared. Her face still wet, Amee looked out and saw a large, acre-sized, field of tall grass.

A tall, thin woman with weary eyes approached Amee and handed her a sickle. The short handle was made of wood and the shiny metal blade was curved. It felt heavy in her hand. "Walk with me", said the woman, and Amee fell in pace behind her as they and the other women walked to the field in the cool morning breeze. The woman kept her eyes focused straight ahead and spoke to Amee without looking at her. "You're new here, aren't you?"

"Yes", said Amee.

"The rules are simple. Take your sickle and cut the grass to the ground. It will be fodder for farm animals. The men will come behind and dig up the roots with their shovels."

When they reached the field, the tall woman fell to her haunches, grabbed a bunch of grass, used her sickle to cut through the grass close to the ground and laid the grass on the side of the field. Amee and other women did the same. The sky was a cloudless blue. Soon, the morning breezes gave way to harsh, relentless sun that was so bright that Amee had to squint to keep her eyes from burning from the sweat running down her face.

After a while, the grass started cutting into Amee's hands. Stopping was not an option, so she persevered through the stinging pain. The tall woman looked at Amee's hand and nodded in sympathy. "You will get used to it. The skin gets stronger, and it does not hurt as much." Amee only hoped this was true.

"Keep working! Work or you pay!" Amee heard the crack of a whip in the air, followed by a horrendous scream as the whip hit a resting woman's back. She glanced up and saw Scarface marching through the field, scanning for anyone pausing to take a deep breath in the stifling heat. She lowered her head and got back to work before he could notice her. Amee's stomach grumbled. Her mouth was dry, and her sickle was too heavy to wield, but she focused on the steady rhythm of her work; grab, cut, throw. Don't think about food or water. Grab, cut, throw…

Finally, the sun set in the distance, turning the sky vivid shades of orange, pink and red. Scarface stopped walking and yelled, "Stop working! Time to head back to your huts!"

Amee stood up slowly, her knees and back stiff from hours crouching in the tall grass. Her arms ached from grabbing grass and cutting with the sickle. She would have gladly laid in the field and slept if she weren't so hungry and thirsty. It was only the prospect of food and water that gave Amee the stamina to wearily trudge back, while wincing at the pain from her bleeding hands.

The evening was a repeat of the previous day, except for the greater weariness and pain. The heavy-set woman who everyone called Aunt Anne doled out the same watery stew into the same tin bowls. Scarface sat under a large tree, drinking homemade rum out of a metal cup. He was surrounded by a group of friends.

They talked loudly enough for Amee to hear bits of their conversation. "What Mr. Oliver doesn't know don't hurt him. I take molasses, make a little rum. Sell a little rum. He don't miss it." Scarface laughed and his friends joined in, raising a toast to his cleverness. Periodically, he would glance over to Amee and flash a smile. The scarred part of his mouth barely moved. The other part opened, revealing blackened teeth, making Amee tremble.

All the while, Aunt Anne kept a sharp eye on the men. She then waddled over to Amee, who was finishing her bowl of food. "Come and help me with the pot," Aunt Anne commanded.

Amee wiped up the rest of her stew with her hard bread and helped Aunt Anne carry the pot into the kitchen. "Come here, girl. I've got something you need". Aunt Anne then opened a wooden door. Amee gasped when she saw a pantry stuffed on one side with loaves of fresh bread, dried beans, salted meats, onions, potatoes, ginger root, and other knobby tubers that she didn't know. On the other side was a gleaming collection of knives, spoons, and utensils. Anne grabbed a loaf of bread and cut it in half, placing the bread and the knife on the table. "This is for you" she said and then left the kitchen. Amee instinctively grabbed the bread and the knife, wrapped them in a cloth, and hid them inside her shirt. Aunt Anne stood outside the kitchen peering into the darkness not looking in Amee's direction.

Amee muttered "Thank you" as she passed her and hurried to the room in her hut.

She placed the bread in her bag and slipped the knife under her thin, lumpy mattress. For a while she lay awake, stiffening at any sound heard outside, but eventually she dozed off to sleep.

About two hours later, she awakened suddenly. She knew she wasn't alone. Someone was with her, close by. She opened one eye and stared right into Scarface's face. He was inches away from her and looked meaner and uglier than she could ever have imagined.

He stunk of rum, sweat and mud. Silently, he moved closer to her face, his two hands holding each of her shoulders down, pressing them against the mattress. His body was now on top of her, pushing her into the thin mattress. She reached for the knife she had hidden under her bed. Her hands closed over the wooden handle. "No! leave me! " She shrieked. He placed one of his hands over her mouth. Her shoulder now free, she pushed the knife upwards at Scarface hoping to catch any part of his body. The knife sliced into his upper thigh. Amee was strong for her age, so the knife wedged deep into his flesh. Scarface screamed in agony, toppling over to his side, holding his leg.

Amee jumped up and grabbed her knapsack and shoes. She ran out of the hut, passing a group of astonished women who looked at her through sleepy eyes. As she passed the kitchen, she looked back. Scarface was nowhere to be seen, hopefully still writhing in agony back in the room. She rushed to the pantry and grabbed some salted meat and more bread. On her way out, she took another knife and clutched it in her hands. It was still quiet in the settlement. She started running towards the road.

Suddenly, a figure appeared before her. It was Aunt Anne. Amee halted, thinking how strange she must look in the middle of the night, running with her knapsack over her shoulder, knife clasped in her hand, hair flying in the wind.

Aunt Anne whispered, "Don't go to the road. They will find you. Go towards the field you were working in. Beyond the trees at the end of the field, there is a small path. Follow the path to the river. Hide during the day, walk at night till you reach the sea. God speed my child." She moved forward and gave Amee a tight hug. "Go now, go." Amee ran towards the field and was soon swallowed by the darkness.

She did not see Scarface stumble out of the hut. "Help! I've been stabbed! That girl..." He screamed, blood streaming from his wounded thigh. Aunt Anne ran towards him. So did a few of the men who were awake. "Did anyone see her? " Scarface rasped between screams of pain.

Aunt Anne said, "I saw someone running towards the road. Men, take Mr. Brown back to his hut and boil some water. I'll take care of his wound."

CHAPTER 21:
THE RIVER

Amee stumbled through the field till she saw the trees ahead. On reaching the trees, she could see a small path snaking into the woods. Still clutching the knife, she tied her knap sack firmly around her back and walked into the forest. She was so full of adrenaline that she was not weary despite the previous day's grueling labor, Finally, after hours of walking, the path narrowed into a sliver of a clearing barely wide enough for one step. Then it disappeared into the underbrush. Facing her was a dense forest. She glanced around to see if the path reappeared further ahead. Exhausted, she sat down under a cabralea tree. The smooth bark cooled her back but not her spirit. She glanced up through the dark green leaves at the softly brightening sky and then broke down in tears. Shattered were all her plans and hopes. The dream of a better life after the ship's journey remained an illusion. Jeev's words, man plans, and God laughs, came into her mind. I wonder what he is doing now. Probably coming up with a scheme to fight the British. Her thoughts about him brought a fleeting smile of happiness. Then the dread of her current situation sunk in. She was now in a foreign land, with no money, no plans, a fugitive lost in the jungle. Where would she go? How would she live, even if she could somehow go back to India? The situation there was hopeless. Her situation here was bleak. As reality sank in, she shed another bout of tears.

Up above, the sky was alighted with bright colors. The clouds appeared blood red, while the treetops were a succulent orange. She remembered Aunt Anne's words, *hide during the day,* and scouted for a place to conceal herself. A thick shrub on the side of a rock looked like a good hideaway. She crawled between the shrub and the rock, flattened some leaves on the ground, placed her bag under her head as a pillow and closed her eyes.

The sounds of rustling leaves woke her up. A dark-brown squirrel had wandered into the underbrush and was standing on his hind legs looking inquisitively at her. Amee moved. The squirrel sprang up a tree to safety. She peered out from the bushes. Bright sunlight filtered through the tree leaves dappling the forest floor. Birds chirped. Bugs screeched, and small animals rustled over the leaves. Amee reached into her bag and found the hard bread; Aunt Anne had provided. She would save the dried meat for later, as she needed to conserve her food until she could forage in the woods. She stretched her legs, munched on the chewy bread and waited until dark before making her move.

As the sun started to set, she walked in a circle around her area, trying to figure out which direction to follow. Suddenly, she heard flowing water. Behind a row of trees was a bubbling stream flowing down a ravine. *Follow the river, the stream will lead to the river.* She gingerly followed the flowing water. The going was slow, as rocks on either side of the stream were slippery. Wet clothes and wet hair would not dry quickly in the humid jungle, so she did not want to fall into the stream.

After walking for a couple of hours, she smelled smoke. Amee slowed her pace, her senses on high alert for danger ahead. A brief flicker of light caught her eye. She stopped, crouching in the bushes, holding her breath. In the distance, on the other side of the stream was a fire. Still crouching, she crept closer and noticed huts near the fire and silhouettes of people going to and from between them.

The stream passed close to the huts. She would have to be incredibly quiet so as not to attract any attention. Coming closer, she heard someone walking towards her. She stooped close to the ground and crawled till she could hide behind an enormous tree trunk. A woman carrying a large jar was walking towards the stream on the other side. She knelt by the bank and filled the jar with water from the cold stream. *There is something familiar about the woman.* Amee strained to see her face in the moonlight. Then it hit her. *That's Agni!* Amee got up and whispered to her friend on the other side of the stream, "Agni, it's me, Amee!" The woman froze, scared and uncertain. "It's me, Amee," Amee repeated, in a louder, firmer voice. Agni dropped the jar, which clanked loudly on the rocks.

Another woman appeared on the bank with Agni, "What happened?".

"Nothing" called out Agni, "Just dropped the jar, I will be right there."

She signaled to Amee with her hand to wait, filled the jar with water, and headed back to one of the huts. Amee went back to her hiding place behind the tree, her heart beating wildly. After what seemed to be an eternity, Agni came back with a smaller woman. They crossed the stream taking small steps on the wet stones. Then, Amee gasped, for in the moonlight, she saw Agni and her sister Arti! Crying, the three young women fell into a group hug.

Arti held on to Amee tightly and whispered, "The boat I was in came into Georgetown the day after your boat arrived. They assigned me to a group with Agni."

Amee pressed Arti close to her "I am so sorry I did not keep you with me. I will never let that happen again."

"What are you doing here?" asked Agni.

"I ran away from the farm," said Amee.

Agni's eyes widened with a million unasked questions. "We need to get back before anyone notices we have been gone for too long" worried Agni.

Amee held on to her sister tighter. "Come with me. We can run away from this nightmare together," pleaded Amee.

"A merchant who intends to sell us to the highest bidder has brought us here. He has gone back to the port to pick up another group. The rumor is that he will be back in a few days and then we will all be transported to another place far from here to work on farms," said Agni.

"Look, you must come with me. Together, we can work something out. I do not know what, but it will be a better fate than what awaits us here," Amee continued. "I do not know what we will do, where we will go, but it will be our journey, our hope. It may seem we will wander aimlessly through the jungle, but we will figure something out."

Agni needed a little added convincing. "If we leave now, they will come after us. We will go back and when everyone is asleep tomorrow night we will come back here. I will also gather some clothes and steal food for our trip. Amee forced herself to smile and nodded in agreement. With a quick hug, the two departed, walking across the stream.

Amee trudged back to her hiding place. A few raindrops fell on her forehead. She pulled large banana leaves from a nearby tree and dragged them under the shrubs. A few sturdy branches offered the structure a makeshift cover. Not a moment too soon. As the heavens opened, sheets of rain poured down beating down on the huge leaves like a drum. They kept out most of the rain but not enough to keep her dry. Between the wetness and the noise, sleeping was hard. The rain finally stopped after daybreak. Amee tried to catch some sleep, as she, Arti and Agni would walk the entire night. At one point, she was awakened by what she thought were footsteps, but turned out to be a small animal scurrying through the leaves.

After dark, she gathered her bag and headed out towards the meeting point. The rains had turned the once small stream into a raging river. Crossing it now would be too dangerous. She sat down and waited for Agni and her sister. A few hours passed by, and she wondered if they would come. Then, she noticed a couple of shadows in the distance approaching the stream. She crept back behind the tree trunk out of caution. Soon, she could make out Agni and her sister, both carrying cloth bags over their shoulders, coming towards the stream. Amee walked out from behind the tree and signaled to them to keep walking down stream. They all recognized the stream as too deep to cross. They continued to walk downstream; the progress was slow as shrubs, trees and the rocks around the water often blocked the way, and the stones were slick. Finally, they came to a place where a large tree had fallen across the stream and was securely lodged between the rocks. The water gurgled and roared under the tree trunk. Amee beckoned them to cross over. Apprehensively, the two crawled onto the tree. Agni took the bag from Arti and told her to go first. Terrified by the water below her, she could not stand up. So, she crawled on all fours, slowly moving towards the opposite bank. When she was close enough, Amee held out her hand and pulled her over to solid ground. Agni seemed fearless. With a bag on each shoulder, she stood up on the tree trunk and precariously balancing, took one step after another, quickly crossing over. On reaching the end, she flashed a big smile of victory.

The trio walked on through the night, putting as much distance between them and the encampment as they could. They knew that two different search parties would be looking for them, so they needed to find a hiding place by daybreak. As the first rays of the sun appeared over the horizon, they stopped following the stream and headed towards a hilly area. Climbing upwards, Amee noticed a small cave. It was barely deep enough to fit the three of them. They covered the entrance with branches, drained from the all-night walk, tumbled to the cave floor, where each made a makeshift bed from her own clothes and lay down to rest.

Later in the day, they shared the food each had stolen from the encampments. Agni recited the ordeals she had faced with Scarface.

The story terrified Arti. "We could just live in the forest for the rest of our lives," she chipped. The two older girls looked at her with disdain.

"We need a plan. Something realistic, something we can do.

Somewhere there is a better life for us," Amee philosophized to no one in particular. " We can follow the stream to the river and then follow the river to the sea. We need to get to the sea, where we can get on a ship out of here. I have some gold I could sell to get our tickets. " There was silence.

Amee continued pensively, "No one knows how much it will cost to buy tickets for a ship. No one knows where we want to go. No one knows how we will survive in the jungle or where our food will come from. No one knows if the stream will lead to the river, or the river will lead to the sea. What I do know is that we cannot go back to where we ran from."

The trio continued following the stream for two more nights, not encountering any sign of human habitation. Their food ran out, so they ate berries and other wild fruit they found along the way. Luckily, the stream had plentiful, clean water, which had fish, but they had no way to catch and cook them.

Three nights later, as they continued to follow the stream, the landscape changed, the sides of the stream were steeper and the water rushed down at increasing speed, forcing the women to veer off-course and climb up a steep ravine. Reaching the top, Agni peered into the distance and said, "Look, sugar cane fields. There is definitely a farm there. We may even be close to a village or city."

"What's that loud sound?" asked Arti.

"Sounds like a waterfall," said Amee.

They soon came upon a giant rock formation with water flowing over the rock, falling into a ravine below. Cautiously approaching the edge, they saw the waterfall, and the stream emptying into a wide river. "Be careful these rocks are slippery" said Amee as they made their way down the ravine to the riverbank and rested on a ledge by the waterfall, pondering what to do next. The sky was slowly turning blue. "It will be daylight soon, and we need a place to hide" warned Agni.

"Look up there" said Arti pointing towards numerous holes the waterfall had carved into the cliffside. They climbed up to one of the larger openings, a cave about five feet deep.

"Gather up the fallen leaves so we can use them as a bed. Then place branches at the entrance," said Agni. Collecting leaves by the armful, they spread them across the cave floor to make the ground softer to lie on and then covered the end of the cave, so someone looking up from the river would not see them.

As daylight rose, they were glad they had taken the precautions to hide, as occasional anglers drifted into the area with their fishing poles and nets. A few larger boats also passed by, carrying goods and passengers. They remained hidden, lest someone should see them. The afternoon passed, and they finished their final rations. The first thing they would need to do at nightfall would be to hunt for food.

"It was a miracle seeing you in the forest," said Arti.

Amee cuddled up to Arti as tears welled up in her eyes "It was a miracle for me to see you again. I thought your boat was heading for another island. For you to end up with Agni…I can't even imagine where you could have been."

Agni moved closer to the two sisters, "After we were separated at the harbor, we stayed near the harbor, sleeping out in the open. The next day the boat carrying Arti arrived and she, along with several others, was added to our group. The merchant told us that he was going to deliver us to plantations far away from the harbor. However, there were other boats coming in and he would be taking us to a farm by the stream to wait for a few days until all the boats arrived. We travelled in carriages to the farm. He told us that we had been contracted to work at various plantations. By contract, we would have to work for at least five years to pay their share of the voyage and living expenses in Guyana before they could free us to live our lives. One of the older workers who was guarding us told me that he had been working for fifteen years and still could not earn enough to complete his contracts and pay off the owners. Once someone started to work in the plantation it was usually till, they died." Agni paused to wipe the tears from her eyes "I was scared for Arti. She is too frail for the hard life at the plantation. For me, it was a feeling of hopelessness. I did not know what to do, Amee, until you came along. Now I would rather die escaping than go back to that fate."

After dusk, the three ventured out to survey the area. In the distance was a farmhouse, with a fire burning in the courtyard. As they passed closer, they could smell roasting meat and cassava, making their empty stomachs rumble. Several dogs barked, and they beat a hasty retreat to the riverbank. Arti pointing to the riverbank said "Look, there is a boat tied to the tree."

The three assessed the boat. It was weather beaten with a thatched roof, and a single sail in the front, but was big enough to comfortably hold all three of them. They looked at each other in agreement. "We can take this boat and go downstream. It will get us faster to the sea," exclaimed Agni.

"Other people will spot us," cautioned Amee.

"See what we have here. " Arti held up someone's clothing, obviously belonging to the angler who owned the boat. "We can use this as a disguise. To the people who see us, we will appear to be fishermen."

They untied the boat from the tree and pushed off into the river. Amee and Agni grabbed the two oars in the boat and started rowing. Under the thatched roof was a small mattress for sleeping, some dry food, and a net for catching fish. Amee reached into a pile of clothes and grabbed two shirts, two pairs of pants, and two cloths. "Here, put these on," she said, tossing them to Agni and Arti.

"Eeww... these clothes smell like fish!" Arti exclaimed.

"What do you expect? This is a fishing boat." Amee was stern.

"At least we have a way to travel the river. My sore feet and I are happy for that!" said Agni. Amee and Arti chuckled in agreement.

All three women smiled as they each put on shirts and

pants and tied up their hair with cloths to make crude turbans. The slow-moving current carried them forward with little effort. The moonlight was bright enough for them to see where they were going. Arti steered the boat while Agni and Amee rowed, so they could put as much distance as they could from where they had stolen the boat. "That is going to be one unhappy angler when he finds his boat missing" said Agni laughing.

"It just means more people will be looking for us" warned Amee.

They rowed for several hours before pulling up the oars and letting the current pull them down river. They passed several small islands that were deserted. Agni took the fish net and tossed it overboard, dragging it with a rope. Once she felt something pulling at the net, she yanked it back in. "I caught two fish" exclaimed Agni. Up ahead was a small island, and they pulled into the riverbank. They tied up the boat and covered it with leaves and branches to make it difficult to detect. Agni sliced the fish into very thin pieces and left it on the rocks to dry. As the sun came out, the three settled in to get some sleep.

Waking up in the afternoon, Agni scouted the small island. She saw a fruit that looked like a lemon. She squirted the fruit juice over the fish which was completely dry from the scorching sun. Hesitantly, they ate the protein, the sour juice covering up the fishy taste. A giant otter with black velvety skin, long tail, huge whiskers on his mouth and eyebrows and a white spotted neck who was attracted by the fish smell sat on a rock, staring at them. Agni hurled the fish bones in his direction. The otter, sensing danger, ducked into the water.

They saw a few boats pass the island. They felt increasingly confident that their boat was well hidden, in a secure place. "We should stay here for a few more days, rest and build up our supply of food and wash our clothes," said Amee.

Agni continued to cook fish using the heat of the rocks and the sun. They stocked up on food, and Agni created piles of dried fish soaked in a lemony liquid. Amee and her sister found mangoes and bananas, which they loaded on to the boat along with the fish.

Looking at the now well-stocked boat, Agni suggested, "Why not travel by day? We can disguise ourselves as fishermen..."

Amee placed her hand under her chin, looking pensive. "Also, we can better navigate the river then. There's lots of rocks, shallow banks and islands that make it treacherous sailing by night."

"Let's do that then!" Agni agreed, as did Arti.

In the first light, they uncovered the boat and set off downstream. They glided past thick vegetation covering both sides of the river. The islands in between were equally green and dense. A pink dolphin jumped in front of the boat, playfully splashing water over them. "Ah! What was that?" exclaimed Amee.

"It looks like a dolphin, but I've never seen a pink one before," said Agni.

"Look, we've got company," said Arti pointing to the right side of the boat where there were three more dolphins swimming alongside.

"Well, I guess we've got bodyguards," said Amee, laughing.

A few hours later, they saw another boat in the distance. All three women checked to make sure their heads were covered. Agni took some mud that was stuck to the side of the boat and smudged their faces with the muck. "It will make you look more like fishermen," she chuckled. The boat ahead was another fishing boat like theirs. Two fishermen were throwing nets into the water. As they passed them, they stared straight ahead. One man in the boat waved his hand, Agni waved her hand back. Once they rounded a bend in the river, and the boat and fishermen were no longer visible, all three heaved sighs of relief. *Their disguises were working.* They travelled all day and as darkness set in, they stopped at another small island, camouflaged their boat, and settled in for the night.

The next few days passed without incident. They flowed past many small villages and boats. No one gave a second glance at the fishing boat passing by. It blended perfectly with the surroundings and to observers on the riverbank or other boats. It was no different from hundreds of other small fishing boats with crews of two or three.

A few days later, however, Arti noticed something different. "Is it just me, or is the river getting wider?"

Amee and Agni looked. "Yes, the river is getting wider," both said in unison.

"What's that ahead?' Arti pointed. "It looks like a big town." Soon, they were floating by lots of boats tied to wooden moorings, and a riverbank crowded with timber frame buildings on both sides. A group of boys were jumping from a steep embankment into the river. Several soldiers loitered around the houses on the riverbank.

One man on a nearby boat called out, "Hey! Would you like to buy some guavas? Extremely sweet!" Agni shook her head, and they continued forward.

They saw women washing clothes or filling their pots with water. Many nets were strewn across the river, and Amee and Agni had to use all their recently acquired skills to navigate around them.

Suddenly, a large boat appeared behind them. A man stood on the side, looking over at the river. Amee glanced up at him and a shiver ran down her spine. *It was Scarface.* She could recognize that face anywhere. He glanced in her direction. She expected him to yell at her. Instead, he looked blankly at her and the boat and then turned his gaze in the other direction. As the large boat glided past them, Amee's heart thumped wildly, while the other two were unaware of the danger they had just passed.

CHAPTER 22:
THE FLOOD

"Can you see any place to stop? I'm tired," whined Arti.

"Don't worry, Arti. We'll find a place soon enough," Amee's voice was soft and reassuring, but the lowering sun cast shadows along the riverbank, which wherever they looked, was full of people.

"Look there!" exclaimed Agni, pointing to a deserted piece of land with plenty of shady trees, perfect for hiding the boat and themselves. "Pull the boat in Arti. I think we've found our resting place." They pulled the boat close to the riverbank and tied it to a tree trunk.

"What do you think, ladies? Shall we spend the night in the forest or on the boat?" asked Agni, gazing deeply into the forest.

"We don't know what's in there," replied Amee, still shaken from seeing Scarface. "Nobody will see us here, so we should be safe." Arti and Agni nodded in agreement, and the three bedded down on a pallet of clothes on the boat sole.

Early the next morning, Amee woke suddenly to a roaring sound in the distance. "Arti, Agni, what is that?" The other two women sat up, rubbing their eyes. The roaring sound was getting closer.

"I don't know..." replied Agni, yawning. Before she could finish, however, the boat started shaking as the river water got rough. It was as if the river was flowing backward.

"Grab your bags! We've got to get out!" cried Amee, as the

waves became larger and rushed towards the higher ground of the riverbank. All three women snatched what they could and jumped out of the boat and scrambled up the wet ground. They watched in horrified fascination as enormous waves barreled down the river ripping the boat from its mooring and pushing it upstream. Soon it tipped over and was swallowed by the rushing water.

Suddenly, a gruff voice yelled, breaking the women out of their trance. "Move up higher!" Climb up! You're going to drown!" Turning around, they saw a man wildly waving his arms. They looked down. The water was twirling at their feet. The women turned, climbing higher up the riverbank. Arti slipped on the wet grass, her arms flailing in every direction, Amee and Agni grabbed a hand each and pulled her up. Rushing up the slope, their knees scraped against the tall grass, feet slipping on the muddy bank, as the water level kept rising. At the top of the bank, where the man was standing, they halted, gasping for breath, and looked down at the rough, muddy water as it churned where they had been standing just a few minutes before.

The man walked towards them asking, "Are you all OK?". They looked at him and nodded. "I have never seen a flood like that," he continued. "All the rain we have been getting, the high tide from the sea must have created those waves."

Amee swallowed but remained outwardly calm as the man looked over the at the trio standing in front of him. Her wet, baggy clothes felt heavy as did the mud on her face. Her makeshift turban had fallen off during her climb up the bank, and her long black hair fell free to her shoulders. Her arms itched from the dirt lining them. She wanted nothing more than to grab her knapsack and run, but she could not leave Arti and Agni, no matter how horrible their fate. Agni's wet clothes clung tightly to her curvy body, her fisherman disguise now in disarray.

Finally, the man spoke. "I thought you were fishermen. Who are you and where are you from?"

The three young women stood in silence, unsure of what to say. The man came close to Amee. Her hand reached into her knapsack, where her fingers wrapped around the wooden handle of her knife. His skin was mahogany brown, sharply contrasting with the grey and white hair on his head and beard. He wore strangely familiar Indian clothing and spoke with an accent not unlike what Amee had heard at home.

He looked her straight in the eye and asked, "Did you all come on a ship from India recently?" Amee nodded her head. The man wrinkled his brow. "Are you all in trouble? Are you running away from a plantation?"

Amee hesitated. Could she trust this stranger? Did she have any choice? Had she ever had any choice? She stayed frozen, as did Arti and Agni.

The man noticed their hesitation, and said, "Listen my name is Amir Chowdhary, I too came on a ship a long time ago. Now I am a free man. I live with my wife and children on my farm just over the hill over there. It is not safe for you here. Come with me. We will try to help you." He started to walk towards a farm in the distance.

Amee and Agni looked at each other. Agni moved close to Amee's ear and whispered, "Can we trust him?"

"He is from our country, and he said he would try to help. It would be nice to have a roof over our heads. Also, we are near a big town and getting close to the sea. We need a plan and somebody to help us reach a safe location" replied Amee. Arti looked at both with fearful eyes.

The man had started to move ahead. Amee grabbed Arti's hand and pulled her forward. The three followed the man though a freshly cut sugar cane field, until they reached a stone house. Blocks of thick white rock made up the front and sides of the house. Stone steps led up to a small patio and black door. There was a large wooden roof and windows on the first floor. Two dogs came tearing from behind the house to greet their master, both wagging their tails so rapidly they looked like they would jump out of their skin. A plump lady wearing a large white apron opened the door. She looked inquisitively at her husband, who was leading the three girls inside the house. " I will explain," he whispered. "Let's get these girls inside the house." Turning to the girls he said, "This is my wife, Meera."

Amir opened the door, releasing a wave of warm air. The girls stepped over the threshold and took off their muddy shoes, placing them on a rack beside the door. Inside it was warm and cozy, with a smooth, wooden floor and a large, crackling fire burning in a gray stone fireplace at the end of the room. A massive wooden table with chairs was in the center and four plush blue velvet covered chairs faced the fireplace. Two small children, a girl and a boy, sat on the floor playing with wooden toys. Meera and Amir led the three girls into the kitchen, a cavernous room with a red brick floor, which felt rough and warm to Amee's bare feet. At the end of the room was a stone hearth blackened by years of soot. A pot, from which came tantalizing smells of chicken, ginger, and garlic, hung above the fire, supported by two iron beams over burning wood. Pots and pans were neatly lined up on shelves on the wall. Sacks of grain were stacked below the shelves. Across from the shelves was a table used for cutting and preparing food, with several ironwood stools lining both sides.

Meera smiled and gestured toward the stools. "Ladies, put down your sacks and take a seat." Amee, Arti, and Agni placed their knapsacks on the floor and climbed onto three adjoining stools.

Meera and Amir took two stools across from them. Amir's posture was straight but calm. Meera leaned forward, clasping her hands loosely together. She looked directly at the girls, her warm brown eyes showing no deceit. "So, tell us your story," she asked.

Amee took a deep breath and looked at Arti and Agni. Both girls were relaxed, with shoulders slightly bent, arms open, and slightly smiles. She then decided to trust this family and began her story. "My sister Arti and I were brought on a ship from Calcutta. We thought we would be living with an aunt, who would provide a better life for us. Unfortunately, we then found out that we were going to be contracted to a plantation owner. I was willing to do the demanding work, but the foreman had other intentions. I feared for my life, so I ran away. By a miracle I met Agni and my sister in the forest. We traveled on foot and by boat for days. We wanted to make it to the sea, so we could take a ship back home."

The husband and wife nodded in understanding "We understand" said Amir, "thousands of people have been brought here from India. Most have led dangerous and miserable lives on the plantations. Very few have been able to escape the country."

Amee looked anxiously at her newfound acquaintances and asked, "Can you help us?"

The woman spoke "Yes, we will help you. We too came here with a story like yours. I met my husband on the boat on the voyage here. We came from different villages, but on the same boat, we became friends and married a few years later. We were lucky to be employed by a man who was true to his word. After five years of working for him, he set us free. We continued to work for him for another fifteen years till he passed away. He did not have any heirs. His wife and son had died during childbirth. He left this house and farm for us. So, we have been living here for the last few years." She then gestured towards the two children playing in the living room. "The two small children are orphans. Their parents were our neighbors, who both died after getting sick from mosquito bites, so we are looking after them."

Amir then added, "You are not safe out in the open. There will be people looking for you. The people here do not take kindly to runaways. They are always caught and punished to teach them a lesson and warn others not to do the same," he paused for a minute, looking at his wife for permission. She nodded, and he continued. "You can stay here, while we can determine what you should do next. There is a hidden room upstairs that you can use. The room must stay dark during the night, no candles. People cannot know we have you staying in our house."

Outside, the wind had picked up and they could hear it howling as it whipped around the house. Amir rose from his stool and looked towards the door. "I've got to go out and make sure that the livestock and carriage are safe." Meera nodded, as he walked out.

She opened a door leading to the backyard patio, "I will get you some hot water, you can wash up here, and put on some dry clothes."

The girls soon returned feeling fresh. "Would you like some tea? We always have some when Amir finishes his evening chores." The young women nodded gratefully.

When Amir came back inside, he groaned with effort to bolt the door shut, and the girls could see that rain was falling in torrential sheets. They were glad to be indoors, enjoying hot green tea on a night like this.

After they finished their tea, Meera led the girls to a room behind the kitchen. She opened a door that led to a closet, which held a few bags of grain. Then, extending her arms into the dark closet, she pulled out a wooden panel about two feet wide. Amir walked up carrying a lit candle, which showed the girls a ladder that was hidden behind the panel. "You can climb up that ladder and it leads to a room upstairs. You can hide there. My old master built this room as a place to hide from troops. He had a friend who had deserted the British Army. They were after him and his family. My master hid them here for several months before they eventually could catch a ship to America," he explained.

Meera placed the wooden panel back in its fitted position. Someone looking in would only see the bags of grain. "Come, let's eat," she commanded. Amir and the girls followed her into the kitchen, where the children joined them. Meera ladled out bowls of steaming hot chicken soup served with fresh chapatis and fried plantains. The food tasted better than any Amee had ever tasted. Meera smiled as she watched the girls eat. When they finished, she asked, "Do you want more? We have plenty."

Amee said, "Yes, please." Arti and Agni enthusiastically agreed, and Meera ladled more soup and served them extra bread. Later, with their bellies full for the first time since they could remember, the girls climbed up the ladder into their new room in the attic. The room had a small window overlooking the farm. There were four cots lined up against the wall, a small low table in the middle of the room with a pitcher of water and several cups. On the other side of the window, the storm raged on. Torrential rain hit the wooden roof, trees swayed wildly in the wind, and flashes of lightning illuminated the landscape, followed by ear shattering thunder. Standing near the window, Amee peered out into the darkness and saw a pair of shining blue eyes. Startled, she kept staring at the spot. Lightning struck again, revealing a fox staring directly at her window. When the next bolt of lightning struck, the fox was gone. The trio settled in for the night, the cots and blankets a soothing respite from the raggedy clothing pallets on the boat floor. That night, Amee dreamt of being locked up in a prison and a fox with blue eyes coming to rescue her.

They woke just before sunrise to a rooster crowing loudly, and dogs barking, they climbed down the ladder into the kitchen, where Meera cheerfully greeted them and offered them warm tea and some freshly baked biscuits. Outside, the storm had passed, yielding to clear skies and bright sunshine.

Amir, who had been at work since well before dawn, came into the house looking tired and distraught. "The storm has damaged our cattle barn."

"We'll help you clean up and get fixed up," said Agni, taking the initiative. Amir looked at Amee and Arti.

Amee said, "We're happy to help. Show us what to do."

Amir's face relaxed. "Follow me," he said. "I'll show you what needs to be done and thank you for your help. It will make the work much easier." They spent the rest of the day picking up the broken pieces of wood, cleaning the animal stalls, and reorganizing the barn. It was tedious work but satisfying as they quickly saw the progress they made.

CHAPTER 23: LONDON (1909)

Jeev approached the massive front door of the run-down house with quiet steps and all senses on high alert. When he reached the entrance, he stood up straight, holding his satchel with a firm grip in his left hand, and knocked with a large, ornate iron knocker, dislodging chips of peeling red paint. Jeev waited, breathing in a steady rhythm to keep calm.

After two minutes that seemed like two hours, the door swung open. Jeev gazed up at a giant. The man was a foot taller than Jeev and muscular as well. His brown face and dark eyes showed no emotion. "I am Peekay, I am the caretaker of India House". He spoke with a with a Punjabi accent and had a gruff voice, which matched his strapping physique.

Jeev remained calm, and said in a firm businesslike voice, "Hello. I am Stephen Pereira".

Peekay's expression did not change. He said, "Welcome, Mr. Pereira. We have been expecting you." He stood aside, letting Jeev enter an enormous foyer with an elaborately carved oaken staircase. Peekay, staying silent, led Jeev up the stairs to a small room with a round window through which the sun shone, illuminating dust particles dancing in the air. "This is our guest room", he stated. "You can only stay here for one week. Then you must find other suitable accommodation. There are many people living in the India House, all from the Indian subcontinent. It will be better for all if you don't talk to them about your background." He then left the room, only to turn around and say, "Also, Mr. Sarkar will be here at 9:00

tomorrow morning to see you. Don't be late."

Now alone, Jeev studied his new accommodations. They were basic, with a thin cot, flimsy table with a chipped porcelain bowl and pitcher, an old, cracked mirror above it, a chair with one broken leg propped up by a brick, and a small wardrobe, with warped doors that did not shut evenly. Jeev set his bag on the hardwood floor, took off his shoes, and stretched out on the cot, falling into fitful but needed sleep.

Jeev woke up just after 8 a.m. the next morning. He shivered when he threw off his wool blanket. What he had heard about England was true. It was damp and chilly. There was, however, no choice but to get ready for his appointment. Hot tea and breakfast would have to wait. He splashed some water on his face, careful not to overly wet his beard and mustache, brushed his teeth, and selected a clean white shirt. After dressing, he combed his hair, straightened his necktie, and walked downstairs where Peekay was waiting for him.

Peekay nodded and started walking. Jeev followed him down a long hall to a parlor with dark green damask wallpaper. Peekay turned and left Jeev standing on an intricately patterned red, cream, and green rug, A fire blazed in a large fireplace, taking the edge of the damp chill. Jeev saw two tall dark red velvet chairs on either side of the fire facing a long mahogany table in and a dark red leather sofa on the opposite side. Jeev stood near the fire, musing as he watched the flames.

"Stephen Pereira? I'm Mr. Sarkar" A deep, cultured voice with a West Bengali accent startled Jeev out of his trance. Jeev turned to see a man who looked not much older than him. He carried an eagle headed cane, wore a white linen shirt, black bowtie, black double-breasted suit over white trousers, tall black boots, and an elegant silk top hat. If not for his brown face, Mr. Sarkar could have been mistaken for English aristocracy.

He took off his top hat, revealing a full head of black

hair as he sat down in one of the tall velvet chairs, He waved his hands towards the sofa. Jeev sat. Mr. Sarkar clasped his hands and leaned back slightly, stretching his legs, and studied Jeev for a few moments. Jeev looked at Mr. Sarkar and then politely averted his gaze, looking into the burning fire. Finally, Mr. Sarkar soke. "So, you are the man who will undertake this mission."

"I am still unsure of all the players and what my part is," said Jeev.

"Well, Stephen, we are having a meeting tonight. I will pick you up in my car. I will then explain all to you." He then rose and left the house in an unhurried, aristocratic fashion.

That evening, Jeev stood outside the India house in his best suit and tie, his hands clean, and every hair in place. He looked down the street and saw a black car slow down as it approached the house, where it pulled up alongside him. Jeev had never seen anything like it. It was long, open, with ebony leather seats, gold trim, all gleaming. Mr. Sarkar, as elegant as before, sat at the wheel, seeming not to notice Jeev's gaping mouth and staring eyes. "Climb aboard, Stephen! Sit here in the front with me so we can talk easily."

Still in shock, Jeev moved his legs, stepped on the running board and into the front seat beside Mr. Sarkar. He watched as Sarkar pulled the choke, threw the gears into action and the car lurched forward. The ride was smoother and more comfortable than Jeev expected. "This is an automobile built by a friend of mine from Trinity College, Charles Rolls." The engine purred rather than roared, so Sarkar spoke at normal volume. "This is the future, Stephen. All the horse-drawn carriages are going away. One day I want to build machines like these in our own country."

Half an hour later, they arrived in a neighborhood of large, ornate houses with trees lining both sides of the street. Mr. Sarkar stopped the car in front of a white brick house.

Each window had a balcony surrounding it. A marble staircase led up to a massive teak door carved with dancing figures. To Jeev's surprise, a large, turbaned Sikh opened the door.

Jeev gasped as he entered the foyer, which had a gleaming white marble floor, ornate gold and crystal chandeliers, and a sweeping brown teak double staircase.

"Follow me," commanded Mr. Sarkar.

Jeev followed with some effort to keep up with the other man's long stride. They walked down a long hallway lit with sconces without flame or heat. Despite the hurried pace, Jeev managed to glance into some of the rooms as they passed. They were filled with colorful Rajasthani furniture, intricately woven Arabian carpets, walls covered with paintings depicting scenes from Indian history and mythology, and a treasure trove of artifacts collected from various parts of the Indian sub-continent. Jeev wanted to stop and admire the sights, but there was no time to linger.

Finally, they arrived in a windowless inner room where a group of fifteen men and women had gathered around an oval mahogany table. Some were smoking. Most had snifters with whiskey or gin, and all were noisily chatting in English and several Indian languages. When Sarkar and Jeev entered the room, the drinking and conversations stopped, and all eyes focused on Jeev, making the hairs on his arms and the back of his neck stand up.

A fat man with slicked-back hair stood up and announced, "They are here, let's get started." He extended an arm towards Jeev with a flourish. "This is Stephen Pereira. He is our envoy from India and will be going to Germany to meet the committee in Berlin."

Jeev walked around the table, as the participants

introduced themselves. The men wore well-tailored Western suits or silk kurtas; the women brightly colored silk saris accented with exquisite jewelry. All of them were pleasant, but Jeev suspected that the names he was given were as false as the name that was given for him. One man, however, stood out. He was the only European in the room. "Good evening, Herr Pereira. My name is Franz Von Oppenheim" he said in a heavy, but understandable, German accent. He held his hand out to Jeev, who shook it firmly, not wanting to show any lack of confidence. He was acutely aware that Sarkar was standing in the background watching him. There was no room for missteps.

Finally, Sarkar approached the table. Everyone, including Jeev, took a seat. Sarkar started the meeting with "I bring the India Liberation Committee meeting to order", clapping his hands to bring attention to himself. "We are here to discuss the Berlin agenda. I have introduced you to Stephen Pereira. He will go to Germany to meet with the Berlin-India Committee. Over the next few months, we will prepare a detailed plan on the arms we need, where those arms will ship and the mobilization of the domestic forces. Each of you will have input into the plan. I must warn you that our sources in the War Office have told us that there is going to be added scrutiny for South Asian affairs and alerted us to be incredibly careful of our clandestine activities. The agenda for today is to discuss the list of weapons to be obtained. This is an inventory of weapons we could use, " Sarkar brandished a stack of papers, which he then passed around the table, giving everyone a copy of the list. There were lengthy discussions on the suitability of the weapons for the Indian climate, transportation nuances, availability of ammunition and supply chain planning. The turbaned butler glided smoothly carrying large silver trays piled with various fritters, samosas, chutneys, and drinks.

After the meeting was over, Jeev's head spun with the effort of digesting all he had learned in the last few hours.

Franz pulled him aside and said, "You have become something of a hero with what you tried to pull off with the Viceroy Train."

Jeev was startled "How did you know?"

"We make it our business to know," said Franz. "Sometimes a revolution needs a spark. That's what you are trying to do. I was in India in 1895. I met Swamy and Ramu. Glad you are learning from them. I have travelled extensively from Bombay to Calcutta to Delhi, crossed the desert in Egypt, and toured the Ottoman Empire. I speak Farsi, Arabic and Urdu." He then spoke in Urdu to Jeev, who only knew a few shared words between Hindi and Urdu. He understood enough to realize that Franz would be his contact in Berlin, and that he would help him once he got there.

Over the next few weeks, more meetings to hash out details of the plan were held at the Sarkar residence. Franz outlined the plan to the committee "A small group of militants will take over Port Blair in the Andaman Nicobar Islands in the Bay of Bengal. The port is about eight hundred miles from Calcutta, so there will be a significant distance between the rebel forces and the British. These islands are to form the base for the war against the English in the Indian sub-continent. We will smuggle arms from there, in boats, to villages near Calcutta on the East coast and Bombay on the west coast. The capture of these two cities would be the start of a battle to recapture the rest of the country. There is an inherent hope in this plan that the fall of the two principal ports will motivate the local population to rise and take arms against the British, joining our rebel forces." The committee agreed to the plan. The key to implementation was the procurement of arms from Germany, without which nothing could happen.

About six weeks later as Jeev was leaving a meeting at the mansion, Sarkar placed his hand on his arm. "Stephen, I must talk to you. It's urgent." Jeev nodded, and followed

Sarkar to his office, an imposing room lined with groaning bookshelves and dominated by a massive mahogany desk. Jeev sat in a maroon leather armchair facing the desk. Sarkar came straight to the point. "India House is being watched by the War Office. It's not safe for you to stay there."

"Where will I go?" asked Jeev.

"You'll go to Cambridge, just as Stephen Pereira planned." Sarkar handed him a train ticket and a slip of paper with an address. "Your accommodations are settled. You will be near Trinity College. Pack your bag and go to the address on the paper. Most of all, keep a low profile."

Jeev rose, shook Sarkar's hand, and left. He packed his bag and caught the train. When he arrived at the address, it was a small Tudor style home with lace curtains and red geraniums in the window boxes. He knocked on the door. A small, pale woman with blonde hair in a tight bun answered. "Hello. You must be Stephen Pereira. I'm Mrs. Carter, the landlady."

"Yes, I am he", said Jeev.

"Come in. I'll show you to your room." Mrs. Carter led Jeev upstairs to a small room with a single bed, oak wood desk, chair, and wardrobe. The room was free of dust and smelled fresh. There was a nightstand with a kerosene lamp and a small table with a pitcher and bowl underneath a clean, scratch-free mirror. A large window let in the weak sunlight, and a brown rug cushioned his steps. "Rent is due on the first of the month. Cooking your meals and cleaning your room are your responsibility. You share a common toilet, bath, and kitchen with four other students. Two are from India, like you, and two are from Egypt. The doors are locked after 9:00 p.m., so don't stay out too late. Women, gambling, alcohol, and opium in the house will not be tolerated."

"I understand," said Jeev. Mrs. Carter smiled briefly and left the room. Jeev unpacked his bag, ready to start another new life.

This new life meant keeping erratic hours to avoid his housemates. Jeev spent his days in the Wren Library, where he read, updated his plans, and documented the meetings held at the Sarkar home. To all appearances, he was indistinguishable from the other foreign students studying at Trinity.

One day, while walking out of the library, he walked into a group of well-dressed young Indian men standing outside the building. Jeev walked around them, avoiding eye contact, as he did not want to answer unnecessary questions. However, one man in the group tapped him on the shoulder as he passed. "Hello, are you new here?" he asked.

"Yes, I am a new student" Jeev replied, "Stephen Pereira" and stretched his hand.

"Raj Patel," replied the young man, shaking Jeev's hand firmly. "This is Amrit Bakhtar." Amrit smiled and shook Jeev's hand. "And this is Joe Nehru." Jeev looked at Joe, who was elegantly dressed in a navy-blue suit, white shirt, and blue silk tie, fitting in with the other Trinity men.

The elegant man corrected the introduction with a smile. "Jawaharlal not Joe. Pleased to meet you." Jeev shook his hand and wondered what Jawaharlal's views were on the British occupation. He was obviously wealthy and would have a personal stake in the status quo.

"I am from Calcutta. The partition of Bengal and the famines have left my hometown in shatters" said Jeev, testing the conversational waters.

Jawaharlal's face turned somber "It is directly a result of the British policies that have caused the suffering of our people. My hometown of Allahabad has experienced no less a toll. The only solution that I see is self-rule. Indians must be able to oversee their country." Both young men professed their nationalist tendencies and spoke cautiously about their hopes for an independent nation, resolving to meet again to continue their discussion. Jeev left the brief encounter with renewed hope. There was something about Jawaharlal that made him proud of his homeland, giving him an extra burst of energy to fulfill his plans. He looked forward to meeting him at Trinity again. Unfortunately, Trinity was soon going to become too dangerous for Jeev to stay.

CHAPTER 24: RED COATS AND BLUE EYES (1902)

One afternoon, Amir came rushing into the barn as the Amee, Arti and Agni were helping to feed and milk the cows. "Hurry, you need to hide, there are soldiers headed this way." The girls ran to the house and scrambled up the hidden ladder.

Breathless, Amee commanded "Lie down on the bed and don't move," as Meera closed the wooden panel and dragged sacks of grain into the closet to conceal the wall opening. Amee prayed with silent fervor to the elephant-headed god, Ganesh, Remover of Obstacles. She knew now with certainty that the nagging prompting that she had felt that she, her sister, and her friend could not stay indefinitely with Amir and Meera was correct. They needed a more permanent solution, but what could it be? Amee could not fathom a resolution, but right now her hope was that the soldiers would not find them.

Amee soon heard a tapping sound, followed by English speaking voices as Amir opened the door to a group of British soldiers. In her mind's eye, Amee could see their red coats and black pants with gold stripes down the sides. She strained to hear what she could. The sounds were muffled but still distinct. She heard Amir greet one of the troops. "Welcome Corporal Thomas. What can we do for you, today?"

"Mr. Chowdhary, we are sorry to intrude on your home. Three women have run away from the plantation, and we are searching for them. A fisherman's boat was stolen and was found close to your farm. We think the three runaways may have stolen the boat and are hiding somewhere in this area."

"Thank you for letting me know," said Amir. "You have my utmost cooperation. If I see something, I will let you know. Do you know if they found any bodies, it is possible the runaways drowned in the flood?".

"That is a possibility." The corporal hesitated then continued. "We will search all the local houses, nonetheless. Private Burke, Private Griffin, go search the barns and outhouses. " Amee heard heavy footsteps walking away from the house. "With your permission, Sir?" Amee heard footsteps walking toward the kitchen. One pair of feet continued walking past the stove and stopped. Amee's heart rose into her throat as she heard the closet door holding the hidden stairs open.

She heard the grain sacks shift a bit as the soldier prodded them, with a bayonet. He then moved on.

The three girls held their breaths. They lay on their cots without moving, lest the slightest sound give them away. After what seemed like an eternity, they heard the soldiers leave the house. As they heard the voices move outside, Agni slowly crawled to the small window and peeked out. "A red coated soldier, probably the corporal, is talking to Amir," she whispered. "The other soldiers are looking through the stables, springhouse, and woods."

"When will they go away?" Arti moaned softly. "I'm scared."

"We all are," replied Amee, moving over to stroke her sister's head. "But we must be brave. There is no other choice."

Agni whispered, in a rising cadence, "They're leaving! We're safe... for now." Amee and Arti sighed deeply with relief, but the fear remained, as a cold, gnawing pain in their stomachs.

Meera came to closet, opened the door, and pulled down the ladder. "Girls, it's safe now. Come down to the kitchen and have some tea and papadums."

Amee's stomach growled. She, Arti, and Agni eagerly moved

the grain sacks, spilling some wheat from the hole where the soldier had poked his bayonet. Amee shivered when she saw it, realizing how close she and the other two girls had come to being caught... and Amir and Meera. Tears stung her eyes as she realized what they must do.

A few minutes later, the girls were sitting in the kitchen, drinking hot green tea, and eating crunchy papadums with mango chutney.

Amir entered the kitchen smiling. "Good news. The soldiers are gone." He sat down with a sigh. "We will need to come up with a plan for you," he looked at the girls, his expression becoming serious. "Those soldiers will be back and will not be as polite as before. Also, if the neighbors notice you and they will let the authorities know."

Amee, spoke up. "We will leave tonight. You have been exceedingly kind to us. We do not want to cause more trouble for you."

Amir raised his palms. "Not yet. I know someone who can help. I will see if he can come here tonight." Amir left, saddled his horse, and rode into town. He soon returned, saying "Everything is taken care of. You girls will be safe."

Later that night, as the girls and Meera sat by the fire, there was a knock on the door. Meera opened it and a man dressed in an oversize black overcoat entered. His pale face was barely visible under a floppy brimmed black hat and a gray wool scarf that covered his mouth. He had bright blue eyes that twinkled in the glow of the candles. "It better for you if you don't know who I am or cannot recognize me," he said, looking at the girls. "Amir has told me about your escapades. One day, this country will be safe for you, but not today. There is a ship leaving soon for the island of St. Thomas. I know a family on the island who will keep you safe. They will provide you with food and lodging in exchange for fair and safe work. I will come to get you early tomorrow morning. There is a sailor on board the ship who will help you hide." With that, he took his leave. Amir walked out with him, profusely thanking him for his help.

The girls were up before daylight the next morning. When they came down from their room, Amir was attending to early morning chores and Meera was in the kitchen preparing breakfast. "You ladies need a delicious meal. You've got a busy day ahead of you." A single tear ran down Amee's cheek. She took a deep breath and sucked back the rest. Crying was a luxury none of them could afford.

"Can we help you?" asked Agni, feigning brightness.

"No, sit down and have some tea. I've got it about ready." Amee realized that Meera was keeping her head down, not letting them see her face. The girls poured themselves steaming Darjeeling tea from the white teapot on the table. A few minutes later, Meera served them fresh roti, mint cilantro chutney, mango chutney, steamed fish, and fried plantains. "Eat hearty, girls. You won't be getting home cooking on the ship." Meera wiped her eyes. Although Amee, Arti, and Agni were not hungry, they ate greedily, and made Meera smile.

Just as they were finishing breakfast, Amir came in with the blue-eyed man, whom the girls had decided to call Mr. Blue Eyes. He looked at the girls and said, "Good morning, ladies. Are you ready to go?" His eyes twinkled. Amee could almost see him smiling underneath his scarf.

"Yes, we're ready," said Agni, picking up her knapsack. She looked at Meera who was softly crying, walked over, and gave her a big hug. Amee and Arti did the same.

"Girls, we wish you all the best in your new lives," said Amir, dry-eyed but subdued. He shook their hands, and he and Meera stood in the doorway watching as Amee, Arti, and Agni walked away.

"Ladies, your coach awaits," said Mr. Blue Eyes with a flourish towards a black carriage with two sturdy brown horses at the reigns. He opened the doors. "Step inside." The girls climbed in, and he shut the door. The seats on the coach were dark red cloth, and there were matching curtains that allowed no one to see in or to Amee's dismay, the girls to see out. Amee pulled back a small section of the curtains and peered out. She saw Mr. Blue Eyes climb into the driver's seat and pull the reins. The coach moved forward, and they were on their way.

After about half an hour, the coach stopped. Mr. Blue Eyes opened the door. "Ladies, grab your bags and get inside *quickly*," he whispered. They did. Amee barely had time to notice the outside of their new lodgings. She did see a tall, whitewashed brick house, with a large, bright blue wooden door flanked by thin windows, also painted the same blue. The second and third floor had three windows each, with two chimneys protruding from either side of the roof.

Inside, the walls were papered with green and black wallpaper, while faded red carpet covered the floor. Amee noticed the sparsely furnished living room with a writing desk, a few chairs, and a sofa facing the fireplace. Mr. Blue Eyes led them up a circular oak stairway to a bedroom that had three beds. "You will stay here till your ship leaves in a few days. I am going to buy your tickets for the journey," he said.

Amee reached into her bag and pulled out her gold earrings. "Please use these to help pay for the tickets, that's all we have."

The man looked at the earrings in amusement, the twinkle in his eyes brightening, pressing her hand to close around the earrings "That's all right, I do what I can and more importantly what I must."

Amee insisted, placing the earrings into his hands "Then use these to help the next person."

With a sigh, he nodded his head. "You are young, yet you understand the concept of paying it forward. I will accept this as a token of your kindness and put it to good use." He placed the earrings in his pocket and walked downstairs.

Later that day, Mr. Blue Eyes returned. The girls met him in the living room, where they sat on the threadbare linen sofa, while he pulled up a chair to face them. His eyes no longer twinkled, but Amee could still see the kindness in them. He sighed. "I have some news, ladies. Your ship is delayed for a few weeks." Before any of them could respond, he continued.

"Don't worry. This is not unusual. Many things, including storms, problems with the crew, or equipment damage can delay voyages for weeks or even months. You will be safe here until you sail. You will be supplied with plenty of fresh food. Most importantly... whatever you do, *don't go outside under any circumstances.*"

"We understand, don't we?" said Agni, looking at Amee and Arti, who both nodded their assent.

From then on, Mr. Blue Eyes mostly left the girls to themselves in the big house. They opened windows late at night just to stare out into the empty street and breathe in some fresh air. During the day, they peered out of upstairs windows, watching the people pass by, while being ultra-careful to not be seen. Mr. Blue Eyes would come by occasionally to check on them and assure them that the ship was on its way. Initially, they spent their time exploring all the rooms in the house. Most were empty.

Late one afternoon, Amee spied a door near the kitchen. "Agni, Arti, what do you think is behind here?"

Agni shrugged her shoulders. "Probably the cellar?"

Arti's eyes, however, were full of curiosity. Amee put her hand on the round iron doorknob, and slowly turned it, pulling the door open to reveal stairs, descending into pitch black darkness. Amee gulped. Agni grew pale. Arti begged, "Amee, shut the door! The bhoot might live down there!"

Amee imagined, not a ghostly boogeyman, but rather the all too real Scarface climbing up through the blackness. She shivered.

A scraping sound from behind her made Amee jump and slam the door. "Amee, help us!" shouted Agni and Arti. Amee turned to see the two girls pushing a massive oaken chair across the dusty wooden floor. Quickly, she went to the back of the chair and pushed while Agni and Arti pulled from the sides. With effort, they turned the chair around, and braced it against the cellar door. No bhoot or Scarface would get through that.

Later that day, Mr. Blue Eyes came in with a bag stuffed with clothes, some sewing needles and thread. "Here are some clothes for your trip. Since these are too big for you, you can cut and sew them so they will fit".

Amee grabbed a faded blue cotton dress from the bag and held it out in front of her. "Whew..."

Arti's eyes grew wide. "That's two dresses!" Agni nodded in agreement.

Mr. Blue Eyes chuckled. "You ladies are talented and resourceful. The clothes are faded but there are no holes or tears. You can cut and stitch these clothes and have lovely, comfortable apparel for your journey."

Amee smiled. It would be lovely indeed to toss away the baggy fishermen's shirts and trousers and have proper dresses. The girls spent the next few days hours cutting and stitching the hand-me-down clothes, their excitement about their journey and new lives growing.

About a week later, the sun was up. Its brightness and warmth beckoned Amee to the third-floor window. Recklessly, she stared out, her mind lost as if in a trance, when suddenly she saw the boogeyman. It was unmistakably Scarface. He had a cane in his hand and walked with a slight limp down the street towards their house. She pressed her nose against the window glass to get a better look. To her horror, he glanced upward and stopped walking. Amee dropped to the floor, breathlessly wondering if he had seen her. Would he knock at the door? Hopefully, he would think he was seeing things and continue walking. Amee fervently prayed to Durga for protection. She stayed on the floor for several minutes before cautiously peering out of the window. She breathed a deep sigh of relief to see that he was no longer there.

Later that evening, Mr. Blue Eyes came, his eyes twinkling more brightly than usual. "Ladies, I've got good news. I've heard from the ship! A storm damaged the hull, which had to be repaired. It's now fixed and will be in port tomorrow. It will be there for a week and then leave."

The next few days passed in a blur as the girls got everything ready and soon it was the day of their departure. Mr. Blue Eyes pulled up with his horse-drawn carriage with curtained windows. The girls climbed aboard and rode into town towards the port. There in front of them was a long black ship tied to the docks. It had one big funnel in the center, emitting thick black smoke. On either side of the ship's stack were several one-story cabins with life rafts on top. There were two cannons on the stern and two cannons on the bow of the ship. "That's your ship, we will wait here until it is time to board," said Mr. Blue Eyes.

"Why do they have cannons?" inquired Arti.

Mr. Blue Eyes explained, "They are for protection from pirates. You will be sailing the Caribbean Sea which is infested with scumbags. Don't worry though. The ship can defend itself."

Suddenly, there was a knock at the carriage door, and a sailor came inside. He wore a black uniform with a round cap and a bandana around his neck. He looked at the girls and said in an American accent, "Hello, I am Jimmy Riley, Welcome to the Cheshire, that's the name of the ship. I will take you to your quarters. Do not speak to any of the other passengers. Stay inside the cabin and only come out when I am able to go with you. Do not come looking for me. I will check up on you from time to time. The crew or other passengers cannot know I am helping you. Is that understood?" All three nodded in compliance. He looked out of the carriage to see if the way was clear. Satisfied, he asked them to follow him. Mr. Blue Eyes waved a solemn goodbye and guided his carriage away. They entered the ship through a gangway, walked on the deck for a few feet and then went down a stairwell. Jimmy stopped at a cabin with the number 15 on the door. He held the door open so they could step inside. The cabin had four bunk beds, two on either side, a small table in the middle, and a porthole to the outside. "We will leave in a few hours. You'll hear a long whistle before the ship's engines start. There is a sack of food in the closet, enough for the trip, and the jar over by the bed has water. Remember what I told you." And with that, he left.

Just as Jimmy said, after a few hours, there was a long whistle. The ship's engines roared to life, and the boat set out into the ocean.

On the second day, Arti cried. "Why do we have to eat this thick, hard bread? This fish is too salty, and I'm sick of mangoes!"

Amee put an arm around her. "It's all we have, I'm afraid. We can't go to the kitchen…"

"With our brown skins, would stick out like sore thumbs among all the pale, white passengers," added Agni. Arti dried her tears and took a bite of hardtack and dried fish. Amee sighed. Hopefully, things will be much better soon.

The weather held out, and they passed many islands with crystal white beaches and clear blue waters. Colorful yellow, red, and blue fish were visible through the translucent sea. Often, dolphins would swim close to the ship, diving gracefully in and out of the water. They passed large turtles lazily swimming by. One night they glanced out of the porthole, which illuminated the entire sea with a sparkling blue color, as if lit by a mystical, glowing sea creature.

As they sat admiring the scene outside, Agni turned to Jimmy, who had come to check on them, and asked, "So what do you do on the ship?"

"I am the first officer on the ship. The only person higher than me is the captain. All the crew members report to me. I supervise the loading of the cargo and the passengers. If something were to happen to the captain, then I would oversee the entire ship. My father is a captain in the American Navy."

Agni looked intently at Jimmy's thin but tall body as he leaned against the window. His face was tanned by the hot Caribbean sun and his black hair tussled by the wind. She was taken in by his quiet and soft-spoken manner.

Her eyes wide open, she rested her chin on the palm of

her hand "Do you have any brothers or sisters?" Jimmy's deep brown eyes clouded momentarily "I had one older brother."

Agni whispered "Had?"

"Yes, my elder brother Samuel, followed in the footsteps of my father in the Navy. He rose rapidly through the ranks, becoming one of the youngest captains. We were sure he would become an Admiral one day. However, when on a routine mission near the Island of Hispaniola his ship was attacked unprovoked by two Spanish vessels. In the battle that ensued, he was hit by an exploding cannonball and killed."

Agni placed her hand on Jimmy's hand. "Your father must have been devastated."

"Yes, he blamed himself for pushing Samuel to join the Navy. We grew up in a small seaside town in Delaware. Our house overlooked the Atlantic Ocean, the sea was our playground. Samuel and I spent our free time rowing, sailing, and diving in the ocean. I too wanted to become a Navy captain, but my father made sure I could not join." Jimmy's face softened, but he soon regained his composure, and sighed. "Finally, after a lot of persuasion, my father allowed me to work on a merchant ship."

The three girls listened in silence as Jimmy narrated his life story, occasionally interrupting when they did not understand some words. He mentioned some places and events that were so foreign to them that they did not even try to understand. Words such as Delaware, Civil War, Mexico, or President Lincoln were beyond their knowledge. They did eventually learn some American history, but most of the conversation dealt with Jimmy and his relationships with his father, his brother, and his love of the sea. "The sea is *freedom*." He spoke with passion, his hands outstretched as if to express the vastness of the ocean itself. "To be on the ocean is to be in control of your own destiny. I love freedom, and I want to help others escape tyranny and have their own freedom."

"Wow," Agni spoke softly. How do you do this? I see how you got us on the ship, but what about after? How are we going to start and live our new lives?"

Jimmy looked her straight in the eye, his expression now serious. "My father accumulated a small fortune through the spoils of war. I was the sole heir to his wealth. One of the spoils was a plantation in Saint Thomas. My father gained it by dubious means, but I've placed the land to beneficial use. It is now a sanctuary for escaped slaves and indentured laborers."

"Like us?" said Amee,

Jimmy smiled, "Yes, Amee, like you and your friends."

Sometimes, late at night, after most of the passengers were in their cabins and the crew had retired for the night, Jimmy would allow them to come up the deck, weather allowing. On clear nights, he would point at various stars and their importance for navigation. "Imagine if you don't know where you are going," he explained, the three pairs of eyes glued to him in fascination. You look up into the sky and find the Plough. "There," pointing into the cloudless sky, "that's the Plough. Now follow the Plough to its handle and you will see the two stars pointing upwards. Those are the seven stars of the Plough. From the last two stars, go directly upward in a straight line, about five times the distance between the two stars, and you will see the North Star. See the bright one there!" The girls nodded, "That star sits directly above the North Pole. Once you know where north is, you know the other directions. I can even tell what latitude we are just using my wrist and measuring the degrees based on the star." He then named other stars and then pointed out Jupiter, Saturn, and Mars, explaining as he went along that those were "planets and not stars." As they stared in fascination at the heavens above, they heard voices and saw two crew members heading in their direction from the other end of the ship. Not wanting the crew to ask unnecessary questions, he quickly herded them back to the cabin.

During the day, as they looked out the porthole, they passed strings of islands in the distance. Jimmy explained that the captain kept clear of the land, firstly to avoid the danger of rocks, reefs, and sandbars, and secondly, many of the islands were pirate strongholds. "We are following the Antilles current," Agni imitated, trying to recreate Jimmy's accent.

CHAPTER 25: THE VIRGIN ISLANDS

Jimmy squinted in the bright sunlight and smiled at the girls. "This calm, sunny weather and a strong current in the right direction means that we'll be making port tomorrow, well ahead of schedule. You will be in the Danish Antilles. Also known as the Danish Virgin Islands. Christopher Columbus named them after Saint Ursula and the eleven thousand virgins. People shortened it to Virgin Islands."

"Who was Saint Ursula?" inquired Agni, again imitating Jimmy's accent.

Not to be outdone, Arti asked, "What is a virgin?" Jimmy replied with a smirk on his face. "Well, Ursula was an English princess who was to marry a German prince. She set out to meet him with eleven thousand virgins." He paused, then continued, "A virgin is a girl who has never been with a man." Amee and Agni snickered. Arti looked befuddled. "Ursula decided first to go on a holy pilgrimage to Rome. There she met the pope, the most powerful man in the church. From there she and the pope continued their journey, but when they reached their destination, the Huns had besieged the city of the German prince and they killed Ursula and her eleven thousand virgins. Later she was canonized a saint." Arti had many more questions to ask. *Who was the Pope? Who were the Huns? And why would someone take eleven thousand unmarried girls on a journey?* But she was too polite to ask questions. "Anyway, we will disembark at the port, and I will take you to my plantation where you will be safe."

Upon reaching the port of Charlotte Amalie, they waited until all the passengers had disembarked. It was getting dark by the time Jimmy came to their cabin and asked them to follow him. Going down the gangplank, they felt the warm Caribbean breeze around them. There was a sense of freshness and a new beginning. An open horse-drawn carriage awaited them. Around them was a bustling town of white buildings and cobblestone streets. Most of the inhabitants were dark-skinned. A few well-dressed, European looking men and women strolled the streets. In the distance was a large fort, which towered above the town with its white and red walls. A Danish flag flew from the main tower.

The carriage carried them up a steep cobblestone road and then veered off to the left, where the road was mostly dirt and gravel. They continued to travel upward into the hills. On one side was a steep drop to the ocean. They could now see the ship they had traveled on and the fort and the town below them. Soon they came to a wooden gate with a sign 'Riley Plantation'. Jimmy opened the gate and led the horses up a steep slope. On the left was a long single-story house with a porch along the front. On the right was a barn and two smaller houses.

A woman walked out, smiling, to greet them. She was blonde-haired, looked European but well-tanned from the Caribbean sun. "Welcome back, Master Jimmy," said the woman as she unharnessed the horses. The woman beckoned to the girls to follow her to one of the smaller row houses, where a few steps up, a stone and brick landing led them into a room with three beds. "I am Freja, the manager of this plantation," she said. Her blue eyes twinkled, revealing crows' feet, showing that she was older than she looked. "This is where you will live," she said matter-of-factly, as if Jimmy bringing strangers back from his trip was routine. "Rest for now. I will be back in the morning to show you your duties."

The girls woke up to roosters crowing before sunrise. Shortly thereafter, there was a gentle knock on the door. Agni got up, splashed some water on her face, patted it with a hand towel, and answered the door. It was Freya, her long hair braided at the back. She carried a sack and a basket of sweet-smelling fresh bread with butter. Agni touched it. It was still warm from the oven. Agni stood aside and let Freya enter. The older woman moved fast, like an athlete. She set the bread down on a large pine table in the center of the room and pulled out three plates, butter knives, a slab of butter, jars of jam and honey from her sack. "I brought you girls some food. I'll be back with a pot of tea. Meanwhile, go ahead and help yourselves." Freya turned around and left, and the girls eagerly helped themselves to chunks of warm, crusty bread. A few minutes later, Freya returned with a tray with a full tea pot, sugar, a pitcher of milk, and three cups. She sat it down, and the girls poured themselves cups of steaming tea.

Freya pulled up a rattan chair to the table and sat down. "Well, girls. I guess that you're wondering what you're going to be doing here." Amee, Arti, and Agni looked at her with expectation. She pointed at Amee and Agni. "You two are assigned to the barn where will take care of the goats, cows, and horses. You little girl", pointing at Arti, "will go to school during the day and help in the kitchen later in the afternoon." Arti smiled back at Freja, unable to hide the joy in her face "Go to school?"

"Yes, we have a school at the bottom of the hill, you will learn English, Danish, History and Arithmetic." Arti gasped. Amee and Agni began to cry.

Freya looked at them with concern. "Is everything all right?"

"Yes," gulped Amee. "I'm so happy for my little sister. She's never had a chance to go to school."

Freya's blue eyes softened. "She does now." She then straightened her back and folded her hands on the table. "Let me tell you about your new home. There are about seventy people living on the plantation. Everyone works, has opportunities for education, and most importantly, everyone is free."

"Free?" Amee could not believe she heard Freya correctly.

"Yes, *free*. Jimmy has rescued several hundred slaves and indentured laborers, mostly from St. Thomas and the neighboring island of St. Croix, but also from Trinidad, Georgetown, and several Brazilian ports. He comes and goes as his journeys take him, as do those he has rescued. Many have left for work on ships. Others settle in the Northern American states or the islands around St. Thomas."

After breakfast, Freya helped Arti get ready for school, and Amee and Agni went to the barn. The barn was warm, dim, and smelled earthy, like clean straw and animals. A lean framed, wrinkled old man with chestnut brown skin and white eyebrows approached them. His head was bald. "Hello girls. I'm Mo. I'll show you around here." He walked them through the structure, showing them how to clean the stalls, runs, paddocks, and aisles, feed pigs, goats, and make sure that the horses had clean water and hay. While lifting a large pitchfork full of straw, Mo groaned, and placed his hand on his back. "Oh... I'm not the man I used to be. More than seventy years are catching up with me."

"Let me take that," said Amee, grabbing the pitchfork. Agni took ahold of Mo's arm, led him to a hay bale, and helped him sit down. She placed another bale behind his back.

Mo smiled at her. "Thank you, Miss. You are kind."

The corners of Agni's mouth turned up. "You are welcome, Sir." She sat down on a bale beside him. "Tell me more about yourself. How did you get here?"

Mo became solemn. His eyes looking far into the distant past. "I don't remember much before I came to this island. I wasn't more than a child when I came here. According to the ship's register and the records at Fort Christian, my name is Mukamo Momanyi, but everyone calls me Mo. I've lived here and been working for over sixty years now."

"What did you do before you came to this plantation?" Agni

asked in a soft, gentle voice.

"Hard work. Lots of it, and there were no comforts. Hard beds, moldy bread, thin soup. If I didn't work hard enough or well enough, then…"

Agni lightly placed her hand on his arm. "It's okay."

"Thank you, Miss," replied Mo. He then rose and went back to work. Later that morning, he took Agni and Amee out to the grassy fields and taught them how to herd the animals both with and without the help of dogs.

One evening after a long day's work, Mo brought a bunch of grilled corn and gave them to Agni and Amee. They gladly accepted the warm treat. He then brushed the corn with a spicy paste he had ground. As they savored the corn, Agni asked him "Do you remember your childhood?"

Mo replied in his raspy voice "I no longer remember my village in West Africa, just that it was a bunch of huts surrounded by dense forest. I was only eight when my family of four, Father, Mother, and brother and I, were captured by a neighboring tribe during a raid, sold to the British, and taken to a jail in Lagos. Then along with many other slaves, placed on a ship to the Caribbean. They tied iron chains on all of us and we had to sit chained up. Hardly gave us any food or fresh water. I was the only one who survived the voyage. My parents and brother had already become weak and sick as they waited in a jail in the town of Lagos. Halfway through the ship's journey across the Atlantic, they succumbed to illness. The sailors picked up their bodies and tossed them into the sea." Mo pointed his index finger at his head "That incident, of the three bodies being unceremoniously tossed into the sea, was burned into my memory even though I was only eight years old." Mo paused, heaved a sigh, and continued "Strangely, rather than breaking me, it reinforced my resilience. I resolved to survive, if only to preserve the memory of my family. I told myself I would be stronger than my captors. When the ship arrived in St. Thomas, they sold me to a sugarcane plantation owner. Life was hard for me, but I survived for another ten years.

Then slavery was abolished on the islands under the Dutch protectorate. I was now free, paid a little more, yet still under the clutches of the owners. By a stroke of luck, my owner died, and they passed the plantation on to Jimmy's mother, and father. They eventually bequeathed the plantation to Jimmy after the death of his brother. So, I began to work for the new owner - Jimmy."

As he narrated the story of his life, Mo asked Amee and Agni about their lives. Most of the plantation workers had come from Africa, however, there were a few from the Indian subcontinent. Mo introduced the girls to them. They quickly made friends with whom they could share memories of home, home cooking, and other things.

Mo performed his tasks with pride, and his face basked with joy at the sight of a clean and well-maintained barn. As Amee and Agni worked with him, they, too, took pride in their work.

As the months turned into years, Mo became weaker and could do less and less. Amee and Agni learned from Mo how to ride the horses, take care of sick and injured animals, milk the goats and cows, make cheese, store salted meat, and reuse manure for fertilizer. Mo taught them the business of farming. How to buy and sell, to negotiate the best prices and keep their customers happy. Mo's knowledge and motivation and Agni and Amee's energy and enthusiasm made the barn the plantation's most profitable venture. They not only provided supplies to the nearby townspeople, but also served most of the ships that passed through the port. The Dutch army also started buying meat, eggs, honey, and cheese from them. While the economies in the region were suffering because of the abolition of slavery, Jimmy's plantation continued to prosper. He kept his workers happy, provided them with good working conditions, and treated them all with respect. Amee's deep respect for him had deepened even more because he allowed her sister to get an education rather than be forced to work on the farm.

Arti was a quick learner. She learned English and Dutch

and was soon reading books in both languages. She ravenously devoured any knowledge she could get from Freya, Jimmy, Mo, or anyone else who would lend her books or talk about any subject from astronomy to zoology. She soon surpassed the knowledge of her teachers and instead of working in the kitchen, started as a schoolteacher for younger children on the island. Jimmy brought books for her whenever he came back from his trips, which were becoming less frequent.

One evening, as the sun was setting, Arti saw Jimmy on the beach staring out at sea, his face wistful. Not wishing to disturb him, she turned around to head back to the house.

"Please stay, Arti. I'd like someone to talk to." Jimmy's voice startled Arti.

"How did you know it was me?" she asked.

"I saw you approach. I knew it was you because you're carrying a book."

"Oh…" Arti blushed and looked down at blue leather volume she held in the crook of her left arm. It was Jane Austen's *Mansfield Park*. She went and stood beside Jimmy.

"You know I've been offered a captaincy on a merchant ship- a big one."

"That's wonderful!" exclaimed Arti, thinking of all the exotic places Jimmy would go.

"I'm not taking it," said Jimmy. "I'd much rather be here."

"Why?" asked Arti, totally confused.

"Because life is more than a journey. When you find what you want, you don't go searching for something else."

Suddenly, Arti realized someone was watching them. She glanced at where the path from the house exited the forest and saw Agni approach. Jimmy turned, and his face lit up. Arti quietly made her exit, looking back to see in silhouette, the two standing close together, touching each other's faces. Arti's heart warmed with happiness for her friends.

Two nights later, Amee and Arti were sleeping when Agni entered the house. "Amee! Arti! Wake up! I've got something to tell you!" Amee and Arti rubbed their eyes and opened them to see Agni, still in her blue cotton dress even though it was past 10 o'clock at night. Amee lit a candle. Agni stretched out her left hand, which had a large ruby ring on her ring finger.

"Agni! What is going on?" said Amee, startled into sudden wakefulness.

"What do you think? Jimmy and I are getting married!"

"Married?", exclaimed Arti.

"Yes. I'm going to be Mrs. James Riley."

Amee took a deep breath. "I'm shocked, but I'm not shocked. You've been spending a lot of time with him, riding horses, walking on the cliffs to see the sunsets."

Arti added, "You two are a good match. He's got that American swagger and sophistication. You've got unbridled curiosity and you're mischievous."

"Mischievous?" said Agni, her eyes narrowing while she grinned. "I'll get you for that!" She took a playful swipe at Arti, who started giggling, causing the other two to join in.

"Oh, there's something else I've got to tell you." Agni spoke quickly in her excitement. "You both will be living in the main house with Jimmy and me."

"What?" exclaimed Amee. "We're comfortable here. We don't have much, so why do we need more space?"

"Because I want you there. You both are my oldest, dearest friends. I want to share my wealth and happiness with you."

A few months later, it was Jimmy and Agni's wedding day. Amee stared at her friend in her long white silk dress and lace veil, contrasting elegantly with her black hair and dark skin. "You are gorgeous! Freya made you the loveliest dress I've ever seen."

"Thanks Amee. I've never felt so beautiful as I do today." Agni beamed, as she gazed at her reflection in the full-length mirror. "Freya has magic and lots of patience."

Amee laughed remembering the many fittings it took to get the dress exactly right. "That's true!" Suddenly, her expression became serious. "Agni, are you sure you're doing the right thing?"

"What do you mean?"

Amee gulped, "Well, the gods..."

"You mean my becoming Christian?"

"Yes."

"What have the Hindu gods done for me? As a Hindu I was enslaved. As a Christian, I have love, stability, and happiness. Which would you choose?"

Amee was quiet, then said, "It's not a choice I have to make, so I don't know."

"That's right. So, I'm not going to ask you to."

"Thank you," said Amee, giving her friend a gentle hug so as not to wrinkle her dress.

Agni looked around, making sure that she and Amee were alone. Amee sensed her friend's thoughts and shut the door. She then came and sat next to Agni, who whispered, "There is one thing that concerns me."

"What's that?" Amee whispered back.

"Jimmy's parents... especially his father. What they think."

"Captain Riley wasn't happy to start with, but you've won him over."

"Do you really think so? Jimmy can't go home to Delaware again. Not with me. He can't be married to a dark-skinned woman like me. It's against the law there. Also, his father's health isn't good..."

Amee chuckled. "Do you really think that the law in Delaware matters to him? St. Thomas is his home now. So, why does it matter what people in Delaware think?"

"I guess it doesn't. Captain Riley wasn't thrilled when he first met me..."

"But he did come. So, let's go. You've got the rest of your life to start."

Agni grinned, and the two friends walked out.

The wedding ceremony took place on a bluff overlooking an isolated beach, with waves crashing on to rocks that resembled steppingstones to the ocean. Jimmy wore a white tuxedo and a ruffled shirt with matching white leather boots. Dinner plate sized Dahlia's of many colors were used to make a canopy of flowers. Bougainvillea and lilies, which naturally grew around the bluff, added even more color. Father Brandon from the Episcopal Church performed the service. The entire workforce of the plantation and many townspeople attended the ceremony.

Captain Riley dressed up for the wedding in his full naval white service dress uniform, complete with his shiny polished cutlass and a string of medals clasped to his chest. His white coat had a standing collar and shoulder marks showed his officer status.

"Let me adjust that dear" said Mrs. Riley as she correctly positioned the three stripes of half inch gold lace with a gold star.

"You know our Church back home will never accept Jimmy and his wife. Just last month the priest gave a sermon about God creating different races for a reason and God never intended for these races to intermingle and marry."

Captain Riley adjusted his white cap which also had gold oak leaves and acorns on the visor. "I know dear. I did not tell anyone why we were coming here, precisely for that reason. They will not understand why a white man is marrying a brown girl. We both have accepted Jimmy's choice and quite frankly I am enjoying the warm air of the Caribbean. We will stay here for a while." Mrs. Riley slipped her hand into the captains and they both walked out towards the wedding venue.

Agni walked down the aisle holding on to Mo's hand. To Agni's surprise Captain Riley tipped his hat to Agni, which made her walk with greater confidence into her new life.

As the sun set over the ocean, a large table filled with all kinds of fish, meats, fruits, pastries and varieties of rum extended the festivities well into the night. Workers brought out tin drums and sticks and broke out into song. They were gentle peaceful tunes, although they had a rhythm that got the celebrants' feet to dance. Jimmy called it 'kaiso music'. It had been brought over from Africa and then adapted to the Caribbean. As the evening wore on, and the rum took effect, everyone was gyrating to the joyful music. Even Captain Riley and his wife danced, waltzing to the rhythmic beat. Amee and her sister joined Jimmy and Agni along with Mo and Freya and danced, ate, and drank through the night.

Jimmy gave all the workers a day off the next day, although the animals had to be attended to and cooking done. Amee was shocked when she entered the barn and saw Agni tossing hay to the horses. "What are you doing? Don't you know it's your honeymoon?"

Agni laughed. "Honeymoon or not, horses get hungry!"

A few minutes later, Captain Riley entered. "Agni, can you help me get a horse? I want one with some spirit but not a wild beast."

"Sure, Gunpowder will be a good one. Do you want me to saddle him for you?"

"No, I'll do it. Just show me where he is." Arti pointed out a dark gray horse and retrieved a black leather saddle for her father-in-law. "Thank you, Agni. Jimmy has done a really outstanding job with this place. I think I'll stay longer than I'd planned."

Agni had a sudden thought. Taking a deep breath, she spoke quickly, lest she lose her courage. "Captain Riley, why did you change your mind about me?"

The captain stopped. He turned to Agni. "Dear lady, you may call me "Father" if you wish. First, you have made my only living son incredibly happy. Not only do you love him, but you also love this plantation as well. Why else would you be out here the morning after your wedding?"

"Is that all?" asked Agni, sensing there was more to the story.

"Well, no," said the captain, with a dreamy look in his steel blue eyes. "It's a long story. Back many years ago, when I was younger than Jimmy, I sailed through these islands. I was a good-looking man back then. I certainly had my pick of the ladies." He chuckled. "There was one, however, Rekha, who was truly special. She won my heart, but I was already engaged to Margaret, and I had my career..." Agni thought she saw a stray tear in the corner of the old man's eye, but it never rolled down his cheek. Agni bowed her head, then looked up and said, her voice soft, "Have a good ride, Father. It's a beautiful day for it."

The captain smiled briefly, then saddled his horse, mounted, and rode away, as Agni and Amee gave thanks to their respective gods, their hearts bursting with gratitude tinged with sadness.

CHAPTER 26: A NEW BEGINNING IN NEW YORK (1910)

Arti's education had gone as far as she could on the small island. She wanted to learn more, but there was no route for added formal education. Captain Riley, on his way back from his daily rides, stopped by the school where Arti taught. He crept in and sat in the shaded back row, motioned to the few students sitting there to be silent, and observed Arti instruct the children. After class was over, he joined Arti as she walked back to the house.

"Captain Riley, what may I do for you?" said Arti, startled by his sudden appearance.

"Young lady, you have impressive teaching skills."

"Why thank you Sir," she replied. "I am enjoying teaching the children and I'm doing a lot of reading to teach myself." Arti stared straight through him, her wide-open eyes reading each body movement, dissecting every syllable spoken while her brain processed millions of thoughts in rapid succession.

"What books have you read?" asked Captain Riley.

Arti rattled off "Shakespeare, Charles Dickens, Mark Twain, Homer, Socrates. I enjoy books that have philosophical elements to them."

Captain Riley was dumbstruck. He stared back at the diminutive figure in front of him, at once realizing this was no ordinary farm worker. There was an intelligence and a thirst for knowledge that needed to be quenched hidden behind her dark, sparkling eyes. Arti's eyes widened with concern. "Captain Riley, are you okay?"

The captain took a deep breath and found his voice. "Arti, you should get a higher education, and I know there are no colleges here that you could attend. Let me see what I can do."

It was now Arti's turn to be shocked. "Yes, I would certainly like to study more."

"I'll see what I can do." Captain Riley walked back in long brisk strides to his study, took out a pen and paper, and wrote a letter to a friend.

Dear Professor Hunter,

I hope this letter finds you in good health and spirits. I am currently living on my son's plantation in St. Thomas in the Virgin Islands. In the local school here, a young teacher by the name of Arti Ray, has outlasted any education opportunities available to her. She would like to be trained in the humanities and educational arts.

Your college, originally founded to train women teachers, now enables women to pursue studies in a variety of academic fields. It is open to ladies of all religions, races, and ethnicities and will provide Arti with the opportunities she needs to further her studies and fulfill her immense potential.

Also, we have a need for teachers on the Island of St. Thomas and in providing Arti with an education you will be doing us a service. I will bear all the costs associated with the education.

Yours Sincerely

Captain Riley

A few days later, Arti was sitting on the steps of the front porch when a young black man rode a black stallion through the plantation gates. He wore a tailored black suit, a white shirt, and a black bow tie. His brown riding shoes shone in the sunlight. His curly black hair was parted in the middle and his mustache turned upwards as he flashed Arti a big smile, revealing big, milky, white teeth. Arti returned his smile.

Jimmy then walked out on the porch; his arms stretched out wide. "David Jackson, it is a pleasure to see you. How are things in St. Croix?"

David dismounted from his horse, strode up the porch steps and gave Jimmy a big hug. "As well as can be my brother." Arti stayed silent and intently watched the two men. "I have heard some rumors that could be good for the island. In the halls of Congress, there is a bill in circulation for the United States to buy the islands from the Danish."

"During the Civil War, there was also a bill that proposed the purchase of the islands from the Danish, but that did not pass congress. Why do you think this time around they will agree?" asked Jimmy.

"The Senate did not ratify the bill almost sixty years ago as there were many warring factions in the Senate and they could not agree on anything, even if it were in the best interests of the country. Today, the Danish government is finding it increasingly expensive to govern these islands from thousands of miles away. They have been negotiating with the US government for years to find a good deal. There has been increased German and Spanish activity in the area, as you are aware, this has raised concerns in US Navy circles. They do not want the islands to become a base for a foreign power."

If the islands become American territories, it would certainly be good for the native population, thought Jimmy. "How soon do you think this will happen?"

"It takes time, but I think in a few years." David smiled. Then echoing Jimmy's thoughts, he said "If all the people living on these islands eventually become American citizens, it will be good for us all. I have been admiring the progress you're making on your plantation. It is so productive and professionally managed. I see the same faces every time I visit, and everyone looks healthy and happy. I can't say that about most places I visit."

"Thank you, David. Riley Plantation wouldn't be without

the workers. They are the life and soul of this place." Jimmy's voice was soft, his eyes gazing at Agni, who was gathering flowers at the edge of the yard. His house was built on the highest part of the plantation, they had a bird's eye view of the acres of sugar cane fields, the barn animals, and the cattle. The Caribbean Sea stretched out before them in all directions and on a bright day they could see St John and even Tortola.

David glanced at Agni but kept his focus on Jimmy and his task. "You know that your plantation is a model for how farms should be run. Workers in all Danish territories should be so content."

Jimmy turned back and looked at David, his expression now alert and serious. "Contentment requires good management, which the Danish lack."

"I don't know if they lack management skills. They see these islands as a burden."

"And you as a troublemaker…" said Jimmy, grinning.

"Sometimes it takes a troublemaker to get things done. To them I am a rebel who should be punished because I am trying to ameliorate the lives of the local population. Organized workers can speak for not only themselves, but the good of the farms as well. Of course, it will be much easier to speak as Americans…" Arti kept on listening. Captain Riley soon joined the two men, and their conversation became even deeper, with more details about American legislation and citizenship. The men continued conversing over the next few days. Since Arti now lived in the main house, eavesdropping while pretending to read was easy.

A few weeks later, Captain Riley summoned Arti and Amee to his study. They entered his office with trepidation, their feet silent on the ornately patterned red, brown, and cream Persian rug that covered the hardwood floor. "Have a seat, ladies," said the captain, gesturing to two maroon leather upholstered mahogany chairs in front of his massive desk made from the same wood. Arti and Amee sat down. Captain Riley pulled out a drawer in his desk and retrieved an envelope. He put on his reading glasses and took a letter out of the envelope. "This is a letter from my friend, Thomas Hunter. He is founder and former president of the Normal College of the City of New York, and he is pleased to grant you, Arti, a place at his institution." Arti gasped. Amee's eyes widened. The captain continued. "I'm going to ask Jimmy to arrange your trip, Arti. Tuition is free, but I'll pay for your travel, living, and extra expenses."

Arti was speechless. Amee, however, spoke up. "New York? How far away is that?"

"1,637 miles," the captain replied.

"That's too far. How can she go there, to a strange country, *alone*?" Tears rolled down Amee's cheeks as she looked at her younger sister.

The captain spoke in a calm, measured tone. "She won't be alone. Jimmy and I have numerous contacts in the city who will make sure that your sister is safe and well cared for. You have no reason to worry."

Arti found her voice. "Amee, this is my dream, not the nightmare into which we were sold. I'm still young, but I'm old enough to take care of myself. Besides, it will be just a few years, not forever. I love it here, and most of all, I love you, so I'm coming back."

Amee sobbed, as she and Arti hugged. "Just make sure you do!" Arti looked up at the captain and smiled.

Once the arrangements were made, the day finally came for Arti to travel to New York.

Arti boarded a ship bound for New York from St. Thomas. A few days later, Arti stood on the deck, gazing in awe at the Statue of Liberty. The massive blue-green edifice scraped the still dim dawn sky with her crown and torch, reaching as high as Arti's dreams. Tears welled in Arti's eyes.

"Magnifique...yes?" Startled, Arti turned to see a slender, blonde woman in an elegant white lace shawl staring at the statue.

"Oh, yes. It is magnificent indeed." Arti looked at her brown hands. "Whoever would think that I, a poor country girl from a village near Calcutta, would come to New York to go to college?"

The woman's eyes flickered with surprise, but her expression was soon serene again. "Mon Dieu works in ways mysterious." She walked away and Arti never saw her again.

The ship docked at Ellis Island, where all the passengers, including Arti, disembarked. Standing in one of the many long lines, Arti did her best to remain inconspicuous among all the pale and olive-skinned people. She heard a multitude of languages, none of which she could clearly decipher. She held on tightly to her single bag, inching ahead every few minutes as the line squeezed forward. Finally, she reached the front of the first line, and presented her Danish travel papers along with letters from Captain Riley and Thomas Hunter.

A young immigration officer, in a blue suit with gold buttons and a blue cap, looked closely at the papers. "What is the purpose of your trip to the United States, Miss Ray?" His voice was stern. He did not even glance up at her.

"I am here to study at the Normal College of the City of New York." Arti spoke slowly, making sure to articulate each word well. The official asked her a few more questions, stamped her papers, and wished her well in her studies.

Arti then joined another line for a physical examination, followed by another for a mental test. By the time that she joined the line for the ferry across the Hudson River to Manhattan, she was exhausted. She no longer cared if the crowds pressed against her, or how their unwashed bodies smelled, or how noisy and strange they sounded. The people blurred with the sounds of engines, moving cargo, and seagulls and the smells of seawater, burning coal, and dust.

She stood by the railing as the ferry slowly made its way to the pier. Sea water gently splashed around the boat. Fog settled over the water as the silhouette of Lady Liberty gradually faded into the distance. She instinctively knew that she was embarking on a new journey. The joy of this sent goosebumps up her arms, even though she wasn't cold. She alighted at Pier A, seeing the circular sandstone walls of Clinton Castle to her north. She reached into her skirt pocket and felt a for piece of paper. Pulling it out, she read the instructions on how to take a streetcar to the college. With the sun still high in the sky on a warm July day, Arti walked from the port to the college

building on 68th and Park Avenue. She had studied a map of New York City before her trip. The grid layout was imprinted in her brain. Why should she take a streetcar when she could walk? Arti lifted her bag and began her trudge up Broadway. Farm work had made her strong. She would likely be there in less than 90 minutes.

What should have taken her no more than an hour and a half, however, took her over three hours as she often stopped to stare at the tall buildings, the rush of street cars, horse-drawn carriages, and pedestrians all moving together in seamless harmony. The energy of the city excited her, the diversity of the neighborhoods, the people and their clothing were enthralling.

The first neighborhood was filled with vegetable and fruit vendors lined up on the side of the street. Large carriages were carrying supplies. Throngs of children ran around the vendors as their mothers yelled at them from their apartment balconies. Three to five story townhouses lined the streets. The first floor of the townhouses were stores. There were produce stores, clothing, food, and cafes unlike any she had ever seen before. Then she had to let out a gasp as she passed the Woolworth building. Straining her neck upwards, she almost toppled over. The building seemed to touch the clouds. She counted thirty stories on the base tower and another thirty on the upper tower. She resolved one day to visit the building and ascend to the top. The view from there must be fantastic! As she moved further uptown, the streets became wider, and she saw more cars than she had ever seen in her life. The townhouses were opulent with fewer people on the street. Elegantly dressed ladies with fancy hats were driven in their cars by chauffeurs She heard many foreign accents and languages as she passed, including Hebrew, German, Irish Gaelic, Dutch, and, of course, English.

Finally, Arti came to a large gothic building with huge stained-glass windows. Arti stopped walking, lifted her head, and gasped in amazement. This was her college! Intricate designs of birds, animals, and mythical creatures were cut into the glass. Tall, thin pointed arches surrounded each of the windows and the building. A single pointed arch marked the entrance. Above the arch, a tower extended a few hundred feet into the air, with flying buttresses supporting the massive roof. A wide stone staircase led up to the main entrance of the structure. She climbed up the stairs with anticipation. Inside was a large room, a tall, vaulted ceiling, chairs, and a large reception desk with a young woman sitting behind it. Her auburn hair was piled high on her head, and she wore a high-necked white blouse. Arti took a deep breath, stood up straight and approached the desk.

"May I help you?" asked the woman in a lilting Irish brogue.

"Yes, my name is Arti Ray. I'm here to see Dr. Hunter," Arti replied.

The young woman smiled. "Dr. Hunter is with someone now. Please take a seat, and he will be with you shortly." Arti took a seat and waited and waited some more. Tired from standing in lines and her long walk, she fell asleep.

About an hour later, someone shook Arti's shoulder. "Miss Ray? Dr. Hunter is ready to see you now." Arti opened her eyes to see the Irish receptionist's freckled face. She blushed with embarrassment, stood up and gathered her bag.

"Don't worry," said the receptionist. "I can see that you've had a long journey. I had one myself to get here." She quickly scanned Arti from head to toe. "You look good, but you have a few stray hairs you may want to slick back." She took a compact mirror out of her skirt pocket, and handed it to Arti, who patted back a few rouge strands that had escaped her braided bun.

"Thank you," said Arti, handing the compact back.

"You're welcome. Now, if you'll follow me…" The receptionist turned around, and Arti walked behind her, up a winding flight of stairs, past several classrooms filled with students, to a large office with a big brass sign on the door reading "Thomas Hunter, LL. D, President Emeritus". The receptionist opened the door and Arti entered Dr. Hunter's office, a soft-white walled room with green carpet, oaken bookshelves with tomes spilling out of engorged shelves, and at the center, a massive roll top desk, behind which sat Dr. Hunter. Arti was taken aback by how old he looked. He was a grizzled old man with gray hair, an unkempt beard, wrinkled forehead, and hands that trembled as he reached out to read the letter, she handed to him. He gestured towards a chair for her to sit down. Adjusting his glasses, he read Captain Riley's letter, along with the acceptance letter from the college.

"How is my good friend the captain? " He rasped.

"He's doing well, "Arti replied.

"Welcome to the college. I am impressed by what the captain has said about you." His trembling hands grasped a bell, and he rang it briefly. A young woman opened the door. "Mary, please take this young lady to the registrar and bursar to get her set up" and then looking at Arti, "God speed, young lady. Do well."

Arti rose and followed Mary to the registrar's office, where with Mary's help, she completed her paperwork. "You've had a long journey. I'm sure you want to rest."

Arti's stomach rumbled, reminding her that she had not eaten since early that morning. "That would be wonderful, but where could I get some food?"

Mary's face reddened slightly. "I'm so sorry! I didn't think. You haven't had anything to eat for a while, have you?"

Arti shook her head. "No, not since early this morning."

"Well, let's get you settled, and then I'll show you where to get food." Mary led her to a five-story brick building, with a sign that read "Women's Dormitory". Mary told her, "This is where many of the students who go to the college live. Women run and manage the entire building. You will share your room with two other girls and the bathrooms are at the end of the corridor." She led her to a room on the third floor with a hardwood floor, three single beds, three desks, and three wardrobes. The walls were white, and a single large window with blue and white flowered curtains let in sunlight, making the sparse room look cheerful. "Put your bag on that bed." Mary pointed to an unoccupied bed against the wall. Arti did so. "Now, how about some tea and sandwiches? I know a good place around the corner. It'll be my treat."

Arti's face brightened. "That is so nice! Thank you!" The two women left, Arti carefully locking the door with her new key.

CHAPTER 27: A LEAGUE OF THEIR OWN

"Elizabeth, what are McBride and I going to do about Emily? We've offered her the finest education with the best tutors we could find. She won't get better instruction anywhere she could go, but she is determined to go somewhere." Claire Calvert began sobbing. She held her head down, face in handkerchief, lest her friend see her red eyes and snotty nose.

Elizabeth Burke put her flowered China cup in its saucer, with a slight clink. "Claire, you know that Emily's of age to make her own choices." Elizabeth spoke softly in her dulcet English accent.

"But will she make the right ones? She's hardly ever been away from the estate. She knows nothing of the world…"

Elizabeth reached out, and put her slim, white hand on top of Claire's trembling fingers. "You know that Emily can't spend the rest of her life at home. She's a young woman now, not a girl."

Claire dried her eyes. "She's still my baby girl."

"All babies grow up, if they live long enough." Elizabeth thought of her son, Sean, now a captain in the British Army. She handed her friend a clean, white handkerchief, and poured her a fresh cup of Darjeeling tea. "Drink your tea and have a cucumber sandwich. You'll feel better."

Claire sipped the hot sugared tea. The warmth and

sweetness made her feel more alert. She bit into a sandwich, the crisp coolness of the cucumber contrasted nicely with the salted butter and soft crustless bread. She took a deep breath before speaking again. "I just want Emily to be happy."

"Then you must respect what she wants. She's made such an effort…"

"I know. She's written every college on the East Coast, and in the South and Midwest as well."

Elizabeth sighed. "It's too bad that her options are so limited. If she were a man, the world would be a much wider and welcoming place. 'He' could easily go to Oxford or Cambridge as well as Harvard or Yale." Elizabeth's mind wandered. *And I could be working for the Foreign Office as a diplomat instead of organizing social events and helping embassy staff settle…*

"That's true. For Emily, it's Boston or New York. I'd prefer the latter. It's closer to her home, and McBride and me."

"Lionel and I have a house in New York. We know the city well. You know that I'll do whatever I can to see that Emily is safe and happy."

Claire's face brightened. "Really? You don't know what a relief that is!"

Elizabeth laughed softly. "I know more than you think. You know I have a child too. He's a son, but I worry about him all the same." She flashed a brief, brittle smile, not wanting Claire to know the depth of her concern. *If Sean is injured in the army, like his father was in the navy, that would be the end of him. Deskwork and diplomacy are not his fortes…*

"McBride says that he's going to buy a townhouse for Emily to live in, so that she has more space and privacy than she would in the dormitory."

Elizabeth was shocked. "Are you sure that's wise? Leaving her to her own devices? Freedom is one thing, license another."

"No, no, it won't be like that at all. She'll have maids and a guard outside. Also, I'll be coming to New York from time to time to see how she's doing."

"And you can catch up on the latest fashions, theater, and concerts as well."

Claire laughed. "I guess freedom is a good thing."

"It is, for all of us. Emily will enjoy her new life, and so shall we."

"Can you really take time away from your embassy work to visit New York?" Claire asked eagerly.

Elizabeth smiled. "Not during the busy season, but after fresh staff have been settled in, yes. I'd come on my own, of course. Lionel's duties at the embassy preclude him traveling much outside Washington. Our ambassador does so rely on his organizational and planning skills."

"Shouldn't that be *ambassadors?*"

Elizabeth laughed. "Of course, it should. We are fixtures here. Everyone else comes and goes…"

"That would be lovely!" Claire's face brightened.

It was thus decided that Emily Calvert would attend Hunter College, to which she enthusiastically agreed.

In one of Emily's classes on history, there was a discussion about colonialism and the pros and cons of this subject. One student stole the show with her debating skills. Emily was in awe of the breadth of knowledge and ran after class to introduce herself.

"Hey! Wait, Wait!" While walking down the hall after a history class, Arti turned to see a tall, blonde-haired girl running up to her, her high laced shoes clacking on the marble floor. The girl stopped, breathless. "I really appreciated what you said about colonialism in class today. How do you know so much about it?"

Arti smiled, while trying hard not to laugh. "Let's just say I have experience."

"Oh, by the way, I'm Emily Calvert. I'm from Maryland."

"I'm Arti Ray. I'm from St. Thomas."

"That's a Danish colony in the Caribbean, isn't it?"

"Correct, "said Arti, impressed. "Not many people know where it is or who rules it."

"Well, the United States is a big country. We Americans aren't that good with geography."

Arti chuckled. "I'm finding that to be quite true."

"I'm off to the library; do you want to work on the upcoming project together?" Emily's speech was rapid and slightly high pitched.

"Sure! That would be great!" said Arti.

Despite their differences in ethnicity and social status, Arti and Emily soon became fast friends due to their similar personalities, veracious reading, and being intelligent enough to challenge each other academically. As the semester progressed, Arti spent vast amounts of time at Emily's townhouse, as her cramped living quarters lacked the space and privacy needed for lengthy, avid philosophical discussions.

One evening, after a light supper of cold chicken salad, Arti and Emily sat on the green velvet sofa in Emily's parlor, enjoying glasses of Bordeaux. Arti held the delicate glass stem and gently swirled the red liquid in the large glass bowl. The light of the gas lamps highlighted the wine's vivid red color, making it almost too pretty to drink.

"How would you define *feministe* Arti?" asked Emily, taking a small sip of her wine.

"Well, I know it's French, and means the characteristics of being female, but the definition is changing. It's the concept that women and men are equal, and that once we have guaranteed political equality, we can achieve whatever we want."

Emily smiled slightly as she rubbed the rim of her wine glass with her index finger. "You have a good point, Arti, but do you really think anything can be achieved through *politics*, especially considering that we can't vote?"

"How else are we going to get anything done?" Arti was confused.

"By social change. The primary source of the persecution and subservience of women is the family. As long as women are forced to marry, hand over all assets to their husbands, and risk their lives in childbirth, then they have no means of attaining political or economic power, nor can they fully express their intellects and talents. Women must thus be equal, or superior to men in family dynamics. That's the only way the goals of feminism can be achieved."

"How are you going to achieve all that without gaining political power first?"

Emily laughed. "I guess it's like the chicken and the egg..."

Arti sipped her wine, which warmed her chest and abdomen, making her relaxed and loquacious. "I think we can agree that as women we face restrictions that men don't. After all, if we were differently gendered, we could be at Harvard, Yale, or even Cambridge or Oxford. We both are certainly intelligent enough."

Emily sighed. "It's not just getting into the universities. It's the career opportunities that come after. What can we do? Go to law school? Go to medical school? Start a business? Run for office? All these choices are open to men, but we must be teachers, librarians, or secretaries."

Arti's voice was sharp. "What is wrong with being a teacher?"

"Nothing, unless you want to do something else."

Arti calmed down. "You have a point. We should have

choices, like men do. I think we can agree that feminism is the goal of achieving equality. We haven't yet figured out how it is to be accomplished, and exactly what justice is? Those are still open questions."

"That's about as good as we're going to do tonight!" said Emily, raising her glass in a toast. Arti raised hers, clinking Emily's in agreement.

Soon, other like-minded women joined Emily's and Arti's discussions, eventually forming a loosely organized group that met weekly to discuss feminism, feminist history, women's plights around the world, and authors who championed women's rights. At first, the conversations were academic, but soon developed into calls for action. They formed a Women's Rights Society and began publishing a monthly newspaper. Emily funded the organization with her own money. Soon the newspaper gained notoriety, first in New York, and then further afield as academics carried the print to Boston, Washington, and Philadelphia and eventually across the Atlantic, where other women's organizations read the newspaper in London, Paris, and Amsterdam.

"Arti, Arti!" Emily, her skirts flying, chased Arti down the hall as she walked to class. You won't believe it! I've got some fantastic news!" Emily was red-faced from running but grinning from ear to ear.

"What is it?" Arti asked, eager to know.

"I've received an invitation from the Women's Social and Political Union."

"You're kidding? Not the group that founded the Women's Press in London?"

"Yes, the very one! The want *me* to come to London and speak about women's rights!"

"That's wonderful!" Arti squealed with excitement.

"I've never been abroad before."

Arti laughed. "There's nothing to be afraid of. Not for you."

Emily scowled. "Scared? Me? No way! It's going to be a grand adventure, not just for me, but eventually for all women who want to be free."

Arti put down her books and hugged her friend, whispering in her ear, "I'm so proud of you."

News of her trip, however, did not sit well with Emily's parents. Two weeks later, Arti was in Emily's study, reading letters from her friend's father. "He's really not happy with you."

Tears welled in Emily's eyes, but she refused to cry. "I'm an only child. He and my mother are overprotective. They didn't want me to come to New York. If they had their way, I would have never left the farm."

"You aren't going to get anything settled like this," said Arti, placing the letters back in their envelopes. "Why not go home and talk to them in person? Let them see how much you want to make this trip."

"On one condition," said Emily, dobbing her eyes with a blue silk handkerchief.

"What's that?"

"That you come with me. It'll be over the holidays, so it won't interfere with your studies, or mine."

"I accept your invitation! I've never been out of New York."

"You're going to go now." Emily smiled and squeezed her friend's hand. Arti was thrilled. America was an even more exciting place than she had imagined.

There was one other ace Emily played. She wrote a letter to Elizabeth Burke, her mother's friend:

Dear Mrs. Burke,

I hope that you and your husband are doing well. I would like to request your help regarding a dispute with my parents. I have been invited to travel to London to speak at the Women's Political and Social Union. This is a tremendous opportunity for my life, education, and career. My parents, however, do not want me to go as they are concerned about my safety. Would you, on my behalf, assure them that London is safe, and I will not be in danger? I would be extremely grateful for your help.

Yours Truly,

Miss Emily Calvert

Once the college was closed for the holidays, Emily and Arti took a carriage across the Hudson River to Jersey City. There, they boarded the Baltimore and Ohio Railroad train to Washington D.C. Traveling in richly appointed cars, they dined on oysters, fresh fish, and champagne before arriving in Washington a few hours later. McBride sent a car to pick them up and take them to the Burke's home, where they would stay overnight. A driver pulled up outside the station, in a Cadillac Model Thirty, a black and silver car with two seats up front, two seats in the back, a cloth top, and a spare tire attached to the rear bumper. While Emily was used to car travel, for Arti, it was a luxury. She and Emily sat in the leather upholstered backseat and listened to the engine purr as they rolled through tree-lined streets.

Just as Arti was about to fall asleep, the car stopped in front of a brick mansion with dark blue shutters on the windows. The chauffeur opened the car door for the girls and carried their luggage up the brick steps to the dark blue front door. He tapped a large brass knocker shaped like a lion's head.

The door was opened by a stout, bald man in a dark suit. "Good evening, how may I help you?" His voice was deep, and words measured.

The chauffeur spoke. "Miss Emily Calvert and Miss Arti Ray. The Burkes are expecting them."

The man looked at Emily and Arti. Arti saw a flicker of shock in his eyes when he looked at her. He quickly gained his composure, stood aside, and said, "Welcome to the Burke residence ladies. I will take your coats, and I will have the footman take your luggage to your rooms." The chauffeur was thus dismissed, turned, and left. Arti and Emily entered a black and white marble paved foyer, with strategically placed fresh flowers, and a massive golden chandelier surrounded on both sides by a curving double staircase. They followed the bald man into a richly appointed sitting room with an oriental carpet in shades of red, purple, orange, and cream, mahogany furniture, and red striped papered walls. A welcoming fire was burning in the fireplace.

A middle-aged couple rose from a maroon leather armchair and maroon velvet settee. "Emily! How are you doing my dear? It's wonderful to see you!" said the man with a plummy English accent. He held out his hand, which Emily shook. The woman stretched out her arms and gave Emily a brief hug. Once again, as with the butler, Arti noticed a flicker of shock in their eyes when they looked saw her.

Emily spoke up. "Mr. and Mrs. Burke, this is my friend, Miss Arti Ray from St. Thomas. She is also a student at Hunter College. Arti, this is Mr. Lionel Burke and his wife, Elizabeth Burke." The Burkes both smiled, a bit too broadly, Arti thought.

"Welcome, Miss Ray," said Mr. Burke, with false joviality, holding out his hand. Arti shook it. His hard grip crushed Arti's hand, but she smiled and did not flinch. Mrs. Burke gave Arti a brief embrace, barely touching the girl's shoulders. Arti smiled. If the Burkes could pretend to be nice, so could she.

Mr. Burke then rang a small silver bell standing on a side table. The butler appeared almost at once. "Smithers, would you show the ladies to their rooms?" He then turned to Emily and Arti. "Dinner is at 6:00. You can go rest and get freshened up."

Emily and Arti nodded in agreement and followed Smithers up the curved staircase up to their night lodgings. Arti gasped when Smithers opened the door to her chamber. It was a giant room with a canopy bed with lace curtains, an attached balcony overlooking the gardens, a sitting room, and a bathroom with an enormous bathtub. Arti took a bath, combed out and restyled her hair into her usual tight bun. She changed into her smartest outfit, a high necked light blue wool dress and black boots with silver buttons.

She then made her way downstairs to the sitting room where Emily and Mrs. Burke were talking. The door was open, so Arti heard their conversation clearly. "I know you want to go to England, but it's a voyage by sea, the weather could be unpredictable, also a young woman travelling by herself may not be wise," recommended Mrs. Burke.

"It's an opportunity I do not want to pass up. You could make some arrangements so my safety would not concern my parents," pleaded Emily.

Emily turned her head and saw Arti hesitating in the doorway. "What if you come with me, Arti?" Emily brightened.

"To England?" Arti asked, entering the room, and slowly taking a chair.

"Of course! It would be perfect. You could help me with my speech, and we can see London together."

Arti thought for a moment and then shook her head. "I cannot afford to miss any college. My scholarship depends on it, also I cannot leave the United States till my education is over. They may not let me back in."

Emily continued to plead until Mrs. Burke sided with Arti, saying, "She is right to be cautious about leaving the country." Emily slumped in the chair with a sad face, looking out of the window to hide her tears.

Finally, Elizabeth gave in. "All right, my dear, I will ask my son to make the arrangements for you. He is a captain in the army and will ensure your safety. I will talk to your parents when we meet in a few days." Emily jumped up with a gigantic smile, wiped away her tears, and gave Elizabeth a big hug. The joyful party then retreated to the dining room for a sumptuous meal of venison, potatoes, and peas, followed by a decadent Eve's pudding consisting of spiced apples topped with sponge cake and smothered with rich, gooey custard.

The next morning, the chauffeur returned in the Model Thirty Cadillac, and the girls said their goodbyes to the Burkes. They rode through the Maryland countryside to the Calvert farm. The dirt road snaked for miles as they passed small towns in between large tracts of farmland. Grazing cows, horses, green fields, rolling hills, thick forests, the sweet smell of the country road was intoxicating. Emily broke out in a song about the 'Good old summer'. The chauffeur joined in. Arti did not know the lyrics, but the tune was catchy and by the third time they sang the song she was singing too. They continued to sing loudly, scaring a few of the cows that were grazing close to the road. Soon, the car stopped at a wooden gate. There was a sign next to the gate reading 'Fox Hollow Farms'. The driver got out, swung the gate open, drove the car past the gate and then stopped again to close the gate behind them. The road became narrower and steeper as it curved upwards. They drove for a few miles before veering to the right, where Arti saw two buildings. The first was a huge circular barn and the second, a small distance away, down a cobblestone pathway, was a large brick and stone mansion with a circular driveway and fountain. The car drove around the driveway with the fountain and pulled in front of a large, carved, wooden front door.

The large door swung open, revealing another smiling middle-aged couple. This time, however, the smiles were genuine. "Emily! you are home!" exclaimed the man. The woman ran out and gave Emily a big hug, as three large collies came out and jumped on the girl.

"You must be Miss Arti Ray", said the man, finally noticing Arti. "I'm Emily's father, McBride Calvert. This is my wife, Claire." Mrs. Calvert, having finished greeting her daughter, smiled warmly at Arti.

"Hello, Mr. and Mrs. Calvert. I'm pleased to meet you," replied Arti, and this time she meant it.

As she entered the house, Arti studied the intricate carvings on the large door as she passed through, making a mental note to ask for an explanation. The foyer was three stories high, with a chandelier made from antlers hanging from the ceiling. The entire interior was framed in wood, hardwood floors and wood paneling, with a stone fireplace at one end. A circular stairway led to the upper two floors. Cushy, comfortable leather couches and chairs were placed around the fireplace.

They followed the dogs to the kitchen where Claire had prepared apple pies, blackberry tarts, a tray of cheese and fresh bread, along with cups of hot tea. One collie sat next to Arti and followed each bite that she took, licking her lips every time Arti chewed on her pies.

"That is Lady, the naughty one. Toss her some bread and then she will go away," said Claire. Arti tossed a slice of bread in Lady's direction. The collie grabbed the bread and scampered away. They sat in the warm kitchen, talking about life on campus. They omitted talking about the trip to England. That subject would be broached the next night when the Burkes were invited over for dinner.

Emily grabbed Arti's arm. "Come with me! I want to show you, our farm." They ran towards the stable where Emily's favorite horse, Sugar, was already saddled and waiting.

"Uhm... Emily, I've never ridden such a tall horse

before..." Arti said, looking up in awe at Sugar's high flanks.

"Don't worry! I'll have Jasper saddled for you. He's old and is the friendliest, gentlest animal in this barn."

Arti grinned. "Great." One of the stable hands saddled the ancient brown horse and helped Arti mount.

The two girls then rode out to explore the countryside. Jasper seemed to know how fast to go, where to go, and followed Sugar down the hill. At the bottom of the hill, they turned onto a narrow path leading into the woods.

They passed a dense section of the woods, which Emily called 'Fox Hollow'. "My father named the farm after this section. We call it Fox Hollow because of the shape of the ground and the fox families that have lived in this area for decades or centuries. They were here long before my grandfather built the place. These foxes were sacred to the natives who lived on this land before the settlers pushed them out," explained Emily.

Arti pulled Jasper's reins and came to a halt. There was a peculiar silence in the place, the trees were so thick they formed a canopy that blocked out most of the sunlight. The ground was littered with fallen leaves, moss grew around the tree trunks, and roots intertwined in the lush undergrowth. Despite the darkness, there was a peacefulness in the surreal atmosphere. The stillness of the woodland permeated through the leaves, the slow trickle of moisture on the trees, the occasional rustling of a squirrel, and the gentle flapping wings of a songbird. Emily had moved further away, and Jasper gently shook his head, urging Arti forward. From the corner of her eye, she saw a silver creature slowly crawling towards her. Turning around, she saw a fox staring right at her. It had bright blue eyes. Memories of her, Amee's and Agni's harrowing escape came back to her, making her shiver. The fox sat down on its haunches, pushed his front legs forward, and nestled his head between them, still staring straight at her. The motion brought her back to the present. A feeling of calmness returned.

"Come on," yelled Emily. Arti turned around to see Emily off in the distance, barely visible through the light fog. When she looked back in the fox's direction, it was no longer there. She nudged Jasper forward and then trotted out to the clearing ahead.

They rode to the location of the abandoned campsite of the Patawomeck tribe. McBride had left the area untouched. Nature had reclaimed most of the land. There were still visible ruins of burnt wood. The large firepit in the middle of the village was now a randomly scattered heap of stones. They dismounted from the horses and tied them to a tree. As they walked among the ruins, Emily told Arti the story of the shoot out of the place by her grandfather. Arti was shocked to hear the story of the near massacre and the ingenuity of the natives who escaped. Like her, they left behind the land that has sustained them for ages, to face an uncertain future out west. She pondered on the fate of the villagers who had moved, only to encounter other Benjamin Calverts, who claimed ownership of their homeland.

"Why so somber, Arti?" Emily looked puzzled.

"The American Indians had a different concept of land ownership from the Europeans. For them, land belonged to everyone, the humans, the animals, and the plants."

"Where did you learn this?" asked Emily.

Arti was shocked. "Didn't you know this as well?"

"No, I didn't…" Emily looked pale.

Arti took a deep breath. "I learned this from reading at the college library. I also visited the new public library, the one on Fifth Ave and 40th, and researched more there. The number of books and artifacts that have been donated to the library is quite extensive."

"Tell me more, please," asked Emily.

"According to American Indian chieftains, land is a gift from the Great Spirit. It is sacred, and must be respected, along with the trees and animals. Deforestation is wasteful. Planting crops is an affront to the purity of the soil. The mindless hunting of bison is beyond their comprehension."

"You mean, shooting buffalo from trains? I've seen photos of their carcasses, littering train tracks…"

Arti nodded. "They were used for target practice. When the natives hunt, it is for food, and every part of the animal is respectfully used."

"There were millions of them and now there are only a few hundred left, mostly in Yellowstone and a few private herds."

"Exactly."

"Why, why would anybody do such a thing?" Emily was ready to cry.

"Why do you think? Men love shooting. Also, without buffalo, there could be no American Indians, at least not as they have been. Buffalo was their primary source for food and clothing." Emily was silent. Arti had nothing else to say. The girls wandered around the old encampment lost in thoughts of natives, buffalo, and things that had been lost.

McBride had instilled in Emily a reverence for the place, and she often came to Fox Hollow to sit and think. Emily and Arti could hear the roar of the river as it poured downstream. Walking to the edge of the cliff, they looked down as the water churned around rocks, foaming through channels in the ravine, relentlessly moving to its destination. The water knew its place and where it wanted to go. The pair sat on the rocks, transfixed by the beauty of the scene, music of the rushing river and the floating white clouds in the distance. Jasper, deciding he had given the girls enough time, neighed in the distance. The two got up smiling and headed to the horses to start their trek back to the house.

Taking a meandering way back, they passed a meadow with grazing cattle. The cattle recognized Emily and the horses, and the herd walked towards them. Arti plucked some grass and offered it to the cows. A series of barks made the cattle nervous as the three collies came tearing through the meadow towards them.

An old, but strong and sinewy, cowhand rode up to them, tipping his hat politely in their direction. "Welcome Back, Miss Emily. We missed you," smiled Louis, showing his white teeth.

"Louis, good to see you! " Emily shouted Emily and introduced Arti to him. "Louis runs the farm with Chet, as he has since my grandfather's day," she explained. "Everything functions smoothly because of him."

Louis smiled back at her. "You are, like your father, too kind." The three rode back to the house with the collies speeding ahead of them. Louis explained how the farm worked along the way. It impressed Arti to see a black person in charge of a farm, when her experience so far had been the opposite.

CHAPTER 28:
LONDON CALLING
(1912)

"**W**hat have you done to my kitchen" exclaimed Claire. Emily and Arti were covered with flour as were the kitchen islands, tables, and floor. "We are making a fluffy chocolate cake, fudge brownies with nuts and a steamed bread pudding" said Emily proudly. "We have all the ingredients here, fresh eggs, butter, sugar, containers of flour, salt, lard, and milk."

"Don't worry" said one of the cooks "We are helping Miss Emily and her friend. We will make sure all is done correctly, and the place is cleaned up."

Claire raised her eyebrows in disbelief and walked out of the kitchen.

The Burkes arrived later that evening, for dinner, and after the pleasantries, they all retired to one of the living rooms. McBride added wood and stoked the fire until it was roaring. Arti stared into the fireplace fascinated by the dancing flames. As glasses of red wine were passed to the gathered, Emily dropped the bombshell "I want to accept the invitation to speak at a convention in London in a few weeks."

McBride put down his wine glass "Absolutely not, it is unsafe for a young girl to travel by herself across the ocean."

Claire readily agreed "Send someone else or just decline

the invitation."

Emily sipped her wine and pushed her legs higher on the couch "It is an honor to be invited, also it raises the profile of my magazine and my women's organization. I want to meet my compatriots in England and exchange ideas with them. I may even want to visit Paris."

"There is a war in the Balkans" said Claire "You cannot go." Emily's voice rose to a high-pitched squeal "Mom! The Balkans are far away! She looked pleadingly at Lionel Burke. He got up walked over to the fireplace and said "Yes, there is a war being fought in the Ottoman Empire, however that is a couple of thousand miles away, about the distance from Washington to San Francisco."

"If there was a war in San Francisco, the war would come to Washington very soon" said Claire, proud of herself for defeating the argument being made by Lionel.

Unperturbed with the interruption Lionel continued "The Ottoman empire has been in decline. There are nationalist movements in Serbia, Bulgaria, Romania, and Greece that want independence from the Ottomans. At the same time the Austria-Hungary empire ruled by the Hapsburgs, which conquered Bosnia-Herzegovina from the Ottomans, does not want the entire Empire to crumble as they are equally afraid of the nationalist movements. Especially Serbia which believes Austria-Hungary has usurped land belonging to them. It is an extremely dangerous part of the world. The German and Italian empires are also watching the situation closely. Germany is an ally of Austria-Hungary and will go to war if Austria desires. Italy which has fought the Ottomans before does not trust them."

Lionel continued his monologue into the intricacies of each of the countries involved and the politics that were in play. Arti and Emily were fascinated by his grasp of history hung on to his every word. Claire's who had stopped listening, her eyes glazed over as she twirled the wine in her glass. McBride put on a polite listening face, periodically drowning his boredom in Bourbon. Elizabeth twisted her body on the couch to catch her husband's eyes to make him stop, but his history lesson train was chugging on full speed ahead with no station in sight.

One of the kitchen staff announcing that dinner was ready was the catalyst that finally broke the dialogue. Over dinner, Elizabeth looked at both Claire and McBride. "I have a solution. You know Sean is now in London working for the War Office. He previously oversaw the security of the Viceroy of India. I will ask him to make all the arrangements for Emily's journey and to ensure her safety. It will also be an opportunity for Emily to meet Sean."

Claire nodded approvingly at the suggestion, "That is an excellent suggestion Elizabeth" much to the consternation of McBride and left him wondering why his wife had just agreed. Emily looked anxiously at her father for approval. "Ok, just be careful" McBride sighed. While Emily and Arti had big smiles on their faces, Claire and Elizabeth looked at each other with eyes of conspiracy. They had both secretly hoped that their children would meet each other, hoping they could join the two families in marriage. Emily's visit to England would supply justification for that encounter.

Lionel, meanwhile, upon talking to Arti about her life in St. Thomas, told her "The United States had been trying to buy some of those islands since the Civil War. In the 1860s the US actually made a formal proposal to buy the island, but that deal fell through when Congress did not fully support it. Since then, there have been proposals floating around. I think the US will take over the island because it's a good strategic decision for the US and there would be benefits to the islanders to become part of the US territory as well." As with any tidbits of knowledge she got, she filed it away in the back of her mind, with a resolve to read more about this matter later.

With their mission accomplished, Emily and Arti spent a few days on the farm before catching a train back to New York. A few weeks later, Emily sailed for England on the RMS Lusitania. Pier fifty-four was bustling with activity as Emily, Arti, McBride, and Claire arrived. Her parents had arrived from Maryland to see her off. Carts filled with luggage were being pushed, hundreds of passengers in line to board, other passengers saying their goodbyes to well-wishers, a few stray dogs wandering by, seagulls fighting over tossed food and the waves of the Hudson lapping against the pier. Towering above the mayhem were the four tall smokestacks of the RMS Lusitania. The ship had a black hull; the smokestacks were painted red, white lifeboats were strapped on the deck. Black smoke poured from the smokestacks, as passengers lined up on the deck to catch a view of the New York City skyline on departure. After a long-protracted goodbye and many promises on communication and safety, Emily boarded the gangplank where an attendant escorted her to the assigned cabin. The first-class cabin where she was staying was on the top deck. A one bedroom with a parlor and bathroom. Windows in the bedroom and parlor looked outward towards the ocean. Not bothering to unpack, she ran to the deck to wave goodbye. In the sea of people on the pier, hundreds of horse carriages, and cars, she had a tough time locating her parents. Finally, seeing them, she waved in their direction. To her astonishment, they saw her too, reciprocating the waves.

With a loud horn blast, a barge towed the ship out of the harbor and then let go as the ship sailed into the North Atlantic. Inside her cabin, Emily tried to pull a chair closer to the window. Unfortunately, she realized they had bolted all the furniture down to the floor. Undoubtedly to assure the welfare of the passengers in inclement weather. The journey took a little over five days. Mostly the weather was pleasant, however on the third day gale force winds, rain and thunderstorms caused the boat to lurch from side to side. It soon vetted the practicality of bolting the furniture. However, passengers were on their own in the opulent ambiance of the first-class dining room. Many passengers went sprawling across the floor, spilling their wine on their posh wardrobes.

The RMS Lusitania docked at Liverpool, where arrangements had been made for Emily to board a train to London's Kings Cross Station. On her arrival at the station, a smartly dressed British officer, Captain Sean Burke, met her.

CHAPTER 29: THE WAR OFFICE (1912)

C aptain Sean Burke strode into his new office in the War Office building in Whitehall. He had hoped they would place him on one of the upper floors, but he did not have the seniority, nor were his potential contributions recognized, let alone valued. To reach his office, he had to go down a flight of stairs, through a dark corridor, into a room that had once been a wine cellar. Although someone had done a respectable job of whitewashing the walls, the smell of oak barrels and fermenting wine still hung in the air. There were no windows. Someone artfully arranged the desks in rows, where soldiers in uniform were busy typing their reports. Sean classified his subordinates as analysts or agents. An analyst's job was primarily desk based, while an agent mostly worked in the field. The war department, however, was insistent on the continued use of the titles of the army hierarchy. He stopped by the desk of one agent, "Second Lieutenant Cooper, get me the report on the India house surveillance" he commanded as he continued walking, then, before the officer could respond, went back to the desk, and added "Also find out about a new student at Trinity college, a Stephen Pereira."

"Yes sir! Captain Burke!" responded Cooper, who then got up with alacrity and stepped over to the file cabinets to retrieve the requested information.

About five minutes later, he walked into Sean's office with a file. It had the names and brief summaries of all the students and visitors to India House. The young officer handed the file to Sean. "Thank you, Second Lieutenant Cooper, you may go now." Cooper nodded in acknowledgement, pivoted towards the door, and left.

He glanced through the names. No Stephen Pereira. There were guest visitors, their names were unknown. There also were some visits from Mr. Sarkar, a prominent business owner. Sean made a note to start surveillance on his house as well. A few hours later, there was a knock on the door. "Come in," Sean barked.

The door opened and Cooper walked in. "Captain Burke, sir. Here is the list you requested of all the new students at Trinity College."

"Thank you, Cooper." Sean took hold of the list and scanned it, and then scanned it again. "Hmm... there is no Stephen Pereira listed. I'm going to give you a description of Mr. Pereira and I want you to go to Trinity and India House to see if anyone has seen him."

"Yes sir," replied Cooper, taking a pencil, and writing tablet out of his inner jacket pocket.

"He's a young Indian man, under thirty. Tall, brown-skinned, with deep brown eyes. He has short, straight black hair with a center part, a mustache, and a small goatee. Oh, and he wears black rimmed glasses."

Cooper looked up from his tablet. "Is that all, sir?"

"Let me see your notes," requested Sean, holding out his hand. Cooper handed over his tablet, and Sean quickly read the description the junior officer had written.

"Everything is correct," said Sean. "Now go and find out what you can about this man."

"Will do, Captain Burke, sir." Cooper stood up smartly, saluted, and left the office.

Later that evening Sean walked out of his office, got

in his Model T roadster, and headed to Kings Cross Station. Once there, he stood outside the clock tower entrance, staring up at the twin arches that formed the front facade of the station. He periodically looked at the picture of Emily his mother had sent him. The young woman was standing by a decorated Christmas tree, curly blonde hair, clear white skin, mischievous eyes, and a big smile. She wore a high-necked, puffy sleeved white blouse, a dark ankle-length skirt, and black boots. Her prettiness had captured his fancy, along with his mother's letters with glowing praise of Emily's kindness, vivacity, and intelligence.

Sean glanced up from Emily's picture to see a young blonde woman walking with a porter, pushing a steamer trunk on a dolly. Sean immediately recognized her. It was Emily. He put her photo in his pocket and rushed to meet her. "Hello, Miss Calvert. I'm Captain Sean Burke. I hope you had a pleasant journey."

Emily smiled at him, revealing perfectly pearly white teeth. "I did. Thank you for asking." She pulled a photo of him out of her skirt pocket. "I knew it was you. You look just like your photograph, except more colorful."

Sean laughed. "I can say the same about you!" He led Emily and the porter to the waiting car. Sean helped Emily into the front seat and then he and the porter put Emily's trunk in the rear of the vehicle. He then got in the car. Before starting the engine, he asked, "You're staying at the Savoy, aren't you?"

"Yes," replied Emily.

Sean then started the engine. As they rode to the hotel, conversation was brief, as they had to shout to be heard clearly above the engine noise. He gathered, however, that her journey had been pleasant but uneventful.

When they arrived at the Savoy, after a porter had collected his trunk, Emily asked, "I need to let my parents know that I made it here safely. Could I send them a message?"

Her eyes were wide open, giving her a look of helpless innocence.

Sean resisted the urge to fold her in his arms. "I'll be happy to take care of that for you. I can telegraph my parents from the War Office, and they will let your parents know you are safe and well. Also, I have arranged for you to have a car and chauffeur at your disposal while you are here."

"Thank you, Captain Burke." Emily turned to enter the hotel.

"Wait a minute, Miss Calvert." Sean raised his hand. Emily turned around to face him. "Would you do me the honor of dining with me here at the Grill tomorrow evening?"

"Why yes, that would be a pleasure."

"Shall we say 6:30, or would 7:00 be better?"

"Let's make it 7:00. I've got a speech to work on."

"Good. I look forward to seeing you then." Sean turned and left Emily standing, watching him as he turned his back and left. As Sean drove off, Emily thought, *damn! What a good-looking man!* turned and entered the Savoy.

The Savoy Grill was lavish, noisy, and smoky all at the same time. The dark wood paneling, plain white linen tablecloths, and smoke from diners' pipes and cigars gave it a masculine atmosphere even though there were numerous women diners, many wearing their hats while seated. Sean and Emily sat by a wall near the bar. Sean glanced around the room and saw three men seated around a table across the room, earnestly engaged in conversation. He instantly recognized the student, Stephen Pereira. The other two were unfamiliar. One looked European, possibly Dutch, or German, the other was an Asian in a well-tailored navy-blue suit, from Savile Row.

Jeev took a long draw on his cigar and sipped his whiskey, as Mr. Sarkar laid out the plans for Jeev's visit to Germany. "You will take a boat from Southampton to Amsterdam in a few weeks. It's too dangerous for you to leave from London. Franz will travel to Amsterdam separately and meet you there, then together, you both travel to Berlin. You will present the plan to the Berlin Committee and stay there until you can get the arms. If all goes well, you will board a ship with arms and head to the Andaman Islands in the Bay of Bengal. Once we know you are on board, we will give the signal for our hidden troops on the island to take over the city of Port Blair, the capital of the island. The troops will first attack the main jail, where the British troops are holding thousands of political prisoners. This will create a diversion as well as supply additional troops. The port will be secured by the time the ship arrives with the arms. From there we can launch an assault on the mainland." The three men lifted their glasses to celebrate.

Sean desperately wanted to know what the three men were talking about. His attention kept moving from Emily to the table across the room. Emily noticed. She stopped talking and her gaze hardened into a steely blue. "Please excuse me," said Sean, getting up from the table. "I've got to retrieve something from my car." Emily nodded.

A few minutes later, Sean returned and pulled out a Vest Pocket Kodak camera from his jacket. Emily's face brightened. "Let's take a picture to send back to your parents," he offered.

"That would be lovely!" Emily beamed and clasped her hands together.

"Come this way, Miss." Sean led Emily to a position where Pereira and his companions were clearly visible in the background.

Seeing a passing waiter, Sean raised his hand. "Waiter, would you please take a photo of the lady and me?"

"I would be happy to, sir." Sean handed him the camera.

The waiter took a few pictures and Sean and Emily returned to their table, in a better, more jovial, mood.

Sean's actions did not go unnoticed. Jeev at once recognized the captain and warned his companions. "Gentlemen, I must warn you. We are being watched, and we have been photographed. The man who is watching us is sitting across the room with an elegant blonde lady. He is a captain in the British Army, whom I met on the ship to England."

"What's his name?" asked Mr. Sarkar, taking out a pen and small notepad.

"Captain Sean Burke," replied Jeev.

Sarkar wrote down the name. "I'll see what I can find out about him," he promised.

"Should we leave, perhaps?" asked von Oppenheim.

Sarkar took a drag on his cigar. "I don't think that's necessary. If we leave, we will just draw more attention to ourselves. Captain Burke probably recognizes Pereira from the sea voyage. Besides, the lobster here is excellent." The three men thus continued with their meals and their plans.

Emily noticed Sean periodically glancing over at the corner table, and once again, became irritated. "Do you know those three people sitting there? You keep looking at them." Sean sighed. "Sorry, Emily, my work never leaves me. Let us just say that they are persons of interest for the British government and leave it at that. I don't think I am allowed or should say anymore." Emily nodded in agreement and changed the conversation topic to her speech that she planned to give at the women's organization meeting. Sean listened politely, feigning interest. However, his thoughts were on the conversation happening in the background.

After leaving the hotel, Sean dropped off the camera at the military intelligence unit of the War Office, which was always open. He left instructions to have the photos developed before he arrived in the morning.

The next morning, Sean arrived at his office to find three men around his desk, laughing. He stopped in his office doorway and looked at them. They all stood up as he walked in. "Something funny?" he questioned. "No, sir, just looking at pictures of your friend from last night. She is quite a looker, sir," smiled a beefy brown-haired man with lieutenant insignia on his jacket sleeves.

"You idiots," Sean grumbled, snatching the pictures off the table. "I am interested in the three people in the background. I want a report on my desk by the end of the day. Who they are, where they live, everything! Now scram off to work and start earning your wages."

Jeev had left the Trinity area and was now living in a small Victorian house that was owned by Mr. Sarkar, near the King's College Campus by the Thames.

"Mr. Pereira! Wipe your feet before coming in! I can't be mopping up mud all day."

"Sorry, Mrs. Pearl," Jeev replied, inferring his guilt from looking at his muddy footprints, as he could not understand his new landlady's thick Irish brogue. Mrs. Pearl threw up her pale pudgy arms in exasperation, as Jeev took off his shoes and carried them upstairs, with only thin socks to cover his feet while walking upstairs. The house was always slightly damp and musty smelling. It was, however, near King's College and its library. Jeev chuckled. He could not remain irritated with Mrs. Pearl, who managed the house for Mr. Sarkar. She was always smiling and smelled of freshly baked goodies, which she freely shared with him and the other four house residents. Jeev patted his expanding stomach. If he didn't stop eating her Cornish pasties and cream cakes, he would soon be as round as her.

When not at his lodging house consuming baked

goodies, Jeev was at the Library at King's College reading books and newspapers about South Asia and the world. He also read works by his favorite philosophers: Karl Marx, Friedrich Nietzsche, Thomas Aquinas, Rene Descartes, and Immanuel Kant.

One day, while Jeev was sitting at a long table in the library, immersed in a book on rational thinking and reasoning, he heard someone come and sit a few chairs down at the same table. Preoccupied, he did not bother to look up until his aching eyes demanded a rest. Sitting across from him was an oddly familiar blonde girl with blue eyes. He smiled at her and then went back to reading. The philosophical writing suddenly seemed way too complex to decipher. Epistemological issues of rationalism and empiricism collided with dogmatism and conventionalism. The confusion of seeing the girl's face in his thoughts replaced his ability to interpret intricate sentences. Hurriedly, he packed up his books and left. The blonde girl's eyes followed him out. It was Emily. She recognized Pereira from the restaurant encounter. Her first impulse was to contact Sean and let him know. Yet something inside her, the sense of danger and adventure, made her stall her instinct.

The next day, Jeev entered the library and saw the blonde girl seated at the same table. Emily was finishing her speech and noticed Jeev coming in her direction. Jeev walked up and took the same seat he had the day before. Without glancing at her, he sat down, opened his book, and pretended to read. Just as the day before, the words did not make any sense. They rose and reassembled on the pages in random configurations. He looked up and noticed Emily studying him. He shifted in his seat and nervously whispered, "Hi I am Stephen Pereira."

"Emily Calvert" said in a soft voice with an accent he could not recognize.

"You are not English?" he asked.

"American, from Maryland," Emily replied, blushing slightly.

A library matron suddenly materialized as if out of nowhere, "You cannot talk here, please take it outside." Embarrassed, the pair gathered their belongings and walked out of the library. They strolled towards the river and sat on the steps of a garden facing the Thames.

"You are from India, Stephen?" Emily continued the conversation.

"Yes, I'm from Goa." Jeev took a deep breath. He had almost said Bengal. No matter how intoxicating Emily's beauty, he must keep the Stephen Pereira story straight. Conversation then turned to Emily's college and her work on women's rights. Jeev told her briefly about Stephen Pereira's life in India and now as a student in England.

"For an American woman, you know a lot about India," he remarked, impressed with the depth and detail of Emily's knowledge about his home country.

Emily grinned. "Why, thank you! My best friend was born in India, but she later immigrated to the island of St. Thomas in the Caribbean."

Not wanting to reveal too much of himself or his lack of knowledge regarding Goa, Jeev changed the conversation topic to his philosophical readings. "I have been studying the concept of rationalism. You know, Descartes said, 'I think, therefore I am'. If I am thinking and if I am approving or I am doubting, I am thinking so the rational thought is that I exist. And because I exist, I am a thinking thing." Emily was a bit lost at his circular logic but continued to listen without interruption. "Since I am a thinking thing, I can consider myself as a freethinker. I can think about whether I should believe things that are told to me the absolute truth. Are you with me so far, Emily?"

Emily nodded. "Keep going."

Jeev continued, "I think of myself as a rational being, and I possess intellectual logic. So, I can choose to believe something if it is presented to me with the use of reason and rationality. I do not have to believe something solely because it is preached to me. I am not necessarily arguing against religion, I am arguing for morality. If reasoning is the foundation of morality, then what I see happening in India is not moral. There can be no justification for the subjugation of the population. There are no morals in allowing people to die in famines. There is no reason for women to be sold as indentured workers. So, because I am a thinking person, and I do not see any morality in the British colonial rule, I am within my rights and within my logic, to remove them one way or another."

"Is it morally right for one person to use whatever means possible, even if the other person is morally wrong?" inquired Emily.

"Well, what you have to remember is that this is not about the individual, it is about two societies that are in conflict with each other," explained Jeev. "One society has imposed its will and cruelty on another society. The suppressed now have the moral upper hand to struggle against the suppressor. It does not differ from your George Washington. I am sure you and most Americans hold him in high regard. He used whatever means he could to fight the redcoats. I do not think anyone has questioned Washington's tactics; his reasoning, let alone his morality. On the contrary, he is praised and revered."

"So, are you the George Washington of India?" a smiling Emily asked.

Jeev laughed out aloud, "Well, maybe I could think of myself as an Alexander Hamilton. A thinking man, as a strategical person, someone who makes things happen," He paused as an image of Ramu came to his mind, then in a more serious tone "There is someone back home, much braver, much stronger. He would be the George Washington of India."

All Jeev could think about for the rest of the day, was Emily. However, he had not recognized her as the girl accompanying Sean Burke. Her face appeared on the windows of the buildings he passed, even when he peered into the Thames, he saw her reflection in the water. He could clearly see her thick rich blonde hair, parted in the middle, cascading down to her shoulders. Her milky white complexion, large blue eyes, full pink lips, high cheekbones that formed a perfectly symmetrical face enhancing her beauty.

A few miles downstream, in the war office building, Sean was sitting in a large conference room, listening to a general drone about current affairs around the world. He had been called to the War office to discuss the death of the Japanese emperor. His son Yoshihito had taken over. The Prime Minister needed to be briefed on Yoshihito, and Sean's office was tasked with creating the reports for the briefing. His entire staff had to place their other less immediate duties on hold while they complied data from various Asian and European sources on the new Japanese Emperor.

Emily did not tell Sean about her meeting with Jeev. She visited the library as often as she could, and Jeev was there daily while he waited for his ticket to Amsterdam. They talked often, mostly about philosophy. Emily was not sure why she did not tell Sean about Jeev or (Stephen as she knew him). It could have been the adventure of knowing someone who was a freedom fighter in her eyes while being a militant in the eyes of Sean, the thrill of knowing someone involved in a plot to overthrow a colonial power or her own feelings about equality. While these primarily applied to women's equality, it was hard for her not to empathize with other races and nationalities. In her eyes, everyone deserved to be treated equally. Stephen was thus fighting for something that was near and dear to her heart.

CHAPTER 30: THE WOMEN'S MOVEMENT

Emily gazed in awe at the massive King's College lecture hall. The soaring ceilings, dark paneled walls, large, high windows, and stone floor contributed to a stately, religious atmosphere, further enhanced as she climbed the steps up to the podium to give her speech to the Women's Social and Political Union (WSPU). Looking out at the audience, she saw a sea of faces, mostly women with one notable exception, a familiar looking man in a military uniform in the second row. Emily blinked while trying not to look at him. A quick glance confirmed it was Sean. Oh well, Emily thought, if he thinks he has to protect me, let him. He isn't going to stop me from saying what I came here to say.

Taking a deep breath, she began to speak. "Ladies and gentlemen, my name is Emily Calvert. I am deeply honored to be one of several speakers here today at the invitation of the Women's Social and Political Union. I am a student at Hunter College in New York and the publisher of *The New American Woman*. I am here to speak about suffrage in America. As in the United Kingdom, our struggle is not only for our right to vote, but also for our right to own property, enter professions, and choose how we live our lives…"

Unknown to Emily, Stephen Pereira was also there, discreetly standing in a corner, hanging on to every word in Emily's speech. He pulled out a notepad and pencil and made notes so that he could hopefully discuss some of the finer philosophical points with her later.

"...and that is why we have more in common as *women* than we have differences as Americans and British. We are fighting in our own countries for the same goal, freedom for all women to exercise their God-given rights and live their lives in freedom." Emily stopped speaking. The audience started applauding.

"Bravo! Well said!" a female voice called out from one of the back rows. The audience then stood up, and the applause grew louder. Emily smiled and nodded until the clapping died down. She then stepped down from the podium and took a seat in the front row, careful not to look back at Sean.

More speakers followed, including the founder of the WSPU. The speeches became progressively fiercer and more provocative. Many members of the audience became uneasy with the violent rhetoric. Sean stayed calm, looked straight ahead, and did not respond to the stares, glares, and muffled comments about him and his uniform. He kept his eye on Emily, who sat straight-backed with her hands and her speech papers in her lap. Like him, she was staring straight ahead.

Finally, the last speaker left the podium. Before Sean could sigh with relief, however, a loud female voice behind him yelled, "Votes for women!" The others in the audience, including Emily, took up the chant and streamed outside, continuing the recitation at increasing volume. Sean moved into the crowd with quick discretion, keeping sight of Emily. Jeev, curious to see what would happen, also melded into the crowd. Banners appeared out of nowhere and the audience marched toward Ten Downing Street.

"Halt!" cried a strong male voice, as police officers with truncheons appeared and blockaded the streets ahead.

"Here, take this," someone said to Emily, thrusting a "Votes for Women" picket sign in her hand. She took it and headed to the front of the line. Sean was several yards deep into the crowd, but seeing Emily move to the front, he pushed through to get a better view of her and to better help her if necessary.

Suddenly, the mob stopped moving, stopped by a line of police officers mounted on horses with more lines behind them on foot, all armed with wooden batons. Jeev, who had lost sight of Emily, saw them, turned around, and headed back to his rooming house. He could feel the energy of the crowd changing. The protesters were growing restless, and the chants were turning into screams. Staying in the crowd would put him, his trip to Germany, and the weapons purchase scheme at risk. Emily would have to fend for herself. India was more important.

Just after Jeev exited the crowd, someone threw a stone at a nearby store window, shattering the glass. The women picked up what stones and bricks they could find and threw them at more windows. The sound of shattering glass echoed through the streets. Still, the police hesitated. "Fire!" someone screamed as flames spouted through the broken windows of a store.

"Charge!" yelled the commanding police officer. The mounted police then moved as a single unit, charging into the crowd, batons drawn. Police horses smashed through the mob, batons swinging wildly, cracking skulls and shoulders, and anything else they contacted. The throng, mostly women, retreated in panic, many trampling each other.

Emily attempted to move through the heaving throng, doing her best to avoid both the police and her fellow protestors. Suddenly, she felt a sharp pain at the side of her head and then on her shoulder. When she reached up and then over to feel her wounds, her hands felt warm and sticky. Looking at her hands, and down at her white blouse, she saw blood. Suddenly, she felt nauseous. Throwing up, however, was not an option, so she continued to push through the crowd until she found a streetlamp post to lean on.

Sean, meanwhile, took advantage of his military uniform to walk past the police while he looked for Emily. Suddenly, he saw her, leaning against a streetlamp post, groggy from the hits to her head. Blood had flowed from her scalp to her ear, over her neck and drenched part of her white blouse, red. "Emily! It's Captain Burke. I'm going to help you get out of here." Emily groaned. She did not resist when Sean grabbed her arm, placed it around his shoulder and helped her move past the police. With one glance at Sean's uniform, the police let him through. Sean got Emily to the Savoy Hotel, called a doctor to examine her and bandage her head to stop the bleeding. He also requested a lady's maid.

After bandaging Emily's head, the doctor left, and the maid helped her change into her nightgown and tucked her into bed. Sean waited in the sitting room until the maid opened the bedroom door. "You may come in now, sir." The maid bowed her head slightly. Revealing the tight chestnut bun at the back of her head.

"Thank you..." Sean paused, unsure of her name.

"Agnes, sir. Miss Agnes Brown," the maid said rushing her words.

"Thank you, Miss Brown." Sean replied with a smile. Agnes relaxed, let Sean enter the room and followed behind. She pulled up a chair to Emily's bed and moved to a discreet distance as Sean sat down. Emily was laid on her back, her covers pulled up over her shoulders. Her eyes flickered open as she sensed Sean's presence.

"Miss Calvert, it's Captain Burke."

Emily groaned, feeling the bandage on her head. "What happened?"

"You were injured in a riot. I found you and took you to

the Savoy. I called a doctor and found you a lady's maid who will stay with you until you are feeling better."

Emily glanced across the room and saw Agnes. "Oh, that's nice."

Sean took a deep breath. "Emily, listen. What I'm about to say is especially important. Do you understand?"

"Understand what? You haven't said anything yet." Her voice was weak, yet Sean still sensed aggravation.

"It's vital that you stay inside this hotel. The police are roaming the streets looking for rioters, but they will not come here."

"Why not?"

"The Savoy is too opulent, and its residents are too well connected to be questioned."

"Why would they suspect me? I'm just a tourist."

"A tourist with bandages…"

Emily's face darkened. "That's right. I'd draw attention, wouldn't I?"

"You would indeed," said Sean, thinking to himself *only a bit more attention than she would be from her beauty alone.* He stood up. "I'd better get back to the War Office. Please let me know if you need anything."

"Will do," said Emily, as she closed her eyes and drifted off to sleep.

As he walked back to his office, Sean frowned, and his feet hit the pavement harder than usual. Why had he not done a better job of protecting Emily? Once his mother heard about Emily's injuries, he would never hear the last of it. Reaching his office, he faced a stack of reports waiting to be read. Sean sighed. Would his work never end? Sean sat down in his chair and picked up the first report. It was titled *Mr. Ikbal Sarkar*:

Mr. Sarkar is 35 years old, married, with two children, a boy, and a girl. His wife does not work and is rarely seen outside her home. He is a wealthy diamond trader. He came to the United Kingdom as a young man, looking to expand his father's diamond business as the supply of diamonds in India dwindled while the supply of diamonds from South Africa increased, Mr. Sarkar started a business buying African diamonds in England, shipping them to Surat, Gujarat for cutting and polishing, and then selling them in London, Paris, and other places in Europe. The venture was profitable, and Mr. Sarkar settled in England to run the business.

His siblings continue to help his father run the business in Surat. He has constant contact with the Indian subcontinent as his employee couriers carry diamonds back and forth between the ports of Surat and London. His wealth has made him many friends in high places in London. He has financed many politicians, so he must be handled with care. At this point, the military intelligence does not recommend placing a constant surveillance on Mr. Sarkar as it could cause issues with the Prime Minsters office.

The second report was titled *Franz von Oppenheim:*

Herr von Oppenheim is a German citizen and is 52 years old. There is no available information about his family. He has travelled extensively in Asia, the Middle East and Africa. He has contacts in Cairo. He is closely affiliated with the regime in Berlin and is a frequent visitor to the German Embassy. He has homes in Berlin and Vienna. He is currently in England, staying at a small hotel in Central London. We have placed a surveillance detail on him. He has been observed entering a home that is owned by Mr. Sarkar. The war office has a file on him. He is known to be an Arab and Muslim sympathizer and now the Asian Indians.

The third report was on Stephen Pereira:

Mr. Stephen Pereira came to the United Kingdom to study at Trinity College, Cambridge. According to the college, however, no one with that name was registered as a student. One student at India House stated that Mr. Pereira lived there briefly. He then moved to Cambridge where he stayed in a boarding house with Trinity College students. Mr. Pereira spent most of his days in the libraries. He was not seen attending any lectures that were not open to the public. A few days ago, he abruptly left Cambridge without telling anyone or leaving a forwarding address. He left behind some clothing and personal items which indicated his departure was sudden. His current location is unknown. A photo of him has been given to the Metropolitan Police.

Sean looked at the picture of Stephen Pereira and covered the mustache and beard with his thumb. That face looked so familiar. Could he be the same person who attacked the Viceroy train? "Damn, these Indians all look the same," Sean blurted out aloud.

He stepped out of his office and called one of his agents. "If you see Stephen Pereira, detain him immediately. Let the Metropolitan police know as well. Continue tailing Herr von Oppenheim. For now, we cannot do much about him or Mr. Sarkar. We do not have enough information about them. We can, however, hold Mr. Pereira for false documents."

The next day, Sean was sitting in his office, musing over Stephen Pereira, when he heard a sharp knock on his door. "Enter!" he barked, annoyed at being disturbed. Second Lieutenant Cooper entered, holding a piece of paper in his hand. The hairs on the back of Sean's neck prickled. Something was up. "What is it, Cooper?" he inquired, lowering his voice.

"It's a telegram, sir, from our embassy in Germany. The Berlin-India Committee is active again. They met a fortnight ago. They will have another meeting later this month, which an emissary from India will attend. He will present a plan to obtain German arms to use against our troops in India.

"Who is this emissary? Do we have a name?" Sean tried to contain his excitement, but his words came out more rapidly than he intended.

"Jeev Sen", replied Cooper, "also known as Stephen Pereira."

So, I was right! Sean felt the thrill of satisfaction. "Arrest him at once for espionage! Let the Metropolitan police know about him as well" he commanded.

"Sir, Herr von Oppenheim has also been identified as working with the committee."

"Keep monitoring his activities. We'll eventually catch him for something, and what about Mr. Sarkar?"

Cooper grimaced. "Nothing, sir. He's covered his tracks well."

This did not dampen Sean's renewed enthusiasm. Now was the time to act. "Cooper, I want you to gather a team and go to known hiding places that militants use. It will be like looking for a needle in a haystack, but we must start somewhere."

"Yes sir, Captain Burke," said Cooper, saluting. "I'll do so right now." He turned sharply and walked out of the room.

After Cooper left, Sean looked at his watch. It was just after 2:00 p.m., time to go to the Savoy and check on Emily. He put on his wool overcoat, and since the weather was pleasant, he decided to walk to the hotel. The stroll would help him clear his mind.

This did not happen, however. Instead of thinking about Jeev, aka Stephen Pereira, he thought of Emily. He smiled when he thought about how beautiful she was, with her large blue eyes, luxuriant blonde hair, and slim, yet womanly, figure, just the type of woman to attract envious glances from his fellow officers at military balls... Suddenly, he frowned. Emily was too independent thinking and free spirited to be an army officer's wife. For them to live peacefully in a house in the English countryside, raising kids and interacting with the local aristocracy would be an impossible dream. He shuddered to think of how his colleagues and their wives would react to Emily advocating the causes of the so-called poor, the oppressed and her feminist views, the very people whose upliftment would mean the destruction of the status quo that he had dedicated his life to uphold. Sean sighed in disappointment. He knew his mother would be displeased. He would, however, ensure Emily's safety until she boarded her ship back to New York, which would be the next one available, as London was no longer safe for her. Before he could work out his plans for Emily in detail, Sean arrived at the Savoy. He entered the lobby and approached the front desk.

"Good evening, Captain," said the man at the reception desk, noticing the rank insignia on Sean's jacket. "What may I do for you?"

"I'm here to see Miss Emily Calvert."

The desk clerk picked up a telephone. "Who shall I say is calling on her, sir?"

"Captain Sean Burke."

The clerk circled the rotary dial and lifted the receiver to his ear. After about two minutes, he laid down the receiver. "Nobody is answering, sir.

Sean sighed. "I'll go to her room. Don't worry. I know her room number." Sean moved towards the stairs and walked rapidly up them as he could without knocking down hotel guests. He reached Emily's room on the fourth floor and rapped on the door. No answer. He tried again, with a bit more force. Still no answer. *Where is Emily? What kind of game is she playing?* Sean turned around, went back to reception, left a message, and walked out of the hotel with a sinking feeling in the pit of his stomach. Something was not right, and it was something to do with him. *Please, God, help Emily, and help me help myself...*

While Sean was fretting over her absence from the Savoy, Emily was sitting on the bank of the Thames, apprising Jeev of the events of the riot. She wore a broad-brimmed blue hat, to hide her bandaged head.

"Can you believe I was in a riot!" she said excitedly shaking her head, causing a sharp pain at the top of the skull. Her expressive simile turned into a wince, as Jeev looked at her and asked, "Does it hurt badly?" Emily replied "Not much, only when I move my head. And I was assaulted by a policeman!" her voice again rising with excitement "I feel as if I accomplished something yesterday. That I took a hit for a cause. That I am suffering for something that is meaningful to my existence as a human being. I don't mind the pain at all, in fact I now have the courage to face more adversity if it is for the cause I believe in."

Jeev hung on every word of Emily's story, while patting the envelope in his jacket pocket to verify it was still safe. He had received an envelope the previous day with his ticket to Amsterdam, a wad of cash and travel documents indicting his name as Tony Fernandes, again with Portuguese seals. This time, his profession was that of a trader.

"That's enough about me," Emily spoke softly, her eyes growing wider as she looked at Jeev. His heart skipped a beat. Somehow, he knew he could trust her, but how much? "I'm going to Germany. I'll be speaking at a meeting there."

"Ooh... that sounds interesting! Who invited you? Who else is speaking?"

Jeev laughed nervously and raised his palms as if to push away Emily's barrage of questions. "Whoa! I don't know who else is speaking, and as for who invited me, let's just say it was a friend of a friend."

Emily made a sad face. "Oh, okay. You're not going to tell me much, are you?"

Jeev sighed. "I'm afraid not.". Emily looked at the tall lanky figure stretched out on the stone steps facing the river, a rare bright London sun shining on his brown skin. "You are quite confident in your ability to achieve your goals." Jeev sat up on his elbows and shielded the sun from his eyes as he looked at Emily's glowing white face and supple lips, "Confident yes, life however had a way of adding many twists and turns. The puppet master up there" he said pointing upwards at the sky "has many tricks to play on us. So, what actually happens we will have to wait and see. All I know is that I have to keep trying no matter the odds."

He then switched topics to Nietzsche. As they continued their discussion, Jeev was half present, thinking about how he would miss the time spent with Emily.

"Jeev... are you alright?" asked Emily, her blue eyes wide with concern.

"Ah, yes. I'm only tired."

"Well, I need to get back to the Savoy, before that busybody Agnes returns from running errands."

"Tomorrow in the library, then?" asked Jeev

"Yes, see you then." Emily flashed him a smile, and Jeev almost forgot to breathe.

Emily returned to the Savoy and went to the front desk to get her key. "Miss Emily Calvert?" asked a male clerk.

"Yes, I'm Emily Calvert."

"A gentleman called on you today and left you a note." The clerk handed her a piece of paper. Emily did not recognize the handwriting. She thanked the clerk and went up to her room. Agnes had not yet returned, so she had the entire suite to herself. She sat down at the tea table and read the note. It was from Captain Burke:

> *Dear Miss Calvert, I called on you today,*
> *but you were not present. It is vital for your health*
> *and safety that you stay inside the hotel and*
> *not leave for any reason until I come back to see*
> *you this evening. I have booked a table for 7:00*
> *at the Grill. Regards, Captain Sean Burke*

Emily clenched her teeth and balled her fist, crumpling up the note. *Damn Captain Burke! Who does he think I am? Some weak little woman who has to be protected...* Emily took a deep breath. Sean only had her best interests at heart. However, his overbearing sense of responsibility was demeaning to her own sense of individuality. Before she could continue musing, Agnes returned with armloads of shopping bags. Emily helped her sort through the various stockings, handkerchiefs, tea cannisters, and other random items that Emily had put on her list to keep Agnes busy while she enjoyed Jeev's company.

When Captain Burke arrived promptly at 6:55, Emily was ready.

"Hello, Captain Burke," said Emily, rising before Agnes could announce Sean's arrival. "I'm ready." Sean smiled as she took his arm and they walked to the restaurant.

When they were seated at their table, Sean began to speak. "There's a search going on for all the suffragette rioters." Sean swirled the whiskey in his glass. Emily took a small sip of her sherry. He continued. "Some of the key members of the organization have fled to France. Since you are on the list of speakers, the authorities want to interrogate you. It's just a matter of time before they come here to the Savoy. Also, you need to be careful about your friends. Being associated with the wrong people can create more problems than you could imagine."

"What am I to do then?" asked Emily, suddenly alert, thinking of Jeev. *How could Captain Burke know? Has he been spying on me?* Then she remembered the men that Sean was watching during their first dinner at the Savoy Grill. One of them was Jeev! Emily almost gasped in astonishment.

"I've managed to pull some strings with people I know. Your name will be removed from the list. On the one condition that you leave the country now. There will be no further problems from the police. The RMS Mauretania leaves Southampton in three days. I've got you a ticket."

Emily swallowed. She felt sad. "Is there no other choice?"

"No, Emily. There isn't."

Emily held back her tears and looked defiantly at Sean. "Well, *Sean*, then I'll leave."

"Good", Sean replied. He reached for Emily's hand, but she withdrew it. Her speech was over. She did not want to be a prisoner in England, and her head still hurt from the blows, but she would not shame herself by asking for help. She was a modern woman. She did not need some damn fool riding in on a white horse to rescue her. The food came, and Emily and Sean ate mostly in silence, which they only broke intermittently to talk about the weather and flower gardens.

CHAPTER 31: GIVE ME LIBERTY

Emily wanted to cry as she walked to the library to bid Jeev goodbye. Being with him, whether in the library or walking along the Thames, was both comforting and thrilling, something she dared not think about as she strode briskly down the street, head held high. Then she saw Jeev, at the top of the library steps. He walked down to meet her. One tear fell loose from her eye, she wiped it away with her silk handkerchief, hoping Jeev would not notice.

"Emily, how are you?"

Emily did her best to smile. "I'm fine."

"Why don't we walk along the Thames? I want to talk without being thrown out of the library."

Emily chuckled. "Sounds good to me." In the chilly morning, the area was deserted and quiet. A light fog hung over the water like a curtain that covered the windows but did not reach the floor. Emily slipped her hand in Jeev's hand, to his surprise, and they walked quietly, neither one speaking. The silence said it all. They strolled to their usual spot, overlooking the river.

"I have to tell you something" Emily blurted "You need to be careful, there is someone looking for you." Jeev stared at her in shock. "Captain Sean Burke, a friend of my family, saw you at the Savoy having dinner. I know you are a militant." Emily stared right at Jeev with her wide eyes.

Jeev felt a mixture of astonishment and gratitude. He

struggled to find the words. They had stopped walking and were facing each other. He placed both his hands lightly on her shoulders. "You knew and did not tell him about me?" Emily shook her head.

"Why? I may be dangerous," he retorted, there was a moment of silence and they both burst out laughing. The morning sun struggled against the thick mist that lay over the river. Chimney smoke filled the air and mingled with the mist. The two friends walked, hands clasped, on the banks of the river, with the Tower of London in the distance. Goodbyes are never easy.

Two days later, Emily strode along the bustling Southampton docks. The steady flow of passengers and cargo kept her moving in a zig-zag pattern. Sean had driven her to a hotel near the port the previous day. Neither of them talked about anything during the trip, as the road noise hindered conversation, and neither of them wanted to talk. Emily's mind wandered. She wondered what Jeev was doing. Where exactly was he going? Could he be here at this port, right now?

Suddenly, she gasped. All thoughts of Jeev vanished. Emily stared up at the largest ship she had ever seen. It had RMS Titanic in huge letters across its hull. *Why didn't Sean book me on that ship instead? That would be a* dream *trip! What else can I expect from him? Nothing but disappointment.* Scowling, she walked towards the Mauretania, which to her surprise, was not much smaller than the Titanic. *Well, maybe my journey won't be so bad at all... If only I had gotten to go to Paris!* Emily sighed. After all, life never went as planned.

While Emily wandered along the Southampton docks, Sean was at a nearby building, reading a telegram from the Royal Army Intelligence Corps. After reading, he folded the paper and tucked it in his brown, civilian jacket. It confirmed exactly what he had expected. He drove to a run-down café near the docks where he met some of his fellow officers, also dressed in civilian clothes. Sitting down at a corner table, out of earshot of other customers, Sean spoke in hushed tones. "Men, I just received a telegram from the Intelligence Corps. The ship, RMS Patterson, has a passenger named Tony Fernandez heading to Amsterdam. Fernandez fits the description of Stephen Pereira. Fernandez was seen by a Metropolitan Police officer in London yesterday boarding a train for Southampton."

"Sir," a short, balding man whispered, "this sounds like the man we followed to a cheap hotel nearby. He's in his room right now, and we are awaiting your instructions."

Sean smiled and was careful not to shout. "First, board the boat and search it inside out. I do not want him to slip aboard and leave. Next, three of us will go into the hotel and arrest him. "

Sean nodded at the short balding man, who stood up. "I will get the local constabulary and go to the Patterson, sir."

Sean again nodded and rose up with the other three men and walked to the hotel where Jeev was staying. A bored clerk, half asleep, looked warily at the four men when they walked in. "What do you want?" The man glared at them with blurry gray eyes.

"Do you have a Tony Fernandez staying here?" asked Sean.

"Who want to know?" growled the clerk.

Sean whipped out his dog tags from underneath his shirt. "Captain Sean Burke, His Majesty's Armed Forces."

The clerk did not look impressed. "No, we've got no one here by that name."

"Well then, do you have a short guest with brown skin, black hair, glasses, and a goatee?"

"No, no goat man here."

Sean sighed. "What about a brown-skinned with black hair, a beard, mustache and no glasses?"

"We've got more than one of those." The clerk smirked.

"Our man arrived sometime yesterday," Sean added.

"Room 204" replied the clerk nonchalantly, handing Sean a key to Jeev's room.

Two floors above, Jeev was peering through his streaky, net curtained window, when he saw Sean and his men head towards the hotel. The hairs on the back of his neck prickled. He knew trouble was coming. Grabbing his bag, he ran out of the room and took the stairs, two at a time, to the roof and jumped to the adjoining building. Opening a door to that building, he rushed down the stairs and out into the streets.

By the time Sean opened the door, hotel room 204 was empty. "Damn! He's flown the coop!" Sean and his men briefly searched the room, but there was no trace of Jeev or his belongings. They ran outside, but once again, Jeev was nowhere to be seen.

Meanwhile, Jeev was running towards the dock, heading out to the RMS Patterson. As Jeev approached the ship, he saw police officers guarding the gangplank and several on the deck, arguing with the captain. His cover blown, he rushed in the opposite direction, towards the other side of the dock. Two humongous ships were up ahead. Slowing down, and taking a deep breath, Jeev walked into the first ticket booth. He pulled out his wallet. "Give me a ticket for that ship," he said, pointing at the Titanic.

"You want a ticket on the RMS Titanic?" the collector laughed at Jeev. "Those tickets have been sold out for months." Still chuckling, he continued, "I have a few tickets left for the Mauretania, also going to New York. "

"Yes, one adult please," requested Jeev.

"First class?" asked the collector, having fun with Jeev.

When Jeev opened his wallet, he was shocked at the amount of money he had, which was more than enough for a first-class ticket. Splurging on luxury, however, would be foolish, as the last thing he needed was to draw attention to himself. Also, the future was uncertain and extra money would be useful. "The cheapest one, please," Jeev politely replied, presenting his travel documents. Suddenly, Jeev realized that he still had his ticket for Amsterdam. After collecting his ticket for the Mauretania, he asked, "I have a ticket to Amsterdam on the RMS Patterson. Could you give me a refund?"

The ticket collector frowned. "I'm afraid not." He pointed to a group of men standing across from the docks and lowered his voice. "I am not supposed to say this, but those people may buy the ticket from you."

Jeev strolled over to the men and sold his Amsterdam ticket at a steep discount and headed towards the Mauretania, which had three separate gangways, first class, second class, and the third class. Each was appropriately decorated, the first with polished mahogany walkways and stairs, fresh white flowers and ship's officers greeting the passengers, the second with shiny metal railings and a carpeted walkway, and the third with a solid unpainted slippery staircase. Jeev presented his papers and climbed up the slippery staircase. On boarding the ship, he was handed a bedding and a blanket and directed toward a large hall deep in the bowels of the ship. When he entered the room, families had already started claiming their places, staking out areas for the journey ahead. Jeev placed his blanket and bedding near an unoccupied porthole and sat down on the floor, wondering where this journey was going to take him. England was no longer safe but what trials and tribulations would his next destination bring?

While Jeev pondered, Emily walked towards the Mauretania, wondering where Sean was. She assumed that he would be there to see her off if only to make sure that she got on the ship. The hotel had arranged for her bags to be transferred to the ship. An attendant then unpacked and hung her clothes in her cabin, ready for her to wear.

Sean, meanwhile, having lost track of Jeev, rushed to the RMS Paterson. *Why, why didn't I lay a trap for Pereira, Sen, Fernandez, whatever the hell his name is instead of rushing to that hotel?* He glanced at his watch and nearly jumped. It was time for Emily's ship to sail. Sean sprinted to the main docks. Emily had already boarded the ship. He looked up and scanned the ship's deck, where he saw Emily waving at him. He grinned and waved back. The Mauretania sailed away, black smoke bellowing from its smokestacks. Sean watched it vanish onto the horizon with regret. He hated to see Emily go, as she was beautiful and charming. At the same time, however, he was relieved that he did not have to be accountable for her risky, capricious behavior.

As he turned away, one of his officers ran up to him. "A man matching our description bought a third-class ticket on that ship," pointing toward the Mauretania.

Sean slapped his hand on his forehead in frustration. "Too late to stop that ship. Send a message to the captain to search and detain him. He won't be hard to spot. There can't be many people who look like him on board. They make a stop in Liverpool before crossing the Atlantic. We can pick him up there."

Emily stood on the deck, watching the shoreline in the distance. It certainly had been an interesting trip. She had grown as a person; the girl had turned into a woman. She was confident about what she was doing in life and who she would become. She would become a lawyer and fight for the right for women to vote in America. She would expand her organization to cater not only to white women but to colored people, Asians, and American Indians.

While Emily was musing, a well-built blonde ship officer

strolled up to her and talked to her about the ship. "We recently crossed the Atlantic in the shortest amount of time ever " he proudly explained and went into details around how big the ship was, how many passengers and crew it carried and how many tons of coal it needed to cross the Atlantic. "I have all the numbers in my head," he told Emily. She smiled and politely asked a few relevant questions.

In the middle of his description of the cargo area of the ship, a deckhand ran up to him and gave him a note. Emily glanced at the paper, and the officer made no attempt to hide it.

"Ooh, what do you have there?" Emily did her best to appear innocent and wide-eyed.

"It seems we have a 'Person of Interest' the officer said puffing out his chest with self-importance.

"Can I read it?" asked Emily, trying not to appear too eager. The officer handed her the paper. Emily quickly scanned the contents, which described a Tony Fernandez, an Indian with Portuguese papers, travelling in third class, who was a dangerous militant and was to be apprehended right away. There was a description of him as tall, thin, with black hair, brown skin, long mustache, and beard. Emily shivered. The wanted man was Jeev. She must find him and warn him.

The officer misinterpreted Emily's reaction. "He should not be hard to find," said the officer, "Don't worry, you are in no danger, Miss Calvert. Now you must excuse me".

As he turned and left, Emily took a deep breath, pulled up her skirts, and hurried toward the second- and third-class areas. Catching a deck hand looking at her oddly, she let down her skirts, approached him, and grinned. "I'm just getting some exercise."

"That's fine, ma'am." May I do anything for you?" the sailor asked.

"Yes, where is the third-class section? I want to avoid it,

if possible, when walking."

He pointed to a door leading down to the lower decks, "Don't go down that steep flight of stairs and you will be fine."

Once the deckhand was out of sight, she opened the door and descended. She came to the large hall holding the third-class passengers, frantically searching for Jeev. None of the ship's officers were there. They all had other things to do, and considering they were an entire day away from reaching Liverpool, they had plenty of time to search for and apprehend the person of interest. Everyone on board was trapped until the next port of call.

Then she saw Jeev staring out of a small porthole. Walking up to him, she called out "Stephen".

He turned around, shocked, surprised, and happy at the same time. "Emily, you are going back on this ship".

Emily grasped his hand. "Come with me, you are in danger," she whispered. "Say nothing. Gather your things and come with me. " He grabbed his bag, leaving the blanket and mattress on the floor. "Keep your money and documents with you. Toss everything else overboard," commanded Emily. He placed his documents and money envelope in his pockets. As they passed one of the lower decks, he looked around and discreetly threw his bag into the water. Emily then held out her hand. "Lock your hands in mine, as if we are a couple and walk confidently with me." They walked right up to the guard at the entrance in the first-class section. Jeev felt nervous as they approached the guard. Emily smiled at the guard. He tipped his hat, greeting them, and opened the door to let them in. She guided him into her cabin and locked the door behind them. They both felt relieved and sat down.

"Well," said Emily, "Now I too have broken the law, so you better tell me everything, Stephen. What have I gotten myself into?"

Jeev sighed. "My name is Jeev Sen, not Stephen." He started with the assassination attempt on the Viceroy. Emily was stunned. Had she acted in haste, harboring a wanted person, a spy, or even a terrorist? She looked deeply into Jeev's eyes. There was nothing malicious, nor did she feel any danger. She had sought him out to save him from prison and likely death. Morality is a two-sided coin, she assessed. She was dedicating her life to fight for the oppressed, and so was Jeev. While the ends may not always justify the means, he was morally justified in his actions. Encouraged by her continued attention, Jeev kept talking and then described his ongoing attempts to buy weapons from Germany. He had already explained the philosophy of his life to Emily. Now he gave her the details.

As he laid bare his soul to Emily, he felt he owed it to her, as this was the second time, she had saved his life. If she wanted, she could have easily told Sean about him and had him captured. His only regret was that he was now involving her in an international conspiracy. "So now you know everything about me. If you continue to hide me here and we are discovered, there could be severe consequences for you. I think it would be best if I left, and I will find some way out," pleaded Jeev.

Emily was silent for a moment, considering all the options. Shaking her head, she explained, "They will find you. This is the only place you can hide. I will help you get to New York, where you can better conceal yourself." Having little choice, Jeev agreed. If he were caught and sent to India or England, he would certainly hang.

"Just a minute, Emily…" Emily caught a brief flicker of fear in Jeev's eyes that vanished as quickly as it appeared. "We need a signal, a secret knock."

Emily looked perplexed. "A secret knock? For what?"

"So that I know it's you, and you know it's me."

"Oh, I get it." The seriousness of Jeev's circumstances hit Emily. This was not the adventurous game she had imagined when she led him to her room.

"Are you okay?" Jeev asked, looking concerned.

"I'm fine!" Emily's face brightened with a forced smile. "Why not this?" Emily rapped her knuckles twice quickly on her writing desk, paused briefly, and then knocked once more.

"Umm... I think this would be clearer." Jeev repeated Emily's knock, adding another quick knock at the end, for a total of four knocks in all.

"I hear what you mean." The second knock at the end leaves no doubt."

Jeev grinned. "Good. We've got our signal."

Emily looked out her cabin window at the darkening sky. "Jeev, you stay here. I'm going out to get us some food." Jeev nodded, picked up a book and began to read. Emily rose and left the room. While on her way to the dining room, she passed a cabin left open by a cleaning attendant. Seeing no one around, she casually stepped inside. It was empty. She went into the bathroom and grabbed a razor, a brush and shaving soap. On a whim she also stepped into a closet bursting full of shirts, pants, and jackets, all, in her estimation, in Jeev's size. Emily gasped. *There is no way this man will miss a few of these clothes!* Emily quickly scanned the hallway and room. They were still empty, so she grabbed a few items and went back to her cabin, knocking the pattern of the secret knock, before opening the door. She handed the loot to a surprised Jeev. "Here, shave your mustache and beard, and put on these clothes. I'm going out again to get us some food."

The ship's officer's search for Tony Fernandez was futile. While the ship's manifest showed that Fernandez boarded the ship, he was nowhere to be found. A thorough search of the entire third-class section yielded nothing, not even his luggage. Another passenger had taken Fernandez's blanket and mattress, so there was no evidence left. The officers concluded he likely decided not to sail and left the ship. They sent a telegram to the Intelligence Corps informing them the man was not on board.

When Sean heard of the search, he was furious. "They must search the entire ship! Cargo, boiler room, second, and even first class! I don't care what the captain says!" Sean balled his fist and struck his desk.

The private who had brought him the message gulped. "Sir, what are we to do now?"

Sean picked up his telephone. "I'm going make a call." The private turned and left the room. Sean dialed the undersecretary of the War Office, who then commanded the captain to search the entire ship, including the first-class cabins. The captain was unwilling to have his first-class passengers subjected to a search and refused. He knew, however, that when the ship docked at Liverpool, he would have to comply whether he wanted to or not.

Meanwhile, Jeev stayed hidden in Emily's cabin, sleeping comfortably on her sitting room sofa, and hiding in the bathroom when strangers came to the door. Emily sweet-talked the cabin attendant into not cleaning her rooms and delivering food to her cabin, giving him a generous tip for his discretion. The attendant gladly acquiesced, as he was used to the eccentricities of the leisure class. Oh, the tales he could tell of some of the strangest requests he had received over the years.

Three days later, the Mauretania docked at Liverpool, where Sean, with a group of military intelligence officers and the local police, boarded the ship and conducted an exhaustive search, looking everywhere from the lifeboats to the engine rooms, to the first-class cabins.

Emily soon heard the officers knocking on the first-class

cabins down the hallway, along with angry protests of elite passengers. "Jeev! They'll be here soon! Hide in the bathroom closet."

"Umm... won't they be looking in all the closets?"

"Don't worry! I've got a plan." Jeev went and hid. Emily ran to her bath, took off all her clothes, and jumped in the tub, just as there was a knock at her door. Emily did not answer.

"Captain Burke, there is no answer. Should we use the master key to enter?" inquired the officer.

Sean looked at the room number and sighed. It was Emily's room. "Yes, give me the key." Sean unlocked the door and entered the cabin. Everything was neat and orderly, although there was a slight lingering odor of coffee and oranges. The officer began going through drawers, opening closets, and making a careful, efficient search with a minimum of disruption.

Seeing no sign of his former charge, Sean called out, "Emily, are you here?"

"In the bath," Emily replied. Sean gently opened the bathroom door and peeked inside. Emily sat up and grinned at him. She was naked. Sean gasped, quickly averted his eyes, and shut the bathroom door. He heard Emily laughing.

"Sorry, sorry," he apologized from behind the door. "Have a pleasant trip," he called out, hastily retreating. "Come on, Cooper. We're done here." Sean hoped that Cooper had not heard his conversation with Emily. Sean glanced at him. There was no sniggering, blushing, or any other sign that Cooper had heard anything untoward. Sean beckoned him and the two men left.

Jeev heard the front door of the cabin close and came out of the closet. Emily lay in the tub, the water barely covering her legs. Her head leant back against the side as she smiled in relief. He moved towards her, kissing her soft lips. "Thank you, thank you," he whispered to her. They held each other tight as the stress ebbed away. Jeev took off his clothes and climbed into the bathtub with her. The water level rose with the weight of another body in the warm tub. They clasped each other firmly, reassured of their safety.

Suddenly, a loud horn blew, and the engines of the ship trembled to life. The huge steam powered turbines pushed the pistons, steam flowing out with each push. Slowly, the pistons gathered speed as the vibrations of the engine shook the skin of the ship. Propellers churned the waters of the sea frothy as the ship slowly moved forward, gently parting the waters as it made its way into the ocean. The pistons pushed faster and harder till the ship achieved its cruising speed. The two lovers in the warm bath water relaxed, still locked in a snug embrace.

CHAPTER 32: NEW YORK SOCIALISTS

Sean, infuriated at losing Stephen, drove back to London. When he arrived at his office, he was greeted by a colonel from the War Office. Sean saluted. "Let's go into your office, Captain Burke. I've got some news." Sean led the way and let the colonel sit at his desk while he took a chair in front. The colonel spoke. "The Amsterdam Office has found Herr Franz von Oppenheim. He arrived in Amsterdam yesterday and checked into a hotel by the docks."

"That's good news, sir," replied Sean. "We'll be able to keep an eye on him."

"Now, take charge captain. Don't lose your Indian again" The colonel rose and left. Sean sent a telegraph to the Amsterdam Office requesting a full-time shadow on von Oppenheim, hoping that Jeev or Stephen or Tony would also appear in Holland.

Emily stared out her cabin window watching the gentle breeze blowing across calm waves. The sky was a vivid light blue and sunlight sparkled on the crests of the waves.

Jeev came over and sat beside her. He gently put his arm over her shoulders and pulled her towards him. "It's hard to believe that danger could be so near."

Emily choked up. "Yes. All those people... and I was so irritated that Captain Burke didn't get me a ticket for the Titanic."

"I tried to buy a ticket on that ship, myself. The ticket

collector laughed and said all the tickets were sold months ago."

Emily gave a hollow laugh. "I guess that we're both lucky despite ourselves."

Jeev chuckled. "That means that this ship won't sink, then."

"Tell that to all the passengers who disembarked in Ireland when they heard the news... Maybe we should have too. Ireland is so beautiful..."

"But like so many beautiful places, it's troubled. Besides, what would we do with ourselves there? We both have our causes to fight for, and Ireland's not one of them."

Emily sighed. "You're right. I'm only glad this ship is moving slowly and alert for icebergs. I need to get myself together before I get home."

"I think that you're very 'together'," said Jeev, whispering as he kissed her.

Later that afternoon, Emily entered the cabin after a foray for food. She closed the door and went over to Jeev, who was sitting on the drawing room sofa, reading. "Jeev! Look what I found!" She then dumped the contents of the white canvas bag she was carrying onto the coffee table in front of Jeev.

"Emily, where did you get these?" asked Jeev, looking at the shoes, clothing, and jacket.

Emily smirked. "I found them in an unoccupied cabin. People really should be more careful about shutting and locking their doors."

"And so should the attendants," added Jeev.

"I've taken care of that," said Emily. "A little generosity goes a long way."

Jeev tried on a pair of black leather shoes, which fit

perfectly. "You don't think these items will be missed? What if someone sees me wearing them?"

Emily laughed. "Men and women travelling first class have so many clothes and shoes that they don't even know what they have. Besides, I take a little here, a little there, and I don't take anything loud, monogrammed, or too distinctive."

"All the better for discretion," added Jeev.

Emily looked at him over from head to toe. "Not only for discretion." Emily reached over and stroked Jeev's now clean-shaven face. "You're much more handsome as well. Captain Burke would never recognize you, now."

A tightening in Jeev's stomach reminded him that Burke knew exactly what he looked like without the mustache and beard, but he did not tell Emily. Instead, he smiled and said, "Nor would the officers on this ship."

"Well, then kind sir, you may escort me to dinner." Jeev took her hand and they walked to the first-class dining room. To all appearances, they were just another wealthy couple, keeping a low profile while enjoying all the luxurious amenities on offer.

After a few days of peaceful weather and pampering, Emily and Jeev looked out their cabin window and saw the New York City skyline, distinctly visible against the cloudless sky. When they docked, Jeev assumed the identity of Tony Fernandez, the Portuguese trader and was quickly processed through immigration. He and Emily then caught a horse-drawn carriage to Emily's townhouse.

Three days after arriving at Emily's home, Jeev and Emily were enjoying a light lunch of tea and sandwiches. Jeev nibbled the crustless white bread, and barely tasted the chicken salad filling, which was a bit too salty for his taste. Emily noticed his hesitation and asked, "What's the matter, Jeev? Are the sandwiches all right?"

Jeev straightened up and finished chewing. "Everything's fine. I just don't feel right taking advantage of your hospitality."

Emily laughed. "That's not the only thing you're taking advantage of, and it's no problem at all."

"I don't mean your kindness, Emily," said Jeev. "I care for you, and I don't want you put in danger because of me."

"You can hide. You did on the ship. Besides, no one knows about you here in America."

"But they do know you. It's best that you don't let anyone know about me." Emily started to protest, but before she could speak, Jeev said, "if they find out about me, I could be in danger too."

Emily gulped and lowered her head. "I'm sorry. I just enjoy having you're here so much... and I really want you to meet Arti."

"Your parents are arriving in a few days. I've found a small apartment in Harlem. The rent is cheap, and I've got the money to cover it. I'll be moving out tomorrow. Please, Emily, don't tell anyone about me."

Emily pouted. "Even Arti?"

"Yes, even Arti. The fewer people know about me, the safer we both are."

"What will you do?"

Jeev did his best to remain calm. "I've written to Mr. Sarkar, explaining what happened and asking if he has any contacts in New York. I should hear something back soon."

Emily walked over to Jeev, and he folded her into his arms and stroked her hair. "It's all right, Emily. It's going to be all right." Jeev wished he could believe so himself.

Jeev received no reply from Mr. Sarkar, until a few weeks later when someone knocked on his apartment door. Jeev crept to the door and looked through the peephole. He saw a stocky, middle-aged man in a brown suit and brown bowler hat with a rolled brim. Jeev unlocked the door, and opened it slightly, keeping the chain on. "Hello? How may I help you?"

"Hello, Mr. Fernandez. My name is Norman Harrington from the Democratic Socialist Party. Our mutual acquaintance, Mr. Iqbal Sarkar, sent me."

Jeev unfastened the chain and opened the door just enough for Harrington to enter. "Come in Mr. Harrington. My home is small, and I have nothing to offer you." Harrington scanned Jeev's dingy apartment, with its ratty sofa, straight backed wood chairs, and worn carpet.

"Why don't we go to the café around the corner and talk? They've got good roast beef sandwiches and coffee." Jeev agreed, and followed Harrington to the restaurant, making sure to lock his door on the way out.

Once at the restaurant, the men settled at a table in the center of the restaurant, away from the many white net curtained windows. "What do you know about political philosophy?" asked Harrington, taking a sip of strong black coffee.

Jeev took a sip of his sweet black tea and replied. "I find it fascinating. I've read Marx, Mill, Locke, and many others."

"Are you familiar with the Democratic Socialist Party?"

"No, not exactly, but I know what democracy and socialism are. I'm going to venture that your organization favors labor unions and the advancement of the oppressed as do I."

Harrington smiled. "You've got it right. I think that we're going to get along well, very well indeed. That doesn't mean, however, that you don't have lots to learn. Why not attend some of our meetings and get to know us and what we stand for?"

"Sounds interesting," said Jeev, slightly disappointed. Attending party meetings would not help him get arms from Germany to support his cause.

Harrington took another sip of coffee. "Of course, you need a job. There's a place open at our newspaper. You'd be a journalist. Think you could handle that?"

Jeev was thrilled. "Yes, I can." While not conducive to his original goal, a job would help his finances stretch further until he could figure out the next step of his plan.

"Good then..." Their food arrived; two massive roast beef sandwiches accompanied by potato salad. Both men dug in, saving further conversation for after the meal.

As they finished their meal, and drank the last of their coffee and tea, Norman said to Jeev, "You will meet a lot of interesting people working at the newspaper, and most of them are German immigrants" he winked at Jeev. He handed him a slip of paper with an address written on it. "Report here tomorrow morning at 9:00."

"I will," Jeev said with enthusiasm. Harrington grinned. Both men left the restaurant and went their respective ways.

Jeev arrived at the address at 8:50 the next morning, having given himself extra time to find the location and get used to walking in a new city. Jeev looked around. He took out the slip of paper Harrington had given him. It was the right address... Then he saw a small wooden board with 'The Working Man' written on it on the entrance to a four-story walkup building on the corner of 20th and 3rd Avenue. *This must be it.* Jeev entered the building and walked up the four flights to the top floor, where he saw a door with a sign reading 'The Workingman.'

He opened the door to a long, narrow corridor. Four people, all hunched over typewriters, barely looked up when he walked in. At the end of the corridor was a closed door with a sign reading 'Editor'. On the left side of the corridor was a large glass window. Peering through it, he saw a variety of idle printing machines. Jeev knocked on the editor's door. A gruff voice called out "yes?" Jeev entered the office. Seated inside, behind a desk, was a large bald man with thick glasses, parts of his body protruded from gaps in the chair. If the man got up, the chair would remain attached to him. He had an unlit cigar in his mouth and a stack of handwritten papers in front of him. Periodically, he crossed out words and sentences with a red pencil.

Norman was sitting in front of the desk, and he pointed towards a chair where he could sit. Jeev sat in silence until the heavy-set man stopped his corrections, adjusted his glasses, and studied Jeev. "So, this is the Hindu we are hiring?" He looked at Norman and then back at Jeev, who wanted to point out that the name Tony Fernandez would make him a Roman Catholic but thought better of saying anything. "Stan Wagner," he introduced himself. "Norman will give you your assignments and show you around the place. All your work will go through him. Here are your notepad and pencil," he said handing Jeev the two items. "Good luck."

Norman walked him to an empty desk with a typewriter. "This will be your desk. On the other side of the wall is the printing press and the cutting and folding machines. The machines start in the evening and work throughout the night, so we can send out the newspapers early in the morning. We used to publish once a week. We are now publishing every weekday. Five papers a week. You will follow me for the first week while I show you the ropes." He introduced Jeev to the four people in the office. The two women working there were typists The other two were journalists. Norman then grabbed his hat and jacket saying, "Let's go Tony, we have a meeting to cover."

"A Democratic Socialist meeting?"

"Yes, a meeting of the Democratic Socialist Party of New York. It's a short walk over in Midtown."

When they arrived, the hall was sparsely filled, with people scattered in small groups throughout the hall. A speaker was droning on about the recent victory of the Socialist Party of Germany in the Reichstag elections. Thumping his fist on the podium, the speaker called out, "The Kaiser's power is in danger! The Liberals and Conservatives will soon be defeated, and the Socialists will take over Germany and most of Europe! It is time for the Socialist Party to rise and contest all American elections! The next few years will be the rise of Socialism..."

Norman and Jeev took seats at the back of the hall. "Tony, take out your notebook and pencil and take notes on what all the speakers are saying." Jeev took out his pad and pencil and started writing. He struggled to understand all the words due to the speakers strong accents as they spoke about " a world in which workers rights were supreme...curtailing the ability of the rich to take profits...in order to maximize profits cost have to be minimized...the biggest cost is labor.....so capitalism exploits the laborers.....that's why slavery had been a great model for capitalism....own the labor as well as the machines and raw materials...the politicians have given power to and written laws to favor the rich factory owners.....we need to change this by electing our own politicians and rewriting the laws...."

When he got back to the office, Jeev looked over his notes, which mainly covered one long speech. The speaker had railed against capitalism and painted socialism as a blissful utopia of well-paying, secure jobs and free education and healthcare for all. Jeev realized why the hall was nearly empty. The speaker did not tell how utopia could be achieved. Jeev put some paper in his typewriter and began typing his first article as Tony Fernandez, journalist.

The problem with the socialist agenda is that it strives for perfection. It creates a vision of a utopian society that can never be achieved because the vision so disrupts existing society that it can never gain the support it needs to manifest itself. The vision can only be achieved through absolute power and control over every aspect of the nation, the military, the factories, and the entire economy.

The problem with this scenario is that absolute power corrupts absolutely. Once a party or person attains that power, the incentive is no longer for the betterment of the people but rather the preservation of existing power. Today's corrupt Democratic politicians would merely be replaced by tomorrow's corrupt Socialist leaders.

The only way forward is to reform the current government by evolution not revolution. Karl Marx himself did not approve of drastic changes, rather he recommended implementing changes slowly and verifying those changes helped rather than harm. To win elections, Socialists must address this issue and provide pathways to achieve this without collapsing a productive economy.

Jeev presented his finished article to Stan Wagner for approval. The editor read it, then chewed on his cigar, then read it again, before throwing it on the floor. Dejected, Jeev bent down to pick up his article and walked out of the room. Stan yelled after him, "I want that printed in tomorrow's paper." Jeev's mood raced from sad to ecstatic. He was going to be published!

Norman patted him on the back, "Good going son, now go find something else to write." The article, while controversial, established Tony Fernandez's reputation as a journalist.

Meanwhile in London, Sean stared at the telegram

from the Royal Intelligence Corps office in New York. He had requested that they let him know if Stephen Pereira or Tony Fernandez had disembarked from the Mauretania. It took several long weeks to obtain the paperwork from the Cunard Cruise Line. According to the telegram, a Portuguese trader named Tony Fernandez matching his militant's name had indeed disembarked in New York. Sean balled his fist, crumpling the telegram. How could this Jeev Sen or Stephen Pereira or Tony Fernandez keep escaping his clutches? Sean would get him, someday, somehow.

"How are things going at the paper?" Emily asked Jeev as she poured him a cup of tea.

Jeev leaned back on Emily's green velvet settee, took a sip of tea, and smiled. "I'm doing something useful, covering politics, while earning enough to support myself and save a bit. I feel that I've done more here in the few months than I did in all the time I was in England."

Emily looked pensive. "I just wish we had more time together."

"I do to, Emily, but you've got your Women's Rights Society, final exams, and you'll be going to law school this autumn."

"Don't remind me," Emily sighed. "Sometimes it seems overwhelming, but the work has to be done. Our causes are much bigger than we are."

"We agree on that." Jeev concurred.

"Can't you get some coverage in your paper for women's rights? If women aren't free…"

"You do know that if I did… it wouldn't be me covering the story."

Emily looked downcast. "You don't want to be seen with me… for my safety."

"And mine. I've got to keep a low profile, and we've got to be discreet."

"I know, but I don't like it." Jeev put down his tea and pulled her close. If only...

The next day, Jeev was in Stan Wagner's office. "Stan, what about some stories about the women's rights movement? They have some interesting angles on workers' rights."

Stan burst out laughing. "Our newspaper is the Workingman, not the Workingwoman!" He kept laughing until he choked on the unlit cigar that was always in his mouth. Jeev secretly hoped that Stan would swallow the cigar and end his tenure as editor.

A few months later, Jeev stood on a railroad platform, staring at the tracks. His mind wandered back to when he last talked to Stan. Having several months and several noteworthy articles published, Jeev, or Tony as his co-workers knew him, had significant credibility. Jeev remembered taking a deep breath and knocking on Stan's door.

"Come in!" the editor barked. Jeev entered. "What do you want?" Stan growled.

Jeev stood tall and remained calm. "I'm sure you know about the Women's March in Washington DC on March 3."

"Yes. What about it?"

"We should have someone to go there and cover it. It's a major event."

Stan leaned back in his chair, as much as his girth allowed. "You think it'll be the biggest story of 1913, do you?" Stan laughed raucously.

"I don't know about that, but it is significant. Bedsides, were would the Socialist Party be without our women members?"

Stan stopped laughing. "You do have a point. The story

would appeal to our female readers." He then leaned forward and resumed his stern expression. "You can go to Washington, but on your own dime. The paper's not going to cover your expenses."

"Thank you, Stan. I'll make my own arrangements to go. "You won't regret this," Jeev said, thankful that he had enough money saved to cover the trip.

"I certainly hope so. If not, your head is on the block, no matter how high and mighty you think you are." Jeev nodded and left.

A tap on his shoulder brought Jeev back to the present. Startled, he turned around to see Emily with a big smile on her face and next to her, a pretty Indian girl, her body filled out in all the right places, wearing a white blouse, a dark blue jacket over a matching long skirt, leather shoes and a light blue hat with an embroidered blue rose.

"Hello, Tony. I'd like you to meet Arti, my close friend and fellow student at Hunter College. Arti, this is Tony Fernandez, a journalist for The Working Man newspaper, which I believe needs to change its name to The Working People or just The People." Emily laughed.

Arti and Jeev shook hands. Jeev looked at Arti. There was something familiar about her. Arti also looked at Jeev. Had she seen him somewhere before? Who was this tall, brown-skinned man with a clean-shaven face, dark suit with a bow tie, glasses, a bowler hat over broad shoulders?

They sat in the train, Jeev on one side, Emily and Arti facing him, with a table in between. "So where in India are you from? " Asked Jeev.

Arti chuckled. "I am from St. Thomas Island," replied Arti, who did not want to acknowledge her life before then. Jeev dropped the topic, and conversation turned to the upcoming march and inauguration in Washington DC.

That evening in his Washington DC hotel room, Jeev was grateful that the Women's March had passed without incident. Despite of, or perhaps due to, the enormous number of participants, spectators, and police, peace had been maintained. Emily gave an eloquent speech that was enthusiastically received, and which Jeev, as Tony, covered for The Working Man:

March 3, 1913- Miss Emily Calvert, student at Hunter College and head of The Women's Rights Society of New York, addressed the Women's Suffrage Movement in Washington DC. The crowd numbered in the thousands. The women were all well-dressed, many wearing evening gowns. The colorful spectacle was purposely designed to show that women are unique, intelligent, proud of themselves and their bodies and are not afraid to fight for their rights. There was a large police presence and Miss Calvert addressed that in her speech. She said that violence was not the answer to the problem. She had seen violence in London and, thus, could not advocate such a response. Some say that women do not have the education, the reasoning, or the independent thinking to vote. That such important decisions are better left to the men to decide and that women are better suited for domestic duty. Miss Calvert emphasized that because women excel at domestic duty, they have skills with organization, managing money, leadership and giving instructions. So, the argument that women are unfit to vote is baseless. Rather, women are better suited to vote than men. The speech continued, expanding the demands of the feminists beyond just the right to vote. Miss Calvert argued that feminists should work towards equality of men and women in access to education and jobs and both sexes should have equal pay. She stated that marriage is a legal and spiritual merger between equal partners and women must not be asked to obey their husbands. Also, custom and convention should not be used to classify women into a subservient

*class. Rather, each woman should be free to make
her own choices and have her own property. And
finally, she declared that the feminist movement
is not confined to the United States or England; it
is an international movement, which should lead
to the freedom of all women across the world.*

*If Miss Calvert is right and the
feminist movement is successful, our paper
may change its name to one that better
reflects the equality of all workers.*

After finishing the article, Jeev met Emily at Lafayette Park. He showed her what he had written. "What do you think?"

Emily took a few minutes to read his story, moving her finger underneath each handwritten line. Finally, she looked up, grinning. "Good job, Tony. You chronicled our success very well."

"From what I've heard and read here in Washington, I'm not the only one."

Emily chuckled. "It's certainly a different experience from London."

"That's true..." said Jeev softly, thinking of his walks and talks with Emily along the Thames.

"Tony, Arti, and I are going to take a few days off and visit my parents in Maryland. We would love for you to come with us."

"Thank you, Emily, but I really don't think that would be a good idea."

"Why not?" Emily pouted.

Jeev sighed. "You know why. Besides, I must get back to work."

"If you must." Emily looked disappointed.

Jeev took hold of Emily's hand and kissed it. "Goodbye, Emily. I'll see you in New York."

"Goodbye... Jeev," Emily muttered.

With a lump in his throat, Jeev turned around and headed to the train station, back to his life as Tony Fernandez.

CHAPTER 33:
THE SPARK FOR
FREEDOM (1914)

Sitting at his desk at The Working Man, Jeev stared at the newspaper in front of him. A teenage boy in Serbia had been arrested for assassinating Archduke Franz Ferdinand of Austria-Hungary and his wife, Sophie, the Duchess of Hohenberg. A chill went down Jeev's spine as the thought of his own assassination plot of the Viceroy of India came to his mind. Had he succeeded, would his picture have been splashed across the papers of the world? Would that have been enough of a spark to light the fire of freedom in India?

An alternate reality of events flashed by in Jeev's mind in photographic clarity. The Viceroy was assassinated. All the militants were killed in the attempt, except for him. The British captured him, arrested him for high treason, then sentenced him to death. While imprisoned in Delhi awaiting the execution, he, with help from a group of accomplices, made a daring break. They escaped to the Andaman Islands, where militants had already captured the town of Port Blair. A hero's welcome awaited him, as he was declared the General of the militants. He formed his own army, the Indian Democratic Alliance. Ships bearing arms from Germany and Japan arrived at Port Blair, now renamed Port Jeev. He declared war on Great Britain and sailed a flotilla of ships towards Calcutta. Upon hearing the news of the fleet, a general strike broke out nationwide. Uprisings occurred in every major city.

Fires burned in Delhi, Calcutta, Bombay and Madras. His troops met minimal resistance and quickly assumed control of Calcutta. Throngs of people welcomed him as moved into the Government House the former home of the Viceroy of India. He stood on the steps of the palace and gave a stirring speech to the people of the new democracy. His military swelled into hundreds of thousands of troops. He directed one force to head towards Delhi and another towards Bombay. Within two months, both cities fell, and the British fled. He called the British generals and offered an ultimatum, leave the Indian sub-continent, or face his military to the end. They agreed to leave; the country was now free. He declared national elections and was elected the Prime Minister of Free India.

"Tony, in my office! Now!" Stan's hoarse voice startled Jeev out of his reverie. As he got up and walked to Stan's office, he smiled and thought to himself, *well that was a good daydream!*

Jeev took a seat beside Norman in Stan's office. Stan had several local newspapers, including the New York Times and the New York Post spread on his desk. All papers showed the same story, the assassination of Archduke Ferdinand. Stan's eyes looked weary. He was not his usual irascible self. "There were two attempts on the archduke's life. The first attempt was earlier in the day. Someone tossed a bomb at him which he brushed away only for it to explode after his car had passed, injuring some of his staff."

"What about the second attempt?" asked Norman.

"Later that day, the archduke and the duchess were on the way to the hospital to visit their injured staff members, when they were shot directly by a young Serbian man. I've lived in Germany and Austria. I know these people. This will have consequences. There will definitely be a war. There is much hatred between the Austrians and the Serbians. Austria's ally is Germany and Serbia's ally is Russia. I know Austria will wage war against Serbia to punish them. It will mean Germany and Russia will also join." Norman and Jeev were speechless. Stan straightened up, pulled out a pad of paper and wrote down some names. He tore the paper off the pad and handed it to Jeev. "Tony, get statements from these men. They're all Socialist Party leaders, and many of them are German immigrants." Jeev took the list, nodded, and left the office.

An hour later, Jeev was sitting in a diner eating doughnuts and sipping strong, black coffee with a stout, muscular man in his early forties. After some preliminary niceties, Jeev took out his pad and pencil. "Herr Friedrich, tell me about yourself. When did you come to America?

Herr Friedrich chuckled. "You can call me Ludwig if you want. I do not believe in formality."

Jeev smiled, "Okay, Ludwig, when did you come to America?"

"I came to America twenty years ago. My home was a small village near Berlin. Having experience working with iron, I soon found work in New York, especially as I was willing to work on the most dangerous, hardest projects. I did my job well, and was soon made a foreman, which meant I taught others how to do their jobs well."

"You worked on the Woolworth Tower, didn't you?" asked Jeev.

"Yes, I did. I'm proud of the work my men and I did there, but to do well, is not just knowing how to do the job. To do well is to be well paid and well-treated. That is why I joined the Iron Workers Union and the Democratic Socialist Party." Ludwig put down his coffee and pushed his doughnut plate away. "I know that you did not come here to talk about me."

"Well, you are part of the story," said Jeev.

"No, I am not, but I do know about the story, and I am happy to share what I know with you." Ludwig took a deep breath. "The primary responsibility for this terrible tragedy rests on one man, Kaiser Wilhelm. If Austria punishes Serbia, which they will, they take some land and then stop. There will then be peace in Europe. Otherwise, Austria will annex most of Serbia. It will force Russia to come to aid and attack Austria. Germany will retaliate if Austria is attacked and declare war on Russia. It is just a matter of time before Italy and France are also embroiled in the war. The Imperial German Army should not be taken lightly. They can easily overrun the continent. War will also break out in other parts of the world controlled by the colonial powers," narrated Ludwig. Jeev's pencil moved furiously as he took notes.

Meanwhile, on the other side of the pond, recently promoted Major Sean Burke shuffled the stacks of papers on his desk. The events taking place in continental Europe were disturbing. Britain could soon be at war with Germany. The Royal Intelligence Corps was tasked with gathering information on German sympathizers in England, of which there were many. It was his and his team's job to find and detain them. Sean palmed in forehead in desperation. If only he could capture Jeev or Stephen or Tony or whoever the hell he was! Sean sighed. At least Iqbal Sarkar was no longer protected by the Prime Minister's office. According to the paper Sean was reading, Sarkar and his family had fled to Ireland but had now been apprehended. That was one down. There were many more to go. The jails would soon be full of people who might even have a remote propensity to aid the enemy. The country was hurtling towards war and there was no leniency. A rap on the door broke Sean's musings. "Come in," he commanded, sitting up straight, and jogging the papers on his desk.

Also newly promoted Lieutenant Cooper entered. "Good day, sir." saluted.

"At ease, Cooper. What news do you have?" asked Sean, looking at the telegram in his hand.

"Good news. There was a raid on the Swamy's house in Calcutta. Everyone in the house was arrested and imprisoned."

"Everyone?" Cooper nodded. "Any information divulged?"

"Yes. Some of the boys sang like birds, telling everything they knew."

"Did they have any information about the attack on the viceroy's train?" Sean was so eager he could hardly breathe.

"Yes. We know who was responsible and how they did it. The main instigator was Jeev Sen."

"I knew it!" Sean pounded his fist on the desk and added the information to the growing file on his primary target.

A few weeks later, Sean was on his way to New York. Unable to sleep, he paced the deck and stared out at the star-filled sky and moonlit sea, thinking about the changes to come. War had broken out in Europe and British forces were now in France, holding the Germans back. He would soon be called to fight, and perhaps die, for his country. After disembarking, he planned to catch a train to Washington to stay with his parents. He then thought of Emily. Her blonde beauty and vibrant personality still enchanted him, but now was no time to start courting. His job was to focus on his given task: setting up a joint counter espionage task force with the US Department of Justice. Nothing else mattered now.

A few days later, Sean was sitting in the dark paneled ambience at Old Ebbitt Grill in Washington DC enjoying steak and potatoes washed down with cold beer. "Do you think the United States will enter the war?" he asked his companion, Craig Baker, a special agent with the US Department of Justice Investigations Bureau.

"That remains to be seen. Some Americans are eager to help your side. Others want to stay out what they see as a foreign problem, and still others want a national referendum."

"Hopefully, we won't need your help to fight…"

"You do have our help tracking down people of interest. My job is to track down and apprehend these people. Our government has no interest in harboring agitators or militants." Both men having finished their meals, Sean handed Baker his file on Jeev Sen aka Stephen Pereira aka Tony Fernandez. Baker scanned through the file and looked up at Sean. "Ahh… we've already found him."

"Where is he?" asked Sean, speaking more rapidly than usual.

"He's in New York, working as a reporter under the name Tony Fernandez. Do you want to be present when we arrest him?" he inquired.

Sean was thrilled. "Yes, I will be there."

It was just another day in New York. Jeev walked to the Working Man newspaper offices. He noticed some strange men hanging around outside but thought nothing of them. As soon as he arrived at his desk, however, one of the men, wearing a gray suit, approached him. "Tony Fernandez, I presume?"

Something about the man wasn't right, but Jeev had nowhere to run. "Yes, I'm Tony Fernandez. What can I do for you?" Jeev saw another man enter the room, standing behind the man in the gray suit. The man looked familiar but out of place. Where had he seen him before?

"Mr. Fernandez, or should I say Jeev Sen. He flashed his badge. I am arresting you for grand espionage against the United States." Jeev froze. In a split second, he pulled out a pair of handcuffs and manacled Jeev's hands.

"Just a damn minute! Who do you think you are coming into my paper? Tony's one of my ace reporters!" Stan stood in the doorway and screamed, his face red, and his cigar chewed in half.

Norman stood beside Stan, glowering at the two strange

men. "Who the hell are you? What right do you have to come in here and harass one of the finest reporters in the city?"

The gray-suited man grinned and flashed his badge again. "Good morning, gentlemen. I am Special Agent Craig Baker with the US Department of Justice and I have every right to be here. Like I said, this man is a militant who has committed grand espionage against the United States. Stan and Norman both opened their mouths to protest, but Agent Baker continued. "Also," he said, looking toward the other man who came in with him, "Major Burke here has a petition for Sen's or Fernandez's extradition to the United Kingdom for the murder of two British Army officers and a plot to assassinate the Viceroy of India." Stan and Norman both went silent and backed off. Jeev was on his own.

Jeev looked up, right into Sean Burke's eyes. Burke's eyes were cold, but Jeev saw a small smile of satisfaction on his face. Jeev strove to remain calm. He looked back at Sean with defiance. He would never show Captain, now Major, Burke any sign of weakness even if he were being hanged. Baker and Burke walked Jeev out to a waiting car and drove him to Sing Sing Prison, in Ossining, New York, on the Hudson River, just outside of New York City. Jeev's handcuffs were removed. He was registered, processed, and given a black and white striped prison uniform. He was then led to a small cell, with a cot, small desk, chair, toilet, and sink. Jeev stared at a blank white wall as the cell door was locked behind him.

That evening, Craig and Sean sat, drinking cold beer, and waiting for roast beef sandwiches, in a red leather booth tucked at the back of a wood paneled bar in Manhattan. Muttered conversation surrounded them, interspersed the clink of glasses. Craig leaned forward, so that Sean could clearly hear what he was saying. "I've asked for a quick hearing so that Jeev Sen can be efficiently processed and handed over to you. The only problem is that a hearing here could take weeks to schedule."

Sean sighed. "That's rough. I need to get Jeev Sen back to Britain. We need information about the whereabouts of the Berlin Committee."

"Ah, a little fish to catch the big fish?"

"Correct."

"Well, we can only hope that some liberal judge doesn't allow Sen multiple appeals or let him go. As you may know, there are many judges here who have no sympathy for the British, and strictly speaking, Sen has committed no major crimes in New York."

Sean looked down. How could he have come this far only to have Jeev slip away again? "What are we going to do? I can't return to Britain empty handed."

"Well, there is one judge I know who would be sympathetic to our cause. Let me see what I can do."

A week later, Emily came down to breakfast to see Arti reading the newspaper with intense focus. Arti beckoned her, pointing to her newspaper. "What's so interesting?" she asked her friend.

Arti jumped slightly and turned to face Emily. "It's your friend, Tony. He's been arrested for being a spy."

"What?" Emily froze.

"It's right here, on the front page of the paper. He's going on trial today in Ossining, near the prison.

"What time?"

"This morning at 10:00."

Emily glanced at her watch. "It's 7:00 now, so we've got time to get there. Let's eat quickly and go."

Emily drove quickly and nimbly, but recklessly enough to make Arti feel nauseous. She was relieved when they reached the courthouse, about fifteen minutes before the trial was to start. The Ossining courthouse was a small white two story building shaped like a barn with a bell tower on top and a wraparound porch in the front and side. On the day of the trial, people were gathered outside the courthouse waiting to get in and the normally empty street was packed with parked cars and carriages. The sleepy hamlet on the Hudson River had been thrust into the spotlight with the trial of the Indian terrorist. They sat in Emily's car and stared at the crowd entering the courthouse.

"Wow, who knew an Asian Indian spy would be such a big story?" Arti said, her voice trembling.

"I think it's the fact that it's unexpected. What serious grievances would somebody from India have against the United States? None of which I can think."

"Do you think he's guilty?" asked Arti.

Emily looked pensive. "No, Arti, I don't." *And whatever he did, his actions were morally justified. All people deserve dignity and freedom.*

The train of Emily's thoughts came to a crashing halt when she saw the prison van pull up to the courthouse steps. As Jeev stepped out of the vehicle, he looked out and noticed Emily and Arti. He gave them a courageous smile before being pushed inside the courthouse. The bailiff asked the prison guards to stay outside. He then removed Jeev's handcuffs and led him to a waiting room "You will sit here until we are ready to bring you into the courtroom."

After Jeev entered the courthouse, Emily and Arti got out of the car and followed him. The courtroom was packed. Emily and Arti saw Stan and Norman sitting close to the front row. Just as she started to approach them, she saw Sean Burke sitting at the front with a gray-suited man. Emily put her hand on Arti's arm. "Arti let's get a seat at the back. We'll be more comfortable there." Arti nodded, and the women discretely slid into the back of the public gallery. They sat next to an elderly woman who at once turned to Emma "I came to see the Indian terrorist. I imagine he must look like Gunga Din; you know from the Rudyard Kipling poem." Emily turned her face away from the woman in disgust.

Jeev stared straight ahead, avoiding the gaze of the passing public as he was escorted towards the now filled courtroom. There had to be some way to escape… Then Jeev saw the toilet signs. "Please Sir, I need to use the lavatory." Jeev pleaded.

The guard, at first, hesitated, then led him to the restroom, peering inside to make sure no one was there. He then said, "Make it quick, " closed the door, and stood outside. There was a small window above the toilet. It was jammed shut, but he was able to pry it open. Jeev glanced around to make sure he was alone. Glancing outside, he realized he was looking at the backyard of the building. There was no one visible. He pulled himself up to the window and twisted and turned till he squeezed out. The drop to the bottom was much more than he had predicted, the grass, however, cushioned his fall. In front of him was the river, behind him the courthouse. Peering from the corner of the building he saw Emily's bright blue car parked by the curb. Stooping low, he followed a tall hedge till he was close, then ran to the car and opened the trunk. *Luck is on my side,* thought Jeev, *first the window in the bathroom and now the open trunk.* He slid inside the trunk slowly, closing the lid and waited. *Now I have to hope for a miracle.*

It took a few minutes for the bailiff to notice that Jeev was not coming out. He rushed into the stall and saw the open window, then ran into the courtroom. "He escaped!" He yelled. Sean, Craig, and the guards rushed outside, spreading out in all directions.

"Come on Arti, let's go," said Emily, keeping her eye on Sean. Arti did not protest, and they exited the courtroom and walked back to the car as unobtrusively as possible.

They reached the car without any hassle. Emily took a deep breath and went around to the back of the car. The trunk door was ajar. She glanced around to see if anyone was watching. Then she knocked twice quickly on the trunk, waited, and then repeated the same knock. She then heard the same knock in response. *Their secret knock, Jeev was inside.* Calmly, she pushed the trunk shut. "Come on, Arti. We're leaving." Arti climbed into the passenger seat and Emily got in on the driver's side, started the car, and drove away.

Meanwhile, the courthouse was in chaos. "Where in the hell is Sen?" exclaimed Sean. "He can't just have vanished, again."

"The most likely place is the Hudson River. It's wide, with forests and cliffs on both sides, which means lots of places to hide. We'll get a search party and search every nook and cranny of the riverbanks until we find him."

"Do it!" commanded Sean. Soon a search party was organized, complete with bloodhounds. Despite their best efforts, Jeev was not found. "Could he have swam to the other side?" Sean speculated.

Craig Baker looked out at the wide river. "Not likely, but we'll search there just in case." The search party broke up into two parts, and one part searched the other side of the river to no avail.

Emily drove for a few minutes before she looked at Arti and said, "He is in the trunk." Arti opened her mouth to speak but was too shocked, she closed her mouth and stared ahead. They drove in silence until they reached the townhouse Emily and Arti remained silent until they reached the townhouse. Emily scanned the street and houses. When she was sure no one was looking, she and Arti went around to the trunk and opened it. Jeev's hand flew up to his eyes, as the sun blinded him. "Emily, thank God it's you."

"You need to get out, Jeev, quickly, now." Emily and Arti both held their noses, as the sour smell of Jeev's sweat wafted out of the trunk. Jeev sat up. With Emily taking him by one wet arm and Arti the other, he managed to climb out and stand up straight. They then moved as rapidly as possible into the townhouse. Once inside, Emily locked the door. "Arti, I have a job for you." Emily took some money out of her purse and handed it to Arti. "I want you to go buy Jeev some nice clothes. Get him a suit, shirt, shoes, and hat. Don't forget to get underwear and socks." Arti blushed, put the money in her purse, and left. Emily then went to the backyard, which was a courtyard fenced off with a high stone wall. There were also tall shade trees giving extra privacy as well as shade. She started a fire. "Take off your clothes," Emily ordered Jeev. Jeev complied. Emily threw them on the fire. They both watched his prison garments go up in flames. Jeev looked at Emily with immense gratitude. She looked back at him and smiled. No words needed to be said, nor would they have sufficed.

Emily then led Jeev back inside and ran a bath for him. The hot water soothed his aching, cramped muscles, making him feel strong and healthy enough to take on not only Major Sean Burke, but the whole British Army.

After bathing, Emily provided Jeev with a dark red velvet robe that while roomy, felt smooth and soft against his skin. He walked into the drawing room and sat on the sofa. Emily was pouring hot Darjeeling tea from a silver teapot.

"Ah, I haven't had a cup of hot tea in days." Jeev said. The steaming sweet liquid coursed through his body, going right to his toes.

"Enjoy. There's plenty where that came from." Emily looked at Jeev with soft eyes. Jeev put down his tea, leaned over… Then the door opened.

"Emily, I'm back!" called out Arti. Both Emily and Jeev let out sighs of relief. Arti came into the sitting room with several shopping bags, which she placed on the coffee table. She then sat down. Emily poured her a cup of tea, and the three sat in silence, exhausted by the turn of events.

The next day, after a good night's sleep, Jeev realized that he needed to get in touch with Norman. After breakfast, he put on a long trench coat, hat, and gloves, and walked to Norman's house. Jeev took a circuitous route, moving down alleys and side streets, to avoid being seen. Finally, he arrived at Norman's apartment building, went up to the second floor, and knocked on his friend's door. Norman opened the door a crack, keeping on the chain. "Who is it?" he asked.

"Tony Fernandez," whispered Jeev. Norman took off the chain and let him in.

"How are you?" asked Norman breathlessly. Jeev caught a brief flash of fear in his expression. How could his friend be afraid of him?

Jeev remained calm. "I'm well, thank you."

"Well, why don't you take off your coat and sit down?" Jeev pulled off his trench coat and sat down in Norman's worn, brown, tufted leather sofa. Norman sat across from Jeev in a big oxblood leather armchair. "Do you have a place to hide for a few days?" Norman asked. Jeev nodded. "The less I tell you the better it will be for you, but I do need travel papers can you get them for me?"

"Come back in two weeks. I will have some papers for you. For now, do not go outside. They're looking for you everywhere." Norman rose and walked to the door. Jeev took the hint, put on his coat, and left, tipping his hat to thank his friend.

Unfortunately for Sean and Craig, they were not looking everywhere for Jeev. "Why can't the Justice Department step in and do a statewide search? Why not a regional search? We British wouldn't put up with such foolishness," said Sean, staring out Craig's office window at the street outside.

"I didn't follow normal protocols and cut too many corners trying to get the case rushed through." Craig did not even try to look at Sean. "Also, the Sing-Sing Prison authorities didn't want their failure publicized. I've been called back to DC."

"I'm going back home to England. There's nothing else I can do here." Sean continued looking out the window.

"You may not have caught your man, but he is now wanted by the Bureau of Investigation in New York."

Sean gave a hollow laugh. "What good is that?"

"Well, he can't work as a journalist or appear in public. His face is on posters across the country. Somebody will see him."

"I certainly hope so," said Sean, as he got up and left.

Jeev, meanwhile, stayed hidden in Emily's townhouse. Jeev entered the dining room one morning, to see Emily reading the morning paper, holding a piece of toast with grape jelly aloft, a cup of cold coffee by her side. "Good morning, Emily. What is going on?"

Emily looked up; her face paler than usual. "Take a look at this." She held up the front page of the paper. The headline read 'RMS Lusitania sunk by U-boat." Jeev looked at her quizzically. What did this mean?

Emily swallowed and explained. "There were several hundred Americans on board the ship and are feared lost."

"Oh, Emily... that's terrible..." Jeev walked over and hugged Emily as she leaned her head into his chest.

That afternoon, Arti brought over a copy of the Working Man paper. Jeev turned the pages and found Stan's editorial. According to Stan, Germany was justified in the ship's sinking as it was carrying munitions from the United States to Britain.

Since the passenger ship had been converted into or used partially for military purposes, Germany was within its rights to sink the ship. "Arti don't let Emily see this," said Jeev.

Arti came over and scanned the article. "That's rough! You know though, that you can't hide anything from her."

"She was so upset this morning reading about the Lusitania."

"She'll be even more upset if you try to shield her from anything."

"You're right." Jeev sighed in frustration.

About a week later, while they were having tea in the drawing room, Emily presented Jeev with new travel papers. "Your friend Norman came through for you. He met me at the University yesterday and gave me this package. He told me to tell you not to try and contact him as he is going away for a while. The Workingman has been shut down."

Jeev blinked back tears. "Do you have any idea where he might be?"

"No," sighed Emily. "He's gone underground, like Stan did."

"Stan risked everything for that editorial and lost. I thought you were supposed to have freedom of speech."

"Sedition is a limit. You can't instigate violence against the government, and that's what the paper was advocating, at least according to the FBI."

"What do you think? You're going to be a lawyer."

Emily sighed. "I don't know. Stan's editorial was wrong and foolish, but not worth destroying his life for. I'm glad he and Norman escaped before their trials. I just hope that wherever they are, they are free."

"Me too," said Jeev.

Jeev opened his travel papers. They identified him as Miguel Sanchez. Inside the passport was a folded note. Jeev opened it. It was from Norman:

Tony, the safest place for you is Mexico. Germany has operations there, so you can make contacts. German operations in the US are being decimated as the US will soon join the war in Europe. There is no room here for German sympathizers, and there is great suspicion of Germans, especially recent immigrants. – Norman

Jeev asked Emily, "How am I going to get out of the US? If I could escape to Canada, that would be easy, but it's a long way from New York to Mexico."

"That's what these are for," said Emily, pulling out a stack of railway timetables from a small cabinet. She placed them on the coffee table. "The best way to get to Mexico is by train from New York to San Antonio, which is on the border, cross the Rio Grande and then on to Mexico City."

"Sounds like a sensible plan," said Jeev.

"Oh, by the way... I'm coming with you."

Jeev, horrified, drew in his breath rapidly, and exclaimed, "Definitely not. It is far too dangerous."

"What if I come with you to the Mexican border and you can go from there? " Emily insisted.

"Will you then go back to New York?"

"Of course!" said Emily, with a sweet smile, crossing her fingers behind her back.

Jeev sighed. "Oh, all right..." He knew there was no point in arguing. He also knew that she would not leave him at the border. She was too reckless and headstrong for her own, and his own, good.

"Goody!" Emily face brightened with anticipation. "Now,

let's get to the details."

Jeev reached into the documents Norman sent, and found a sizeable amount of cash, in US dollars. Counting the money, he calculated that it would last him a few months in the US and longer in Mexico, where things were cheaper. "Money's not a problem," he told Emily.

"I have money" Emily said softly without looking at Jeev "I've contacted a professor and mentor of mine, Enrico Garcia. He's an acclaimed lawyer who's practiced both in the US and Mexico. He's currently on an extended assignment in New York, teaching at my university and giving speeches at various law schools around the country."

"How is that going to help?" Jeev was skeptical.

Emily looked smug. "He's advised and defended many top politicians and military officers, so he has excellent connections and is highly respected." Jeev started to speak, but Emily put a finger on his mouth and shushed him. "I told him I was going to Mexico City. I asked him to provide me with a contact in Mexico who could help me If needed."

"Who?" asked Jeev, wondering where the tale was leading.

Emily then reached into the cabinet and took out a letter. "This is a letter addressed to General Alvaro Obregon, one of Professor Garcia's closest friends. He is the leader of the Mexican Revolutionary Army and served under President Carranza."

"That's good," said Jeev, relieved that Emily at least had some protection.

Arti stopped the next day to help them plan the trip. The three of them gathered around the dining room table, where they spread out the train timetables and writing pads. "You did a good job organizing all this, Arti," Emily beamed with approval.

Arti chuckled. "That's my job. We law clerks have to have everything in the right place."

"As you will when you go to law school, and later when you practice," added Emily.

"If only..." said Arti, wistfully.

Before Emily could reply, Jeev entered the room. Emily looked up at him and smiled. He took a chair. He saw that the timetables were arranged in two separate groupings. "What is this? Are there two separate journeys or a choice of routes?"

"The latter," replied Arti. She pointed to the first grouping. "This route takes you from New Jersey to Washington, DC, where you'll change to a train to Atlanta. You'll then go from Atlanta to New Orleans, where you'll catch a slow train to San Antonio and then get a train to Laredo, where you'll cross the border."

"And the other option?" asked Jeev.

Arti pointed to the other grouping of timetables. "You leave from New York on an express train to Chicago. Then you go from Chicago to Fort Worth via either St. Louis or Kansas City. Then you catch a train from Fort Worth to San Antonio and then Laredo."

Jeev looked at Arti and her beautiful brown skin, the same color as his... "I think the train to Chicago will be best, don't you, Emily?" he asked, turning to face her.

"Yes, I think that would be wise. We've never been to Chicago, but we have been to Washington, so we might be recognized there."

"And going from there into the Deep South is not something I would do, and I definitely wouldn't recommend it for Jeev." Arti spoke in a soft, but authoritative, voice.

"The Chicago route, it is," said Jeev.

"I'll get the tickets. We can leave in a few days," said

Emily.

Arti's brow furrowed with concern. "What about your parents, Emily? They'll be worried about you."

Emily scowled. "Then I won't tell them! Why is it their business anyway? They can just assume I'm here in New York." Arti and Jeev looked doubtful. Emily took out a pen and started writing on her tablet. "Arti, I'm writing some brief notes. I want you to mail them to my parents at regular intervals. That way, they won't come here to check on me." Once again, Jeev sighed. The journey would be long, mostly uncomfortable, and dangerous, and like it or not, Emily would be with him.

The first leg of the journey was comfortable. Jeev and Emily travelled in first-class all the way to San Antonio. The train to Laredo, however, had no first-class accommodations, only wooden benches, and stifling heat. Along the way, Jeev and Emily spent endless hours in scintillating conversation. He stared at her hair now dyed a raven black. "It will help me blend it with the locals" she had said. Jeev knew the Emily was going to come with him all the way to Mexico City. She was enjoying traveling, the sights, the people, the smells, and the thrills. She loved adventure. He could see it in the brightness of her eyes, her frequent smiles, and relentless curiosity.

Disembarking at Laredo, they walked towards the river and stood on the north bank of the Rio Grande. As they stared at the moving water, a middle-aged man with a pronounced paunch, a broad-brimmed cowboy hat and long black mustache approached them. "Do you want to cross the river?" he asked. Jeev and Emily looked at each other and nodded in agreement. The man picked up their suitcases and walked towards a small wooden boat. Jeev and Emily followed.

"You help your wife get in the boat. I will load the suitcases," said the man, who assumed the two were husband and wife. Jeev and Emily smiled. That would be the perfect story as they entered Mexico.

CHAPTER 34: CROSSING THE RIO GRANDE

The low boat wobbled as the man in the cowboy hat and then Jeev stepped in. Once the luggage had been sorted and boat stopped shaking, Jeev held out his arms, took Emily by her waist, and lifted her into the boat, which the man gently rowed across the Rio Grande.

Jeev stood on the bow, looking back at the American shoreline as the boat moved towards Mexico. With his dark skin, six-foot height, round, black-rimmed glasses, and stubble on his face, Jeev looked quite athletic. His white shirt flapping against the wind contrasted with his black pants and black shoes. Emily sat near the stern. Under her wide cut, her black hair sporadically blew onto her face and her pale, ivory skin. Her black silk dress clung in all the right places to emphasize her womanly curves. She gazed in awe at the scenery as they crossed the river. The man with the cowboy hat sat on the center board, sweat rolling down his face as he worked on getting Jeev and Emily and the two leather suitcases containing everything they owned to the other side. In the distance was the town of Laredo, Texas, where a low bridge crossed the river. Looking at the bridge, Jeev told the man rowing the boat, "Do not take us to the border crossing at the bridge. We will get off further down the shoreline."

"Si, yes, Senor" replied the man, steering the boat in a slightly different direction. Emily looked confused at first, but soon realized what Jeev was thinking. *If we don't cross at the border, there will be no record of us leaving the US or entering Mexico. Much better to be sight unseen.*

They soon landed on the Mexican shoreline. Jeev and the man in the cowboy hat scrambled out of the boat with the luggage. Jeev than lifted Emily onto the riverbank. "Walk a mile that way" pointing at a dirt road, "it's about a mile to the town of Nuevo Laredo." "Thank you" said Jeev and handed him money, much more than he had asked for. "Gracias" said the man "be careful here. You are in bandido territory. Pancho Villa controls the land near here and Emiliano Zapata is in the South of the country." Emily and Jeev nodded nervously, picked up their suitcases and trudged down the dry sandy road towards the town in the distance. The man got back in his boat and rowed down the river looking for more passengers.

Jeev then turned to Emily and whispered, "Stay close, we have a long way to go." She looked at him and smiled. Jeev picked up the two suitcases, and they made their way down the dirt path towards Nuevo Laredo.

Emily looked around. The land was dry and desolate, as if no humans had ever crossed there. The sun was relentless. She had to squint her eyes to see, and the dry heat parched what delicate skin remained uncovered. Jeev, seeing her start to stumble, pulled her closer. "Be careful. We're in bandit territory."

"You mean, like Pancho Villa?"

"Yes, he's one, but there are many others. Even the Mexican Army is ruthless, and two foreigners, like us, would be easy pickings." Emily tapped her corset to verify that the letter from Professor Garcia was still there. She sighed with relief when she felt the paper nestled on her left side.

"Are you okay?" asked Jeev, concerned.

Emily smiled at him. "Yes, I'm fine..." Suddenly, she stopped and stared straight ahead. "What is that?" she said, pointing to a group of brick and adobe structures rising out the landscape ahead.

"That's Nuevo Laredo. Keep calm." Emily straightened her back and neutralized her facial expression. As they got closer to the town, they noticed that some buildings were piles of rubble, while others had large cracks, boarded windows, or other signs of damage. The people looked jaded, rarely smiling. Jeev and Emily were largely ignored, except for a few curious stares from local peasants. They headed down the main street and asked for directions to the railway station, where they found that the next train to Mexico City was in two days. They then found a small, nondescript hotel nearby and settled in.

Once in the simple plank floored room, Emily collapsed into a wooden armchair and unlaced and pulled off her boots. "What a walk! My feet are sore," she said, rubbing her narrow arches. I need a hot bath. You can join me if you wish."

"Sounds good," said Jeev, also weary and sweaty. Emily smiled, got up, and ran the bath.

Half an hour later, Jeev sat on the small pine bed, toweling off his naked body with a large, white cotton towel. Emily sat beside him, on the white cotton bedspread. Jeev looked at his "wife", smiled, and commented, "Who would have thought you would travel with me into Mexico."

Emily, however, did not look at him. Instead, she pulled her towel tightly around her body, as though she was about to freeze. "Professor Garcia told me that the problem is that Obregon is in the city of Merida in the Yucatan peninsula. That is all the way in the Southeast of Mexico. Not a simple place to get to, especially with the activities of Zapata. I am worried about how we can get that letter to him."

Jeev replied, "We first need to get to Mexico City. I will make some inquiries there on how to reach the General. There has to be a way of communicating with him from the military office there."

Emily relaxed and loosened her towel, but she still did not look at Jeev. She was silent, trying to take in the enormity of the changes in her life. She had traveled with Jeev to Mexico, naïve about the consequences. The danger was real.

Yet somehow, she was truly living her life, even if she was sitting on a rickety bed in the El Coyote Hotel in Nuevo Laredo, overlooking a dusty street. That night she heard random gunfire as horses galloped down the street. She kept her eyes closed tight and hoped the bullets did not come through the flimsy wooden walls.

Emily and Jeev spent the next day in the room. They dared not venture out, lest they get robbed or caught up in rebel activity. Jeev brought up some coffee and tacos from the bar downstairs, which they wolfed down with gusto.

Jeev and Emily rose early the next morning, packed their suitcases, and were at the station by 9:00 a.m. although the train to Mexico City did not leave for another hour. Much to their surprise, the Mexico City train was already there. Emily raced toward the ticket booth to get a seat. Jeev put a hand on her arm to restrain her. "Emily, let me buy the tickets."

"Okay," she said, looking puzzled. She waited as Jeev stood in line and paid for their passage.

He came back brandishing two tickets and handed one to Emily. "I got us a private cabin."

Emily pouted. "But I wanted to ride with the people! Everything and everyone is so colorful here!"

Jeev wanted to laugh but resisted. "You will be much more comfortable and much safer in our own cabin. With a hundred stops along the way, it doesn't make sense to expose ourselves to thieves or... worse."

"Would it really be that bad?" Emily whined.

"You would be riding on rough pine benches with extremely poor, desperate people. The second-class seats are for soldiers only, and I don't think you want to ride with the horses."

Emily chuckled, then sighed. "I guess you're right. Four days is a long journey, and who knows what could happen if we're not careful?"

Jeev pulled her close. "I wouldn't let anything happen to you. You know that don't you?"

"Yes, I do" whispered Emily.

The train whistle blew, startling Emily and Jeev out of their embrace. They rushed to board the luxury car and entered their richly appointed cabin, complete with dark teak bed, red leather armchairs, and a red and green patterned rug. "This isn't so bad," said Emily, cheering up.

"No, it isn't", agreed Jeev, thinking about the hunger and yearning of the peasants sitting on pine benches.

A long whistle and the groaning of the railroad cars as they moved forward broke Jeev's reverie. He glanced out the window to see if anyone was watching, but only saw a sleepy dog woken up by the train laying his head down in disgust to go back to sleep. The train chugged away towards Monterrey, the first major stop. The scattered farmhouses soon turned into vast forests and plains with mesquite, oak, cacti, and orchids.

Jeev took out a notebook and wrote the last few days' activities. He then looked out of the window, his hand supporting his chin and his mind drifted to another time and place–Bengal a few years ago. He was sitting with his friend Ramu, listening to Swamy give his usual anti-colonialism lecture. After the lecture was over, Swamy called the two of them over. "I have an assignment for you," he instructed. "You two will travel to Rangoon to meet with some men. They will supply us with arms. You will be our contacts there." Swamy rose from his seat and beckoned the boys. "Come with me. I have something to show you."

The three of them left in a horse-drawn carriage and traveled until Jeev lost track of time. Jeev stayed silent. He knew better than to ask questions. He devoted his life to the cause of independence at a youthful age and went along with any task that was placed before him. His easy-going manner and adaptability earned him the trust of Ramu and Swamy. As the sun was setting, they arrived at a small village. They stopped at a cowshed. Walking inside the shed, they were greeted with the smell of cow dung, hay, spilt milk, and mud.

There were a few red Sindhi cows tied by ropes to the side of the barn. An old frail man with a stick sat in the corner. He rose to greet them, and Jeev noticed that he was unshaven and wearing stained clothing. Swamy greeted him warmly, as did Ramu, and they introduced Jeev.

Swamy asked, "Is everything finished with the construction?" The man answered, "Yes, all is ready. Let me show you. " He walked over one of the cows and struck her with his stick, making her move toward the wall. He then took his stick and scraped the hay and cow dung on the ground, revealing a trapdoor. On the end of his stick was a hook that he inserted into a small hole in the door and swung the door upward, exposing a wooden staircase. They climbed down the stairs, and the man lit a kerosene lantern, illuminating a wide hall more than a hundred feet long. "This is where you will bring the arms from Rangoon," showed Swamy, pointing toward the large, empty room. They then walked out behind the barn, where Jeev could see a large lake. "These are the backwaters of the bay. During high tide, we can bring a boat right up to the barn. We can easily hide the arms underground until we are ready to use them," explained Swamy.

The next morning, they walked to the village dock. The tide was low, and many sailboats lay on their sides in the mud. All the boats were brightly painted in reds, greens, and blues, with colorful flags and pictures of Indian gods and goddesses. Many were named after Hindu deities, such as Durga, Laxmi, Arjun, and Krishna. The man they had met the night before came running down the path towards them. "Your boat is ready. Please come with me," he asked.

They walked to one of the fishing boats, still stuck in the mud. A crew of five shirtless, muscular men were shifting the boat into the water. "We will leave as soon as the tide comes in," said one of the men. Jeev realized he was going to Rangoon much sooner than he thought.

The trip to Rangoon lasted a few days, with stops to drag fishing nets. They sailed into the harbor with a hull full of shrimp and crabs. Jeev was shocked to see that most of the population of Rangoon was Indian. "Indian immigrant's control everything here, stores, trading, laborers, merchants... even the soldiers are Indian," explained Ramu. They asked a local for the location of the 'Shaw and Sah' store and then walked into the city.

The 'Shaw and Sah' store stood on busy Strand Street. Entering the store, Ramu and Jeev smelled ginger, cinnamon, cardamon, turmeric, and other spices, which along with various grains and sugar were stacked on shelves on one side of the store. The other side was piled high with brightly colored textiles and clothing. Two short, fat, bald men dressed in identical blue pants and white shirts navigated the store in bare feet, jumping from one customer to another. Ramu whispered to Jeev, "Those men are the store owners. They are identical twin brothers, named Shawarilal and Saharilal, hence the 'Shaw and Sah' name." Jeev nodded in assent.

Jeev's attention was soon drawn to a curvaceous young Burmese girl in the corner. She wore her hair in a large bun decorated with white jewelry and was dressed in a tight blouse with side buttons and a snug flowered skirt. She was busy taking customers' money and giving receipts, so she did not notice the two young men who had just come into the store.

Ramu and Jeev pretended to look at the merchandise, in between stealing glances at the pretty young woman, waiting for an opportune moment when either of the brothers would be free. It was not long before one brother approached Ramu. "What do you need?" he inquired.

"Swamy sent us," said Ramu.

The brother looked at them suspiciously, then told them, "Go wander around town, never come back to the store. I will meet you in the park in front of the Strand Hotel after the store closes around eight o'clock. By the way, my name is Shawarilal."

Jeev and Ramu strolled around the city, eating food from street vendors, marveling at the similarities between Rangoon and Calcutta, the stark contrasts of living standards between the impoverished and the elites, the muddy single room dwellings where large families somehow found room to sleep, and the mansions hidden behind lofty walls. Tired of walking, they found their way to a hotel and sat on a bench overlooking the river. Behind them was a large clock tower. Periodically they glanced backward, checking on the time. "It's amazing how time slows down when you are watching it," remarked Jeev. "And when you don't want it to slow down, it speeds up."

"Time goes at its own pace, always," Ramu stated. "It's the perception in the human mind that changes. You know, the Vedas discuss perception as a way of the attainment of a higher self. We study to gain knowledge, but that knowledge is based on our senses, which limits us to what we can see, hear, smell, or touch. Enhancement of our understanding of perception allows us to interpret the world beyond our senses. By extending our comprehension of the universe, we can raise our inner awareness and function as a being on a higher level."

One of the twin brothers approached them interrupting the conversation. "Mr. Shawarilal, good to see you," Ramu said as he came close.

"I am Mr. Saharilal," corrected the brother.

"It is easy to confuse you two," said an embarrassed Ramu. *Just our luck to get contacts who are identical twins*, thought Jeev. Mr. Saharilal sat down facing them and asked Jeev and Ramu many questions about Swamy. They answered him, not knowing where this line of questioning was going.

Finally, the man explained, "I needed to know you both are who you say you are. I am satisfied with your answers." Ramu and Jeev sighed in relief. He continued, "There is tremendous animosity towards the British here. We have been able to get arms from Japan and can arrange for them to be transported with you. Once the fight against the English starts in Calcutta, we have people who will rise against them in Rangoon as well. They will have to fight on multiple fronts. There are also Indian battalion leaders who will stop their soldiers from fighting for the British. Meet me here in three days at the same time. I will have instructions for you on the arms and the transport back to Calcutta." With a curt goodbye, he disappeared into the darkness. Jeev and Ramu, pleased to hear the news, strolled into the city's center to find a cheap hotel. They found a small inn run by a man who introduced himself as Deven Patel. Ramu paid him in cash for three nights, then asked for directions to the nearest bar.

Jeev, meanwhile, strolled around the neighborhood. As he walked down Merchant Avenue, he noticed a bookstore and at once stopped. "What in the hell do you think you're doing?" Ramu sneered.

"Looking at books!" Jeev exclaimed, exasperated.

"Well, go ahead. I'll be down at the bar further down the street. Meet me there when you're through." Ramu turned his back and walked off.

Jeev looked up at the bookstore's English language sign, which said 'Smart and Mookerdum: English Books'. Jeev entered the store and perused the used books section looking for something that was both interesting and affordable. He found two books, Descartes ' First meditations on Philosophy' and Baruch Espinosa's 'Ethics'. The books were worn out, with dog-eared pages and writing in the margins. He understood little of what was written, but that was the challenge for Jeev. The more difficult a book was to understand, the greater its value to him.

Ramu, meanwhile, walked into the bar, relieved to see a mixed crowd of Indians, British and Burmese. He sat at a table for two, ordered a beer, and looked around. A woman sitting at a table with an English officer looked familiar. As he peered through the murky light, he realized it was the young girl from the twin brothers' store. She was engaged in an earnest conversation with the officer. Ramu gulped down his beer and snuck out of the bar, not wanting her to recognize him, especially if she was friends with the enemy. As he walked out of the bar, he ran into Jeev, walking down the road with the books in his arms. "Jeev! Turn around and walk the other way! We've got to get out of here." Jeev looked shocked but did as Ramu said.

As they headed down the street, the young woman came out of the bar along with the officer. The young woman and the officer watched as the two men hurriedly walked away from the bar.

On the third day, they sat on the same bench and as one of the brothers approached, Ramu hailed him. "Mr. Saharilal, good to see you".

The man replied, "I am Mr. Shawarilal". Ramu muttered an apology, cursing under his breath for having identical twins as a contact on a shady arms deal. "Follow me," he commanded. They walked to a waiting carriage, and Mr. Shawarilal muttered something to the driver. The carriage started, and they rode out of the city into a forest, where they stopped by a river in front of a sawmill. Jeev and Ramu observed men steering makeshift rafts up to the riverbank, where the rafts were disassembled and the logs stacked into neat piles about twenty feet high, waiting to be cut, dried, treated and then loaded on ships to England or other parts of the empire.

Mr. Shawarilal led them to a large, weathered wood storage shed and opened the door. Inside was a single room with two small windows and a dirty floor piled with wooden crates. He grabbed a nearby crowbar and opened one crate to reveal several rifles and boxes of ammunition. "You will take ten of these boxes with you," he proudly said. Just then, the door of the shed opened again, and the young woman from the store came in. "Ah Miss Kyi Kyi, you are here," he exclaimed. "Miss Kyi Kyi will make a checklist of everything being delivered and will make the arrangements to load the cargo on the ship." Kyi Kyi smiled that them in a manner that was provocative and condescending at the same time. Ramu looked at her suspiciously. Jeev gave her a big smile and happily greeted her, still struck by her beauty, but most of all, not wanting to give away what he knew and Ramu had seen. They then examined the contents of the crate. Ramu and Jeev, thrilled at seeing the treasure trove of arms in front of them, were ecstatic that their mission was going well. Kyi Kyi and Mr. Shawarilal hastened towards the front door, "We are going to check on the second shed to see if there are any more boxes" said Kyi Kyi as they walked out.

Jeev paused. Something wasn't right. "Why are they in such a hurry?" he asked Ramu in a soft voice.

"Let's see..." said Ramu whispering. He moved to a window and looked out. He saw a soldier hiding behind a mound of logs. He saw glints of bayonets amongst other log piles as well. They were going to capture them as soon as they stepped outside the sheds. He strode over the Jeev and muttered. "It's a trap. Get a rifle and some bullets," he commanded. Jeev grabbed one rifle, but only the butt came in his hand. *Damn! Why can't they have them assembled?*

Kyi Kyi called out to them, "Come outside and look at the second shed."

Ramu shouted, "Coming!" to buy some time, and ran to the back of the shed, towards the other window. He gestured to Jeev, and they ran to the opening and climbed out. The shed was now behind them. In front was an open space and beyond that, the river. They ran towards the water. Suddenly, they heard shouts at the rear. "Come on! Faster!" commanded Ramu. They picked up speed. By the time their feet hit the water, the soldiers were at the back of the shed. They dove into the water. The soldiers pointed their rifles and started shooting at them.

Bullets struck and splashed around the boys in the surrounding water. Fortunately, both were excellent swimmers. They dove deep into the murky water and made sharp turns to swim with the current. Jeev stayed under water as long as he could, and then when he felt his lungs were about to burst, he surfaced and looked towards the shore. He saw the soldiers, along with Kyi Kyi, scanning the river. Up ahead, Ramu surfaced as well. The soldiers spotted them and fired again. The two at once submerged. When they reappeared, they were out of shooting range. They swam to the opposite riverbank and dragged themselves onshore, exhausted. The other side of the river was thickly forested. They scrambled through the underbrush, finally collapsing in a ditch surrounded by tall trees. They peered over the edge. Not seeing or hearing any gunshots or footsteps, they started walking upstream, away from the town.

The Irrawaddy riverbank was muddy, and the stench of stale fish permeated the air. The rainy season had just ended, and flood waters from a month ago had left the surrounding jungle wet, mossy, and putrid. Insects of all shapes and species crawled everywhere in search of food. The two men at first relentlessly smacked their clothes to get rid of the creepy crawlies. After a few hours of flailing their arms in desperation, they only scraped off the bugs that had attached themselves to their skin. As they continued their walk, Jeev saw a straight line ahead. "Look! What is that?", he said, pointing.

Ramu squinted his eyes and stared at the line, which now had something moving across it. "It's a bridge. A railroad bridge. Look how slowly the train moves over the bridge," observed Ramu. "We could board one easily."

"Sounds like a good plan to me," said Jeev, scraping more bugs off his skin.

"We'll have to wait until dark, so that no one sees us board." Later that night, as they were sitting next to the tracks, they heard a distant rumble followed by a light vibration. "A train is coming" announced Ramu, "get ready." They crouched in a ditch at the end of the bridge. As the last carriage passed them, they got up and ran towards the train, easily grabbing hold of the rails on the rear car. They pulled themselves up and, to their surprise, a couple of helping hands hauled them to the roof. The top of the train sloped slightly downwards in both directions. In the middle was a small flat area where someone could sit without sliding down. People sat on the roof over the entire length of the train. Jeev and Ramu found places to sit, nodding in appreciation at the people who helped them.

Up ahead, the engine horn sounded, and the roof passengers laid down flat and urged the two new passengers to do the same. Ahead, loomed an approaching tunnel. As they passed through the tunnel, the roof of the structure was just a few inches from their faces. Anyone who sat up would literally have their head handed to them. The smoke from the engine filled the shaft. They held their breaths until the short tunnel ended, then sat up gasping for air.

The train travelled through the night and most of the next day, often stopping at small stations. No one paid attention to the stowaways on the top of the train. They were told the last stop was the city of Mandalay. They discreetly asked one passenger how they could get back to Calcutta. He told them there were groups of people who travelled from Mandalay to Calcutta, and he would tell them where the groups started their journey.

On reaching Mandalay, they walked with the man they had met on the train to the outskirts of the town, where groups of people gathered around several bullock carts. He introduced them to the leader of the group, a gruffy, coarse man, constantly spitting and wiping his mouth on his shoulder. The leader looked at Jeev and Ramu with piercing dark eyes. "Do you want to walk or ride in the cart?"

"Which is cheaper?" asked Ramu.

The man scowled. "Walking of course"

"Then we'll walk," said Ramu. Jeev nodded in agreement, knowing that they did not have much money.

The group set out, walking towards the city of Chittagong in Bengal, about 310 miles away. They walked seven to eight hours every day, men, women, and children, with a few lucky, wealthy travelers riding the carts. The food was dry rice and chilies twice a day. Water came from the streams and rivers that they crossed.

For the first week, the group followed a flat dirt road, passing fields, small towns and rolling grassy hills. The ground, however, soon got steeper. A narrow path replaced the flat dirt track carved out by the wheels of bygone carts. They reached a village in the foothills of a mountain range. The group leader announced, "All carts stop here, at this village. Everyone must continue on foot from here!" Many of the cart passengers grumbled, while some of those traveling on foot smiled.

The next day, they all set out in single file, following a meandering path. One side of the mountain rose steeply skyward. On the other side, a rocky ravine led to a gurgling stream. The elderly in the group soon lagged as the precipitous incline and stifling heat took its toll. Jeev and Ramu trudged ahead, right behind the leader, who pointed at a towering peak in the distance. "This is the most dangerous part of the crossing. There are tribal people who live in the valley of that mountain who will not hesitate to take us prisoners."

Jeev suddenly looked up. He had broken into a sweat from his reminiscences of his young days. The train had stopped. A few soldiers were struggling to load horses onto the train. Emily was curled up on the bench, fast asleep. He heaved a sigh of relief.

CHAPTER 35: MEXICO CITY

By the third day on the train, the novelty of grand adventure had worn off. Although Jeev and Emily were insulated in their enclosed cabin, forays to the dining car reminded them of how raw life was for the unprivileged. Stepping outside their first-class compartment, they smelled the stench of coal, urine, tacos, and horses and saw how thoroughly soot had penetrated every inch of the train, including seats, clothing, and passengers' skin. Jeev and Emily got off at every station they could to get some fresh air and water. A guard told them, "We should be in Mexico City by nightfall." Both strained to understand his accent but got enough information out of his sentence for their spirits to rise. They spoke as little as possible to the locals or the guards, lest it become known that they were not Mexican. It was best to keep their identities hidden until they were safe.

The train chugged into Buenavista Station a little after sundown. A large sign reading 'Ferrocarriles Nacionales de Mexico' welcomed the arriving passengers. "Wow," Emily gasped. "This is so modern looking!"

"It was built just a few years ago as a hub for intercity travel," replied Jeev. They gathered their luggage, alighted from the train, and wove through the crowds to the main entrance.

As soon as they stepped out into the gaslit walkway, a carriage pulled by a pair of high-stepping black horses pulled up. The driver, a trim older man with black sideburns and a handlebar mustache looked at them. Emily asked him in her best Spanish, "We need to go to Hotel Geneva.". He nodded his head towards the two leather upholstered seats in the back.

"Hotel Geneva?" asked Jeev, muttering just loud enough to be heard over the street noise and clopping of horse hooves.

"It's safe," said Emily. "Lots of Americans and Europeans stay there. It's clean and safe with all the comforts of home. Mrs. Burke, a friend of my mother's, talked about it when she visited Mexico City a little while ago..."

Jeev, momentarily startled, looked away, not wanting Emily to see his expression. *Burke? Could it be Burke as in Captain Sean Burke? Surely not!*

"What's the matter, Jeev?" Emily asked softly, touching his arm.

Jeev turned back towards her. "Nothing, I just thought I heard something unusual."

Emily snuggled into the crook of his arm and grinned. "My protector!" They both took in the sights of the city and soon the carriage pulled up to the Geneva Hotel entrance. Both he and Emily gazed in awe at the entrance to the seven-story façade, which was lit with gas lamps. Four guards and several footmen stood outside, straight-backed, standing at attention. They all wore black uniforms, hats, and white gloves. Jeev noticed the footmen were darker skinned than the guards.

Jeev and Emily alighted from the carriage. The footmen glided over and collected their luggage, then led them to the front desk, where they registered, and then up a winding staircase to a second-floor room. On the way, they passed large sitting rooms with intricate wood carvings, wood-paneled walls, a plethora of paintings and large vases filled with flowers. The furniture was distinctively Spanish; huge Toscano writing desks, leather chairs in walnut wood with carved tops, sideboards with ornate designs and paintings of bulls and toreadors. While the hotel was too ornate for Jeev, it was a heaven-sent opportunity to clean up and rest. He knew Emily would enjoy her stay here. After a welcome hot bath, both travelers passed out and slept for twenty hours.

The next evening, they descended the staircase for dinner. "You scrubbed up well," said Emily, looking up smiling at Jeev. Jeev looked down on her. She was wearing a cream silk dress with her luxuriant black hair piled high on her head, with a few soft waves framing her oval face.

"Thank you," said Jeev, pressing the pocket of his navy-blue jacket. His travel documents were secure.

"Oh, there's a line," said Emily, pouting.

"Come over here and have a seat. They will call us when our table is ready." said Jeev, as he perched himself on a round settee sofa, with a plush purple velvet cover and a large flower sculpture in the middle. Emily came and sat beside him.

Jeev looked around, assessing his surroundings while trying not to be obvious about doing so. His ears soon picked up a fascinating discussion. Two men, who he assumed were Texans, based on their twangy speech and their white cowboy hats, were engaged in a fevered conversation about the current state of Mexico. One of them, smoking a cigar, drawled, "I miss the days of Diaz,"

"Ah, yes!" said the other man. "He ruled with an iron fist, but we were always welcome here and comfortable too."

"And the greasers knew their place."

"Amen to that!" Both men laughed. Jeev clenched his teeth. He wanted to speak up, but it was far more important not to draw attention to himself, or Emily.

The man with the cigar continued. "I'm worried about my hacienda. I have over a thousand laborers. There are rumors of a revolt. Cannot afford to lose the land." He took a puff and continued, "I tried to get the general to send some troops to squelch those brown skins. He had the gall to say 'no' to me. This wouldn't have happened under Diaz."

The second man added, "The Zapatistas attacked my hacienda. They ransacked the house and left my guards, dead, hanging from the trees. All the peasants were spared. Good thing none of my family was there."

The man with the cigar nodded. "The same thing happened

to Bill Riley's ranch, just over the border from Laredo. Pancho Villa's men set the whole thing ablaze. Those banditos need to be taught a lesson. The current leader, Carranza, cannot take care of them. The US needs to send forces to slaughter those brigands."

Jeev saw Emily's face redden. She too, was listening to the conversation. That was enough to spur him to speak. He turned to the man with the cigar and said, "You know, Mexico is a great country, but two- thirds of the population lives in poverty. The western powers and the Mexican elite exploit them. Capitalism's goal is to make the rich richer on the backs of the working poor. The entire system is rigged against the working class and the haciendas you speak of are nothing more than slave camps. The workers toil day and night; the owners receive all the benefits. Nothing is done to improve the workers' lives. They work till they cannot anymore and then are just thrown away and replaced. The servitude of the repressed."

As he spoke there were a few gasps of astonishment from the Anglo-Saxon elite. Jeev's voice was calm and coherent, despite his angry words. Some hotel guests wondered about the ethnicity of the dark-skinned, tall man who appeared Mexican but spoke with a strange accent. Most fellow guests moved away from Jeev and Emily. No one replied or challenged Jeev, who was suddenly nauseous from the stench of Anglo-Saxon supremacy permeating the environment. Luckily, their table was ready and a delicious dinner of tamales, tortillas with avocados, chilies, and turkey meat, washed down with some pulque from the maguey plant, put him in a better mood.

The next day, Jeev sat at the writing desk in the sitting room, pen in hand. Emily came behind him, in a cloud of lavender fragrance. "What are you writing?"

Jeev sighed. "I need to contact General Obregon. We've got the letter of introduction, but how are we going to get it to him when he's eight hundred miles away in Merida?"

"I know the roads are unsafe. There are too many thick

forests and mountains..." Then Emily's face brightened. "But what about boats? It is on the Yucatan peninsula."

"Emily, with the war going on, there are no passenger ships available, not on the river or in the Gulf."

"Well, we'll just have to figure out something else."

Jeev stretched his back and arms. "I need a break. I'm going out for a minute."

"Good idea," said Emily. "Maybe you'll think of a solution when you're not trying so hard." Jeev smiled, already feeling better.

As he was leaving the hotel, he noticed a tall, lanky photographer in a top hat setting up his equipment outside the building. He set up a huge tripod, attached the camera and unfolded the front of the camera. He then attached a flash to the top of the camera and studied the structure of the edifice. Jeev, always curious, walked towards him. As he approached, Jeev noticed the photographer's coat strewn on the grass behind him. A young girl, about ten years old, sat next to the jacket.

"Fine building," said Jeev to the photographer. He answered without looking at Jeev, "Yes, the finest hotel in Mexico City." He then turned around and extended his hand. "Guillermo," he said.

Jeev introduced himself as Jeev forgetting his new name was Miguel, and then turned to the young girl and asked, "What's your name?"

"Frida," she answered shyly, looking at her father for approval.

Jeev smiled and shook her hand. He felt there was something special about them. "So, if I were to take pictures of Mexico City, how should I start?"

Guillermo replied without hesitation. "Look at the mountains surrounding the city. Volcanoes surround Mexico City. Start with Iztaccihua, the sleeping woman. You will see the beauty of the city in the mountains."

All three of them glanced over the horizon to look at the

towering skyline. Iztaccihua roughly formed the silhouette of a sleeping woman. "I hope we can meet again to discuss photography Guillermo," said Jeev.

"Yes, I wish you luck with your hobby." replied Guillermo.

CHAPTER 36: THE GERMAN CONNECTION

Jeev's eyes widened in awe as he approached the National Palace, a long stone and brick building spanning an entire side of a city plaza. Somewhere, within this massive edifice was the Ministry of War. Jeev reached in his jacket pocket. The letter to General Obregon was still there. He kept walking and reading signs, until he found the 'Ministerio del la Guerra'. Jeev breathed a sigh of relief. He approached the guard at the door. "Good day, sir. I have a letter for General Obregon," he said using his cursory Spanish, which he had practiced until he could repeat it in his sleep. He pulled out the letter.

The guard glanced at the missive, then said, "This way, sir," and directing him to a waiting area with comfortable leather chairs. Jeev sat down.

Shortly thereafter, two army officers approached him. "Excuse me sir, may we have the letter for General Obregon?" one of the officers asked in heavily accented but understandable English. Jeev reluctantly handed the letter to him. "Follow me," he said, and they walked down a long tile floored corridor lined with photographs and paintings of past wars. At the end of the corridor was a large double door. One of the officers rapped his knuckles on the door in three short bursts. The doors opened. The officer turned to Jeev and said, "Follow me."

They entered a large room. Jeev saw a middle-aged woman with graying hair pulled back in a tight bun sitting at a mahogany desk addressing envelopes. The sitting area was filled with tufted dark green leather sofas and chairs. Four armed guards stood at attention by the closed door at the end of the room.

A few minutes later, the door opened, and Jeev was escorted through the door into an enormous office lushly decorated in green and gold. Tall emerald-green silk curtains lined the windows. A balcony overlooked the street in front of which was a highly polished ornately carved teak desk. A man wearing a monocle, an enormous sword and a general's uniform sat behind the desk. The officer handed the letter to him. He promptly opened the sealed envelope and Jeev began to sweat. He was suddenly aware how quickly everything he was working for could collapse. The general read the letter carefully, taking what seemed an hour, but was only a few minutes. He then beckoned Jeev to sit down. He then smiled and then shook his hand. "We will deliver this letter to General Obregon as soon as he arrives in Mexico City," Jeev internally sighed with relief. The next sentence surprised him. "We welcome you to the Republic of Mexico. You will be safe here." He winked, and continued, "We have known about your arrival for a few days. You are free in this country. You are among friends."

"Thank you very much, sir!" said Jeev, full of gratitude.

"You are welcome", the general replied, smiling. Jeev walked out of the office at a brisk pace, eager to share the good news with Emily.

As he passed the reception desk, an attendant called out, "Senor Miguel, a letter for you," and gave him an envelope. Jeev read the brief note. It was an invitation from the editor of a local newspaper requesting a meeting. He penned a reply, saying he would meet the editor at his convenience and handed the note to the receptionist. "Please send this back to the man who sent the letter to me," he requested. The attendant smiled and nodded.

Later that afternoon, during siesta time, Jeev and Emily were spooning, relaxing in the bliss of newfound safety and freedom when there was a knock at the door. Alerted, Jeev sprung out of bed, putting his finger to his lips signaling Emily to be quiet. Jeev opened the door just a crack, keeping the chain on. A stocky middle-aged man with pale skin wearing a black suit stood in the hallway. "Senor Sanchez?", he asked in a thick German accent.

"Yes?" replied Jeev, hesitantly.

"May I come in?"

Looking back at Emily, Jeev replied. "No, I'll meet you outside." Jeev's mind raced. *Why are Germans contacting me in Mexico? What do they know about me?* Jeev shut the door. "I'm going out for a few minutes," he whispered to Emily. "Be quiet. Stay here. I'll be okay." He straightened his clothes, slicked back his hair, and slipped on his shoes. Before she could protest, he stepped out of the room, locking the door behind him.

Then he noticed another man at the end of the corridor keeping guard. The first man relayed the message "The people you were supposed to meet before want to meet you now. Here is the address. Meet us there tonight. Your Berlin friends will be there, but this time without the traitors."

"I'll be there," confirmed Jeev.

A few hours later, Jeev and Emily sat in the dining room, enjoying a pleasant dinner of carne asada and green salad with a bottle of malbec. Jeev barely sipped his wine, as he wanted to have a clear head later in the evening.

Emily was initially silent, but halfway through the meal, she plucked up her courage and looked at him with wide-eyed concern. "What's going on? Who was that man that came to our room today?"

"Emily, please trust me. I really can't tell you anything, as I don't know anything yet myself."

"This is about that German stuff, isn't it?" She spoke in a lowered voice.

Jeev sighed. "Yes, it is. I really can't say anything more."

"I understand," said Emily pouting.

After dinner, Jeev walked Emily back to their room, and then stepped out of the hotel, heading for the address he was given. Feeling the need to clear his head, he walked into the clear, cool night. It was dark outside, except for a lone light coming out of a bar at the far end of the street. The cobblestone pavement echoed his footsteps as he turned into a dark alley. He thought he heard footsteps and some rustling of leaves. Glancing back, he saw no one, but there were enough shadows to hide an army. Moving ahead, he stepped into a small grove of trees and waited. Two figures were moving towards him. One wore a top hat and a long cloak. *Could they be dangerous?* He wondered, feeling the hairs on the back of his neck standing up. He quickened his pace. The two figures behind him sped up as well. He turned left into a street and ran. His pursuers ran after him, making no effort to conceal themselves. The night seemed to have taken a wrong turn. He wondered how many other bandits were there in the shadows, waiting for him. He turned around another corner. Suddenly a hand was placed over his mouth, preventing him from screaming, and another pinned his arms back. Someone grabbed his feet, and they hustled him past the trees into a courtyard. His hands and feet were immobilized. It was useless to struggle. He heard a door open and close, then they gently placed him on a sofa. As his eyes adjusted to the darkness of the room, he recognized the two Germans who met him in the hotel. One had his hands to his lips, indicating to be quiet. The other was peering out the side of a window. Finally, the second person seemed to signal an all clear.

"That was close," said the German, whispering, "Those were English agents. They must have followed you from the Hotel. That hotel is not safe for you anymore."

"Let us go," said the second man. "He is waiting for us." They guided Jeev to the back of the house, into a narrow street. Then, verifying all was safe, they walked a block down to a large house, which was dark with curtains covering all the windows. As they entered the house, Jeev's eyes squinted from the glare of many candles. The shadows from their flames danced across the walls and the curtains.

Almost at once, two men walked in. One a tall, muscular man, the second short and pudgy. Even though he was dressed in civilian clothes, he had the bearing of an army officer. *"Guten Abend,* gentlemen. I am Commander von Koenig." The pudgy man introduced himself as Captain Mueller. Commander von Koenig continued, "Our job is to create diversions in parts of the world where Germany can influence the fight against the Allied Powers and spread German influence."

The commander turned to gather some documents. Captain Mueller took the opportunity to hastily whisper in Jeev's ear. "This man is very well connected to the elite, the Reichsbank, and the Kaiser himself."

A butler appeared with a silver tray holding a crystal decanter of dark brown liquid and two snifters. The two Germans who had brought Jeev there retired to a back room. Commander von Koenig poured the liquor and asked, "Why did you not come to Berlin after New York?"

Jeev took a sip of the liquor, which turned out to be a smooth brandy, and replied, "United States Agents and the British Secret Service found and arrested me. I was on trial. There was no way to get to Berlin. I barely escaped to Mexico. The alternative was jail temporarily in New York and then the British would take me back to India where I would face life imprisonment or death." He continued, "What are you doing in

Mexico? How did you get here?"

Koenig, with his eyebrows permanently arched and his saint-like eyes piercing through the candlelight, "Why on the *Deutschland* of course," he smiled.

"You came on a U-boat?" asked a surprised Jeev.

"Just till the coast, of course. We took a train after that. We have many sympathizers in Mexico. There is much anger towards the US for taking away Mexican land."

Jeev was not sure if Koenig was joking with him, but he thought he better not push it further. The fact of the matter was, they were present, having a discussion.

"We have some deals we are trying to do with the Mexicans, as this is a good place for us to conduct espionage activities on American agents. When America enters the war, we need to hit them in their own backyard. There are discussions at the highest levels in Berlin on the plans for Mexico and other areas around the world. We heard you were in the country and are still interested in working with you on the India project. Germany is looking to extend its influence into the India and help you drive out the English. India can be an independent country and an ally of Germany."

Jeev sat up in his chair, interested in where the conversation was going. "You know, I tried to make contact in New York, but no one was listening."

"What happened in New York?" inquired the commander.

"When I went to New York, looking for my German contacts, I was literally stranded amongst the skyscrapers. My first contact, who claimed to be working for the Berlin Committee, seemed to be depressed and uninterested in any kind of dialog. Eventually, after much prodding, he told me he had fallen out of favor from Berlin and someone else had taken over. I did get an address in New York from him. That address was an impressive three-story brownstone. The man told me he had been expecting me. I told him I needed to get to Germany, and he should help me with the arrangements. They said they would get in touch with Berlin and let me know.

I waited for many weeks to hear from them. It was always the same message - waiting for instructions from Germany. Meanwhile, I was arrested by the American authorities and consequently ended up fleeing to Mexico."

The commander's face reddened, and his eyes narrowed to dark slits. "Such incompetence on our side is inexcusable! Look, we want to help you get arms from Germany to the Indian revolutionaries. I promise to do whatever it takes to help you. I will contact Berlin and get you some money so you can get started. We will together work on getting large shipments of arms into India, so with the help of the Indian revolutionaries we can fight the English. The war for us has not gone well, however we would like to hit the British where it hurts. The bread baskets and money generator of Asia. This will divert the attention from Europe to India. An independent India as an ally of Germany will be quite attractive to the Kaiser. I assure you I will work on getting the funds so we can ship arms to India in a big way. I am thinking some Erhhardt mountain guns that we used in Africa, some Krupp field cannons, which are old but can be effective against the British infantry, the Steilhandgrante, stick in hand grenade, Bergmann machine guns for the foot soldiers and Lugers for the officers. Once some territory has been captured, we can also send some Daimler Marienhagen armored halftracks and Uberlandwagens to carry supplies. Now tell me again your plan for India."

Jeev looked incredulously at Koenig, only half believing what he was being told. If this were true, an entire army could be activated, starting the battle for India. "The way I see this happening is taking out the jewel of India for the British, which is Calcutta. We gather the arms and ships at the Andaman and Nicobar Islands in the Indian Ocean. Follow this with a three-pronged attack, one from the North through the Assamese hills, a second one from the South, moving up from the State of Orissa and forcing the British to escape into the Bay of Bengal as their ships try to flee Calcutta. There in the Bay would be German submarines waiting to torpedo the British Navy as they came out of the safe harbor of Calcutta. The devastation of the British would be massive, troop losses and ships lost. Once Calcutta is captured, the army can march towards Delhi. Meanwhile, the Indo-German Navy can lay siege to Bombay. The local population will revolt against the British there. We will send squads of guerrilla fighters inland. They will have no problems getting to the villages as the beaches are poorly guarded. The British will have to flee inland towards the South. If they go North, the army marching towards Delhi will deal with them. With the three principal cities falling. Calcutta, Delhi and Bombay, the British will flee with their tails between their legs. They draw most of their strength from the sepoys, who are all Indian. The sepoys will abandon them in large numbers. The rest of the provinces will either surrender or become allies of the Indo-German forces."

This time, it was Koenig's turn to look at Jeev incredulously. The passion and intensity on Jeev's face and his words were captivating. The ease of the victory, however, was another story. He was battle scarred. The British had been fighting in India for centuries. They knew the land, the people and in Europe had mostly beaten Kaiser's army. There was silence in the room as each man digested the other one's point of view. Both were smart enough to know that much was unsaid and would not be brought up for debate. Also, they mutually understood the uncertainty of the situation. Commander Koenig was a man of his words and did not take things lightly, but somehow, he trusted the dark-skinned man sitting in front of him. He thought about his contacts in the military and how he would present this proposition. In the back of his head, he knew the Kaiser Wilhelm II was losing his support in the military. He could not directly approach the Kaiser and would have to play a delicate balancing game between the Kaiser and the opposing generals.

Koenig narrowed his eyes, wrinkling his crow's feet, smiled with his thin lips, and gently nodded his approval. "Let us do this. I will get you some money for immediate needs, so you can start the operation rolling. You need to stay in Mexico till I can go back to Berlin and talk to my people. It is too dangerous for you to come to Berlin now and you will be jailed or even killed if you go back to India. Wait for my signal and I will arrange for you to come to Berlin soon." The German got up, indicating the meeting was over.

After giving Jeev a firm handshake, he led him towards the entrance. The men who had kidnapped him were waiting by the entrance. They stubbed the cigarettes they were smoking and opened the door, checked the street, verified it was clear and accompanied him to a waiting car. Jeev slid into the back seat. The men nodded at the driver and the car sped off towards the hotel.

CHAPTER 37: STRANGE BEDFELLOWS (1915)

Emily was fast asleep when Jeev entered the room. It was a sweltering summer night, and she had left the window open to let the breeze in and was sleeping uncovered. Jeev smiled as he realized she had been shopping as she was sleeping in a new nightgown. It was made in a Spanish style from sheer white cotton, with light embroidery around the cuffs and neckline. Her legs, now tanned from the southern sun, were sprawled across the bed. He slid on top of the sheets, nuzzling her legs away, and in seconds, was out like a light.

He woke up the next morning, with Emily sleeping on his shoulder, her hair on his neck and bright sunlight streaking through the window. Still wary after the previous evening, Jeev glanced across the room. Someone had slid an envelope under the door. Jeev rolled away from Emily with slow, careful movements, so as not to disturb her. He walked over to the door, picked up the envelope, and opened it. The address on the note was of a street close to the city center. Jeev, still drowsy, rubbed his eyes. The letter was from a newspaper publisher asking if Miguel Sanchez could visit him that day. Jeev refolded the letter and put in back in the envelope. The prospect was intriguing. Jeev looked over at Emily, who was still sound asleep. He attended to his toilet, dressed, and wrote a note to Emily explaining what had happened.

He then left the room, carefully locking the door behind him. A baggage handler standing by the hotel's front door gave him directions to the address, which was only a few blocks away from the hotel. The warmth, sunshine, and fresh breeze put Jeev in a good mood. Soon he arrived at a small whitewashed two-story building with a bell tower and its windows highlighted with bright blue paint. A small, barely visible plaque on the front door read *La Voz del Pueblo.*

Jeev pushed the door open and entered a small open room with wooden floors and white walls. A stocky balding man with a furrowed brow sat at a typewriter punching keys using his index fingers. He did not notice Jeev, until Jeev approached the desk, and coughed.

"*Si...*" he said, continuing to peck at the typewriter.

Jeev interrupted. "*Buenos dias, senor.* My name is Miguel Sanchez..."

"Oh!" The man stopped pecking, stood up, and shook Jeev's hand. "Take a seat," he said in English, gesturing to a rickety wooden chair against the wall at the side of the room. Jeev pulled the chair in front of the desk and sat down. The man grinned and said, "I am Juan Morales, publisher of *La Voz del Pueblo.* When I heard you were in our country, I immediately wanted to get in touch with you."

Jeev was shocked. How many people knew about him? Why, whenever he went to a meeting, did everyone know who he was? As if Juan had read his thoughts, he said, "The Hotel Geneva is not safe for you; you need to move out. Here is the address of a house you can rent. Move out as soon as you can." He handed Jeev a slip of paper, which Jeev, still speechless, took.

Juan continued. "My newspaper fights for the cause of the Mexican people. We fought the Spanish colonists, only to have power usurped by the landowners. Mexican Indians and mixed-race people are second-class citizens who are exploited in every way. There is a feeling of superiority among the 'Spanish blooded' people. I have read some of the articles you wrote in New York and was wondering if you would like to write for *La Voz del Pueblo*."

Jeev relaxed and took a deep breath before replying. "Mexico does not differ from other countries. The universality of a suppression of people and the creation of unequal political systems is a common thread across all nations. Religion, social classes, ethnicity, and geographic locations break people down into segments that are easily exploited. It is necessary to have a system that works for all."

"Yes, I am very much interested in your ideas," said Juan. "We have a diverse ancestry from the Mayas, the Aztecs, to many smaller indigenous groups, to, of course, the white Spanish. There were also black slaves from Africa, brought by the Spanish, who settled here after we the slave trade was abolished." He took a deep breath and spoke slower, in a more serious tone. "I am going to insist on two things. "Tomorrow, you need to move to the new address I gave you and, at night, come to my house for dinner. I will send a car to pick you up tomorrow evening."

Jeev stood up and shook Juan's hand. *"Muchas gracias, Senor Morales!* Thank you very much."

"De nada," Juan replied. "We're glad to have you writing for us."

Jeev walked out of the office, happy that things were moving along. He relished the idea of moving out of the Hotel Geneva with its capitalist trash. Emily would be happy to settle down for a while, but he also knew in the back of his mind that settling down was not compatible with his life and his ambitions.

The next morning, Jeev and Emily checked out of the hotel and took a taxi to the corner of Avenida Merida and San Luis Potosi in the Roma district. "Ooh!" exclaimed Emily. "It's lovely!" Jeev looked up at the house, a two-story Spanish-style structure. A small red awning covered the entrance. Light beige plaster covered the front walls, and the sides were white-painted brick. The two upper stories had balconies with curved grid iron railings. They walked inside to a hardwood floored foyer, beyond which were a large sitting room with a fireplace, a kitchen, and what appeared to be a dining room converted into a library and office. A winding staircase led upstairs, which had two bedrooms and an enormous, tiled bathroom with a claw footed tub. The master bedroom had a balcony overlooking a green, wooded backyard. In the distance, the snow-covered volcanic mountain Popocatepetl towered over the city and following the Paso de Cortes, they could also see the majestic peak of another volcano, Iztaccihuatl.

Jeev and Emily walked out on the balcony to better take in the magnificent view. Jeev put his arm around Emily's shoulders and drew her close. She looked up at him and smiled. "I'm so grateful for this place. It's much more than I expected. We don't even have to worry about furniture. Just think how far we've come since we got on the train in New York…"

"Me too," said Jeev softly. He could feel tears welling up in his eyes, but Emily would never understand just how far he had come and how far he still had to go.

Later that evening, dinner with Juan Morales and his wife Isabella was a homey affair. After enjoying chicken tortilla soup and fish tacos, they settled in the library with flan. Juan and Jeev indulged in cigars and mezcal while Isabella and Emily sipped horchata.

Jeev held his glass up to the gas lamp. The mezcal was as clear as water but tasted subtly smoky. He offered Emily a sip. She tried it, grimaced, and shook her head. Juan laughed. "Most women prefer sweet, milky horchata. Mezcal is a man's drink."

Emily glared at him, but quickly gained her composure. "A man's drink?" Emily smiled sweetly. "Please tell us what it is and how it is made."

Juan took a puff of his cigar and started talking in a professorial tone. "Mezcal is made from the *pina* or heart of the agave plant, a succulent native to the Americas and the Caribbean."

"Isn't that the same plant tequila is made from?" asked

Emily.

Juan looked surprised. "Why, yes, it is. Tequila is a type of mezcal, made from blue agave plants only grown in Mexico." Emily smiled again and nodded. Encouraged, Juan continued. "To make mezcal, the *pinas* are roasted on lava stones, then grounded and distilled, which gives it a strong smoky taste."

Jeev noticed Isabella's eyes narrowing and her jawline clenching as Juan responded to Emily's questions. When Juan paused for breath, Jeev spoke up. "This is excellent liquor. You chose well." Juan grinned and nodded. Jeev continued. "I enjoyed your talk about how it was made. We have similar drinks, such as *handia*, a rice beer and *tharra*, which is made from sugar cane."

"So, tell us something about your young days in India?" asked Juan, suddenly switching the subject.

Jeev took a sip of the mezcal and replied, "As a teenager, I saw the atrocities committed by the British. I had burning anger against the imperialist power that was using the country, nay exploiting the country for its own gain. I saw the devastation of famine, of Indians being enslaved. I saw the violence against the local population and something inside me could not hold back anymore. A friend of mine introduced me to a man known just as 'Swamy'. I never knew his real name. He had set up a safe house in the suburbs of Calcutta. Many teenage boys and young men lived there. Swamy gave us patriotic lectures on the greatness of India and provided us with details of the atrocities committed by the British. He organized us into small groups, primarily to spy on British troop movements and the actions of local politicians. We inconspicuously blended into crowds and reported back to him. Over the next few months, I gained his trust.

He called me and my friend Ramu into his office. He started out by saying, "You are ready for bigger things." Looking straight into my eyes, he asked, "Do you feel you are ready?"

I gulped and said, "Yes."

He continued, "The British conquered us using violence. We

317

can only defeat them using violence. We must hurt them so much that they will leave. You must become a warrior for the cause. I have faith in you, and I see your strength". With that he laid his hand on my head and said, "Go with God."

"We tried several strategies," continued Jeev, "however, we were no match for the British forces. Their trained military and arms overwhelmed us." Jeev stopped talking. He did not want to go into any further details. Juan, Isabella, and Emily were staring at him. He quickly changed the subject to the natural beauty around Mexico City.

That night, after they got home, he and Emily stood on the balcony looking at the mountains in the distance. Turning to her, he said, "I did not want to tell Juan the details of what happened in India that night, but it's something that has always bothered me, and I have struggled with the memories. Ramu told me to come to a meeting at the safe house later that night. At the meeting, there were about ten young men gathered around a kerosene lamp. They were debating how to get funds to buy arms. It soon became clear that the funds were to be got through illegal means. The group finally decided that they would rob the local stationmaster. The safe would have the ticket collections along with money that some of the Calcutta workers were sending to the villages. In my youth, I did not question the ethics behind this, and, to the surprise of the group, I volunteered. Ramu and I were to go inside the office after hours and break the safe and abscond with the cash. A third member would be a lookout and had a bird whistle he would use to warn us. The plan was to rob the office the next night."

Emily looked at him, her eyes wide with sympathy. "Go on, I'm listening."

"Around midnight, the three of us set out towards the train station. We used the minor roads, the ones the patrols normally avoided. There were some hoodlums around, but the moment they saw Ramu, they recognized him and left us alone. Ramu, you see, had a reputation on the street. The station office was dark, and we pried open a window and climbed inside. I saw the safe under a table. It was quite old and rusty, so opening it was not a problem. I took a hammer I brought with me and banged away at the handle. It quickly broke, and the safe door swung open. Suddenly, I saw a man come out of an adjacent room. The station master must have slept over at the office. He had a long iron stick with a pointed end in his hand and started yelling and screaming at us. Ramu reached inside his pocket and took out a knife, its steel glistened in the darkness. The station master lunged towards me with the pointed end of his stick. I thought this was the end of me. Then I heard a sharp scream as Ramu pierced the knife into the stationmaster's shoulder. The knife clattered to the floor. The station master, bleeding from his shoulder, swung the rod and hit Ramu across his cheek, sending him reeling to the floor. I grabbed a chair and smashed it over the man's head. He fell to the floor. We grabbed the cash, the knife and jumped out the window. We did not stop running till we reached the safe house."

Jeev took a sip of water. In the darkness, he could see Emily's wide eyes staring at him with a mixture of horror and sympathy.

"The next day, we found out the stationmaster had succumbed to his wounds. A truck filled with Indian soldiers and a jeep with two British officers pulled up in front of the safe house later during the day. They rounded up everyone in the house. Swamy was missing. He must have been able to escape. All the boys were made to stand in a line. Indiscriminately they hit the boys, while asking them if they knew anything about the robbery and killing. I took a few blows to the back and over my head. A few of the older boys were then hauled into the truck and taken away to the police station. One of them was our lookout. We know at some point someone would talk, torture was common, nails would be removed, and they would apply salt to wounds. Ramu and I made our way out of Calcutta to a village a few miles away. There we reunited with Swamy.

He told us we were now all wanted criminals in the eyes of the 'Raj', but our work was just starting. There were many more places to hit. This was the beginning of my participation in the revolution against the imperialist powers."

Emily nodded. "Please continue."

"With the cash we had stolen, they purchased arms, which had been stolen from the army. We practiced using the rifles; however, we could not use live ammunition as the supply was limited. A few times, we attacked and ambushed army trucks as they transported troops and supplies to and from the Calcutta ports. The idea was to strike hard at the commerce being conducted. The British economy relied on India for exports and the money went directly into the British exchequer."

"I see, robbing from the poor to give to the rich." Emily didn't shift her gaze.

"For the next few years, I was actively involved in guerrilla tactics and strikes, but being poorly equipped and the counter strikes coming with overwhelming force, we took heavy losses. I was lucky enough to not get wounded. My colleagues who got hurt soon succumbed to infection and disease."

"Despite these losses and setbacks, I become more convinced than ever that only force would drive the English from India. We just needed better armaments and funding. I had long conversations with Ramu, Swamy and others about how we should continue next. Swamy had said, "The enemy of my enemy is my friend." The big enemy of Britain is Germany. China too may help. Even though Japan has an alliance with Britain, there are many anti-British sympathizers in Japan. We needed to reach out to these countries to solicit their help."

"So Ramu and I set out to the city of Rangoon. We contacted an operative to supply us with boxes of rifles. Unfortunately, were betrayed by them. I am assuming they sold us out to the British. We escaped just in time and had to make a long and arduous journey through the Burmese forests before coming back to Calcutta. As I had the most experience in these types of communications, they agreed I would travel once more to get the funds and arms. This time my journey led me to England and you know the rest." Smiling at Emily in the darkness, he said, "The death of the station master still haunts me every day. He was an innocent man who did not need to have a violent end. And now, the rest is our story. The saga of life continues."

Emily embraced Jeev, gently kissing him on the cheek and whispered in his ear, "I'm so glad that you're here with me, now."

CHAPTER 38: THE WOMAN IN THE MOUNTAINS (1917)

Jeev woke up looking out the window towards the snow-covered dormant volcano, Iztaccihuatl, the White Woman, and roughly made out the feet, knees, breasts, and head of the eternally sleeping figure. He then carefully turned over and studied the silhouette of Emily sleeping to compare it to the sleeping woman of the mountains.

Later that morning, Emily and Jeev walked toward the mountains. The air was dry, and the sky was blue and cloudless. Emily gazed up at the Iztaccihuatl peaks. "It's all so serene, so beautiful. I wish we could go further into the woods. It's hard to believe that there's bandidos around here."

Jeev placed his arm around Emily's waist, pulling her close. "Sometimes beauty can be deceptive."

Emily grinned, and a mischievous sparkle lit her eyes. "That's what makes exploration such fun! What's life without risk?" Jeev shook his head and said nothing. Like Emily, he too wanted a closer look. They soon found a man with a carraige who took them to the start of a narrow trail.

There was something about the mountains, an energy vortex that attracted Jeev. It was a mystical energy that grabbed his soul and squeezed his heart, searching for the truth that lay deep within. Seeing the mountains left him with a feeling of incompleteness, yet it was not a feeling of sadness, but rather one of a thirst needing to be quenched.

They walked up the narrow trail, peering up at the majestic peaks. Birds chirped, squirrels scurried across the tree limbs, a large hawk flying overhead peered down at the open meadows in search of prey, and in the distance a herd of deer munched on fresh grass while furtively watching for danger.

"Jeev," a booming voice pierced the natural calm. Surprised at being called out amid the wilderness, Jeev and Emily saw a man waving at them from a perch above. He had a large camera set up, pointing at the mountain. Another man and a little girl sat close by. Approaching closer, they saw the trio had picked a spectacular lookout that provided a panoramic view of the volcano and the Paso de Cortes.

"Hola, Guillermo, Senorita Frida!" called out Jeev. Emily looked at him quizzically. Frida smiled at them and waved a shy hello, while the bodyguard had his hands on his revolver ready to confront them.

Guillermo told the bodyguard in Spanish, "Jaime, all is well. I know these people." Jaime took his hand off his gun and relaxed. Guillermo strolled over to greet the walking couple. "Hello my friend, Jeev! Who is this lovely senorita?" he said, turning to Emily.

"This is my companion, Miss Emily Calvert from the United States," said Jeev. Turning to Emily, he said, "I met Guillermo and his daughter, Frida outside the hotel. Guillermo is a photographer."

Emily smiled, and Guillermo delicately took hold of her hand and brushed it lightly with his lips. Emily blushed. "Come join us. We've got plenty of chorizo and chicken tortas and Syrah," he said, gesturing to a large hamper. Jeev looked at Emily, who nodded. They both sat down on the large, colorful blanket covering the ground near Guillermo's tripod.

Sipping the wine, Jeev commented to Guillermo, "Such a wonder of nature, such a peaceful place. One could almost believe in the forces of creation."

"You don't believe in God?" asked Guillermo.

"If you have seen what I have seen, the concept of a

benevolent God is incomprehensible. I only accept what can be defined by rational thought," said Jeev.

"If you speak of man's cruelty and suffering that humankind causes on one another, there are theological explanations for this behavior. Good and evil are always at play in this world. If we are to turn to Him, and to Mary of Guadalupe, we can see that God is with us and will give us the strength to overcome that suffering. He does not always provide us with the answers but is always there for us to bring our suffering to him."

"I think we are on two different planes of thought. You derive your morality from a book written a long time ago. Man derives his morality from experience and human nature. Man deserves to live in a society that is built for him, of him and by him. That humans have an obligation to build a society based on truth and decency. If we are free in the truest sense, then humans will use rational thought and ethics to create a utopian society that works for them. The problem is that we are not free. Imperialism, colonialism, capitalism, political parties, and the bourgeoisie have throttled the human spirit. The fiber of humanity may not develop into a world of caring and empathy. The structures of power that have been created reward selfish motives, squelching the human faith which is built on selfless service, a true democracy and independent thought."

"So as an atheist, how do you explain things you don't understand?"

"I would say I am not an atheist, because an atheist is just someone who does not believe in a higher authority and does not rely on faith for the existence of a God-like figure. My philosophies and beliefs go beyond that. I have faith in humanity. I believe humans can shape their own lives and moral values as long as they are given the freedom to live their lives based on truth. They need to have political freedom, economic freedom, and freedom of thought. When these conditions exist, humans will shape their own destinies, working within an ethical and moral framework, all based on rational thinking."

"As to things that cannot be explained, we as humans are always searching for the truth. Logic can explain some things we know today. The Renaissance movement made great strides in the fields of science, art, and philosophy. Many things were explained, old myths destroyed. We now know the Earth is not the center of the universe, that the Earth revolves around the sun.-Religious leaders thought otherwise, and science proved them wrong. So too, other unexplained things will reveal themselves. Knowledge is something that has to be used by humans and as we search, the mysteries of the universe will be revealed to us. This is our life, the one and only life that we live. There is no reincarnation or afterlife. We must live the best life we can."

"So, for you, we come from dust, and to dust we shall return," said Guillermo with a note of pity in his voice. "Let us enjoy what we have in front of us. Here, let me show you some magnificent views. I see you have a camera; you can get some wonderful pictures from this vantage point."

Jeev looked down at the weathered leather camera bag at his side. "Oh, this? It's just a Kodak, nothing spectacular."

Guillermo took hold of the bag, and carefully extricated the camera. He held it up to the light, examining every surface. "I can tell from the scratches and wear on it that you often carry this bag, but the camera is clean and unscratched, but not unused, as the leather on the outside and the shutter are soft, which shows you have used it. It must be valuable to you." Jeev nodded. They spent the rest of the afternoon eating, enjoying the view, taking pictures, and playing with Frida.

On the way back from the mountains, full of wine and sandwiches, and basking in the glow of newfound friendship, Emily told Jeev, "I received a letter from Arti. The women's organization wants to know when I'm coming back, as do some of my professors. You know, I am enjoying my time here and with you, but at some point, I need to go back to New York and my work," pondered Emily.

"I agree. That makes sense," agreed Jeev, with a twinge of sadness in his words.

"Did you know Arti has a sister in St. Thomas who is coming to New York to visit her?" Emily chatted on, changing the subject. "Amee and Arti are originally from a small village outside of Calcutta."

"Did you say Amee?" gasped Jeev. "I knew Amee and Arti. They were my neighbors. Their father sent them away, telling them they would stay with a well to do relative who would take care of them, but I hate to say this, he sold them as indentured servants to some landlord in British Guyana.

Emily stared, astonished at the revelation. "I know Arti told me never to reveal this to anyone, and she is very hesitant to talk about her younger life, but the two sisters were in Guyana for a short while. They soon realized they were slaves in every way to the sugar plantation owners. So, after a harrowing journey through the jungles and with the help of kindhearted locals, they escaped the plantation. Someone near Georgetown helped them get on a ship to St. Thomas. Amee is happily working on a farm there and Arti came to New York to study and now works there."

This news dumbfounded Jeev. He turned his head so that Emily would not see the tears in his eyes. Grief over Amee had killed a small part of his heart. Now, the weight was lifted, and his heart healed. Discretely, he dabbed his eyes with his handkerchief, and turned back to Emily, who looked at him with curiosity. "I've never seen you so happy! You're bouncing down the mountain!" she exclaimed. Jeev just smiled and resolved to write a long letter to Arti and get Amee's address in St. Thomas.

CHAPTER 39: THE JOURNALIST

"**W**ith your background and experience, you should be writing articles about world affairs," said Juan. He and Jeev sat in the La Voz del Pueblo office, drinking steaming hot dark coffee on a cool, damp day.

Jeev chuckled. "I don't think my Spanish is that good."

"Don't worry. Just write. There are people who can translate your stories or correct your grammar. What we need is a journalist with your ability and passion. Especially now."

Jeev placed his coffee cup on Juan's desk. "Everything is changing. Russia is in revolt. The Great War is ending, and Germany is collapsing."

"Yes. Nothing will ever be the same. News about Russia and Germany has reached Mexico, which is why we need experts like you to give a true account of what is happening. You know about die hard nationalism firsthand and you have great insight into why communism is so successful." Juan stood up and moved over to the fireplace and stirred the embers bringing new life into the fire. He then reached up to the mantle, grabbed a bottle of a milky liquid, poured two glasses, and offered one to Jeev. "Try this. It is *pulque*, a drink made from agave plant, like tequila and mezcal. We make it at home."

Jeev looked at the white, opaque liquid in his glass. He sniffed the contents, which smelled like cactus, then fruit, followed by an acidic odor. Curious, he took a small sip. It was fizzy, slightly sour, mild, yet refreshing. He gulped it down, smiled and said, "I think I will have some more."

Juan grinned. "I knew you would like it!" He then quickly drained his glass and walked back to the mantel.

As Juan refilled their glasses, Jeev looked at the fire and spoke pensively, without looking up. "Fire changed the world for humans. We were once no different from other mammals. I'm not sure how we first harnessed fire. Maybe a lightning strike started a fire, and some enterprising person used a burning branch to keep warm. Maybe they ate an animal that had been cooked in a fire and realized meat lasts longer and tastes better when cooked. One day, someone made fire by rubbing two sticks together. Soon, they were using fire for warmth, cooking, and protection. Suddenly Man was on the path to overwhelm all his natural enemies, all except other men. Fire enabled him to melt metals and strengthen tools and weapons. His ability to destroy increased. In the orient, gunpowder was used first for fireworks and then soon for cannon balls. Man's power for destruction increased even more. The more power Man had, the more it was used to subdue and conquer. Man's ability to invent knows no bounds; his ability to use these inventions for nefarious purposes is also limitless. And it all started with fire."

Juan smiled and nodded, the corners of his eyes crinkling. "To fire!" he exclaimed, raising his glass.

"May it forever burn brightly," added Jeev, raising his. The men clinked their tumblers together, downed their pulque and chuckled.

Meanwhile, Emily was sitting at home, waiting for Jeev to come home from the newspaper office. She practiced breathing slowly and deeply, willing herself not to be upset. Lately, Jeev's writing had become all consuming. Emily often found him scrunched over his typewriter. When he was not typing, he was staring out of the window, thinking about his next sentence. Something had to be done. Emily just hoped that Jeev would think so too.

Suddenly, she heard the door open. "Emily?" called out Jeev.

Emily sprang up from the sofa, all irritation forgotten. "Jeev! I'm here." She ran to him, and they hugged. Before she could lose her courage, Emily told Jeev about her idea. "You've been working so hard recently. We need an outing." Jeev started to say something, but Emily pressed her finger against his lips, silencing him. "I've arranged for us to spend a day at the Xochimilco canals. They are just an hour away by carriage." She smiled hopefully.

"That's a great idea!" said Jeev. "I could do with a break."

"Wonderful!" Emily gave Jeev another hug and kissed him on the lips. His passionate response reassured her.

Two days later, Emily and Jeev took a carriage to Xochimilco. The day was bright, sunny, and not too hot. They enjoyed watching the bustling city and smelling the heady mix of horse manure and car fumes. The military was always visible, some mounted on horses, others patrolling on foot. Jeev wrapped his arm around Emily as if he were protecting her from the danger that surrounded them.

After an hour's ride, they pulled up to the banks of the Xochimilco canals and got out of the carriage. A crowd of boatsmen descended on them, all beckoning them to their shallow, colorful vessels. Jeev saw a bright green and yellow one with red and blue flowers on both sides. "Come on, Emily, let's take this one!" He took her hand, led her to the boat, and they settled in. They agreed on a price, and the skipper plunged a long pole into the canal, propelling the boat forward.

Suddenly, a young man jumped into the boat from the shore. Emily screamed. Tensed and ready to spring, Jeev pushed her back and glared at the young man, who held up his hands.

"Excuse me, senor. I did not mean to frighten you." His voice was calm and his English good. Jeev relaxed. "I just want to share the history of these canals with you," the young man said, gesturing to the canal banks.

"Okay," said Jeev cautiously.

"Sounds interesting," said Emily.

The young man smiled. "My name is Ricardo. I don't want any money from you. I just want you to know our history." Jeev and Emily calmed down and listened intently. "These canals were the primary means of transport for the Aztecs as they delivered food and goods to various parts of the region. During the colonial era, draining of the lakes started and while there are still some small lakes, soon all will be drained out." Ricardo peered over the boat and excitedly pointed at a light gray creature with a fish shaped body, four legs, and what looked like six feathers framing its face. "That's an axolotl. Many people call it a fish, but it's actually a salamander." Emily and Jeev stared at the exotic creature. "You are incredibly lucky to see this animal. It is an incarnation of the Aztec God Xolotl, Quetzalcoatl's twin, and giver of heavenly fire."

Jeev turned to Emily and smiled. She smiled back. *Maybe the gods are smiling at me and granting me favor, even if I don't believe in them...* he mused.

As they approached a bend in the canal, they heard Mariachi music. Four men with guitars stood on the canal bank, singing a slow but happy Mexican love song. A couple on a nearby boat was dancing gently to the music. Emily took Jeev's hand and pulled him up. "Jeev, let's dance." She placed her hands on his shoulders and looked up at him with her wide, innocent blue eyes.

Jeev blushed. "I don't know, Emily. I'm not good at dancing."

"Just move to the music. I will help you," she whispered in his ear. Jeev put his arm around her waist, took her hand, and they began to move. Soon, Jeev was taken in by the rhythm and swung his body to the music. An awkward attempt. The boat rocked precariously. The band, seeing this futile yet brave attempt to enjoy their music, started clapping and singing even louder. Soon other onlookers joined in the singing and dancing. The corner of the canal for a short while turned into a music festival of gyrating bodies and soulful singing. Jeev had not experienced such unconditional joy in a long time. For a moment, he was lost in the melody, all cares nonexistent. The world, with all its suffering, revealed its true colors of eternal peace. Amid a canal, with loud music, singing, dancing, the water sparkling in the sun's rays, there was a calm peace that gently soothed the soul.

The calmness and peace, however, did not last long. About a week later, Jeev entered the dining room to find Emily sipping coffee and staring out the window toward the mountains. "Good morning," said Jeev.

"Good morning," Emily mumbled, continuing to look out the window, not turning towards Jeev.

"What's the matter?" asked Jeev.

Emily turned towards him, tears glistening in her eyes. "Jeev, you know Mexico City is beautiful. I've enjoyed my time here, but I miss my work and school. I was doing something important, life changing, there. Here, I'm not. I don't know what I'm supposed to do." Jeev walked over and hugged her. His heart was heavy, and he could not think of what to say. Emily began to sob, creating a large wet splotch on Jeev's freshly ironed white cotton shirt.

He pulled away and handed her a cream silk handkerchief. "Emily, I've got to go to work. I'll be back home soon, and we can have a good talk then."

"Okay," said Emily, without much enthusiasm. Jeev leaned down, kissed her on her forehead and walked away. Emily continued staring out the window.

By early afternoon, Emily decided that doing something, anything, would make her feel better. She could keep a journal of her life in Mexico! She got out a pen and paper and began to write. Just as she was starting to compose her thoughts, the doorbell rang. Emily went to the door and cracked it open, keeping the chain attached.

"Emily?" said a familiar voice.

Startled, Emily peered out and gasped. "Dad?"

"Yes, Emily. Are you going to let me in?" Emily undid the chain and opened the door. McBride strode in and looked around the small, simple foyer.

"Dad, what are you doing in Mexico?" Emily spoke with forced cheerfulness.

"Why, I came to see you." McBride was calm, which only made Emily more nervous.

"Come with me," said Emily, walking to the living room. McBride sat down in a red velvet armchair. "Would you like some coffee? Or perhaps something stronger?"

"I'll take a neat whiskey please, if you have it."

Emily went to the bar and poured him a neat glass of Jack Daniels, then sat down on the sofa, folding her hands primly in her lap. "Why are you here? How did you find me?"

McBride looked her in the eye. There was no anger, merely concern. He took a sip of whiskey, then spoke. "Emily... your mother and I have been very worried about you. You haven't been home for over six months."

"I've been busy..."

McBride's eyes flashed with anger. "Busy?" He laughed. "Yes miss, you certainly have, but not with your studies, for which I'm paying for!" Emily was silent, wanting to scrunch up small enough to fall between the sofa cushions. "I've been to the townhouse in New York. You weren't there. So, I contacted your friend, Arti." Emily's face went white. "She didn't tell me anything, except that you were visiting Mexico City on some kind of journalism project." Emily felt relieved. McBride continued. "I then went home and met with Lionel and Elizabeth Burke. They recommended that I use my Washington contacts to get in touch with the American Embassy here, and they did the same with the British Embassy." Emily gulped. Her stomach was cold. "Do you know what they told me, several telegrams later?" The pitch of McBride's voice rose. "They told me that you were living with a man, a Miguel Sanchez, which is likely not his real name. How could you, Emily? You know that even a liberated woman like you has a reputation to consider..."

Emily looked her father straight in the eye. "My reputation? If I were a man..."

McBride interrupted here. "If you were a man, it would be different, but you're not. I don't make the rules. It's my job, as your father, to see that you're protected and provided for." Emily opened her mouth to retort, but McBride went on. "What do you want Emily? What is important to you? Do you want to stay here, playing house with Miguel, or do you want to finish law school and help change women's lives? What is the *feminist* thing to do?"

Emily was suddenly deflated. She knew what she had to do. "I've been wanting to come home for a while now. Life here has been wonderful, but it's gotten boring."

"Well then, pack up and let's go. Write a letter to Miguel and let that be the end of it."

Emily rose, went to the bedroom, and packed the few personal things she had come with, and a few mementos she had bought in Mexico. She sat down at her dressing table, took a pen and paper, and wrote Jeev a note:

> *My Dearest Jeev, By the time you come home today, I will be gone. My father arrived today from Maryland. He wants me to come home and finish my studies and start my legal career. As you know from our recent conversations, I've been wanting to do this. My father knows about us, but he doesn't know everything. I love you. It hurts me to leave, but my leaving is best for both of us. Take care of yourself. Love, Emily*

Emily folded the letter, stuffed it in an envelope, sealed it, and wrote "Miguel" on the front.

McBride knocked softly on the door. "May I come in?"

"Yes," replied Emily.

Her father entered and picked up her suitcase. "Is this all?"

"Yes, that's all." Emily got up, grabbed her purse, and picked up the letter to Miguel.

They walked out of the house. Emily left the letter on a small shelf next to the front door. She did not notice that there was another letter there, addressed to her in English, but with Jeev's name written in Bangla script underneath.

Two hours later, Jeev arrived home. "Emily, I'm home!" he called out, expecting her to come running and give him a big hug. Instead, he was met by silence. Jeev panicked, running from room to room, only to find them empty. He opened the wardrobe in the bedroom. Her clothes were gone. He walked back to the front door, where he saw two letters, one thin one from Emily to him and the other, a thick envelope, addressed to Emily but with his real name written in Bangla script. His heart skipped a beat. Could it be news about Amee? He took the letters into the living room, sat down at the writing desk, grabbed a letter opener, and opened Emily's letter first. Reading it, Jeev felt a stab of sadness, yet also relief. He was a soldier. He had to move ahead with his plans on his own. As much as he cared for Emily, he must remove her from the dangerous path he was on. He had to travel alone.

He then opened the next letter, which was written in Bengali. It was from Emily's friend, Arti. Suddenly, Jeev remembered, and tears welled up in his eyes. He put the letter aside quickly and grabbed a handkerchief. *Of course! Amee had a little sister, Arti!* The tears flowed. No wonder she had seemed familiar! Jeev took a deep breath, blew his nose, and picked up the letter, and read it. Arti described how she, Amee, and a third woman, Agni, had been sent to the Caribbean as indentured workers, how they escaped, and what they were doing now. Jeev's heart swelled. He felt every emotion, happiness, sadness, anger, but above all, joy to know that Amee was safe, healthy, and happy. He read the letter over and over again and thanked Durga for protecting Amee and Arti and enabling them to prosper.

Finally, he put the letter back in its envelope and tucked it into a side table drawer. He poured himself a glass of mezcal and took a sip, savoring the subtle smoky flavor. "Emily, would you like a glass..." he called out and then realized she was not there. Suddenly, the stillness of the house perturbed him. The zest and cheeriness that Emily brought to every moment, her ability to make something out of nothing, and her smiling face were gone. Now weary, he sat down on the boldly patterned Zapotec rug, placed his hands over his head as tears dropped on his cheeks.

"Aahh! Dios mio! Dios mio!" Jeev was startled awake by a woman screaming. He was sprawled on the floor, his unfinished drink on the rug beside him. He blinked his eyes to clear them, and saw the cleaning lady standing above him, her eyes wide with fear.

Jeev propped himself up on his elbow and rubbed his eyes which were hurting from the bright sunlight streaming through the windows. "Buenos dias, Dolores," he mumbled, recognizing the maid who came to help every day.

Dolores smiled, and her body relaxed. "Make coffee?" she asked in thickly accented English.

"Si, café," replied Jeev. Dolores bustled to the kitchen. Jeev got up and settled into his chair, trying to figure out how he had wound up on the floor. Where was Emily? Then he remembered. Before he could start feeling sorry for himself again, Dolores returned with a large pot of steaming coffee and fresh, buttered bolillos, a crusty bread that was soft and airy inside. The hot coffee and tender, chewy bread rejuvenated him.

During the next few days, Jeev threw himself into his work, authoring articles supporting Socialist reform policies that benefited workers and peasants. He was busy typing a story at the office when Juan Carlos entered with two bottles of beer. "Here, Miguel. I think you could use a break."

"Gracias," Jeev said, smiling.

Juan Carlos sat down in a chair next to Jeev and popped open his beer. "What is the matter, Miguel? You are here all hours, and you are so intense."

"We're living in intense times, amigo. Socialists in Europe and the United States, who used to be pacifists, are now supporting the war. They're not focusing on reforms that would help workers and peasants."

"It's about gaining public support, you know." Juan Carlos looked wistful. "A party is made of people. Without public support, there is no party and no agitation for reforms."

"I know," said Jeev. "At least the Partido Socialista, President Carranza, and General Obregon are advocating for helpful provisions in the new constitution."

Juan took a swallow of beer. "Like requiring landowners to uphold the rights of the farm workers, to pay them on time, access to free and secular education, restrictions on the Church, and better working conditions are radical policies. Oh, I almost forgot. This came for you." He held out a large, square, ivory colored envelope with an official seal on the back.

Jeev sliced it open carefully with his penknife and withdrew a piece of heavy cardstock paper. "It's an invitation to the Presidential Palace."

Juan glanced at the invitation. "I got an invitation to the Castillo too. You and Emily can ride with Isabella and me."

Jeev sighed. "I'm afraid it will just be me. Emily went back home about a week ago."

"So sorry, mi amigo." Juan patted him on the shoulder. "No wonder you have been doing the work of two men. You are still welcome to come with us. Who knows?" Juan's eyes sparkled. "You might just meet some very interesting people."

About a week later, Jeev stared up at the massive, gray stone edifice of the Castillo, rising above the dark green forest of the Bosque de Chapultepec.

"Magnificent, isn't it?" said Juan, his left hand lightly grasping the steering wheel of his glossy black Chevrolet and his right hand holding his wife's hand, which he released as the road curved to the right as they navigated the winding road up to the Castillo.

Jeev leaned back in the rear seat, taking in the glorious reds and golds of the setting sun contrasting with the dark trees in the park. The castle stood out, not just for its height, but for the brightly colored stained-glass windows, illuminated by electric lights. "Yes, indeed." Jeev agreed.

"It's your first time to visit the Castillo, isn't it?" asked Maria.

"Yes, I've walked through the Bosque many times and looked up at the palace, but I've never been on the hill."

Just then, they stopped for another checkpoint. "Papers, please," demanded the stern-faced soldiers. Juan Carlos handed over his documents, as did Maria and Jeev as Miguel. The soldiers glanced over the papers, and then the passengers. Satisfied, they returned the documents and Juan moved on to the next checkpoint.

As they moved out of sight of the soldiers, Maria griped. "Why so many checkpoints? If they don't trust their guests, why invite them?"

"Because, dear, not everyone is as trustworthy as you," replied Juan. "Pancho Villa, the Zapatistas, and even some of the president's own generals would not hesitate to assassinate him if it would further their own causes."

"What about the cause of the Mexican people?" Maria

remonstrated. "Aren't we all supposed to champion that? I just hate greed, pride…"

Juan sighed. "As do we all. Life is much more complicated than it should be. Why not enjoy the time we have now? It's a beautiful evening in a beautiful place."

Maria squeezed Juan's empty right hand. "Yes, it is!" Jeev gazed around at the deepening crimsons and golds of the sunset, and the Castillo windows shining like jewels in the dimming light. He smiled.

As they approached the Castillo, oil torches lit the way, creating a medieval atmosphere. On entering the palace, Jeev nearly gasped at the huge circular staircases adorned with candles and flowers. They were led up one staircase to a ballroom with dozens of sparkling chandeliers, cherry mahogany wood-paneled walls and scores of men in black tuxedos with crisp white shirts and women in ballgowns. A band in one corner played Viennese waltzes, while white-gloved servers milled around offering drinks and tapas. Jeev, Juan Carlos, and Maria mingled with the crowd for a while.

Jeev, however, soon became bored with small talk about horses, houses, other social events, and people he did not know. He began to study the art on and around the walls. Fascinated, he wandered out into a hall, where he meandered and eagerly drank in a dizzying collection of Spanish paintings and sculptures, interspaced with Mayan and Aztec relics.

As he admired an intricately carved round stone over twenty feet tall, he heard a soft voice behind him. "I see you are appreciating the *Piedra del Sol*,". He turned around to see a smiling young woman with long jet-black hair wore down framing her face in flowing waves, tanned skin, and full lips. She wore a long maroon silk dress with a tight bodice, a daring V-shaped neckline, short flutter sleeves, and a flowing skirt. The sleeves, neckline, and skirt were adorned were small embroidered white and gold flowers with dark green stems and leaves. A sash in matching maroon colored silk further emphasized her slim waist and generous curves. The Spanish beauty then explained, "The sun stone".

"Oh yes, the sunstone," babbled Jeev.

"This was found almost five hundred years ago. We think it represents a sundial or a calendar or one of the Aztec kings or the many phases of Aztec history or maybe many things combined," she continued.

"It is an amazing piece of art; I hope to understand its story one day," lauded Jeev.

"Oh, I am Mariana," she introduced herself, extending her hand.

"I am Jeev." Jeev gibbered, forgetting his identity, revealing his real name. He regretted his slip for a second, but then no one really believed that 'Miguel' was his real name, anyway. Her handshake brought him back to reality. It was a hard, firm handshake, the kind you would get from a well-built gentleman, not the soft limp hand he was expecting. They walked down the hallway towards the ballroom, continuing their conversation about the art. Mariana explained the historical significance of both the Spanish paintings and the Aztec artifacts. They stopped in the ballroom before a more than a life size painting of Hernan Cortes astride a horse. In the background, his army of conquistadores were slaughtering the native Aztecs.

At that moment, a soldier announced the entry of President Carranza, and all turned to face the large doors at the entrance of the hall. The guards swung open the two enormous doors to let in the President with his wife at his side. Carranza wore a general's uniform. He was an impressive aristocratic figure with his long white beard, heavy mustache, and round glasses. He greeted his well-wishers as he strode down to the middle of the room, where General Obregon was standing with other military officers. "Jeev, would you like to meet President Carranza?" asked Mariana.

Surprised, Jeev replied, "Yes, yes, I would like to meet him."

"Then follow me," Mariana beckoned, and Jeev followed her to the center of the room, past Juan Carlos, who looked at him with astonishment.

Mariana smiled at Carranza, kissing him on both cheeks. They obviously knew each other well. "*Senor Presidente,* this is my new friend, Jeev Sen, the journalist, he writes under the name of Miguel Sanchez."

How did she know that? wondered Jeev, but he did not have time to think.

"Ah, our socialist journalist, yes, I have read your articles. Thank you for your contribution to our society! Come, you and Mariana must join us for dinner." The small party left the ballroom and entered an intricately decorated ivory and gold dining room.

The long, white clothed table seated over fifty people. Carranza was at the head of the table, with his wife, Obregon, and other generals around him. Mariana and Jeev were seated towards the end of the table. Mariana was to his left and to his surprise, Captain Mueller seated on his right. "Captain Mueller," he blurted, recognizing the man who had kidnapped him when he first arrived in Mexico.

"It is General Mueller, now," said the man with contempt.

"Sorry, I did not know of your promotion. And what about Commander Koenig? " He inquired about the second man of the kidnapping, who had promised to contact him. "Unfortunately, Commander Koenig and his U-boat went missing in the North Atlantic. One presumes he has died in the fight for the Motherland," explained Mueller.

"Oh, that's tragic" said Jeev "for him and for the plans we were making. What do we..." He was interrupted by a Mexican major sitting across the table was who engaged in a lively conversation with Mariana. "Senora Alvarez," pointing towards Mariana, "is the heroine of the Revolution. She is a *soldadora*, a woman soldier. She fought under President Carranza and General Obregon. After Pancho Villa's forces overran her village, she was the only woman who survived.

They killed most of the people in her village. Pancho took the young women, including Mariana, captive. She escaped and then went back and freed the twenty women who were captured. Then she stole guns from Villa, and they formed their own fighting unit. Soon she had over a thousand women fighting for her. President Carranza heard about her and asked her to join him in the revolution. She and her *soldadoras* have fought in many battles in the North." Both General Mueller and Jeev were in awe of what Mariana had accomplished. Something neither of them had ever seen in their lifetime: a brigade or fighting women soldiers. All the conversations for the rest of the night revolved around the exploits of Mariana Alvarez.

As flan was served for dessert, along with sweet wine, Jeev finally got the opportunity to ask Mueller, "Any progress on the arms we need?"

"The war is not going well for Germany; we are expecting the United States to declare war on Germany soon. I am here to talk to the President about Mexico joining the German alliance, if that happens, I can assure you, you will have all the arms you need." He then placed his hand on Jeev's shoulder, "Not a word of this to anyone, you understand." Jeev nodded, understanding perfectly.

"So how would you convince Mexico to support Germany?" inquired Mariana, curious about the bombshell that Mueller had dropped.

"Simple," expounded Mueller, now having consumed more wine than he should have, "What does Mexico want? I will tell you, Texas, California, New Mexico. Right? Well, we can make it happen. United States declares war on Germany, the next day Mexico declares war on the United States. German U-boats wreak havoc on both coasts of the United States. German ships bring tanks, machine guns, ammunition to Mexico. Mexico stops supplying Britain with oil. The army attacks the US in Texas and California. Large parts of the southern US are now back in the hands of Mexico. Works like clockwork, no?" Mariana and Jeev looked nervously at each other, wondering what would happen when this information reached the highest levels of Mexico or, God forbid, the United States. Suddenly, Mueller went quiet, realizing he had said too much, and as the as the dinner was winding down, he excused himself and left.

Jeev turned to Mariana. "Thank you for a lovely evening. I've learned so much and really enjoyed it." He fervently thought, *I only hope that we meet again.*"

Mariana smiled. "Me too, Jeev." Jeev smiled back, rose, and took his leave and went off to find Juan and Maria.

When Jeev entered the newspaper office the following Friday, Juan was sitting at his desk, with his head in his hands, looking unusually pale.

"What is the matter?" asked Jeev, concerned.

Juan looked up. "Haven't you heard? The US has declared war on Germany."

Jeev was shocked. He sat down in the chair in front of Juan's desk, making sure that his rear end was in the chair seat. "Is Mexico still neutral?"

"Yes," declared Juan.

"Good. I'll draft an article about why that is right. After all, we are finally getting peace. The economy has been ravaged by war and the people have suffered enough."

"Excellent points," said Juan. "You could add that war with the US would have been bloody and costly, both in terms of the economic costs and the human life that would be lost. And don't forget, we also supply oil to both the British and Germans. Our economy is finally improving. Why do we want to take sides and miss out?"

"Neutrality is indeed a wise choice for Carranza and Mexico. Of course, you know that there are rumors that a large shipment of gold has been delivered to the National Bank in exchange for neutrality." Juan opened his mouth to speak, but Jeev continued. "I'm not planning on putting that in my story as I can't prove it either way." Juan's face relaxed.

"What about your German contact, General Mueller?" asked Juan, changing the subject.

"Hmm... he could have some interesting information. I'll try to get in touch." Jeev's efforts to do so, however, failed. Mueller had vanished.

Talking to Juan a week later, Jeev commented, "The war is not going well for Germany now that the Americans have entered."

Juan sighed. "I know. With French, British, and now American forces on the Western Front, Germany is losing strength."

Juan's words sent a chill down Jeev's spine. *How long can I be safe here? Well, I don't know where I'll go next. I just have to stay here as long as I can or until I figure out my next steps.* He then put a sheet of paper in his typewriter and started his next article.

CHAPTER 40: PRESIDENTIAL INTRIGUE (1919)

J eev leaned back in his red leather armchair, stretched out his legs and took a sip of mezcal. It had been a long day at the newspaper office, but now he was home, with letters to read. He grabbed the paper knife lying on the side table and opened the first letter, which was from Emily.

Dear Jeev,

As you may (or not) know, I graduated from law school. I am now living and working in Washington DC as a women's rights lawyer. I am not alone, however.

I am sure that you have heard that the US recently purchased the Virgin Islands from Denmark, making it a US territory. This means that my best friend Arti, and her sister, are free to travel, live, and work in the US. Arti is also living here in Washington and has recently joined the law firm where I practice. We have had several prominent cases and are creating names for ourselves! Life has never been so busy or so good.

I hope that you are doing well in Mexico. Say hello to Juan Carlos and Maria for me. Love, Emily

Jeev's heart swelled with happiness, and since he was

alone, he allowed a tear to drop from his eye. Amee and Arti finally had a chance to have the lives they deserved. If only... Jeev sighed. There would be time for him when India was free.

Jeev grabbed the second letter. It was from Amee. His hands started to shake. He took a deep breath and carefully sliced the top of the letter after shaking the contents down so that he would not cut the message in half. He then extracted a single sheet of ivory notepaper covered in Bangla characters. Eagerly he devoured the contents.

> *Dear Jeev, I hope this letter finds you doing well and happy. I was so excited when Arti told me that you were living in Mexico!*
>
> *I am still in St. Thomas, managing the Riley Plantation. I am happy. I enjoy my work, for which I am very well compensated. I have wonderful friends who are more like the family that Arti and I never had.*
>
> *You too, are part of our found family. Mexico is not that far from St. Thomas. (At least it is much closer than India). You are very welcome to come visit me anytime you wish and can do so. I would love to see you and share old stories and fresh news. We have so much to catch up on! Love, Amee*

Jeev's heart finally burst, and he cried like a baby. Amee and Arti were not just safe. They were thriving. What more could he wish for them?

Jeev took another sip of mezcal, blew his nose, and dabbed his eyes with his handkerchief. As he put Amee's letter back in the envelope, he thought of his friends and family back home in India. Unbiased news from there was difficult to get as it was filtered by the British press. He reached into the side table drawer and pulled out a small notebook in which he had written what little he was able to find out about his native country. Glancing through his carefully written and dated notes, he saw that hundreds of thousands of Indian troops fought on the side of the British, which disappointed him. Jeev palmed his face. Why did his countrymen have to die for those who cared nothing for them or their dreams? Why did he have to struggle to put his plans for freedom into action? Why had none of his plans borne fruit? He was too sad to cry. Enough Indian tears had been shed. It was now time for British blood.

A few weeks later, Jeev and Juan arrived at the Presidential Palace. As they entered a large room with straight-backed chairs lined up to face a podium, Jeev asked Juan, "What do you think President Carranza is going to say?"

"I don't know. I don't have enough information to speculate, but it must be important. Look at the crowd that's gathering!"

Jeev looked out and, to his shock, saw Mariana sitting in a few rows in front of them. "Excuse me," he said to Juan. "I'll be back in a minute." He walked toward Mariana, and Juan smiled, chuckling softly to himself. It was good to see his friend happy again.

As Jeev approached her, Mariana looked up and smiled. "Hello, Jeev! I'm glad that you're here. Have a seat," she said, patting the chair next to hers. Jeev grinned at her and sat down. Before he could open his mouth and speak to her, a brass trio began playing the Mexican National Anthem, and everyone stood at attention as President Carranza came into the room, followed by his entourage. After the music stopped and everyone was again seated, the president stepped up to the podium, cleared his throat and began to speak. He spoke at length about his accomplishments, in steering the country through the revolution, in building the economy and in the drafting of the constitution. He talked about labor rights, land reform progress and the freedom and happiness that Mexicans enjoyed during his term as President.

Having heard most of this before, Jeev did not bother to take copious notes. He was soon bored, and his eyes grew heavy. "It is now time for me to leave. I am not running for president in the upcoming election…" Carranza's words jolted Jeev, whose eyelids popped open. He sat up straight and began taking notes as quickly as Carranza could speak. "Instead, I am endorsing our honorable ambassador to the United States, Ignacio Bonillas, for president." The room was briefly silent and then someone began to applaud and everyone, including Jeev and Mariana, joined in.

As the press conference concluded, Jeev took a deep breath, turned to Mariana, and asked, "Mariana, would you like to have dinner with me later this week?"

Mariana's eyes gleamed and she flashed him a brief smile. "Yes, I would. That will be lovely."

Jeev's heart skipped a beat, and he felt a warm glow. He hoped that his face was not as bright as the rest of him felt. "Great, I'll call you later." He nodded and walked back to Juan. He then went back to the office and worked on his article for the next day, which supported the current President and praised his accomplishments. Jeev especially noted the Mexican neutrality in the war and praised Carranza as having the political power and intelligence to stand up to both opposing forces to maintain the non-alignment of Mexico. The article came out the next day, and the newspaper received a note from the President thanking them for his support. Jeev and Juan were pleased to have the backing of the most powerful man in the country.

Later that week, Jeev arrived at the Hosteria de Santo Domingo, a small pink building in the Historic District. Mariana was standing outside, wearing a soft blue silk dress, with her long black hair falling in now familiar soft waves over her shoulders. "Hello, Jeev," she said, with a flirtatious twinkle in her dark eyes. "Shall we go in?" Jeev smiled and took her arm.

As they entered the restaurant, the maître d' exclaimed, "Welcome, senorita. Come this way. Your regular table is ready."

"*Gracias,* Manuel," said Mariana. Manuel led them past the local diners to a secluded corner. The ceiling of the restaurant had large, dark wooden beams in square pattern. Stained glass windows which reflected the light from the outside chandeliers hung from the ceiling, casting shadows on the large hardwood plank floors. Mariachi music played in the background, and behind their table was a large, dark blue arch highlighting a framed painting of a scene from the Yucatan countryside.

"Do you mind if I order for both of us? I know the menu well, and I know what you would like." Her voice was husky, barely above a whisper and made Jeev's head tingle with pleasure.

"I trust you, Madame. Let's have it your way." Jeev saw a brief, wicked glint in Mariana's eyes. Before she could reply, the waiter approached, and she ordered for them. Tequila was served followed by Chiles en Nogada, a huge poblano chile stuffed with chopped pork covered in a white walnut cream sauce and sprinkled with pomegranate seeds and greens, served on a green plate decorated with red flowers.

As they were eating, Mariana told Jeev, "I read your article. It was good at its praise for Carranza, but there is something you need to know. The election will not be as straightforward as people imagine. As you know, General Obregon had left the service of Carranza and gone back to his hacienda in the countryside. However, with the upcoming elections, he has thrown his hat on the ring to challenge Carranza. This will be public knowledge soon. As you know, in Mexico, he who controls the sword, controls the throne. So be careful."

Jeev nodded in agreement as he digested the information and the earthy tasting, savory food. They walked out into the cool night, heading towards Mariana's house, with only streetlamps and the full moon for light. They stopped outside an iron gate surrounded by a tall white wall. Jeev was puzzled. "Where is the house?"

Mariana laughed, but her eyes did not. "It's for protection," she explained. "When you live in Mexico, you never know what will happen. Come on in," she invited Jeev. A guard opened the gate. Inside, a brick pathway led to an orange stucco ranch-style house with a tile roof. Blooming Mexican sunflowers, dahlias, and hibiscus adorned most of the front yard. Mariana unlocked the front door, and Jeev entered a bright tile floored foyer with earthy orange walls. Mariana led the way to a moonlight bathed courtyard in the middle of the house which surrounded a swimming pool.

"Do you swim?" inquired Mariana as she deftly removed all her clothes, waded into the pool, and then dived in, completely submerging in the water. She appeared on the other side of the pool. "The water feels good," she said. Jeev did not need any further encouragement. He undressed and jumped in.

When he woke up the next morning, he was sleeping on a soft white bed. The sun was streaming in through the window and Mariana was lying next to him fast asleep. He gathered up his clothes and walked towards the courtyard, thinking fondly of last night's escapades. "Café, Senor?" asked a maid in a black dress with a frilly white apron.

"Yes, coffee would be nice," said Jeev, nodding his head to make sure she understood him. He wondered if seeing a strange man in the courtyard was not a peculiar occurrence for the maid. He sat down at a small table, gazing out at the sunlit pool. The maid returned, not only with coffee, but also a tray loaded with cheese, meats, and bread.

As he was enjoying his breakfast, Mariana walked out

wearing a sheer nightgown. "I have news for you. General Obregon is coming back to Mexico City."

Jeev nodded. "Well, he was my initial contact when I arrived here, so I should be on good terms with him, right?"

"Politics is a dangerous game. Friends, enemies, acquaintances, family, does not mean much in politics. Enemies become friends, friends become enemies, families fight each other. The only constant is change," prophesied Mariana. "Tell me, Jeev," she continued, "you wrote some articles about the Russian Revolution. What is your opinion on the Revolution now?"

"You know I have a socialist trend in my thoughts and principles," Jeev answered. "For me, socialism is a political system that is for the people, for the workers and for the common person. The capitalist system is for the owners of the factories and services. For a while I thought of communism and socialism as interchangeable. I was quite elated to find that Lenin had risen to power in Moscow. He had spoken about the principles of Marx and Engels. The etymology of socialism is to share, to combine. My understanding of socialism is that profits cannot be concentrated at the top of the food chain by a few people. They must share it with all. The people at the top did not get there by themselves, they got there because of the workers and the consumers. It is the right of all to share in the profits. I have concluded that those who are entrepreneurs, inventors, creators should be allowed up to a certain extent to enjoy the fruits of their labors. The inventor of the car engine has a right to enjoy much more wealth than the worker on the assembly line, but there has to be a sense of proportion. And the government has to have laws around protecting the wellbeing of the workers."

"So, what about what's happening in Russia?" Mariana interjected.

"Yes, I am getting to that. Lenin used the umbrella of communism to establish an authoritarian government. The killing of the czar's family should not have happened. Today, there is a civil war going on between the pro-monarchy White Army and Lenin's Red Army. The Red Army is killing thousands of people for revenge because they may not agree with their political viewpoints. So, yes, I do not think Lenin's communism reflects the socialist values of Marx. In fact, it goes against what socialism stands for."

They continued their conversation for a while. As Jeev was leaving, Mariana asked "I can set up a meeting with Obregon, would you be willing to interview him and write an article about it?"

Jeev hesitated, "That's dangerous, but yes, as a journalist, I would like to hear from him." Mariana agreed to set up the meeting and then, with a wave, walked away from the courtyard. Jeev walked meekly out of the house.

A few days later, Jeev was opening the front door to go to work, when his shoe scuffed on something on the floor. He looked down and saw a letter, it was addressed to Miguel Sanchez with no address. He bent down, picked it up, and opened it with his penknife. Inside was a brief note.

Dear Senor Sanchez, You are requested to meet with General Alvaro Obregon this evening at 8:00. A car will be sent for you at your home. Be ready by 7:15.

The note was unsigned. Jeev tucked the note back in its envelope, placed it in his pocket, and went to work.

That evening, Jeev stood outside his home. He looked at his watch. It was 7:15 but there was no sign of a car. He tapped his feet to distract himself from being nervous. Suddenly, a silent black sedan with a long body glided up to his driveway. Jeev stopped tapping.

A woman in a cream-colored dress with long black hair got out of the car. It was Mariana. "Jeev, come with us," she beckoned. He got inside the car and sat down. In front were two tall, muscular men with blank expressions. He sat in the back with Mariana. Dark curtains were glued to the windows. Jeev reached out to see if he could move them.

The man in the passenger seat at once turned around and told him "Please don't touch the curtains, otherwise I will have to place a bag over your head." Jeev nodded. "We will drive for a while, so get some rest," he continued. He then drew a curtain that was between the front and the back seats of the car so Jeev could no longer see where he was going, although he could see a faint light from time to time through the fabric. Jeev looked over at Mariana, who had lit a cigarette and was smiling at him. Jeev opened his mouth to speak to her, but she placed her finger on her lips and shook her head. The car was soon full of smoke, causing Jeev's eyes to sting and making it hard to breathe. Squinting, he was able to see Mariana's silhouette. She was calm and her fingers were still and empty as she stared straight ahead. Jeev resigned himself to the situation and closed his eyes. They drove throughout the night. He was not sure if they were going straight or in circles.

Several hours later, the car finally came to a halt. Someone opened the door, and Jeev stumbled out. Stretching his legs, he had to shield his eyes from the bright sunlight. He was in a hacienda. There was a small cottage in front of him. The men led him to the cottage. Inside, there was a wood-burning fireplace and three chairs around a table. He looked around and noticed Mariana was no longer with him. Jeev sat on a chair and waited.

About ten minutes later, a tall man in a military uniform approached him. "Senor Sanchez, come with me. The general is ready to see you now." He led Jeev to a brick path which opened out into a large open space. In front of him was a palatial residence. A straight brick walkway led to an entrance framed by a three-story tower. On either side of the tower, a mansion stretched out in both directions. This was certainly a very opulent hacienda, he thought. The man led him into a large office. General Obregon was seated behind a massive teak desk. In front were a few men, some seated, some standing. Mariana was sitting on a couch in an area near the desk.

"Come, my Hindu journalist" boomed Obregon. "Take notes." He pointed to some paper and pens on the table. The general then laid out his platform for election and the reasons he was a better candidate than the puppet being fielded by Carranza. At one point, he got up and jabbed his finger in Jeev's chest, saying, "I have an agenda that will better the lives of the workers and the farmers. You should understand that since you are a socialist." Jeev nodded and continued to take notes. All the men in the room clapped once the General stopped talking, indicating to Jeev the interview was over.

Jeev placed the pen he used back in the table, folded his notes, stood up, and placed them in his jacket pocket. "Thank you very much for your time, General Obregon," he said nodding to the general. The general nodded back, and Jeev left. The car was waiting for him to take him back to Mexico City. This time, he traveled alone. Mariana did not come with him.

Juan and Jeev worked on their opinion page for a few days before publishing what they thought was a very balanced piece of journalism. They compared the Carranza plan and the Obregon plan listing the pros and cons of each.

Public perception, however, was not so balanced. Both Obregon's and Carranza's supporters felt the article showed their respective candidates in a bad light. Sitting in the office about four days after the article was published, Juan laughed half-heartedly. "No presidential invitations for us this time, Jeev. Nobody is saying anything."

"The silence is a bit much," said Jeev, taking a swig of beer. Just then, there was a loud crash. Jeev jumped up, spilling much of the contents of his almost full beer bottle on the hardwood floor.

"What the hell was that?" cried Juan, running out the door only to see a group of men smashing the newspaper sign while shouting *"Viva Carranza!"* Juan quickly closed and bolted the door. "Jeev, we've got to get out of here. Let's take the back door." Going out the rear of the building, they managed to leave undetected, each man scurrying to his own home, while keeping an eye out for anyone who might be watching.

When he arrived home, Jeev tried contacting Mariana, but she did not answer her phone. He then decided to take a chance and go to her house. When he approached the gate, the guard stared at him without blinking. Jeev, acting as relaxed as he could manage, approached him. "Is Senorita Alvarez at home?" he asked.

The guard sneered at him. "No, she is not. Go away!" He then pointed a gun at Jeev who held his hands up and backed away, then turned and walked back to his house at a rapid pace.

Tensions continued to rise. The elections were held, and Obregon lost to Carranza's candidate. However, the General refused to accept the decision. One morning, when Juan and Jeev were working on the morning edition, an employee came running into the office. He was breathless, pale, and his eyes were wide with fear. Juan rose from his desk. "What's the matter, Hernandez? Have you seen a ghost?"

"N...n...no." The young man shook, then gulped, took a deep breath, and spoke. "The General's military has taken over the Presidential Palace. There are soldiers everywhere in the city."

Juan snapped his fingers. "Miguel, grab your jacket. We've got a revolution to cover." Jeev grabbed his coat and followed Juan out onto the streets. Soldiers had taken over all the key areas of the city. Returning to the office that evening, they started the printing presses. The news was that the military had taken over to bring order to the nation. General Obregon was on his way to Mexico City.

Suddenly, Jeev heard a loud noise. "Juan, what is that?"

"Trouble, Jeev," Juan replied. A group of masked men were hammering at their front door. The door soon caved in, and the group entered the office, smashing furniture, breaking windows. One employee protested, and they hit him on the head, sending him reeling to the floor. Juan and Jeev held their arms up in surrender. The masked men smashed the printing presses, dragged equipment, and threw it out of the window. On their way out, one man tossed a flammable liquid on the floor and set it on fire. Juan and his employees ran out through a back entrance. They looked back in shock, seeing their entire newspaper office go up in flames. Juan saw his life's work burning before his eyes. He fell to his knees, tears pouring down his face. Jeev sat down next to the inconsolable Juan. He could see the flames reflecting in his friend's eyes. In the blink of an eye, everything changed. Obregon made his point and established control. Anyone who supported the last regime would pay a stiff price. Juan and Jeev had picked the wrong side.

CHAPTER 41: GO SOUTH, MY FRIEND

That next night, Juan and his wife came to Jeev's house. They were distraught and scared. "I fear for my life and that of my family," confessed Juan. "My entire life is built around this newspaper; All my savings were used to set up the newspaper. Now it is all gone. We came here to inform you we are all leaving. We will cross the border into Texas to start a new life there." He paused, stifling the emotions that he had dammed inside him. "It was not a straightforward decision, but the only one we now have left. Take my advice, my friend. It is no longer safe for you to be here. Leave while you can." With that, Jeev embraced Juan, and they parted.

Jeev was confused with the information that Juan had provided. He did not want to be on the run again. Mexico had been good to him, and he wanted to stay longer. There was one person who would give him the proper advice and who might help. He went to look for Mariana. It was the 'Día de los Muertos' – the day of the dead, in the city. People's graves were being decorated with marigold flowers; small children were running around with ghastly masks. Periodically he would pass areas where skulls and mask offering were placed, decorated with brightly colored cloths and flowers. People wore bright orange, black and red colored clothing. He found himself in front of Mariana's house. He waited till a passing caravan of revelers distracted the guard, then climbed the wall around the side and slipped inside. Cautiously making his way towards the courtyard, hoping he would find her.

Hearing water splashing in the pool, he made his way there. Mariana was gently swimming across the water. He waited till she stopped and saw him standing there. She smiled and walked out of the shallow end of the pool, unperturbed by her nakedness. She was a powerful lady, reminded him of a mythical Amazonian woman, muscular arms, big breasts, flat stomach, beefy thighs. Unhurriedly, she walked over to a gown hanging on a chair and draped it over her wet body. Sitting on the chair, crossing her legs, and wiping her head with a towel, she said, "What brings you here, Jeev?"

"Mariana, I need to know if it's safe for me to stay in Mexico City. You know both sides, I need your advice on what to do."

She looked straight into his eyes. "You should leave. Obregon will soon be in power, and he will remove anyone who could obstruct him." Running her finger over her neck like a knife. "Is there anything you can do? How will you survive?" he anxiously inquired. She smiled at him with a twinkle in her eye. "You know by now that I take care of myself. Always align with the person in power. So far, I have always chosen wisely."

She got up and walked back towards the house her gown sticking to her wet body. Jeev stood transfixed, watching her go. Pausing, she turned to face him. "Listen to me. Make a plan to leave the country. Sometimes you need to head in the direction where they will not expect you. Most people are going North towards the United States to escape. That is where the soldiers are, looking for Carranza supporters. The smart ones will go South, maybe make their way to the Merida in the Yucatan, then take a ship from there to another country." She picked up a piece of paper and wrote a note. "Here is the name and address of a person in Merida who will help. Good luck," and then she handed him the paper and walked into her house. Jeev took the main entrance to leave, walking past the surprised guard.

Jeev rushed back to his house. He had this feeling that someone had followed him from Mariana's house. Walking inside, he locked the door, stuffed his travel papers and money in his jacket, and grabbed a suitcase, then decided it was too risky to come out with a large bag, so he stuffed a few essential items into a canvas bag he used to carry to his office and walked out of the house. There were four soldiers standing outside his house. When they saw him leave, they followed him, not even pretending to hide themselves. Passing a store, he stepped inside and bought a skeleton mask and a long black gown. He waited until a procession of masked revelers passed the store and then unhurriedly joined them. The soldiers had not seen him enter the store but were standing by the corner waiting to see where they had lost him. The revelers went right by them, the soldiers unable to see through his disguise. He followed the party until he could put some distance between him and the soldiers. Then veered off, removed his costume, and dropped it in front of a man sitting by the street. The train station was full of soldiers, but they would not be looking specifically for him. At the ticket booth he asked, "Is there a train that goes to Merida?" The ticket collector replied "You can go as far south as Veracruz. From there you will have to take a boat." Jeev bought a ticket to Veracruz and boarded the train. A steam engine attached to a coal car, several passenger wagons, and cargo cars. He squeezed into a passenger car and sat on a wooden bench which he shared with a family who had loaded hens in cages, a goat, and several large bags. Mariana was right. The soldiers were searching the trains going North. Soon the train was passing through open fields. At one point, a group of teenage boys started running after the train. His thoughts went back to his days in the village when they too would chase down the trains. He wondered what his friend Ramu was doing.

CHAPTER 42: THE LAST STAND (1915)

"I wonder what Jeev is doing?" said Ramu to Swamy. "I heard he had to escape to Mexico to evade the British and American agents." "I know no matter where he is, he will not lose sight of our goals" replied Ramu as he stretched his leg to relieve the pain. He had never fully recovered from the gunshot wound sustained during the Viceroy train attack. "He will come back one day with the arms we need."

"How is the progress here at the camp? asked Swamy as he looked out into the fields where a group of young men lying on the ground were shooting at targets in the distance. Ramu replied "As per your instructions I am continuing to work on assembling a fighting force. We now have almost a thousand boys here in the camp. We have hidden our locations deep in the forest, where they are trained in armed combat. They learn how to dig trenches, to assemble and clean rifles, target practice and set up tents. They are taught to cook and survive in the jungle, making use of whatever resources they can find. I teach them hand to hand combat and make them run for miles to improve their physical strength." Swamy nodded in appreciation "You have made immense progress." "We are ready to head to the Andaman Islands in preparation to take over Port Blair. Actually, we think we could stage an attack on the British anywhere in the country." "You have trained them well" said Swami "our day has finally come to deploy them." Ramu was happy with the news. "So, when do we leave for the

Islands?"

Swamy placed his hand on Ramu's shoulder saying, "You have always placed your trust in me, and these boys trust you. So, what I have to say may go against all your beliefs but trust me on this one. The Indian National Congress has supported the British in the war effort against Germany. We feel, by supporting them, they will be grateful for our support and grant us our demands for self-rule." Ramu's mouth opened and closed, aghast, he could not produce any words. "You are right that goes against everything we believe in!" exclaimed Ramu. "We should join Germany in the war against the British. This is our chance to strike while they are weak."

Swamy shook his head. "You must listen to me. You and your troops will join the British. There are ships coming into the Calcutta harbor which will take you to the battlefront. Decisions have been made at the highest levels. Gather all your troops, I will address them with news of the plans." Ramu was furious, he briskly walked away.

A few weeks later Ramu and his contingent of soldiers travelled to Calcutta. He surveyed the large tent city where hundreds of tents had been set up. Finding the tent where Swamy was located, he walked into find Swamy sitting with two other men. "Ramu, meet Badal Singh of the Sikh regiment and Sher Thapa of the Gurkha regiment. Just like you they have also been training young men for battle," said Swamy.

"Next week the English soldiers and officers arrive. We will meet with the Brigadier General in charge, who will apprise us of the plans" concluded Swamy.

Ramu and a contingent of Indian officers accompanied by a band of drums, bagpipes and trumpets played on the dock as a British naval ship sailed into the port of Calcutta. The fanfare continued as the gangplank was lowered and down walked Brigadier General Sean Burke. He was smartly dressed in a khaki uniform held together by brown leather belt and shoulder straps along with a smattering of multicolored insignia. Ramu whispered to Badal Singh "He looks rather young to be in command." Badal shot Ramu a warning look to be quiet.

Stepping down from the boat, he greeted the assembled officers and troops. "It is good to be back in India. When I was here many years ago the capital was Calcutta, now it has moved to Delhi. I have always had a soft corner in my heart for Calcutta. All officers get your troops ready to depart in two days."

Sean walked into a large house by the port which had been converted into temporary housing for the British officers. He opened a bottle of whiskey and poured himself a large glass. Just then James Mason walked into the room. "I thought I would find you here," said James. "It has been a long time since we worked together with the Viceroy."

Sean saluted James "Major General Mason Sir."

"We can cut the formality Sean, it's just the two of us."

"I was told you would be in charge of the flotilla as we travel to Europe," said Sean. He lifted his glass "congratulations on your new post."

"What made you leave the Intelligence work at the War office Sean?" asked James.

"To be honest, I had become disillusioned with the work at the Military Intelligence war office. After becoming obsessed with tracking some militants all the way to New York, I had to come back disappointed." "Yes, I heard about that incident, "said James. "I pursued many other German sympathizers but after arresting a few of the known associates, there just was not enough intelligence to track the rest of them down. With war breaking down in Europe, the high command offered me the opportunity to be in charge of my own regiment, made up primarily of troops from India. Given my knowledge of the country and eagerness to leave the Intelligence community and primarily to be of service to the nation, I agreed to the new assignment" replied Sean. They stopped talking as other British officers started walking in.

A small boy sat on a broken harbor wall and watched

the organized chaos with sailors and dockworkers scurrying about, loading supplies and ammunition onto the various ships. Thousands of Indian sepoys, several hundred English soldiers and officers marched into the ships. At sundown the flotilla of the ships left the harbor, the boy closed his ears to muffle the deafening sound of the engines as the sky turned black with smoke and the air putrid with the smell of diesel.

Ramu stood on the deck looking longingly back at the rapidly disappearing skyline of his beloved city and the land he was prepared to lay down his life. He turned to Badal Singh who was standing next to him "Fighting for the enemy is tearing my heart apart." "You are now a soldier Ramu and an Indian officer, your duty is to follow orders" said Badal "I heard from one of the English officers that our first destination is Egypt. After that where we will go is a secret and we will get our new orders once we are there."

As the ships left the safety of the harbor, they fell into formation with the larger battleships taking the lead and the smaller ships following behind. At once they encountered rougher waters as the port disappeared from view, replaced by the never-ending breadth of the ocean.

The ships sailed through the Suez Canal and stopped at a campsite on the Mediterranean Sea in Egypt near the city of Alexandria. Other ships soon followed with troops from Australia and New Zealand. Sean and his officers inspected the massive tent city that had been formed on the Mediterranean beach. As he passed the section where the Indian sepoys were living, Ramu and the other Indian officers stood at attention and saluted them. He turned to Ramu "I want your troops to practice digging trenches. You have been assigned the role of creating an intricate layout of trenches to support the land invasion." "Sir, my troops are capable of fighting as well" said Ramu, who was unhappy with serving the British, was now even more dejected as his troops were now being relegated to manual labor. Sean angry at being questioned curtly replied "Dismissed."

"You cannot question a senior office Ramu, they will put you in jail or worse" warned Badal after Sean had left. "Any way I heard that the combined Commonwealth forces will attack the Ottoman empire in the straits of Dardanelles. We are to fight the Turkish troops as we march towards the Ottoman capital of Constantinople."

"Looks like I will be digging my way to Constantinople. I would much rather blow out the brains of these Englishmen." Badal hurriedly moved away from Ramu.

A few days later, all the troops gathered at a large open field to attend a special meeting. They had set up a makeshift stage where several empty chairs were lined. Shortly thereafter, a group of British, Australian and New Zealander officers walked in, including Sean Burke and James Mason, and took their positions on the stage. James spoke briefly, then introduced the First Admiral of the Navy, Winston Churchill. A man wearing a full back naval uniform, white cap and several medals attached to his chest got up to a standing ovation. He removed his hat, revealing a balding head with black hair that was combed back and a round, pudgy face. He spoke with a hoarse voice, "I am the chief strategist of the invasion, I cannot emphasize enough the importance of this military maneuver and how much I value the officers and the soldiers. We must destroy the Turkish menace and supply a new battle ground to attack and defeat Germany. You are the new hope of the war, and your victory would turn the tide against the evil German empire."

A few weeks later, Badal, who had now decided to talk to Ramu again, informed him "the bombing of the coast has started, and they estimate a month of bombing will completely destroy the coastal defenses. Then we will easily defeat the remaining Turks and march into the mainland.".

Four weeks later the troops were ordered to board the ships. As the troops lined up, guns were handed out to all the troops except to those trained by Ramu. As he wondered when they would be armed, an officer ordered them to walk to a large tent where each soldier was given a shovel. "Sir, how are we to defend ourselves?" he protested. "The other soldiers will provide you with cover. I need to use better trained soldiers to fight. Your men can dig and supply the trenches we need. The superior forces will shoot. The others can dig, this order comes directly from the Brigadier General," said the officer. Ramu was hopping mad, however he knew all he could do was follow orders.

As the ships approached the shores of Turkey, they could hear the British and French ships still pounding the land with their cannons. On a clear sunny day, Sean came up to the deck and addressed the soldiers, "Today you will be landing on the beaches. A scouting party will go first followed by the 7th Indian Regiment. They will start digging the trenches. Captain Howard and the 3rd New Zealand Regiment will follow. Once the trenches have been secured by the third regiment, the 4th Australian and the 8th British Regiment will come ashore."

Ramu and his men boarded many small boats and made their way to the beaches. He was the first of his regiment to arrive. The scouting party was pinned down by the dunes engaged in a heavy battle with the enemy. Dozens of soldiers lay dead on the beaches. The beach was narrow with large dunes in front and tall cliffs on either side. His men needed to get beyond the dunes so they could start digging the trenches. The Turks were handily defending the coast from an embankment about fifty feet above the beaches. They had machine guns that were firing at the scouting party, the arrival of the unarmed Indian soldiers carrying only shovel made it seem like target practice for them. The Turks were firmly in control; the bombing had not devastated them, as Ramu had been told. Ramu was the only one who was armed, he fired repeatedly to no avail. The rest of his men started furiously digging holes and trenches for cover. Dozens of his men were downed ever before they hit dry land. Scores of others were wounded or killed as they raced up the beaches. The waters turned red with flowing blood. The New Zealand soldiers now arrived on the beach, supplying the needed fire power before the massacre stopped. By nightfall, the regiments had set up a small base on the beach. Bodies floated in with every wave striking the shore. They had captured the bluffs overlooking the beach at a steep cost. The Turks were fighting on their own soil. There were thousands of Turkish reinforcements further inland. They had dug in, had a ready source of ammunition, food, and shelter. The invaders were wet, wounded, and worn out from just a day of fighting. Ramu's troops had taken a terrible toll. Over a hundred dead, many more wounded.

The digging of trenches continued non-stop. The beaches were heavily mined and often a shovel would hit a mine with disastrous consequences. The Turks had set up their trenches with barbed wire and strategically placed machine guns. The invaders made slow progress, sometimes just yards a day while incurring heavy losses. At night, the fighting continued as flares would go high into the sky, followed by gunfire. More troops poured into the beachhead. After several days of fighting, the troops were bogged down less than a mile from where they had landed. Brigadier General Sean arrived to inspect the situation.

Sean talking to his officers said, "I have devised a plan to charge the Ottoman front under cover of the night." He pointed at several places on the map laid out on the table in front of him. He then picked up a pen with the cap attached to the back. "If you can think of the land in front of us shaped as this fountain pen, the area we have captured is the nib. Our goal is the capture of Gallipoli which is in the clip. We will have a three-pronged attack. The New Zealand Regiment will go straight up the nib and directly confront the Turks. The Indian regiment will be close behind digging trenches to secure our position. The Australian regiment will attack from the left, the British regiment from the right. All three will meet up on the barrel section of the pen and march forward. We attack tomorrow night, get your soldiers ready."

Under cover of darkness that night, thousands of soldiers sprinted out of their hiding holes and ran towards the enemy lines. No sooner had they run a few yards, flares lighted up the sky and the air exploded with bullets. The ground was filled with mines which devastated the invading forces. Ramu at the head of his regiment, sprang forward, his revolver blazing at the enemy in the distance. *The enemy was prepared for the attack,* he thought. A mine exploded in front of him sending him flying through the air and he landed on a barbed wire fortification. He tried to get up, but the more he struggled the tighter the barbed wire entangled him. The Turks killed most of the soldiers who had gone ahead. None of the regiments made it past a few hundred yards. The killing continued through the night. Just before dawn, an officer walked into Sean's tent "Sir, we have taken heavy losses in every regiment. The Turks are firmly defending their line. We need to call back the troops and regroup before we lose them all."

"Sound the retreat and fall back to our old positions," said a dejected Sean.

Badal found Ramu entangled in the barbed wire, bloodied by scratches all over his body. As he thanked Badal for untangling him, he said "the problem with the attack was that the Turks have deployed a barbed wire fortification design that channels the attacking soldiers into areas where the machine guns can easily target them." He surveyed the battlefield, mangled bodies, barbed wire, ground churned up by artillery shells, limbs protruding from bomb craters and debris strewn everywhere. Wounded soldiers cried out in pain, many in Bengali and Hindi. The Indian regiment had endured most of the losses as they charged right up the center of the battle. Ramu's eyes were red with anger, so many of his people had been killed because of the incompetence of his superiors.

Days of fighting turned into weeks. The two sides were at a standstill, with heavy losses on both sides. Soldiers lay in muddy graves out in the open. The stench of death filled the air. Supplies ran low. Ammunition was harder to find.

One night, a group of Turks charged the line using flame throwers. The screams of burning soldiers erupted through the night. Ramu grabbed a rifle and charged at one flamethrower. He fired a couple of shots, killing him. To his right was another flame thrower, his rifle locked when he tried to shoot. Without thinking, he charged at the surprised man, stabbing him with his bayonet. He then grabbed the flame thrower from the wounded man and turned it on the attackers. They soon retreated.

In the next officers meeting, several officers commended Ramu for his bravery. "What you did saved many lives. Was it not for you we might have been forced back into the sea" said the New Zealand commander. Ramu speaking to his newly found admirers suggested "A small group can go behind enemy lines and set fire to their ammunition and food supplies. These frontal attacks are not working. Using guerrilla tactics, my team can weaken the enemy. I just need some ammunition and supplies. Sean overhearing the conversation stepped in "Don't you ever question my authority or my strategy."

The next day, Sean and one of his officers walked over to the trenches where Ramu's regiment was positioned. "I want you to take two hundred of your soldiers and start digging a trench towards the enemy lines." Ramu protested, " Sir, there are mines and barbed wire, the Turks have a clear line to sight to my men, they will slaughter them. At least provide them with rifles so they can fight back."

"I will have you arrested for insubordination. I have had enough of you" Sean pulled out his pistol and pointed it at Ramu. "Arrest this man," he shouted. Ramu unhesitatingly removed his pistol and fired two shots at Sean. The first missed Sean but caught the officer in the chest and he instantly fell to the ground. The second shot hit Sean in his leg and even as he grimaced in pain, fired several shots at Ramu. The injured Sean limped over to Ramu where he was lying on the ground, blood spouting from his mouth. Sean glanced back at the lifeless body of the officer, pointed his pistol at Ramu's head and fired. He then collapsed to the ground as a medic rushed to pick him up and carry him to his tent.

Badal and some of Ramu's troops quietly picked Ramu's body that night and floated it into the Mediterranean Sea, hoping it would find its way back to the Ganges he grew up in.

The invasion took thousands of lives on both sides. Eventually, seeing a stalemate, England called off the invasion. They sent the remaining Indian troops back, with a stopover in Egypt, to recuperate from their wounds. Sean Burke and his officers were awarded the Victoria Cross for their bravery. The name of Ramu was scrubbed from the annals of the British Army.

CHAPTER 43: YUCATAN (1920)

J eev paid the clerk at a small hotel by the port of Veracruz. "Here are your keys Senor" handing them over to Jeev. "Where can I get a newspaper?" asked Jeev. "Just finished reading this, you can have it" replied the clerk. Jeev took out a few notes of currency and tipped the clerk. "Gracias Senor, the name is Pablo if you need anything".

Jeev went up to his room and opened the newspaper. General Obregon had assumed power and was expected to be named as the President of the country shortly. President Carranza had fled Mexico City and was reportedly heading towards Veracruz. Jeev wondered if Carranza would set up a military unit in Veracruz and use that as a base to fight against Obregon.

A few days later as Jeev was sitting in the evening at an outdoor café looking at the people passing by and enjoying his warm coffee and sweet churros stuffed with dolce de leite, he saw Pablo come into the café. "Pablo, come sit here," said Jeev. Pablo ordered tequila and tacos. "Miguel, we just received news that Carranza has been assassinated" said Pablo sipping his tequila. Jeev thought to himself, I need to get out of here and travel to Merida and meet Mariana's contact.

"I want to travel to Merida" said Jeev, deciding he needed to trust somebody, "Do you know anyone who could help?" Pablo replied, "Yes I know some people they can get you there." "Are these people trustworthy?" asked Jeev "I don't want to be robbed or have get into trouble with the authorities." The clerk looked at Jeev judiciously and said "You only have to pay a fixed fee and they don't like the soldados. They will protect you from them. I will let you know at the hotel when the arrangements have been made."

He bought clothes from a local store, so he looked no different than any other worker in the city. "I have arranged passage for you on a fishing the trawler. They leave tomorrow morning for Merida" Pablo told Jeev a few days later. On the morning of the journey, Jeev took out enough money to pay the fishermen for his services, a tip for Pablo and then he packed the rest of his money and documents into a waterproof packet and tied it around his waist.

The boat was about thirty feet long and had a crew of five. Large nets were folded on the deck. The captain, a large man with a scraggly beard, his clothes smelling of fish pointed at the sleeping area that had several hammocks "The blue hammock is where you will sleep. We will travel towards Merida, but our going will be slow since we drag the fishing nets and pull them up from time to time. Once we have enough fish, we will stop at some of the ports along the way to sell the fish." He pulled out a bottle of liquor and two small glasses. He poured a drink for them and said "My friend told me you don't like the soldados. Are you running from something?" Jeev drank the liquor in one gulp, it burnt as it went down his throat, replied, "It would be easier for me if they don't see me and easier for you if I don't tell you." The captain laughed aloud, got up, slapped Jeev on his back and said, "Don't worry, I don't like soldados too."

They set out into the sea, mostly following the coast. The anglers would toss the nets out and drag them for a distance, then pull them up and toss the fish into the hull below. At the end of the day, they would pull into a city or village and sell their fish. In one city, as they were pulling into the dock, the captain walked over to Jeev and pointed at the shore. "Soldados, are searching for the boats here." He called one of his crew "Take Miguel down and hide him" The man led Jeev down a steep staircase near the fish storage area. He removed one floorboard and said, "Get inside and lie flat." Jeev squeezed into a small opening and lay flat on his back. The man slammed the floorboard down above him. The floor was damp, chilly and the fish smell was almost unbearable. Light streamed through the slats on the floor. From time-to-time water would lap against his feet. The boat lurched from side to side as it came into the port, Jeev's head banging against the side of the floor.

The soldiers boarded the boat as soon as it docked and started questioning the captain and the crew. They eventually walked down the steep staircase to the cargo area. Through the floorboards, Jeev could see the soldiers standing right over him. One of them banged his foot on the floorboard. The wood bent enough to slam against Jeev's nose as blood spilled from it and pain shot through his face. He covered his mouth to suppress a scream. After a few minutes, the soldiers left. The crew kept Jeev hidden for a few hours until they had sold their fish. Only after the boat was out to sea, that the crewman came back and removed the floorboard. He grasped Jeev by the hand and pulled him out. Jeev's face was caked in blood, his clothes wet, and had to hold on to the man to stop him from falling down.

The boat reached a port near the city of Merida where he arranged for a carriage to take him to the address Mariana had provided. The place turned out to be a hacienda on the outskirts of the town, reached after almost half a day's ride. "I am here to meet Senor Felix Diaz" said Jeev, recalling the name on Mariana's note. The guard replied "From here you have to go on foot" he signaled to another guard to take Jeev inside. Jeev paid the cart driver and then followed the guard down a small dirt road towards a house in the distance.

"Wait here" said the guard pointing to a chair on the porch. Soon a man appeared, *it was the same military officer he had met when he presented the letter for General Obregon.* "Senor Miguel" we meet again boomed the man. "Senor Diaz" said a surprised Jeev "Mariana gave your name to me and told me to come here," said Jeev. "Yes, yes, I know, we met in Mexico City, and Mariana warned me you may come here." "Come with me and have a drink, we have much to catch up on," stated Diaz. He followed Diaz into a large house, furnished in a colonial Spanish fashion, leading him to a courtyard where two men were sitting, having drinks. He instantly recognized them both, General Mueller, and Commander Koenig !"You are alive," Jeev blurted out as he shook Koenig's hand. He then looked at Mueller and said, "You had told me that the commander perished in a U-boat accident." Mueller got up laughing "Only presumed dead my friend, presumed dead." Diaz poured a drink, then came close to Jeev to hand him the glass and wrinkled his nose. "We have to get you some new clothes. You smell like fish." An embarrassed Jeev replied, "Sorry, I have spent many days on a fishing trawler to get here. The smell has permeated into my skin. I don't know how to get rid of it." Diaz filled the glasses of the other two men and the four raised them, saying 'Salud'. "Ok now go take a bath" commanded Diaz.

Over the next few days. Each recounted their stories. After Jeev had given them a synopsis of his stay in Mexico, he asked Felix, "So tell me about Mariana?". "I have met her a few times. If there is one word to describe her, I would say 'survivor'. As you know, Pancho Villa wiped her entire village out. She lost all her family. To take up arms, organize a small army and fight the battles takes courage. She understands politics and has learnt to move to the power figures. One day she will become the President," replied Felix as he gave Jeev a wrinkled smile.

"How did you end up in Merida?" inquired Jeev. "I was happily serving President Carranza and had risen to the rank of a General. I supported him during the recent election process and tried to help his candidate. When I learnt, Obregon was going to challenge him, I knew I had to make some alternate plans. I own this hacienda; other than a few close friends, no one knows its existence. Mariana was the one who warned me. She must trust you and like you, otherwise she would not have given you, my name. And I trust you because Mariana trusts you. So, I gathered my family and sent them here for safety. When I saw things were getting bad in the Capital, I too left and came here. Actually, General Mueller and I travelled together from Mexico City," explained Felix.

General Mueller drained his drink and walked over to the bar to get another. As he poured the alcohol into his glass, he turned to Jeev and narrated his story. "I actually have been staying in Mexico for many years. My original plan was to come to Mexico and stay as an envoy for an abbreviated time, to persuade Mexico to become an ally of Germany. When it appeared, war was going to break out, I would like to think that it was my efforts that kept Mexico non-aligned during the war. My job changed to getting fuel for the U-boats and supplies for the German troops in France and Russia. I enjoy living here, to be honest. It is a lovely country, the food, the friends, the culture. I have no immediate family in Germany, so when the war went badly for Germany, I decided to just continue to stay here."

It was then commander Koenig's turn to tell his story. "Well, I have been traversing the Atlantic looking for targets. We found many targets, some big, some small, some easy, others hard. I protected ships that carried supplies from Mexico to Germany. I was even in the Mediterranean for a short while. My submarine sank a British destroyer off the coast of the Dardanelles peninsula." He took a sip of his drink, then continued, "Later, the British and Americans became smart, and the merchant ships travelled in large flotillas. They were heavily armed and always on the lookout for us. It became harder to torpedo the ships. They changed the design of the ships to become more resistant to our torpedoes. We started taking heavy losses. Just before the end of the war, we were off the coast of Bermuda, when, as part of a group of U-boats, we attacked an American armada. They somehow knew we were coming and hit us hard. I know at least three submarines were destroyed. We were hit but could close off some compartments and we limped away from the area. At one point, we thought we were going down, so my radio man sent a signal saying we were sinking. However, the submarine continued to function. At that point, I had an idea. We kept radio silence and came close to the Mexican port of Merida. This has been our landing point for many years, so I could come ashore and contacted General Mueller. He contacted Felix and now here we are. My crew is living in neighboring houses that are part of this farm. The German command thinks we sank off the coast of Bermuda, as that was the last communication we sent."

The four men sat in silence, contemplating the circumstances that had brought them together. "Life is so interesting, yet unpredictable. It follows a path; the path seems random and planned and coincidental all at the same time. How all of us from different paths of life have found this intersection and who knows where we will go from here?" prophesied Felix.

General Mueller, who had a habit of talking too much when he drank, said, "We know where we are going," pointing at the Commander and himself. The commander's eyes narrowed, wondering how much information Mueller was going to give up. "We cannot go back to Germany. The war devastated the country. If we go to the United States, they will arrest us for war crimes, and Mexico, while fine for the time being, is an unpredictable place to live. We intend to travel to a place in southern Brazil. A contact there has land we can buy and settle down. We should be quite safe there." The commander nodded. "Felix, we will need your help to get to Brazil. Of course, we will pay well." He turned to Jeev. "You can come with us." Jeev shook his head. "I am not sure where my next path goes. Thank you for the offer though."

CHAPTER 44: THE LEGEND OF THE FOX HOLLOW ENCOUNTERS

That night Jeev could not sleep, so he walked out into the cool night. The air was heavy with mosquitos, the shrill of insects, croaking of frogs and the occasional rustling of leaves as small animals crawled through the under bush. He walked towards a clump of trees and sat down on one of the low branches. Trying to clear his brain so he could think clearly and decide what he should do next. He could not stay too long with Felix; Obregon's soldiers would soon commandeer the city of Merida. Nor did he want to go to Brazil with the Germans. It just did not seem right. He wanted to pursue his goal of fighting for the independence of his country. As he sat on the branch, he noticed a movement in the forest. A small animal was looking at him. It was a fox, looking silverish in the moonlight. It's sparking blue eyes looking directly at him. He stared at the fox, hypnotized by its eyes. Then, in an instant, the fox was gone, and Jeev knew exactly what he would do next.

The next morning, the four men sat at the breakfast table. Before them was a spread of diverse types of bread, a bowl of soft creamy butter, a pot of freshly brewed coffee and a large plate with sliced oranges, berries, bananas berries and grapes. Jeev said, "I saw a silver fox with bright blue eyes in the woods near the house last night.". Commander Koenig raised his eyebrows "That's incredible" swallowing a piece of bread he continued "Have you heard of the Legend of the Fox Hollow Encounters?" Jeev shook his head as did Felix and Mueller.

"My grandmother would tell me this story," recounted Koenig. "It was passed down to her by the generations before her. It happened in the age of the Visigoths, a Germanic tribe that was an offshoot of the Vikings. They lived in what's today Germany and Austria. There was a tribal leader, the chief of the village. He had a young daughter, she had bright blue eyes. One of the kindest, wisest people you could find, always helping others, taking care of small children, sharing her food and clothing. One day, the chieftain from a neighboring village came with a marriage proposal for his son. The chief was pleased as a marriage between the two villages would ensure peace between them. He did not know that his daughter had fallen in love with one of his soldiers. So, when he told the daughter about the marriage, she was distraught and refused to marry. She told her father she wanted to marry the soldier. The chief, in a rage, had the soldier killed. The daughter ran away from the village into the woods. She did not know this, but she was carrying a child, the soldier's child. She ran deep into the woods, where she collapsed in front of a hut that belonged to a mystical being. The villagers called her a witch. The witch, however, was someone who had a deep connection with nature. She possessed magical powers that she used to take care of the forest and its animals. The witch let the girl live with her for many months. One day, the witch was out gathering herbs. When she came back, the girl was dead. But she had given birth to a beautiful boy with bright blue eyes. The witch was the protector of the forest; however, she did not know how to take care of a baby. So, she turned him into a baby fox, gave the baby fox magical powers for its protection and left him near the hollows where a family of foxes lived. The foxes raised the baby as their own and the baby fox grew up to have many more blue-eyed fox babies. Since then, foxes with blue eyes have migrated all over the world. They are special since they want to help humans. The encounters with these foxes only happen to humans who are good at heart. They will not appear if your heart is evil."

"Old wives' tales," joked Felix. "I don't believe in any of this superstitious nonsense. We are solely responsible for our own actions. There are no magic foxes that come out and help us. My destiny is under my control." "You have a right to believe whatever you want, my friend," sighed Koenig. "I can tell you I have seen the blue-eyed fox, and I looked into its eyes. It told me I should not join the Navy, to go down a different path. I joined the Navy anyway. Every time I gave the command to fire the torpedoes, I saw those blue eyes looking at me, searching my soul for some unknown part I could not see. After what I have done, I don't think those foxes will ever visit me again."

General Mueller stayed silent he did not want to get into the argument instead turning to Jeev, he inquired "So what did the Fox tell you to do?"

"To go to St. Thomas, to meet an old friend of mine," responded Jeev.

"The fox told you that! Go to St. Thomas," mimicked Felix.

"Not in those words Felix," Jeev defended, "when the fox speaks to you, it speaks to your soul, these are not human words that come out of his mouth, of course, he cannot speak English, Spanish, or German. The act of looking into the fox's eye brings out the answer that is buried in our soul. He creates a response for you, but that answer was already within you. He just helps you bring it out."

Felix decided not to press the argument anymore, nor did he want to ridicule his guests. He walked up to the window facing the woods looking for the fox. "I have a way to get you to St. Thomas," announced Felix turning around to face Jeev. "I will contact a person I know who can help."

Waking up the next morning, Jeev noticed activity in the house. There were horses outside being saddled up. Felix, Mueller, and Koenig were standing by the horses. Some horses had large bags attached to them. Jeev ambled up to them and patted one horse. "We are going out for a ride. Do you want to come with us?" inquired Koenig. The other two looked at him with disdain. "I think it's better if Jeev stays here," Felix bluntly said. "He can come," Koenig reiterated. His curiosity spiked; Jeev agreed. They saddled another horse for him, and the four, along with a few guards, set out.

At first the ride was through a thick forest. They often ducked to evade branches that could have knocked them off their horses. The trees soon thinned out and were replaced by a tall swamp of grass. The horses were now trotting through the brackish water of the bay. From time one horse would go through a depression, drenching the person riding the horse. They continued for a couple of hours until a white sandy beach replaced the grass. The water in front was clear and calm. Gentle waves splashed on to the deserted beach. The party picked up speed and galloped down the beach. They rounded a large dune and came to a halt. Soon, a boat appeared with two men. The men brought the boat ashore and spoke to Koenig and Mueller in German. They looked suspiciously at Jeev, but then seemed to nod their heads once Koenig had explained Jeev's presence. The group boarded the boat, and they set out.

The beach was surrounded by a coral reef that protected it from the waves. Once past the reef, the boat rocked violently as waves crashed around it. They continued the shaky journey for about an hour, until, out of nowhere, Jeev saw what looked like a large rocky hill in the middle of the ocean. However, as they approached it, an opening was visible on one side. The boat went past the rock wall and turned into a bay surrounded by rocks. On one side of the bay was a small beach, on the other side was a tall rocky wall and there, tied to the rocks, was a U-boat. There were tents set up on the rocky beach and several men were standing by, looking at the approaching boat. Jeev was astonished. "There it is my submarine" said Commander Koenig, "We hid it right off the shore of Mexico. It will take us to Brazil."

Koenig and Mueller greeted the men and unloaded the supplies that that been brought for them. There were about twenty-five men, Jeev assumed, all to be the crew of the U-boat. All the men spoke to each other in German, some even wearing remnants of their uniforms.

Koenig asked Felix and Jeev 'Do you want to see the inside of the boat?" "Yes, of course" said Felix. "Follow me" said Koenig as he led them over a series of long planks, balanced precariously over the rocks, until the last one led to the deck of the submarine. In front of them was the sail with the diving planes, the periscope and a few antennas protruding upwards. A gun, anti-aircraft, was set up behind the sail. They climbed down a steep ladder through an opening in the sail to the control room. The inside was dark and musty with a penetrating smell of diesel fuel. "Watch this magic" said Commander Koenig flipping a lever, and the lights flickered on, showing a long, dimly lit corridor. There were instruments, gauges, and knobs everywhere. Moving further down, they passed the torpedo tubes. Under the tubes were beds for the crew.

"Every inch of the submarine has a purpose" explained Koenig. The further they went, the stench in the submarine became worse.

"I have seen enough" coughed Felix "I need fresh air. "He headed back outside. Mueller followed him to help him out. Commander Koenig led Jeev to one of the torpedo tubes and opened a side compartment. Inside were hundreds of gold coins. "Our ticket to a new life in Brazil," he proudly bragged. He took two coins and placed them in Jeev's hand. "That's for you, it will help with your escape from here." Jeev graciously accepted. Sliding the coins into his pocket, they started their way back to the outside.

Back on deck the crew was loading supplies into the submarine. Jeev watched another boat chug into the hidden harbor. It had two large diesel tanks, and the crew started the refueling process.

"So, when do you leave? " Inquired Jeev as he trotted his horse next to Koenig on their journey back. "In two days," he replied. "We have some minor repairs to finish and then we will be ready to leave." Everyone rode back in silence, Jeev still in amazement at what he had seen.

Jeev stayed in the Hacienda for another week after the Germans had left. One morning Felix told Jeev "I have to go back to Mexico City, where I will join the new government. I have made my peace with the new administration. Also, I have not forgotten about your trip to St. Thomas. In a few days, a man will come to visit you. He will help you." "I cannot thank you enough for your hospitality," said Jeev.

CHAPTER 45:
PYRAMIDS AND
CENOTES

Jeev stared at the thin, short, and dark-skinned man standing in front of him. "My name is Jacinto Kan" the man said. "Senor Felix told me to help you with your journey." Jeev, by now, spoke Spanish as fluently as any Mexican and with his brown skin color, he blended in with the local population. "My name is Miguel" replied Jeev "when do we leave?"

"To get to St. Thomas, we would have to travel by horseback for a few days before getting to a town on the opposite coast. There you can board a cargo ship that will have a stop at St. Thomas. I will come back in a week with the horses." They agreed on a price for Jacinto to take him to the cargo ship. It was a lot more than he had expected, but luckily, he had enough.

Two days later, in the middle of the night, he heard knocks on his door. Groggily, he stumbled to the door to open it. Jacinto was outside. "We need to get going right away. The soldados are on their way here," he explained. "I have received word that they are coming to search the hacienda tomorrow. They are looking for the Germans, but if they find you, they will take you away for questioning. " Jeev hurriedly packed his things and came out of the house. It was pitch dark outside; Jacinto had tied two horses to the tree. "I don't think Senor Felix will mind me taking two of his horses," he said with a smile. They mounted the horses, and Jacinto led the way into the forest. He followed a small stream for a while, so there would be no tracks left behind. They continued riding through the night. When daylight broke, they stopped in a clearing.

Jacinto lit a small fire and made a hot drink. "Champurrado," he explained, handing Jeev a cup. Jeev took a sip of the thick drink. It had a sweet earthy flavor with hints of chocolate, molasses and some type of liquor, both a meal and a hot drink at the same time. "What is in the drink?" he inquired. "Corn, cocoa, sugar, some water," Jacinto replied. After resting for a few hours, they got back on their horses and continued their journey. "You are not Mexican right? Inquired Jacinto. "No, I am from India. My real name is Jeev" deciding that he needed to prove trust with Jacinto. "I have heard about the country, you are far away from home," he said. "Maybe one day I can visit." "What about you? Where are you from?" queried Jeev.

"I was born in a village quite close to here. My entire family is descendants of Mayans. We have no Spanish blood in us. I have two brothers and one sister. I work as a guide. If someone needs to go from one place to another. Mostly people who come from other parts of Mexico or from America. I have found work with Gringo's who come looking for ancient places and artifacts. There are enormous pyramids in the area and archeologists are excavating around them. I know all the cenotes in the area." "What's a Cenote?" interrupted Jeev.

"It's a hole in the ground, leading to a pool of water. I will show you some along the way. You may call them caves; they are deep and go for long distances. My great grandfather told me the story of something that happened a long time ago, before man was on the earth. Giant animals ruled the earth. A huge rock, bigger than a mountain, came crashing into the earth and fell near Mexico. The sea filled that hole with water. Some rocks flew into the area around Yucatan. These rocks came at a high speed and made holes in the ground.

These holes later had water come into them from rain and underground streams. We believe our gods created these holes. When the ancient people died, we buried them in these holes so they could travel easily to the other worlds."

A few hours later, they stopped. Jacinto tied the horses to a tree and gave them some grass to eat. "Follow me," he indicated, and they went through a series of dense bushes. Jeev had to wrestle the leaves and stalks out of his way as tiny insects crawled all over his clothes. Suddenly, out of nowhere appeared a tall stone structure. Vegetation covered most of the structure, but he could clearly see steps stretching upward. Jacinto climbed the steep stairs, from time to time showing Jeev where he could safely place his hands or feet. They climbed a hundred steps before the structure flattened out before them. They were at the top of a Mayan Pyramid. Shrubs and grass covered even the top of the pyramid. "Be careful and follow me, otherwise you will fall a hundred feet straight down." Jeev followed him to a spot where one could see for miles in either direction. They stood there for a while, admiring the scenery. "There are many pyramids like this that only a few of us know about. There are ninety-one steps on each of the four sides and one big step on top. That makes three hundred and sixty-five steps. One solar calendar year. The Mayans were very advanced," described Jacinto.

In the distance, the sun was setting over the horizon transforming the sky into a breathtaking canvas of many shades of red, the light dancing on the intricate carvings and etchings of the structure. They stared at the spectacle transfixed, as the reds grew in intensity and the warm rays of the sun were replaced by tentacles of shadows, the air cooled perceptively. "We need to get down before dark" warned Jacinto and they started the perilous journey downwards. Jeev slipped a couple of times but could grab on to branches growing out of the rocks. By the time they reached the bottom, the canopy overhead had blocked out any remaining light.

Jacinto lit a small fire, and they settled in for the night.

The next morning, a swarm of howling monkeys, disturbed by humans in their territory, were creating quite a racket. Jacinto and Jeev hurriedly packed their items and rode off to avoid the marauding group. The monkeys followed them for a mile before stopping and heading back to their zone. They entered an area cleared out for farming.

"We have to be careful here. A gringo owns the hacienda. There is an enormous pyramid here called the 'El Castillo'. The man has many people digging around the pyramid. They take the things from the pyramid, the jewelry, the pots, statues and send them to America," lamented Jacinto. "Those relics belong to my people and should stay here."

Jeev nodded in acquiescence, "We have the same problem in India where the British have taken enormous amounts of ancient artifacts and stored them in museums and houses of rich people."

"Yes, during the colonial times, before independence from Spain, the likes of Cortez, Guzman, and Alvarado looted the country. They killed thousands of my people. And many thousands more became sick with diseases that we had never heard of like smallpox. They came looking for gold, they found some, but truly little. My people became the resource for the Spanish. We became their slaves, we worked in their fields, we built their buildings, we dug in their mines. They founded iron, silver, and copper mines. The Spanish mistreated us; our lives had no value to them other than to make them money. They came and conquered us and mercilessly used us for profit," an angry Jacinto replied.

"You know, it is not much different in my home country. Millions of workers toil in farms, factories, and mines. The English take the production, paying slave wages and send it to England for massive profits. They even recruited hundreds of thousands of soldiers to fight for them against the Germans."

This time Jacinto nodded, understanding the grief and anger felt by Jeev.

It took Jeev aback at the similarity of both their worlds. Here he was, thousands of miles away from home, in the middle of the Yucatan, riding with another person from a vastly different culture, sharing the evils of colonialism. "What strikes me Jacinto" said Jeev is that "the British exploited one ancient culture, the Spanish exploited another ancient culture, one goal governed the greed behind the exploitation–profit. At the expense of the conquered people, the destruction of its lands, cultural artifacts, and the slavery of the natives. There are many words used interchangeably with slavery to make it appear as less gruesome–indentured labor, abused workers, oppressed laborers. In the end, it comes down to just another form of slavery. The profits are disproportionately allocated to the owners on the backs of the workers."

Suddenly they heard the noise of horses galloping. Looking back, in the distance, Jeev saw a group of soldiers riding in their direction. "Follow me" said Jacinto as he headed towards a small group of trees. Jeev galloped after him. On reaching the trees, Jacinto dismounted, and Jeev followed him. Leading the horses by their reins he walked towards a labyrinth of trees, shadows and foliage. Using his hands, he moved the foliage away, uncovering an opening. Just high enough for a horse to squeeze through. Once both horses were inside, Jacinto pushed the foliage back to cover the entrance. The darkness was overwhelming as Jeev's eyes tried to adjust to the lack of light. The only sound was that of their footsteps and the clanking of the horse's feet. They walked the horses slowly deeper into the cave. Soon they heard water, and the light in the cave became brighter. The cave abruptly ended in a massive cenote. It was about a hundred feet high and wide. At the top was an opening where sunlight streamed in, shimmering on the blue pool of water. The horses at once stopped to drink the water; it was so clear you could see all the way to the bottom. The place seemed magical. "This is just one of many cenotes here. The soldiers will ride past it without even knowing of its existence. We are safe here," said Jacinto. "Look over there in the corner" he whispered pointing with his finger. Jeev looked in that direction. A pair of foxes were sitting under the beam of sunlight. The eyes of one of them were bright blue, mirroring the color of the water. "The ancient people believed the fox with the blue eyes helped the dead go into the afterlife. They guided the way. To see them inside the cenote is a very auspicious occasion," observed Jacinto. The foxes watched the humans for a while, then disappeared into the darkness.

Jacinto waited for an hour, then went outside to see if the way was clear. Verifying it was safe, they continued their journey. Late that night, they rode into a small village. Jeev could smell the ocean breeze and the saltiness in the air. They stopped at a small house on the outskirts of the village. "We will stay here for a few days till we can get you on the ship," informed Jacinto. He knocked softly on the door, and a young woman opened the door. She let out a scream of joy. "Jacinto," and gave him a big hug. She looked suspiciously at Jeev until Jacinto informed her, "he is my friend." "This is my wife; her name is Xochitl" introducing her to Jeev. She smiled at Jeev. Xochitl would have been seen as pretty in any culture. Thick black hair, a small, framed body, smooth suntanned skin, full lips, and a big smile on a perfectly symmetrical face. She was wearing a brightly colored huipil with intricate embroidery and bold patterns. It accentuated her curves in a graceful and elegant way. A spacious living room opened up into a dining room and a smokey kitchen. A corridor led to the bedrooms. Jacinto left to bring the horses into a barn on the side of the house. Xochitl handed Jeev a cup of a hot liquid. "Atole," she explained. Jeev took a sip, expecting a sweet concoction. However, it was savory. "It's a warm corn milk drink with cinnamon and vanilla flavors" she explained. She also put forward a dish of tamales. Jacinto joined in to enjoy the food and drinks.

Waking up the next morning he walked into the kitchen where Jacinto offered him a cup of hot coffee. "Look over there" he said, pointing to the garden outside the kitchen. Xochitl was standing there, holding a small cup. Her long black hair cascading in soft waves, a picture of gentleness and strength. "That's a sweet nectar for the birds in the cup," whispered Jacinto. A hummingbird was drinking the nectar from the cup, while others were sitting on her hand. She spread out her other hand and a few more birds landed on her. The birds were brilliant shades of green, blue, purple, and pink. They fluttered near her, unafraid of the human holding the sweet liquid for them. "They trust her completely," continued Jacinto. "Birds have a way of knowing what's in a person's soul. They know Xochitl's soul is pure. Many birds and animals approach her with no fear. Do you know what a hummingbird signifies? It shows you the path, the path that you follow to make your dreams come true." Xochitl saw them looking at her and beckoned them over. The hummingbirds seemed unafraid of the two men approaching them. Some hummingbirds landed on Jeev and Jacinto. Between the three humans, there were now about forty hummingbirds sitting or flying around them. The sweet nectar had finished, so they turned and walked inside, the birds flying away, looking like a multicolored cloud.

"So how long are you married?" inquired Jeev. "Two years," replied Jacinto. "And how did you meet?" asked Jeev. "That's an interesting story," muttered Jacinto, looking at Xochitl for approval. She nodded. He continued, "about three years ago, I was guiding a group of American archeologists to see a recently discovered pyramid. We were travelling on horseback but often dismounted and lead the horses on foot because the forest was so thick, we had to cut through it. We reached the pyramid, and the archeologists stayed there for two weeks, digging, and taking pictures. On the way back, there was torrential rain and the streams in the area were flooded and were unpassable. We had to circumvent the original path to find areas where we could cross. We were many miles, of course. Late one night, as we were looking for a place to camp, we saw a fire burning in the distance. We walked towards the fire, hoping to find a warm and dry place to stay. We approached with caution, as I had not been to this place before. As we came closer, a group of men suddenly appeared out of the surrounding trees. Some of them were armed with bows and arrows, others carried large swords. They spoke to us in Yucatec Mayan. I was the only one who understood the language, so I answered back. They wanted to know who we were. I explained the group was peaceful, and we were just looking for shelter. Assuring them that we were not Mexican soldiers and that we were all unarmed, except for two guards in our expedition who carried guns, they welcomed us to the village. I told the guards to leave the guns outside the village, the villagers appreciated the gesture. They gave us food and drinks and provided us with huts to sleep in that night. The next day, I saw Xochitl. She was the daughter of the chief of the village. When I saw her, it felt like they hit me on the head with a hammer. I fell in love in an instant. She just looked suspiciously at me. Her long black hair, her white dress with large colorful flowers, and her smile captivated me. I mustered up courage to talk to her. She wanted to know about the expedition, and I told her their purpose was to discover ancient sites and let the world know about the glories of the Mayan civilization. Her response was that they just want to steal the artifacts like the Spanish have done for centuries. I told her that like all races, there are good and bad people, but agreed that many came to this part of the world motivated by greed. We talked for a while and then we were joined by her father. He told me; his clan was centuries old. They were living much further North, however, over the last few decades, they have had to move their village further and further into the forest. At first, it was the Spanish army and now the Mexican soldiers who continued to encroach on their territory. They had moved to their current location about ten years ago after being forced out by warring factions during the revolution. He asked me not to reveal the location of his village. I agreed and passed his message down to all the expedition members. All of whom concurred that it was better to keep the location secret. I purposely led the group in a zig zag way back to the city of Merida so it would be hard for anyone but me to duplicate our path. After that, I visited the village many times and gradually our friendship grew. I also earned the trust of her father. Two years ago, I got enough courage to ask for her hand in marriage. She agreed and I am happy to say her father agreed as well. We visit the village often, but I fear for their survival. There are no more places left to move. The forest is disappearing, being converted into farmland."

"Wow, what an interesting story," Jeev commented. "Do you have a wife?" inquired Xochitl. Jeev replied, "No, I don't." "Wasn't there someone who you loved?" teased Jacinto. "Yes, many" said Jeev, thinking of Emily and Mariana. "There is a girl I knew when I was in India. She was my childhood friend; we grew up together. They tricked her into being sold as indentured labor in Guyana. I blamed myself for not having prevented it. I did not know something like this existed. Luckily, I found out recently that she had escaped as was now living safely on the Island of St. Thomas."

"So that is why you want to go there," pressed Jacinto. Jeev smilingly replied, "Yes, I want to go meet her. What happens after that is up to fate."

"Do you think they wrote our life stories before we are born?" wondered Xochitl "the ancient ones used to tell us that the stars had already determined our fate. What will happen will happen?"

"There is the concept of free will," interjected Jacinto.

"We decide every day, what we eat, which direction to go in, who to trust. How can you say all actions are predetermined?"

"Maybe in the smaller sense of what you will eat or drink," countered Xochitl, "but in the larger sense, those actions will not change destiny. Destiny intended for the three of us to meet. Whatever decisions we have made would not have affected this destiny."

"For me, what is important is my purpose in life. We have been placed here on earth, each of us, to fulfill that purpose. Right now, I feel like I am a boat floating in the ocean, battered by the waves, moving listlessly in the direction of the currents and winds. At one point, there was a purpose to my life. Lately, however, I have become a drifter, living yet not feeling," lamented Jeev.

"My father used to say," commented Xochitl, "sometimes our lives may not feel purposeful, but there is still a reason thing happen, why we go to certain places and why we interact with certain people. We are just a minor cog in the giant wheel of the universe, yes small, but, as my father used to say, not unimportant. If the smallest part of the wheel does not perform its function, it could disrupt the immense cosmos. So, do what you have to do each day, however mundane, because you are achieving not only your goals but helping others achieve their goals."

"How did you become so wise?" gushed Jeev, looking at Xochitl.

"It is not me. It is a tradition to pass down knowledge from one generation to another. My grandfather instructed my father, and my mother and father taught me. We learn about the ways of life as little children. The wise men and women of the village tell us the teachings and stories of our ancestors every night around the fire. We learn about the forest and the sun and the rivers. The wise elders teach us about the stars in the sky, the animals in the jungle, and the rocks in the cave. We learn how to live with nature. That if we respect nature, nature will respect us back. We learn that all things in the village belong to all. It is normal to share with everybody. There is plenty for everyone, so we share freely. The concept of land, property, ownership is that everyone owns everything, and nobody owns anything. What we have are gifts from nature."

CHAPTER 46:
THE CARIBBEAN
SEA (1921)

"The cargo ship is here Jeev" yelled Jacinto "you have to leave now." Jeev picked up his canvas bag and slung it over his shoulder. The three of them headed towards the docks. Jacinto introduced Jeev to the angler who would be taking him to the ship. Jeev turned to Xochitl and Jacinto embracing them both. All three had tears in their eyes. In an abbreviated time, they had created memories and formed friendships. "You two are amazing people, the bond between us will remain unbreakable," said Jeev. "I wish you well on your quest and hope love finds you" said Xochitl.

Jeev jumped aboard the small fishing boat, and they set out towards the open sea. "Where is the ship?" asked Jeev. "We will see it after we leave the bay" replied the fisherman as he adjusted a lever on the engine. "The ship will not stop for us; they will lower a ladder and you will have to climb aboard." Once they left the calm bay into the choppy sea, he saw the cargo ship in the distance. The small boat rocked precariously in the rough waters.

The angler increased his speed and came dangerously close to the ship. A crew man on the ship tossed a rope ladder overboard. The bottom of the ladder was still too high for Jeev. The crewman swung the ladder again, letting more of it come downwards. This time, a wave caught the boat and swung it away from the ship. The fisherman edged closer to try again. "We only have one more chance," he yelled. "After this I can no longer keep up with the ship, the water is too rough." Jeev tightened the canvas bag that was tied to his back and stood on the roof of the boat. The crewman swung the ladder out again. This time, Jeev lunged at the ladder. If he missed, he would fall into the dangerous chasm between the boat and ship. His hands grasped round the round wooden rung of the ladder. It was wet, and he felt his hand slipping. With his other hand, he grasped at the rope attached to the wooden rung. He had a better grip. The boat below him swung away, and it left him momentarily hanging in midair. The ladder swayed towards the ship, and he hit the side of the ship with a thud. Shaken but still holding, he established a firmer grasp and pulled himself upward, eventually getting his feet on the wooden rung. Slowly, he climbed up the ladder. A couple of pairs of hands helped him up when he was close to the top.

He collapsed onto the deck, his legs feeling like jelly. "Good work, young man," laughed a large man with a Scottish accent, red hair, and a long beard. He thrust his big hand out for Jeev to grab and pulled him up like a sack of potatoes. He then smacked him on his back. "Come on, I will take you to the captain," he said. They climbed a steep staircase towards the bridge and then walked down a passageway. The captain was a small thin man with a thin moustache covering even thinner lips. "Do you have the money for the passage" asked the captain getting straight to the point. Jeev took out a wad of counted cash and handed it to him. The captain counted the notes and satisfied with the amount, commanded the crewman, "Logan, take him to Cabin four" before turning to Jeev, "Logan will be your contact. If you need anything, ask Logan. This is a cargo ship, but we have ten passengers on board. They are in the cabins near yours. Logan will show you the cabin and dining room. We will actually stop at St. Thomas so you will not have to swing from a rope ladder," laughing to himself as he ushered them out of his office.

Logan led Jeev down to the main deck, where he opened the door to a small but comfortable cabin. There was a bed, a nightstand and a thin wooden desk and chair. "We are serving lunch in half an hour" said Logan as he closed the cabin door behind him.

Jeev stood on the deck, enjoying the fresh ocean air, then went to the dining room. It was a small place, with no windows and four tables. Passengers had occupied two of the tables, so he went and sat at one of the empty tables. A couple entered and sat at the table occupied by Jeev. Behind them was a tall man. He had a scar that ran across his face, walked with a limp, and had a cloth wrapped around his head. He walked directly to the empty table and sat down. Logan served the passengers a bowl of meat stew, boiled vegetables, pasta and bread. "I am Professor Gunther, and this is my wife Mrs. Gunther" said the elderly couple sitting next to Jeev. The couple sitting with Jeev introduced themselves as Professor and Mrs. Gunther. "Miguel Sanchez, journalist. I spent several years working at a paper in Mexico, now going to St. Thomas to work there."

"We were in Panama, helping with missionary work," said Mrs. Gunther. "Now we are headed back to Boston where my husband teaches theology." As they dug into food, Mrs. Gunther whispered, "That man with the scar is strange. He boarded with us in Panama but does not converse with anyone. I am actually scared of him." Jeev observed the man and decided he would avoid any contact with him.

"We are going towards Cuba and will halt in Havana for two days to load cargo" said Logan as they looked out into the Caribbean Sea. As they neared the shore, miles of sargassum surrounded the ship. The yellow, foul-smelling seaweed stretched as far as the eyes could see. It clogged up the propellers, and the sailors often stopped the ship to remove the tangled weed. The scar face man walked by his eyes fixed on the ground in front of him. He did not make any effort to acknowledge or greet them.

The ship docked at the port of Havana. "Goodbye Miguel" waved Mrs. Gunther "we are leaving to catch a boat to Miami." As Jeeev was walked down the gangplank, Logan joined him. "Come, my friend," he jokingly thumped him on his back, "I will show you the town." The streets were lined with colorful buildings, balconies had intricate iron works and there was a jovial atmosphere in the city. Avoiding the American made cars, they crossed the street to a restaurant that had lively music coming from the inside. As they sat in the restaurant Jeev ordered arroz con pollo and Logan ordered ropa vieja. Jeev asked Logan "How did you get into this position of taking care of guests on a cargo ship? Logan replied "I had originally been hired to load the cargo, however one day I was called to help cater to the needs of the ten passenger cabins as the person who used to do this left to go back to his village in Ireland. I started loading their luggage, helping the passengers, making their meals, and even cleaning the cabins. The cabins usually ran at full capacity, so the captain reassigned me to the position of Cabin Officer along with a new uniform." Logan smiled pointing to his white outfit.

A waiter brought their drinks and food. Logan looked out into the street. "I have seen Havana change from a sleepy town to now becoming a playground for the rich and evil," said Logan. "If you have money, you can come here and do whatever you want. There are no morals, no limits. Just look around. There is richness everywhere." Jeev looked round the place. There were well-dressed people everywhere. Even at an early evening hour, there were men in suites gambling on card tables, impeccably dressed women were ambling through the aisles with their cigarettes in hand, servers were serving drinks and managers in tuxedos watched to assure everything went smoothly. In the corner, he saw the man with the scar huddled in a deep conversation with someone. "What's the story behind that man with the scar?" inquired Jeev. Logan looked over at the table and explained, "His name is Odeyman Brown. He is a manager of sugar plantations. The rumor is he got into some trouble over in Georgetown, somehow made his way to Panama, where he boarded the ship. He is looking to get a job as a plantation manager. Heard he killed someone, probably a white man, otherwise he would not have to leave the country."

Suddenly there was a scuffle at the table where Odeyman was sitting. The man taking to him got up, as did Odeyman. Odeyman shouted at the man. The man pushed Odeyman aside and started walking out. Odeyman rushed at the man. Out of nowhere, two burly men appeared and shoved Odeyman to the floor. "Never come back again," they threatened as they forcibly threw him out of the restaurant. "I guess he is not getting a job in Havana" commented Logan. "He will probably look for a job in St. Thomas as that is our next stop."

The next day, Logan took Jeev further inland to a sugar plantation. "Sugar is the lifeblood of these Caribbean islands. We are loading machines to take to St. Thomas for a sugar plantation there. Those people there," pointing to a group of people sitting under a tree, "they are sugar cane cutters. They only work four or five months in a year. Even when they work, they are hardly paid any money. The owners make tons of money on the back of these workers." Jeev nodded. "I have heard this story repeatedly. The same situation exists across much of the world I have travelled. Profit superseded everything else. Humanity, decency, fairness, or equality has no place in the realm of profits." "Come, I will show you the magnificent mansions where the rich live" said Logan as they passed the rundown shacks of the sugarcane workers.

The next day, all the cargo loaded, the ship proceeded to its next destination. Odeyman, the man with the scar, was back on board in an even grouchier mood. The ship stayed within sight of the shore as it passed hundreds of deserted islands. Logan was busy with ship duties, so Jeev spent his time writing about his journeys. He thought about meeting Amee. There was a sense of joy and excitement mixed in with sadness, regret, and fear. Would she still have the same feelings for him? He fell asleep to the pleasant memories of the two of them running through the fields towards the river.

It was late night by the time the ship docked at the port of Charlotte Amalie. "You can stay on board and leave in the morning" said Logan. Waking up at sunrise, Jeev threw his canvas bag over his shoulder and strolled into the port city of Charlotte Amalie. Storekeepers were setting up their shops, hens and goats meandering the cobblestone streets. A man was sweeping away the debris in front of a tavern from last night's drunkenness. The intoxicating aroma of freshly baked bread rose from a nearby bakery. He followed the cobblestone path, which now rose sharply upwards towards the hills overlooking the plantation. He had been told to follow the road for about a mile and he would then see the plantation house. As he gained elevation, the small port town glistened before him in the morning sun. Walking up hill towards the plantation, the thoughts about meeting Amee resurfaced. He was happy to be reunited with his childhood friend. Would she be happy to see him? Was she married? How would her husband react? What if she was still single? Would he want to spend the rest of his life with her? Would she want to spend the rest of her life with him? These questions swirled through his brain. He finally decided he was overthinking everything. He was simply going to meet his old friend, and that was it. So far, his life had been a series of mishaps, wrong turns, and long journeys in his quest. He would leave it up to fate to determine what happens next. As Xochitl had prophesied, the stars have already written our fate. What is destined will happen.

CHAPTER 47: SCAR FACE RETURNS (1922)

Jeev walked through the gates towards the farmhouse. A man came up to him and asked, "What are you doing here?" "I am here to see Amee" he replied. "Follow me" said the man and they walked up to a big barn behind the farmhouse. The man yelled into the darkened barn, "Amee Madam" there is someone to see you. It was bright sunlight outside, and his eyes could discern nothing inside the barn. He walked inside, squinting his eyes. There was a woman brushing a horse. Even though Amee had grown into a woman, he recognized her. She placed her hands over her eyes to block out the sun, to look at him. "Amee" he gushed as he came closer to her, "Oh my God Jeev" she squealed and ran to give him a hug. They held each other for a long moment. The old friendship rekindled. Jeev held her arm. "Look at you, all grown up." "I would say the same for you," she responded.

She slipped her hand in his and pulled him towards the farmhouse. "Come on, you need to meet everyone. Never did I think you would come here." They walked to the farmhouse where Jimmy, Agni, and two small boys greeted him. Gathered around a large table, they munched on food laid out by Agni as Jeev told them about his journeys through several continents.

That evening, Amee and Jeev sat on a large swing on the front patio. "Do you remember our rope swing tied to the old oak tree by the canal?" said Jeev. "Yes, you pushed me off the swing into the water many times" replied Amee as she fondly punched him in the arm. "I can still recall the sound of water lapping against the canal banks and the leaves of the oak tree rustling gently in the breeze" reminisced Jeev. "And when all the village children lined up to take turns at the swing, the laughter and screams as we splashed into the water." They continued their chatter until Freja appeared. "Let me show you your room" she said.

Freja, now quite old, led him to his room near the barns. As he passed the barn, he saw the man with the scar coming out of the barn. He stopped and asked Freja, "What is that man doing here?" "He came looking for a job. Mo told him about a job looking after the barn." "I was on the ship with him. He does not seem to be a person you would want to have around on the farm," objected Jeev. "Ok I will tell Amee; she has the ultimate word on who gets hired." Jeev's eyes followed the man as he exited the property.

Amee woke up early, just before sunrise, and headed to the barn to feed the horses. She loved her horses and while she could have hired more people to take care of them; she felt personally responsible for their wellbeing. Every morning, she habitually cleaned, fed, and inspected the horses. Freja had told her a man was coming to meet her about a job, and she hurried to finish her chores. The man was supposed to meet her in the horse barn. She cut bundles of hay to toss into the stalls. From the corner of her eye, she saw someone enter the barn. "Hello," said the man, "I was here looking for a job yesterday. They told me to come in the morning and meet someone here in the barn." Darn, thought Amee, this man should not have come so early. She still had a lot of work to finish. Well, I might as well take care of this. "Sure, I will be right there," she shouted.

The morning sun was glaring through the open barn door. She squinted her eyes to get a better look. As she got closer to him, she saw the silhouette of a tall, thin man.

Something deep inside warned her to be careful. He got closer. The man had a slight limp in his leg. She recognized him, it was scar face. She could never forget him. He looked at Amee and did not recognize her. However, the look on her face that caused him to think. Suddenly, his eyes widened. Sometimes, when two humans recognize each other, there is no need for words. The eyes speak to each other. They both knew that they had recognized each other. Odeyman was born in violence and lived in violence. He did the only thing he knew how to do. He pulled out a knife hidden in the small of his back. Amee saw the glint of the knife in the darkened barn. Odeyman tightened his grip on the knife, smiled at Amee and lunged towards her. Amee tossed a handful of hay at him and sprinted towards a ladder leading to the second floor of the barn. She desperately tried to climb up the ladder but could not climb further, as his hand clasped her ankle. With her free leg, she frantically kicked downwards, hoping to connect with his body. She missed widely, and it caused her to lose her balance, crashing into the floor below. The ladder crashed too, making a loud sound as it banged against a few empty tins of water. Amee lay sprawled on the ground. Scarface approached her, knife in hand. Suddenly someone shouted, "Don't move! ". It was Freja, holding a rifle in her hand. Odeyman ignored the command and rushed towards Amee. Freja fired at him, missing, but striking the empty water cans. Odeyman grabbed Amee by the neck and placed his knife around her neck. "Drop your gun or I will kill her," he commanded. Freja dropped her gun. The noise of the gunshot had woken up others on the farm. Jimmy and Agni had come running out, as did Mo and Jeev. Both Jimmy and Mo carried their rifles. Odeyman had one hand around Amee's neck and the other around her waist. He lifted her up with little effort and dragged her outside, facing the people in front of him. He moved backwards, slowly towards the gate. "Nobody move" he shouted, "or I will hurt her."

A tiny figure slithered out of the sugarcane plants

behind the barn. Odeyman did not see the small animal rush at him and sink its teeth into his bad leg. He looked down in horror to see a fox biting into him. He let go of Amee and swung his knife at the fox. Amee stumbled forward onto the ground, as the knife missed the fox. Jimmy and Mo both fired at Odeyman at the same time. Two bullets caught him in the chest. He was dead before he hit the ground, face first. Jeev, who had run out of his room hearing the commotion, saw the fox with blue eyes slink back into the sugarcane field and disappear. Agni rushed to Amee to help her to her feet. "That's the same man you told us about in Georgetown, right?" inquired Agni. "Yes," stammered Amee, still shaken up by the events. Evil had died a dusty death.

CHAPTER 48: THE SUGARCANE PLANTATION

Jeev woke up to the sounds of the farmyard rooster, he headed to the barn to see if Amee was there. Sure enough, she was saddling a horse to go on her rounds of the plantation. "Do you want to come with me?" she inquired. "Yes, absolutely," countered Jeev. Another horse was saddled, and they rode out onto the farmland. The scenery was stunning. Sugarcane plants stretched out as far as the eye could see, surrounded by the blue Caribbean Sea. Coconut trees gently swayed in the ocean breeze. They rode through a small path in the middle of the sugarcane fields. The tall plants came up to their shoulders, even while riding the horse. "We will get into the cutting season soon," remarked Amee. "Once the cane is cut, it has to be quickly transported to the factory." She pointed at a few windmills in the distance. They followed a path that took them toward the windmills. "The cane is taken to the factory that is powered by the windmills. We now also have machines that run on diesel fuel but continue to use the windmills as well." They reached the windmills and dismounted. The machines were idle, but soon they would hum with the production of sugar cane. Amee led Jeev into another large room. Streams of light shone through windows on the side of the room. In the middle were large pots in which the cane juice would be processed.

They both stood in silence, looking out over the fields,

the bright blue sky, lazy clouds floating by the Caribbean sun and the glistening ocean in the distance. "It is so peaceful here and then I think about the famine in our village. I wonder how amma and baba are doing? Are they still alive? Did they get enough money to survive?" Jeev wrapped his arms around her shoulder. "I wonder what would have happened to me on that fateful night int he plantation if I had not fought back. Even worse what would have happened to Arti."

A lonely tear made its way down her cheek. Jeev thought about the continued evils of colonialization. How profits drove all the actions and the inherent evil of one race, deciding that it was superior to other races. The lack of compassion towards another human being. The feelings of anger rose within him.

He looked over at Amee and used his thumb to wipe the tear. She nestled her head on his chest and heaved a sigh of relief. There was no reprieve for Jeev. Feelings of affection towards Amee collided with ambers of rage. He hugged her tightly with both his hands, placing his cheek on her head. Torn between staying here on this paradise island or continuing his search to bring freedom to his homeland. His thoughts were with the millions of his countrymen, women and children who had starved to death under the rule of the British Raj. Images of the squalid labor camps the English had set up in the name of reducing the famine, but the working conditions were so adverse that hundreds of thousands died setting up railway lines or digging irrigation canals, swirled through his mind. He reminisced about those he had left behind to fight, like Bhalu Ramu. He thought about the British aristocracy that had decided that profits and its perverted theories of social Darwinism ruled supreme. In his anger, he wanted to bring the British empire to its knees.

They rode back in silence to the house. One of the plantation dogs, seeing the horses, came running out of the house, followed by three cute brown puppies. Amee jumped off her horse and cradled all three of them, carrying them to a swing that was attached to the rafters on the porch. As she sat down, the furry creatures tumbled all around her, wildly shaking their tails and biting at her fingers. She rocked back and forth on the swing, playing with the puppies. Jeev surveyed the scene and walked out towards the plantation gate. He knew he needed to think about his next steps. Glancing back at Amee, part of him wanted to stay here forever. He was being pulled in two different directions, one a life of affection, love, and comfort, the other an unknown trek into an uncharted, dangerous territory.

Jeev stayed on the plantation for a several months. This was the first time in his life where he experienced peace and happiness. He worked long hours, helping wherever he was needed on the plantation. The tasty food, clean Caribbean air and the friendly family atmosphere were refreshing. One day, as he walked towards the barn to meet Amee and help her with the morning chores, Freja walked up to him and gave him a letter and said "I was in town yesterday, delivering grain to the Tavern and the owner told me there was a man staying there who is looking for you. The owner did not tell him where you live, but the man had left this letter for you in case you came to the Tavern. The man has gone to a neighboring island but will be back in two days." She stood by him as Jeev opened the letter, curious to know the contents, but Jeev walked away to read the letter by himself.

My Dear Friend Jeev,
I know you are staying at a plantation on the Island. Meet me at the Misty Tavern. I will be back in two days. Have a proposition for you. You can come back with me to my fatherland.
Your Friend the Commander.

He wanted Jeev to come back with him to Germany! The plan to buy arms was back on.

Jeev did not share the contents of the letter with Amee. It would be better if she knew nothing. Nor could he bring himself to say goodbye. For two days, he struggled with the competing thoughts in his head. Should he stay or should he go? The note from Commander Koenig seemed to burn in his pocket. He knew Commander Koenig would not have contacted him unless he had a specific plan for him. A journey he would have to embark on, on his own, leaving behind the one he loved.

On the day of the meeting, he silently left the plantation. He continued walking until he arrived at a turn in the road leading down to the town. He walked towards the edge of the cliff and observed a small fishing boat bouncing in the waves below. The rope that held it to the dock was untied as the boat floated aimlessly in the rough waters.

With a sigh, Jeev sauntered down the road towards the Tavern, a brief glance of goodbye towards the plantation, the decision being made. A black car slowly made its way up the hill. A smartly dressed chauffeur in front and in the back seat Sean Burke and his parents Elizabeth and Lionel Burke. Jeev, lost in his thoughts, barely glanced at the passing car. Sean looking out of his window saw a man walking, who looked like any other island native. As the car passed Jeev, a chill passed through Sean, "could that be him" he muttered to himself. Lionel looked at Sean inquisitively. Sean strained his neck to take a better look at the man walking down the hill. He shook his head; it could not be him. The car entered the plantation. The sleek exterior of the car was in sharp contrast to the rustic surroundings of the place. The sound of coconut trees rustling in the wind filled the air, punctuated by the crunch of gravel under the tires. Stopping in front of the farmhouse, the chauffeur hurried to open the back door. The three passengers shielded their eyes from the bright sun as they stretched their legs and looked at the endless rows of sugar cane extending before them. Jimmy and Agni came walking down the steps to greet their guests. Amee who was on the porch, dressed in a wide brimmed hat and long-sleeved shirt rose to see them. Sean stretched his leg to ease the pain of his war injury, as he saw her stand up with her sunkissed skin and long wavy black hair blowing in the gentle wind. There was something about her that captured his attention and made his heart skip a beat.

Jeev, reaching the town at the bottom of the hill strolled in the Tavern. Standing in the doorway, he waited to let his eyes adjust to the darkness, inhaling the smell of whiskey and cigars. He saw Koenig sitting at the table, waving his cigar carrying hand, beckoning him over to a new voyage!

ACKNOWLEDGEMENT

India suffered immeasurably during the colonial years. The famines caused tens of millions of deaths between the 1800s to early 1900s. The causes of these famines were complex, but British colonial policies played a significant role in exacerbating the effects, a tragic reminder of the devastating impact of colonialism.

We cannot forget and must acknowledge those who fought against tyranny, suffered from colonialism and those who died for freedom. Today this fight for liberty continues in many parts of the world and it serves as a reminder to those who have some degree of freedom not to take it for granted.

Researching and authoring this book took longer and was much harder than I anticipated. There are a couple of people I would like to acknowledge without whom this book would not have been possible.

To Victoria Wilhoite for her editing of the book as well as many snippets of wisdom about culture during the 1900's.

To my wife Sona for her encouragement to write and her support to pursue my passion for writing.

ABOUT THE AUTHOR

Nilish Gupte

Nilish Gupte PhD, calls himself a perpetual student. "The day we stop learning is the day we die is his motto."

He is a history buff and uses his educational background of a PhD in Information Studies from Long Island University Palmer School, A Master of Philosophy also from LIU, an MBA from New York Institute of Technology and a bachelor's in electrical engineering from Stony Brook University to research time periods and visually recreate them in vivid details.

His writing reflects his passion of being an avid bird photographer, a champion of natural habitat preservation, an entrepreneur, and an extensive traveler. He has published many articles on Medium, LinkedIn, Thrive Global and various technical publications.

Made in the USA
Coppell, TX
14 May 2023

16834594R10249